WHEN LOVE RETURNS

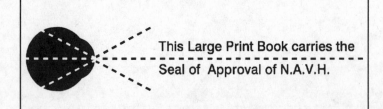

This Large Print Book carries the
Seal of Approval of N.A.V.H.

THE ZIMMERMAN RESTORATION TRILOGY, BOOK 3

WHEN LOVE RETURNS

KIM VOGEL SAWYER

THORNDIKE PRESS

A part of Gale, Cengage Learning

Farmington Hills, Mich • San Francisco • New York • Waterville, Maine
Meriden, Conn • Mason, Ohio • Chicago

GALE
CENGAGE Learning®

Copyright © 2015 by Kim Vogel Sawyer.
Scripture quotations or paraphrases are taken from the King James Version and the Holy Bible, New International Version®, NIV®. Copyright © 1973, 1978, 1984 by Biblica Inc.™ Used by permission of Zondervan. All rights reserved worldwide. www.zondervan.com.
Thorndike Press, a part of Gale, Cengage Learning.

LIBRARY OF CONGRESS CATALOGING-IN-PUBLICATION DATA

Sawyer, Kim Vogel.
  When love returns / Kim Vogel Sawyer.
    pages cm. — (The Zimmerman Restoration trilogy ; 3) (Thorndike Press large print Christian romance)
    ISBN 978-1-4104-8329-4 (hardback) — ISBN 1-4104-8329-0 (hardcover)
    1. Mennonites—Fiction. 2. Large type books. I. Title.
  PS3619.A97W434 2015b
  813'.6—dc23   2015024103

Published in 2015 by arrangement with WaterBrook, an imprint of Crown Publishing Group, a division of Penguin Random House LLC

Printed in Mexico
1 2 3 4 5 6 7 19 18 17 16 15

For the parents who love "someone else's" child as their own; and for the parents who — out of love — allowed someone else to raise their child.

Be ye kind one to another, tenderhearted, forgiving one another, even as God for Christ's sake hath forgiven you.

EPHESIANS 4:32, KJV

CHAPTER 1

Indianapolis, Indiana
Cynthia Allgood

"Mom, it's perfect! I love it!"

Cynthia braced herself as her daughter launched off the floor and into her arms. The cell phone box Darcy clutched narrowly missed a collision with the side of Cynthia's head, but she didn't mind. She laughed and returned the embrace with just as much enthusiasm as it was given. "You're welcome, but remember the stipulations we discussed. No —"

Darcy jolted upright and lifted her palm as if making a pledge. " 'No texting during class, no calls or texts after bedtime, and only approved-by-Mom-and-Dad contacts.' Did I get 'em right?"

"One more," Glenn interjected, pulling Darcy's attention from her mother to her father. " 'No exceeding the allowed minutes, or the penalties will come from my allowance.' "

"Ohhh . . ." Darcy whisked a grin from Cynthia to Glenn. Her eyes — as beautifully blue as her daddy's — sparkled with mischief. "Daddy just said my penalties will come out of his allowance. I like that idea!"

Glenn bopped the top of Darcy's head, his hand descending lightly on her tousled brown tresses. "Nice try, buckaroo, but no dice."

Darcy affected a pretend pout that lasted all of three seconds before she sank back into her spot beside the Christmas tree and broke into laughter. Both Glenn and Cynthia joined in, but their son, Barrett, sat still and unsmiling. Glenn poked him on the shoulder. "What's with you?"

"Just waiting for you to stop horsing around so I can open my last present. It's my turn, you know."

Every Christmas since the kids were old enough to understand the concept of taking turns, they'd opened their packages one at a time in birth order — first Glenn, then Cynthia, then Darcy, and finally Barrett. Glenn held out his hand in invitation. "Go ahead."

Barrett bent over the package, giving them a view of his wavy sandy-blond hair. He resembled a miniature of his father, and

Cynthia's heart swelled with affection as she watched her son meticulously pick at the strips of tape holding the red-and-green plaid paper in place, his face a study of concentration.

Such opposites, these two wonderful children. Darcy dove on her packages — biggest one first — and, like a terrier trying to uncover a bone, sent scraps of paper flying. But Barrett arranged his gifts smallest to largest and worked his way up, carefully removing and then setting aside the nearly intact sheets of wrapping paper. While Darcy was impulsive and mercurial, Barrett had always been philosophical and structured.

Was her first child more like Darcy or Barrett, or was she completely different from both? The familiar ache of regret began to build in her chest.

Glenn eased his arm around Cynthia and drew her snug to his side. Grateful for the distraction from her depressing thoughts, she tipped her cheek against his shoulder and watched her son unwrap the super-sized Lego set she'd located at a thrift store. Even though secondhand, none of the pieces were missing, and the box was still in good shape. After setting up the cell phone service for Darcy — a necessity now that

11

the kids came home to an empty house every day after school — their Christmas budget had been limited. Finding the set at a reasonable price was like finding buried treasure, and she knew Barrett would love it. He amazed her with his ability to create complex buildings, vehicles, and spacecraft from the tiny interlocking blocks.

Barrett slipped the paper off the box. His eyes widened and his mouth dropped open. In an uncharacteristic display, he snatched up the box and hugged it to his chest for a moment before laying it across his knees. He traced the different possible projects printed on the box with his finger. "Oh, man, am I gonna have fun with this. It's the most awesome present ever, Mom and Dad. Thank you!"

Darcy, cradling her pink cell phone beneath her chin, wrinkled her nose. "I'm afraid you're wrong, Batwit. My phone is the most awesome present ever."

Barrett curled his arms protectively around his gift. "You kidding? This is a lot better than a dumb phone, Barfy."

Glenn dislodged Cynthia to lean forward and cup his hands over the kids' shoulders. "Here now, none of that."

"But, Dad." Darcy turned a look of pure innocence on her father. "Batwit would think I didn't like him anymore if I didn't pick on him."

Barrett rolled his eyes. "Yeah, right."

"First of all, your brother's name is Barrett. You learned to say it correctly by the time you were three, so please make use of its proper pronunciation. Second, there are better ways of showing affection than name-calling — and that applies to both of you, as does my third point. This is Christmas." Glenn glanced at Cynthia, and his expression softened. "A time for peace and goodwill among men. Let's practice it, huh?"

Warmth flooded Cynthia's frame. How she loved Glenn. She would never have imagined marrying such a good-hearted, strong, yet tender man. After a childhood of upheaval and disappointments, her life with Glenn was more than she'd ever hoped for. God had certainly blessed her. A loving husband, two wonderful children, a comfortable home in a safe neighborhood . . . Sometimes she thought the dysfunctional family and seedy apartment of her past was only a dream. Until she remembered —

She jumped up. "Now that we've finished opening our gifts, I'll get breakfast started." She rubbed her palms together. "Cream

13

cheese–pumpkin pancakes with chocolate chips, right, guys?"

Glenn caught her hand. "No."

She paused, confused. "No pancakes?" They'd had the same breakfast on Christmas morning since she and Glenn married a little over fifteen years ago. She loved creating happy traditions for her children to remember. She swallowed a lump of disappointment. "What do you want then?"

He drew her back down on the sofa. Excitement glittered in his eyes. "I want you to open your last present."

Darcy and Barrett exchanged secretive looks, their lips twitching with suppressed grins. What had the loves of her life plotted? She released a light laugh and gestured to the small pile at the end of the sofa — new potholders woven from colorful cotton strings from Barrett, a six-pack of animal-print socks from Darcy, and a department store necklace with a silver-plated, filigreed heart pendant from Glenn. "But I already opened my presents, and they're perfect. I don't need anything else."

"Yes, you do." Glenn's expression turned serious. "There's one thing you've needed for as long as I've known you, and I think I finally found a way to give it to you."

14

Apprehension tiptoed up Cynthia's spine. Was he referencing . . . She shook her head. No, he wouldn't do that to her. Not in front of Darcy and Barrett. Not on Christmas, the one day she'd always worked so hard to make perfect for her family to cover up the painful, disappointing, alcohol-drenched Christmases of fighting and heartbreak she'd known as a child. She beseeched him with her eyes, willing him to keep the secret between the two of them, where it belonged.

As if in one accord, Darcy and Barrett moved from their spots on the floor and perched on the edge of the couch, Darcy next to Cynthia, and Barrett next to Glenn. Darcy put her hand on Cynthia's knee, and Barrett rested his cheek against Glenn's bicep. They both looked up at their father with open, expectant faces. Their trust, their innocence, ate a hole in Cynthia's stomach. Tears threatened, and she battled nausea.

Don't say it, Glenn. Please don't say it.

Glenn slipped an envelope from his shirt pocket and pressed it into Cynthia's hands. "Inside this envelope is the receipt for a retainer to a private investigator who specializes in reuniting parents with children given up for adoption."

Cynthia clenched her fist around the envelope and crunched her eyes tight. She gritted her teeth to hold in the moan of agony building deep inside her soul. Behind her closed lids she envisioned the tiny baby girl she'd spent the past two decades trying to forget. But the wailing infant with a shock of black hair and a wrinkled, red face remained embedded in her memory, the image even more painful than the awful scenes she carried of Christmas mornings.

"Oh, Glenn . . ."

A gentle hand cupped her cheek. "Look at me, Cyn."

She jerked free of Glenn's touch, keeping her eyes shut. Darcy's hand tightened on her knee, and a soft whimper sounded next to Cynthia's ear. Her daughter was upset. Mother instinct overrode personal discomfort. Instinctively she opened her eyes and her arms, then pulled Darcy into her embrace. With Darcy locked in her arms the way she'd never held — would never hold — her first daughter, she shot a warning glare at Glenn and mouthed, *Not now.*

But Glenn, a tender smile curving his lips, gave a gentle nod. "Yes, now."

Cynthia tightened her grip on Darcy. She whispered, "The kids —"

Darcy wriggled. "Mom, we know about the baby you gave away."

Cynthia's arms turned to boiled noodles,

and her spine went limp. She released her daughter and flopped against the back of the couch. "Y-you do?"

Darcy pushed her tangled hair behind her ears and nodded.

"How?"

Barrett said, "Dad told us."

Fury roared through Cynthia's chest. He had no right to share something meant to remain between the two of them. But in her stunned, weakened state, she couldn't find the ability to sit up and berate him. Then a swell of shame rose and conquered the anger. How long had her children known? She forced a simple question. "When?"

Darcy touched Cynthia's arm. "Three weeks ago."

Three weeks . . . He must have told them near her baby girl's twentieth birthday. Fresh pain stabbed, the thrust so intense it seared her insides. She felt laid bare in a public arena, and everything within her wanted to run away and hide. But Darcy's hand on her arm, Barrett's open gaze pinned on her face, Glenn's arm along the back of the sofa with his fingers draped on her shoulder, even the bright-colored bulbs blinking their cheerful beat on the limbs of the Christmas tree became shackles.

Cynthia hooded her eyes with her hand

and ducked her head. "I can't believe this."

"Mom?" Darcy pulled Cynthia's hand down and tilted her head a bit to meet her mother's gaze. "She's our sister. Why didn't you ever tell us about her?"

Tears swam in Cynthia's eyes, distorting her vision. She didn't dare look either Darcy or Barrett full in the face or she'd turn into a puddle. A mother should be strong, should be a good example. But now they knew just how weak and foolish she was. How could they ever respect her again? "I . . . I . . ." She gulped. Her dry throat burned. She shot a glare at Glenn before lowering her head again. She ground out, "I didn't want you to ever know how imperfect I am."

"But we already know you're not perfect."

Barrett's blithe comment gave Cynthia a jolt.

Darcy leaned past Cynthia and whacked her brother on the arm. "Batwit, don't say that!"

"Why?"

Her son's genuine confusion coaxed her out of hiding to deliver a touch of comfort. She formed a feeble smile. "It's okay, Barrett."

"I know it is." Resolve creased his boyish face. "Remember the story in the Bible when a man came up to Jesus and called Him 'good teacher,' and Jesus told him nobody's good except for God? Well, you're not God. Neither am I. Or Dad. Or Barf— I mean, Darcy." He gestured as he spoke, his hands jabbing the air as if determined to prove his point. "And then there's that verse in Romans we had to memorize for Sunday school — you know, 'All have sinned and fall short of the glory of God.' That means moms and dads as much as kids."

Glenn caught Barrett in the bend of his elbow and gave the boy's head an affectionate knuckle rub. "You're getting pretty smart on us, buckaroo."

Barrett tipped his head and grinned at his father. "Thanks." He wiggled out of Glenn's grip and offered his mother a sheepish look. "Our name might be Allgood, but we aren't all good. We can't be, 'cause like I said, we're not God."

Cynthia blinked rapidly against the fresh tears filling her eyes. How she wanted to be all good for her children, different from her own mother, whose imperfections and badness had darkened her childhood and pushed her down pathways of poor choices that left her riddled with regrets. "I know I'm not God, Barrett, but I want to be . . . someone you can admire." Her last words emerged on a ragged whisper.

At once both children dove at her. Even Barrett, who'd nearly abandoned giving hugs since his eleventh birthday two months ago, claiming the practice was "babyish." Their arms wrapped around her, holding her tight. Their heads pressed into the curve of her neck, their warm breath offering comfort. She curled her arms around their frames and clung while prayers of both gratitude and pleading spilled from her heart.

Glenn placed his palm on her back, adding the warmth of his presence to the group embrace. "Cyn, I think what the kids are trying to tell you is that something from when you were a teenager doesn't have to define who you are today. You're their mother and they love you. Am I right, buckaroos?"

Both of them nodded, their hair tickling Cynthia's cheeks. She gently set them aside. She'd dropped the envelope, but she reached for it again and smoothed it across her thigh to erase the wrinkles. Despite her efforts the creases remained, a stark reminder of the permanent imprint she wore on her soul. She swallowed. "I love you guys, too." She glanced at Glenn. She wanted to be mad at him for telling her secret, but there was such hopefulness in his eyes. He'd only wanted to please her. She sighed. "And I love you."

His endearing, eye-crinkling smile lit his face. "That's good to know." He caught hold of Barrett and heaved him off the couch. Giggling, Darcy hopped up, too. "You two take your loot to your rooms and then set the table for Mom — help her out with Christmas breakfast, okay?"

"Sure, Dad." The pair scurried to obey.

As soon as the children departed, Glenn pulled Cynthia into his embrace. His stubble pricked her forehead, and the envelope received a few more wrinkles from being pressed between them, but she chose not to pull away. She needed the security his strong arms offered. He whispered against her hair, "Have I upset you?"

He had, but she wouldn't spoil Christmas Day with harsh words or accusations. Determined to bury the ugly memories parading through her mind, she burrowed into his chest. They'd rolled out of bed and scuffed into the living room to open gifts at the crack of dawn, neither bothering to shower before tugging on yesterday's rumpled clothes from the top of the hamper. He smelled of sleep and leftover aftershave and the onions she'd fried to go with last night's liver — one of Glenn's favorites even though Darcy and Barrett made horrible faces when she put the dish on the table. An odd potpourri but somehow right and pleasant.

"Cyn?" His hands caught her shoulders and pulled her from her nestling spot. "I have to warn you . . . The investigator wouldn't guarantee he'll find her or, if he does, that she'll want to meet you. Some adoptees have no desire to reconnect with their birth parents — he told me so. So if you don't want to risk it, I can cancel the investigation."

Cynthia's chest ached with the effort of breathing. Desire to see her daughter, to apologize for leaving her the way she had, to assure herself the helpless baby had been well cared for all these years twisted her heart into knots.

"You won't hurt my feelings if you reject the gift."

She raised one eyebrow.

"Honest."

She sighed and melted against him again. She pulled in his familiar scent, drawing comfort from it. "I do want to know, Glenn. I want to know she's all right."

"I know you do."

"But I'm afraid."

"I know that, too."

Her cheek resting against his firm chest, she fingered the envelope. "If . . . if I say no, don't look for her, do you get your money back?"

"Some. Not all. He required a nonrefundable deposit to reserve his services."

Even though not a hint of worry entered his tone, she knew their finances well enough to realize this gift was a sacrifice. Glenn's job as a high school science teacher paid more in satisfaction than in dollars, and her part-time library position, secured two months ago after years of being a stay-at-home mom, only brought in enough to cover the monthly payment on Darcy's new braces. They couldn't afford to throw away money.

"You don't have to tell me now." Glenn kissed the top of her head and then crushed her close. "Think about it. Pray about it. But, Cyn?" He caught her chin and raised her face. "I really think there's a part of you that will always feel incomplete until you know for sure where she is. I love you, and I want you to be totally whole. Not for me or for the kids but for you. Do you understand?"

How could she have even considered being angry at him? A sob formed, and she

sniffed hard to hold it back. "You're so . . .
so good to me. Thank you. I love you,
Glenn."

He leaned in and delivered a sweet kiss.
When he straightened, he stayed close, his
forehead touching hers. "Does that mean
yes, tell him to find her?"

Cynthia closed her eyes and sucked in a
shuddering breath. She hadn't seen her
baby girl in twenty years and twenty-two
days. Her arms ached with emptiness and
her heart twined with desire, but a deep-
rooted fear rose up to strangle her. If the
investigator found her daughter and she
refused a meeting, Cynthia might never
recover. She'd faced so many rejections in
her life. Could she risk suffering yet another
one?

CHAPTER 2

Arborville, Kansas
Suzanne Zimmerman

Such a hubbub sixteen people created. From her spot on the piano bench, Suzanne glanced around the crowded living room and battled the urge to put her fingers in her ears. The high-pitched squeals of her nieces, the excited jabber of her nephews, the blasting laughter of her brother and brothers-in-law, and the chatter of her daughter, sisters, sister-in-law, and mother combined to create a nearly overwhelming cacophony of confusion.

In the past month since returning to Arborville, she'd adjusted to noisy Sunday dinners with her family again, and she'd even stopped missing the solitude of her apartment. But this influx of assorted voices competing to be heard and crinkling paper and little Isabella fussing about cutting teeth was too much after her years of living with only one other person. She raised her hands, prepared to block the sound, but her gaze fell on her daughter, who sat on the floor in the throng of children with piles of crumpled wrapping paper forming a sea of color around her.

Tears pricked. Alexa's face — her joyful, beaming, nearly-bursting-with-happiness face — squashed the desire to muffle the noise. She would view this Christmas morning through Alexa's eyes instead of her own and celebrate the big-family chaos Alexa had been denied during her growing-up years.

Alexa caught her mother's eye. She winked, her brown eyes shining and her face wreathed in a smile of bliss, and Suzanne couldn't resist releasing a laugh. Her world had been turned upside down in the past months, but she wouldn't reverse all of it now even if she could. Because of Alexa.

Not flesh of my flesh, but the joy of my heart . . . Thank You, Lord, for my precious daughter.

Late that afternoon the girl who was the flesh of her flesh would arrive with her adoptive parents and sister for Christmas supper — the first extended family gathering in years at the Zimmerman farm. Suzanne couldn't deny a fierce stab of apprehension. Sharing the table with the cousins who'd raised the baby she hadn't been allowed to keep would surely be torture. But her mother was over-the-moon happy to resume the long-abandoned tradition, and Suzanne couldn't bear to trample her mother's enthusiasm. Especially considering their newfound reconciliation. She didn't dare create conflict.

"Everyone, everyone!" From her wheelchair beside the sofa, Mother raised both arms and waved her hands. "Quiet down, please! Hush now!"

It took almost a full minute for the three sets of parents to bring their boisterous children under control, but finally — with the exception of six-month-old Isabella's continued muffled grunts around her teething ring — silence descended.

Mother sent a smile across the circle of faces. "Thank you. Before we head to the dining room to enjoy the brunch Alexa prepared for us, I have one more present to give, but it couldn't be wrapped."

Suzanne's oldest nephew, Jay, bounced on his bottom. "Is it for me?"

His father leaned forward and placed a hand on the boy's shoulder. "Didn't Grandmother ask you to be quiet?" Jay shot

Clete a sheepish look and hunkered back down.

Mother chuckled. "No, not for you, Jay."

"Awww . . ."

Clete flicked his son on the back of the head, and Jay scooted closer to his grandmother's wheelchair, out of Clete's reach.

Mother put her hand on the boy's short-cropped blond hair and continued as if there'd been no interruption. "One of the people in this room has faced major upheaval recently. And that person has maintained a cheerful outlook even though all the changes haven't been easy, and I know she's lonesome for her friends."

Suzanne's sisters, brother, and in-laws all glanced in her direction. She squirmed. While giving her a special gift emphasized how much Mother's initial resistance to Suzanne's presence had melted, it put her in an awkward position with her siblings. Her sister Shelley still held a small amount of resentment about Suzanne's return and the way the family and community had accepted her back into the fold. She hoped whatever Mother had selected wasn't too extravagant, or the fragile peace she'd established with Shelley might be shattered.

"So . . ." Mother sat up straight in her

chair, a teasing glint entering her eyes. "Bring in the gift!"

No one moved. Suzanne glanced around in confusion. Who was supposed to heed Mother's instruction? Then she heard the squeak of the stair treads. Her family members from Mother all the way down to three-year-old Ian turned toward the doorway leading to the enclosed staircase. Puzzled, Suzanne looked, too, and she gasped in delight when a pair of impish faces peeked around the corner.

"Tom! Linda!" Happiness exploded in her heart. How had Mother managed to bring her mentors and closest friends from Indiana without anyone spoiling the secret? She jumped up to greet the guests, but out of the corner of her eye, she saw Mother hold her arms toward her. So she went to her mother instead and leaned down for a hug.

Mother's chuckle vibrated against Suzanne's shoulder. "Are you surprised?"

Suzanne choked back a half laugh, half sob. "I'm beyond surprised — I'm shocked!" She straightened and turned to find Linda weaving her way between the children, her round brown face wearing a huge smile and her arms open wide.

"C'mere, girl, and gimme a hug. Mercy,

but I've missed you."

Suzanne stepped eagerly into Linda's embrace. For years this woman had offered motherly advice, sisterly companionship, and countless prayers. Raising a child without a husband or extended family would have been unbearable had it not been for the loving support of Linda and Tom. As Linda rocked her side to side, tears flowed down Suzanne's face.

Tom's throaty chuckle intruded. "Hey, now, I'm needing some of that, too, you know."

With a laugh Suzanne stretched out one arm and tugged Tom into the circle. His neatly trimmed goatee, as snow white as his hair, brushed Suzanne's cheek with a familiar tickle. The hardest part of leaving Indiana had been saying good-bye to her dear friends. Receiving their hugs was the best gift she could have imagined.

Still in the middle of their embrace, Suzanne said, "When did you get here? How could I not know?"

They both laughed and Alexa stepped close. "They flew in to Wichita yesterday afternoon, and Uncle Derek picked them up from the airport. I sneaked them in while you were out in the cottage. Then they just stayed upstairs anytime you came to the house." She giggled. "It's been fun — like hide-and-seek without the seek part."

Behind her, Mother's voice rang out. "All right, everybody, let's get the dining room table ready and let Suzy and the Dennings catch up. Ruby and Pearl, you come, too — no need to sit there staring at your aunt's friends."

Linda gave the pair of blond-haired look-alikes a little finger wave and wink that made the twins giggle. They dashed off, still gazing over their shoulders in wonder at Linda and Tom. Suzanne understood the little girls' fascination. Shelley never took her children to the larger cities for shopping the way many of the other Old Order mothers did. Likely Ruby and Pearl had never seen anyone with chocolate-brown skin and eyes to match.

"I'll go, too." Alexa inched backward. "I already got to visit with them by myself yesterday. Besides, I want to cut that quiche into oblong wedges instead of squares so it'll look prettier on the plate, which means I need to beat Aunt Shelley to the oven." She pulled the antique pocket doors closed behind her.

The moment the doors clicked into place, Linda slung her arm around Suzanne's waist and led her to the sofa. They plopped down side by side and shared another hug while Tom eased into the century-old rocking chair.

Linda pulled back and cupped Suzanne's cheeks between her warm palms. "Heavenly days, girl, it's good to see you. I know you've only been gone since Thanksgiving, but after seeing you and talking to you every day for years on end . . . No sirree, things just haven't felt right. When Alexa called and asked if we'd like to be your mama's Christmas surprise to you, there was no way we could say no. Sure am glad the weather cooperated and didn't keep us snowbound." She sent a slow look around the room, murmuring low in her throat. "Mm-hm, this sure is different from your apartment in Indianapolis, isn't it? But I like it. Homey. That's how it feels — homey."

Suzanne smiled, remembering how cold and somber the room had seemed when she'd arrived to help care for her mother several months ago. Alexa's creative touches — and the restoration of relationships — had worked wonders. "It feels that way to me, too."

"So you're gonna stay?" Tom asked.

Suzanne leaned back so she could talk to both of them at the same time. "Well, I'm still not completely sure. Alexa loves having

32

me here, and it's been good to really get to know my sisters and brother again as well as their spouses and children. It's fun being Aunt Suzy. I've missed out on a lot." The past years of separation loomed wide in her memory, stinging her with regret. She deliberately set the feeling aside. She was making up for lost time now. "But it'll depend on whether or not I can find a job. I've put in applications at the closest hospitals — in Pratt, Kingman, and Wichita — but none have called to request an interview yet."

Linda patted her wrist. "Well, now, when the time is right, a door'll open for you. You just hold tight to your faith and wait."

Suzanne gave her friend a grateful smile. "Thanks to Clete asking me to come help take care of Mother last spring, I had someplace to go when I lost my job. If this had happened a year ago, it would have been much more stressful."

"Mm-hm." Linda nodded, her expression knowing. "God saw it comin' and paved a way for you, didn't He? Kind of nice to look back and see His fingerprints on all these changes."

Tom rocked, the *squeak-squeak* of the runners against the wood floor creating a discordant tune. "Alexa was telling us

33

yesterday how quiet the bed-and-breakfast has been. How's she managing to make any money if she doesn't have guests?"

Suzanne couldn't hold back a short laugh. "You know Alexa and her love for cooking! She ships her homemade cookies and muffins all over the place, caters dinners whenever she gets the chance, and bakes fruit pies five days a week for the little café in Arborville."

Tom smiled indulgently. "Just like her to find a productive way to stay busy. She's a good girl. Always has been."

"Hardly a girl anymore." Linda pursed her full lips into a rueful scowl. "Can't hardly believe she turned twenty already. Where does the time go?"

Suzanne closed her eyes for a moment, remembering. Had twenty years really slipped by since the day she stepped behind the garage at the home for unwed mothers and found the cold, hungry baby squirming in a box?

Linda went on, her tone wistful. "I can still see her as a little bitty thing with lopsided piggytails and missing front teeth." She laughed, and Suzanne automatically smiled. She loved Linda's deep, rumbling chuckle. Linda shook her head. "Remember how she was always trying to climb up high in the apple tree in our backyard?"

"And always falling out, brushing off the dust, and trying it again. Never saw such a determined child." Tom stopped the rocker and reached out to take Suzanne's hand. "Stick-to-itiveness — that's what she's got. It's a trait that'll suit her well in all of life. She inherited that from you, Suzanne, and that's why I know you'll land on your feet with all these changes."

A tiny sting of guilt twinged in Suzanne's chest at Tom's comment.

The pocket doors slid open, and Alexa peeked through the gap. "Are you ready to eat? Grandmother says we need to hurry or we might be late to the Christmas service. It starts at ten o'clock."

Linda heaved herself upright and held her hand to Suzanne. "Been a long time since I had some of Alexa's good cooking. I'm not gonna argue about setting up to the table right now."

Suzanne followed Linda and Tom to the dining room. Alexa had left three chairs in a row between Mother and Sandra. They filled the seats, putting Tom in the middle, and Mother asked him to deliver the blessing for the food.

Without a moment's hesitation he bowed his head. "Our loving heavenly Father, we gather here on Christmas Day to fellowship and to celebrate the most amazing gift the world has ever known — the birth of Your Son, Jesus Christ."

Her head low and eyes closed, Suzanne listened to her friend pray, and a knot formed in her throat. He was such a wonderful man. She couldn't have chosen a better surrogate grandfather for Alexa. He'd assumed a fatherly role in Suzanne's life and served as a wise counselor on more occasions than she could count. And for years she'd deceived him by allowing him — and Linda and everyone else at the church in Franklin — to believe Alexa was her biological child. She'd confessed to her family and to Alexa, but others still needed to hear the truth.

"Amen," Tom's husky voice finished, and everyone echoed, "Amen."

Footed sundae glasses with layers of crushed berries, vanilla yogurt, and homemade granola waited beside each plate. They passed around baskets of crusty herb rolls while Alexa served thick, steaming wedges of the mushroom, spinach, and bacon quiche, the gooey, melted swiss cheese forming strings from the spatula to the plates. Conversation flowed around the table while they ate.

Linda took a hearty bite of her roll and moaned. "Alexa, my favorite bread comes from the farmer's market the Amish put on during the summer months. These rolls are every bit as good as any I've picked up from those bakers. Some of the Old Order must've been passed to you to be able to bake such goo-ood bread."

Alexa grinned her thanks. She shot her mother a brief look, and Suzanne shifted her gaze across the table to prevent silent communication with her daughter. But then she caught Shelley's slight frown, and she knew without even asking what her sister was thinking. Suzanne lowered her gaze to her plate, but the quiche had lost its appeal.

Feigning nonchalance, she turned to Linda. "Will you and Tom have to hurry back home?"

"Now that we've both retired, there's not one thing pressing on us to hurry back, so we intend to stay right here 'til New Year's." Linda beamed. "We wanted a nice, long visit with our two favorite girls, and your mama said we'd be welcome for as long as we wanted to stay."

Suzanne forced her lips into a smile and nodded. She had to tell Linda and Tom the truth about Alexa before one of her family members let it slip. But not today. Not on

Christmas, when they were here as her gift. She wouldn't cloud their time together with her ugly confessions. Maybe tomorrow. Her stomach writhed.

Lord, please don't let them be horrified that I, in essence, stole a baby.

CHAPTER 3

Arborville, Kansas
Paul Aldrich

For as long as Paul could remember, the Christmas service in his fellowship had been his favorite service of all. He'd heard the account in Luke read so many times he had it memorized, but he still experienced a chill of joy when Deacon Muller read aloud the words declared so long ago by an angel of the Lord: "For unto you is born this day in the city of David a Saviour, which is Christ the Lord." Earlier that morning his son had declared his new baseball mitt the best gift ever, but Paul knew better. There had never been — and never would be — a greater gift than the gift of salvation.

He leaned sideways a bit to peer past the back of Eldon Neufeldt's head and located his son, who represented Joseph in this year's depiction of the Nativity. Danny's cheeks sported bold streaks of red, but he held his shoulders square and gazed down in a passable imitation of wonder at the swaddled doll lying in the oldest Thieszen girl's lap.

He swallowed a chuckle, recalling his son's initial resistance to playing the role of Joseph. Not because he was shy about being in front of the fellowship — there'd never been anything shy about Danny — but because he didn't want to give Millicent Thieszen, who chased him around on the playground, any funny ideas.

Paul had assured him he didn't need to worry, but now, in retrospect, maybe Danny's concerns weren't so far off base. After all, it was shortly after the Christmas he and Suzy Zimmerman had filled the roles of Joseph and Mary that he'd begun to look at her as more than just a playmate and frog-catching buddy.

By exercising great self-control, he managed to keep his focus forward instead of turning around to steal a glimpse of Suzy. She was there. Not on the bench she'd shared with her mother and younger sisters when she'd been a part of the fellowship, but clear in the back, where a shorter bench left room for her mother's wheelchair. According to the town's gossips, she was back in Arborville to stay.

So many things had changed since he and Suzy rode bikes, climbed trees, dropped a line in the Heidebrechts' pond, and courted. But that old adage "You never forget your first love" was true. Despite their twenty-year separation, their very different life directions, and even the deep pain of knowing they were robbed of the chance of raising the child they created together, she still held a tiny piece of his heart. And he was pretty certain she always would.

The squeak of weight shifting on the planked floorboards pulled Paul from his musing — the congregation was rising to sing. He jolted up with the others and joined as the song leader started them on "Joy to the World." They transitioned from one carol to another with ease. Paul thrilled to the glorious messages contained within the familiar verses. From angels' voices singing praise, to seeking kings, to shepherds receiving the news of the long-awaited Savior's arrival, the words sank deep into his soul and reminded him of the very heart of Christmas — the coming of the promised Messiah. A smile stretched his lips as he joined his voice with those of his fellow believers.

The singing ended, and in one accord the gathered worshipers turned to kneel at the benches for prayer. As he faced the back of the church, his gaze found Suzy, who had already knelt and bowed her head. Her uncovered hair, twisted into a heavy, braided bun and pinned at the base of her skull, shimmered with gold and bronze in the late-morning sunlight streaming through the windows. His chest went tight. He lowered his head and closed his eyes, but the image of Suzy kneeling in a position of humility with sunlight shimmering on her blond tresses seemed etched inside his eyelids.

The prayer leader said in a somber tone, "Begin with prayers of adoration."

Paul, still holding to the wonderful feelings Christmas evoked, had no difficulty bringing forth words of esteem and appreciation for the One who had saved him from his sins.

After several minutes of silent prayer, the second reminder came. "And now prayers of repentance."

Paul searched himself for any sins he may have committed. Losing patience with Danny, experiencing frustration with a man from a nearby town who'd criticized his work, neglecting his Bible reading one day last week — asking forgiveness for each of these wrongs came easily, and the feeling of being cleansed was like a weight falling from his shoulders. He reached deeper inside for anything else that should be given over in submission to his Father, and an unexpected confession formed in the recesses of his mind.

Lord, I harbor feelings for Suzy Zimmerman. My feelings for her led me down a path of destruction when I was a youth.

"Prayers of petition," the deacon directed.

Paul's prayer flowed without pause. *Give me strength to remain true to Your commands of purity. I'm a man, with the same desires as any other man, and after these many years of living on my own without a wife to meet my physical needs, I fear Suzy's presence in town may prove to be a temptation . . .*

Suzanne

What sweet agony to sit across the table from Anna-Grace. Sweet to watch her interact so kindly with her boisterous younger sister and agony to be unable to acknowledge her as anything other than her cousin's child. Suzanne's stomach ached. No, her womb ached. She should have had the privilege of raising this girl who resembled her so closely.

As conversation, interspersed with laughter, rolled around the table, she sent up one silent prayer after another for God to hold at bay the resentment and anger trying to rise and conquer her. She'd forgiven her mother. Consequently, anger no longer had any place in her thoughts or emotions. But if it wasn't for God's strength, she would still whirl into a tumult of fury. Anna-Grace should be calling her "Mom," not "Cousin Suzy."

"Mom?"

Alexa's subdued voice cut into Suzanne's thoughts. Remorse smote her when she saw tears glimmering in her daughter's brown eyes. Alexa flicked a look across the table — directly at Anna-Grace — then aimed her unsmiling gaze at Suzanne again. "I need to whip the cream and assemble the shortcakes. Will you help me?"

Alexa's request offered an escape from Anna-Grace's presence and the uncomfortable feelings flooding her. "Of course I will." She rose and followed Alexa through the butler's pantry into the kitchen. The moment they rounded the corner, Alexa spun and captured Suzanne in a hug. Suzanne held tight, sensing desperation in the embrace. She whispered, "Are you okay, honey?"

"Oh, Mom . . ." The words choked out on a sob.

Suzanne gripped tighter, her heart aching.

She'd thought it hard to be at the table with Anna-Grace, but it must be even worse for Alexa, whose discovery that she'd not been born into this family was still raw. If only she could find a way to restore Alexa to the happiness she'd exhibited earlier. She brushed a kiss on her daughter's moist cheek and rubbed her hands up and down her shoulder blades. "Shh, sweetheart. It's all right."

Alexa jerked free. She swiped her hand under her nose. "No, it's not." She marched to the refrigerator, pulled out the glass jars of heavy cream, and thunked them onto the worktable. "Do you want to whip the cream or halve the shortcakes on the plates?"

Knowing how particular Alexa was about the appearance of her extravagant desserts, she said, "I'll whip the cream and you arrange the shortcakes."

Alexa gave a brusque nod and headed for the oven. Suzanne stepped into her pathway and placed her hand on her daughter's arm, intending to offer a few words of assurance of how much she was loved. To her surprise Alexa stepped away from her touch and moved on without a pause. Hurt and more than a little confused, Suzanne considered admonishing her for her behavior. But realizing the actions were out of character for her usually tender-hearted daughter, she chose to remain silent.

She poured cream into a chilled bowl and applied a wire whisk with gusto. The cream thickened but didn't form peaks. She switched hands and continued whipping. If it wouldn't be intrusive to those chatting around the table in the next room, she'd use an electric mixer instead. She beat the cream until it resembled a cloud and then, her arms aching, carried the bowl to the counter, where Alexa had set out nearly two dozen dessert plates and centered the bottom half of a dome-shaped sweet biscuit on each plate. A mound of sliced strawberries, bright red and juicy, blanketed the flat half.

Although she'd already enjoyed a hearty dinner, Suzanne's mouth watered. "Mm, those look great."

Alexa glanced up from placing the bumpy top halves, their edges lightly browned, at a jaunty angle against the berries and the rim of the plates, but she didn't say anything.

Suzanne lowered the bowl to the counter and reached for the utensil drawer. "Do you want me to spoon the cream on, or would you rather pipe it on so it's prettier?"

Alexa paused for a moment, her lips sucked in. Then she dropped the biscuit half and faced her mother. "I'm really sorry,

Mom." A burst of laughter from the dining room carried around the corner. Alexa glanced in the direction of the door and cringed. "I acted like I'm mad at you, and I'm not. I'm not mad at all. I'm . . ."

Suzanne tucked a wayward strand of dark hair behind her daughter's ear. "Sad?"

Alexa swallowed. Her pretty face reflected sadness, but she shook her head. "No. Not sad, either. I don't know how to describe it."

Resting her hip against the edge of the counter, Suzanne folded her arms over her chest. "Try."

Alexa imitated Suzanne's pose. Her forehead puckered. "I thought I'd gotten used to having Anna-Grace around. You know, because she stayed here before Thanksgiving. But sitting in there with her again — especially with her parents and you there, too — made me realize how wrong this all is."

Suzanne frowned. "What's wrong?"

Alexa flapped her hand toward the doorway as another round of laughter erupted from the other room. "Us all acting like one big, happy family."

Stung, Suzanne hugged herself. "It's not an act, Alexa. We are happy together." She spoke more sharply than she'd intended, but the acceptance she now experienced from her family was hard won. She needed to acknowledge it. "I agree it was pretty rocky when I first came back, but we've found our peace. I don't understand what you're saying."

For long seconds Alexa stood with her head low, her forehead crunched into a series of furrows. Suzanne stared at her daughter, sympathy twining through her. No matter how settled they'd become, apparently Alexa still felt like the outsider. What would it take to make her precious child realize how very much she was loved and accepted? The blood ties didn't matter at all to Suzanne. Alexa was hers in every way that counted. She'd told her so again and again. Why couldn't Alexa believe it?

She touched her daughter's arm, and Alexa raised her head. Suzanne offered a tender smile. "Sweetheart, it isn't wrong for you to be out there with us, calling yourself a Zimmerman. You do belong. You always will."

Alexa made a face, as if dismissing Suzanne's words. "I know that."

Suzanne's confusion grew. "Then what —"

"It isn't me. It's her." Alexa spoke in a harsh whisper. "It's wrong for her to sit there as your cousin instead of your daughter. It's wrong for everyone to go on acting like nothing has changed when everything has changed. It's wrong because it's the same as lying." She pulled in a short breath, shook her head, then went on in the same raspy tone. "She's going to feel like a fool when she finally finds out. And the longer you wait, the more foolish she'll feel. The harder it will be for her to be comfortable around all of you again." Alexa grabbed Suzanne's hands and squeezed. Firmly. Fervently. Convincingly. "She needs to know the truth about who she is, Mom."

Suzanne started to remind her daughter that she'd opened the door to Anna-Grace to discover the identity of her birth parents, but before she could form the words, Alexa spoke again.

"And I need the same thing for myself."

CHAPTER 4

Suzanne

"Hey, you two, everyone is out there clamoring for Alexa's special strawberry shortcakes."

Both Suzanne and Alexa jumped at the intrusion. Sandra stood halfway in the hall, only her head and shoulders peeking around the corner. Her bright smile was juxtaposed with the serious expression on Alexa's face.

Sandra sent a glance from Suzanne to Alexa, and her smile faded. "What's wrong?"

"Nothing." Alexa gestured toward the shortcakes. "I just need to pipe on the whipped cream, give them a strawberry embellishment, and they'll be ready to serve."

Sandra's lips twitched into a hesitant grin. "Do you need some extra hands?" Orneriness glinted in her eyes — her Zimmerman sky-blue eyes, which Anna-Grace also possessed. "I can send Shelley in."

Suzanne suspected her youngest sister was attempting to lighten the serious mood in the kitchen, and her ploy worked.

Alexa barked a short laugh. "We'll get it, but thanks. Tell everybody to hang on — dessert is coming."

Sandra winked and disappeared around the corner.

Suzanne cupped Alexa's elbow. "Honey —"

"Not now, Mom. Everybody's waiting. We'll talk later." Alexa retrieved the waxed paper and piping tips. "You spoon the cream into the cone and I'll make the swirls, okay?"

If Alexa was willing to drop the topic for the moment, Suzanne wouldn't argue. But the idea of Alexa wanting to discover the roots of her past made her stomach churn. She hoped she'd be able to eat the flaky cinnamon-laced biscuits, honey-and-ginger-sweetened berries, and fresh cream without getting sick.

Suzanne's family proclaimed the strawberry shortcakes and freshly percolated coffee flavored with vanilla, sweet cream, and a touch of caramel the perfect end to a wonderful day, and Alexa did an admirable job of responding positively to their praise.

51

Only Suzanne — and Linda, in all likelihood, based on the way the woman examined Alexa's face — noticed the lack of sparkle in her daughter's eyes as she thanked everyone for their kind comments.

When they'd finished the dessert, Mother pushed her chair away from the table. "Children, you come with me, and I'll read you a story while your mothers, Alexa, and Anna-Grace clean up." She aimed a grin at Suzanne. "Suzy, take Andrew and Olivia out to the cottage and give them a tour."

Suzanne frowned. Showing off the old summer kitchen, which Alexa had magically transformed into a welcoming retreat, should be the decorator's privilege. And she wasn't altogether sure she wanted to be alone with her cousins. She'd barely said two words to them since they arrived. She started to protest.

Mother narrowed her gaze. "Andrew and Olivia will leave for Clete and Tanya's soon and then go home tomorrow morning, so they won't get another chance to see the changes out there. Oh!" Her lips formed an apologetic grimace. "Have Mr. and Mrs. Denning go, too. Of course they'll want to see it." She waved her hand as if shooing flies. "Go on now." She wheeled into the front room, the crowd of children swarming after her.

Suzanne turned to her cousins and then to Linda and Tom. She forced a soft chuckle. "What Mother wants, Mother gets. Grab your coats and let's go." She led them through the kitchen, avoiding meeting Alexa's brown-eyed gaze, onto the back porch, and then across the yard toward the summer kitchen. In the dark the winter air felt even colder, and she hugged herself, hurrying her steps.

Stars glimmered in a black sky, the North Star standing out from the rest. She couldn't help thinking about the Star of Bethlehem that led the shepherds to the manger where the promised Prince of Peace lay. If only a star would guide her to a place of perfect peace concerning the choices made so many years ago.

Andrew moved up beside her, his boots crunching against the snow-crusted grass. "I wasn't sure about driving over on Christmas Day. Especially when my brothers decided not to make the trip. But I'm glad now that Liv and I brought our girls. It was good to be with Aunt Abigail on a holiday again. I hope we'll return to our yearly family get-togethers. Remember how much fun we always had, Suzy?"

She'd buried her memories when she left

Arborville as a scared seventeen-year-old, but at Andrew's simple statement they returned in a rush. Suzanne's heart caught. She remembered playing tag, building tents out of blankets tossed over the clothesline, and having watermelon seed–spitting contests in the summertime. During their Christmas gatherings they made countless snow angels, played hide-and-seek in the barn, and set up a pretend store in the attic. She smiled. "We did have fun, didn't we? Even when we played cowboys and Indians and you and your brothers tied me to a fence post and then ran off to play something else."

"Yes, but I came back and rescued you."

"An hour later!"

They both laughed, their mingled breath forming a cloud of condensation. The shared laughter felt good. Cleansing.

He slung his arm across her shoulders, the way he had when they were kids ambling off to the fishing pond. "You were always more like a little sister than a cousin — my favorite relative on my mom's side." His fingers clamped onto her shoulder. He lowered his voice to a whisper. "And I wish I'd known a long time ago who to thank for the gift of parenthood you gave Livvy and me."

The good feelings dissolved. She stepped free of his touch and gave a little hop onto the cement stoop. She opened the door to the cottage and forced a smile as she gestured them in. "This is it — Alexa's cottage. There's an album of before-and-after photographs on the old sideboard, if you're interested in looking at it."

Linda and Olivia went directly to the sideboard and retrieved the album, while Tom and Andrew wandered the space, pausing to examine the built-in Murphy bed Paul Aldrich had constructed. Suzanne needed to distance herself from Andrew, so even though she would have loved to tell the men that Alexa designed the bed, she joined the women at the white painted table. Maternal pride swelled as she listened to them ooh and aah over the dramatic changes Alexa had made in the old summer kitchen.

Olivia turned sideways in her chair and gave the room a slow inspection. She shook her head, the black ribbons from her cap gently swaying beneath her chin. "Your daughter certainly has a knack for seeing the what-could-be. I'll be honest. If I'd walked into the summer kitchen and seen all this" — she gestured to the pictures in the album — "I would have run away screaming. I'm so glad Alexa didn't. The cottage is charming." She tipped her head and offered Suzanne a pensive look. "Anna-Grace told us how helpful Alexa has been in choosing paint colors and wall coverings for the house she and Steven will live in after they're married. When you adopt a child, you never know what his or her talents might be since they come from a different genetic line. You must be thrilled to have a daughter who is creative in so many ways."

Suzanne scrambled for an appropriate response.

Linda's brow puckered. "You adopted a little girl from China, right? Are you saying you're disappointed in some way by her?"

Olivia's eyes flew wide. "Of course not! We adore both Anna-Grace and Sunny, and we're happy to encourage them to pursue their God-given abilities." She smiled, placing her hand over Linda's. "I wasn't speaking of our girls but of Suzanne's daughter, Alexa." She turned to Suzanne, her expression innocent. "Andrew and I presume you adopted her when she was a young child."

Suzanne's dry mouth resisted forming words, but Linda sputtered to life.

"Adopted her? When she was a young child? Your presumptions are all mixed up.

Why, Tom and I met Suzanne when Alexa was only a few weeks old and Suzanne here was still recovering from childbirth. Young as she was, she had quite a time, but our good friends saw to it she got the rest she needed to recover. We've watched Alexa grow up, and we've watched Suzanne grow up, too." She snorted. "Adopted, my foot . . . Just because Alexa looks more like her father — I presume — than her mama, she's every bit Suzanne's." Linda stared at Suzanne. "Isn't that right?"

"Every bit Suzanne's . . ." Linda's statement resonated through Suzanne's heart. She nodded.

Linda shot a triumphant grin at Olivia. "See there? That girl isn't adopted. You're mistaken."

Olivia stared at Suzanne, her face pursed into a scowl of confusion. "Then how —"

Suzanne leaped up, nearly toppling her chair. She caught the bow-shaped backrest and settled the antique chair into place at the table. Releasing a nervous laugh, she waved at the men, who'd remained beside the Murphy bed, arms folded over their chests, quietly chatting. "I'm sure Mother has finished the story by now, and the children are probably restless. Should we go back to the house?"

Olivia hurried across the floor to Andrew, and Tom moved toward Linda. Suzanne watched her cousins out of the corner of her eye. Her pulse scampered into frantic beats when Olivia whispered something to Andrew, and they both sent puzzled looks in her direction. Before either of them could broach the subject of Alexa's birth again, Suzanne slipped her arm through Linda's and aimed her for the door. Andrew and Olivia followed, and to her great relief they didn't ask any questions.

She led them over the flat steppingstones to the front porch rather than interrupt the kitchen cleanup. In the house Mother had organized a game of "button, button, who has the button" to keep the children occupied. The kids went on playing as Suzanne and the others entered the living room. Mother turned her wheelchair toward the adults and smiled. "What did you think of the cottage? Quite something, isn't it?"

Andrew and Olivia murmured agreement, and Tom boomed, "Doesn't surprise me in the least. That Alexa's been creatin' something out of nothing since she was a little wart. She built a whole town out of appliance boxes in our basement when she was a kindergartner."

"First grader," Linda corrected. "When

she was in kindergarten, she made a worm farm in the backyard."

Tom stuck his hands in his pockets and rocked on his heels, chuckling. "Oh, that's right. I'd forgotten about the worm farm. Fences out of Popsicle sticks and blue yarn. She even named the worms. I couldn't tell Uncle Wiggly from Slim Jim, but she claimed she knew 'em all." His eyes crinkled with his broad smile. "Yessir, that one always had something going. Kept us all hopping, I can tell you, but in a good way. Alexa's always been a joy."

As much as it warmed Suzanne's mother-heart to hear Tom speak so glowingly of her daughter, Andrew's and Olivia's expressions were becoming more confused and curious by the minute. She needed to turn the conversation. "Where are Clete, Derek, and Harper?"

Mother gestured toward the closed pocket doors. "In the dining room sipping a last cup of coffee before everyone leaves." She sighed and reached for Andrew's hand. "It's been a wonderful day — the best Christmas I can remember in years. I'm not ready for it to end."

Andrew went down on one knee beside Mother's chair. "Well, it won't be years until we see you the next time. I already told Suzy we intend to reinstate our annual get-togethers."

Suzanne's stomach twinged, but Mother beamed.

He went on. "And of course we'll all be back in Arborville in less than two months."

"Two months?" Suzanne didn't realize she'd nearly screeched the question until the circle of children paused in their button-passing to gawk up at her. She offered them a feeble smile. "Go ahead and play." Then she inched closer to Andrew. "You're coming back in two months?"

Olivia answered. "Yes, for Anna-Grace and Steven's wedding. They've decided to get married in the Arborville fellowship instead of the one in Sommerfeld. With Steven teaching here now, they decided it was less disruptive to do everything here." Tears glistened in her eyes, but she blinked them away. "Of course, we were disappointed not to have the ceremony at the fellowship where they both grew up, but we understand their reasoning."

Mother nodded slowly. "So the wedding is on . . ."

Andrew and Olivia exchanged a quick look before Andrew spoke. "Yes. Steven's decision to teach in the local school instead of farming his grandfather's land definitely surprised a few people, including Anna-Grace. But when she had time to think about it, she realized God paved the way for him to be able to serve as a teacher."

Olivia placed her hand on Andrew's shoulder, a tender gesture that sent an unexpected shaft of longing through Suzanne. "Even though Steven's decision temporarily rattled her, it didn't take her long to forgive him for holding back his real desires from her. She's a very kind, forgiving girl."

Olivia's final statement echoed inside Suzanne's head. Her vision blurred as tears filled her eyes. Would Anna-Grace have the ability even to forgive Suzanne for not keeping her? Or was her act too hurtful to be forgiven? Her chest grew tight, emotion building.

"And I hope it will be all right for her to come stay with you again in the weeks leading up to the wedding." Olivia sighed. "She said — and she's right — that it will be easier for her to make arrangements from here. I'd like to be directly involved, which will be impossible with me more than three hours away, but at least if she's with you, Aunt Abigail, she'll have the help and support of family."

The pressure built in Suzanne's chest until

she couldn't hold it in. A single sob burst out. She clapped her hand over her mouth, but she couldn't suppress a second sob. Her entire frame shuddered as if she rode a bucking bronco.

The children's game stopped again, every little face turning upward. Mother leaned sideways slightly to look past Andrew. Even through the spurt of tears, Suzanne saw the concern on her mother's face.

Linda touched Suzanne's arm. "What's wrong, girlie?"

Suzanne couldn't bear the kindness in her dear friend's tone. She shook her head, a message of both "I can't talk right now" and "I don't deserve your compassion."

Linda slipped her arm around Suzanne's waist and steered her toward the staircase. "Come upstairs with me. We'll have us a talk."

CHAPTER 5

Suzanne

Suzanne sank down on the edge of the bed and buried her face in her hands. How humiliating to break down that way. She pictured her nieces' and nephews' startled expressions, Mother's furrowed brow, Andrew's and Olivia's confusion. The tightness in her chest grew until drawing a breath was painful. She had to gain control of her emotions. But how, when the source of her anguish would sit across the dining room table every day for the next two months?

The click of the door latch sealed out the mutters traveling up the stairs from the living room. The mattress shifted — Linda settling in beside her — and a heavy arm fell around her shoulders. Then a warm hand, the same thick palm that had offered comfort in countless times of worry over the years, cupped Suzanne's head and gently pulled until her cheek pressed Linda's.

"What is it, girlie? What's got you all upset?" Linda's rumbling whisper sounded next to Suzanne's ear.

Her eyes closed tight, her fist pressed to her mouth, she couldn't answer.

"Is it Anna-Grace?"

The voice wasn't Linda's. Suzanne jolted upright and opened her eyes. Olivia stood a few feet in front of her with her hands clasped in a prayerful position beneath her chin. Olivia had followed her and Linda? Suzanne experienced the very childish desire to hide under the bed.

Compassion glowed in Olivia's eyes. "As hard as it's been for Andrew and me to keep quiet about Anna-Grace's parentage, it must be even worse for you. If you'd like, I'll talk to Anna-Grace about —"

Linda aimed an impatient look at Suzanne. "What is she talking about? Anna-Grace's parentage . . . And earlier she asked about you adopting Alexa." She shook her head. "You two've got me all befuddled."

An expression of both awareness and shock came over Olivia's face. She stepped forward and leaned down to grip Suzanne's hands. The ends of the black ribbons from her cap tickled Suzanne's knuckles, a reminder of what might have been if she'd stayed in Arborville, married Paul, and raised her baby with him. She closed her eyes again.

"Cousin Suzy, I'm so sorry. I just assumed your good friends knew you'd given up your baby girl for adoption."

Suzanne heard the deep apology in Olivia's voice, but she couldn't make herself look her cousin's wife in the face. Because she knew she'd see questions in addition to contrition.

"Gave up?" No apology laced Linda's tart tone.

Suzanne hunkered lower. She hadn't wanted to divulge her secrets on Christmas Day, but firm fingers gripped her chin and forced her head up.

"Suzanne?"

She opened her eyes. Linda's face was only inches from hers, and the set of her lips told Suzanne clearly the woman meant business.

"All right, girlie, it's been a long time since I got all motherly on you. Seems a little silly to be doing it now with your own mama sitting downstairs and you thirty-seven years old instead of seventeen like when we first met. But I'm not gonna be able to sleep tonight unless I understand what in the name of all that's sensible this cousin of yours is talking about." She released Suzanne's chin with a light pinch. "Go ahead now. Talk."

Olivia drew the reproduction Louis XV tapestry chair close and slipped into it. "Yes, Suzy. I'd like to understand, too. The letters you gave us for Anna-Grace identify you and Paul Aldrich as her parents. Yet you have a daughter who's the same age as Anna-Grace. How is that possible?"

Haltingly, her words stumbling out between swallowed sobs, Suzanne explained being sent to the unwed mothers' home in Indianapolis by her mother with the fierce instruction to give her baby to Andrew and Olivia. Reliving the torment of her squalling baby girl being carried away pierced her anew, and she flattened her palms against her aching heart as she continued sharing with the two silent, wide-eyed women closed in the bedroom with her.

"The day I was supposed to leave the home — to go to a 'recovery house' arranged by the home's director — I heard what I thought was a kitten crying behind the garage. But it wasn't a kitten. It was a baby. A brand-new baby girl. Someone had put her in a box and left her there, all alone in the alley. I didn't even think. I just scooped her up and I . . . I kept her."

Linda gasped, and Olivia exclaimed, "You did no such thing!"

Suzanne squared her shoulders and spoke forcefully. "Yes, I did. I took her to the hospital, and because I'd given birth only the day before, everyone assumed she was mine. And I let them believe it. I'd prayed for God to let me keep my baby, but the people at the home took her away anyway. So when I found this little girl, I told myself she was my answered prayer. She was mine. The birth certificate the state sent me proved it. She's always been mine."

She looked from Olivia's astounded face to Linda's, and her firm resolve dissolved. Tears flooded her eyes. She turned away. "I've disappointed you."

In a heartbeat she found herself wrapped in Linda's embrace. Her friend's breath — spice-scented from her longtime habit of munching licorice cats — wafted across her cheek, drying the tears that flowed in a warm trickle. "Oh, honey, no. You've . . . shocked me."

Suzanne could only imagine Linda's shock at being lied to for twenty years.

"All this time I never once suspected Alexa wasn't yours."

Suzanne pulled back, uncertain she'd

heard correctly. "You aren't shocked that I . . . I took a baby that wasn't mine?"

A tender smile tipped up the corners of her full lips. "Knowing your compassionate heart, of course not. Then consider your young age, that you'd just given birth and your hormones were likely running amuck, and you'd been praying for God to let you keep your baby . . . No, doesn't shock me at all that you picked up that helpless little girl and claimed her as yours."

Suzanne threw her arms around Linda and clung hard. "Thank you for not thinking ill of me."

"Think ill of you?" Linda rocked her side to side, chuckling. "Lands, girlie, the things you say. What you told me makes me admire you even more for how much you love Alexa. I've never seen a more dedicated mama."

"Oh, Cousin Suzy . . ." At Olivia's tearful, raspy voice, Suzanne and Linda pulled apart and turned toward her. "I'm so very sorry. We never knew."

"Of course you didn't know." Suzanne's heart felt bruised by the real pain in Olivia's eyes. "No one knew — not even Alexa. My family only recently found out."

"No." Olivia shook her head hard, making her cap ribbons flop furiously against the caped bodice of her deep-maroon Christmas dress. "Not that Alexa isn't yours — that you wanted to keep Anna-Grace. Andrew and I were only told the baby's mother was young, unmarried, and unable to care for her. If we'd known you didn't want to give her up for adoption, we would never have taken her." Her white face spoke clearly of her inner anguish. "I feel as though we . . . we stole her from you."

Suzanne placed her hands on Olivia's knees, praying for the ability to speak assurance to her cousin without divulging the bitter regret still clinging around the edges of her heart. "You didn't take her from me. You and Andrew opened your hearts to a stranger's baby, and you loved her like she was your own. You've done nothing wrong."

"You listen to Suzanne now, you hear?" Linda cupped her hands over Suzanne's and leaned close. "You welcomed that baby girl into your home with a pure heart — same way Suzanne here welcomed an abandoned baby into her heart. Neither one of you has any reason to be ashamed or regretful over what you did."

Olivia sniffed. "Thank you. But . . ." She turned a worried look on Suzanne. "What of Alexa? Since you never adopted her, is she legally your daughter?"

Suzanne's palms began to sweat. She sat up, slipping her hands from beneath Linda's and swiped them along the thighs of her pleated wool skirt. Suzanne feared the answer to Olivia's question was no, but she didn't want to admit it. She didn't even want to think about it. A tap at the door saved her from answering.

Linda said, "Whoever's out there, come on in."

Tom stepped halfway into the room, his curious gaze flicking across the trio of female faces. "Mrs. Braun, your family's ready to go. Your husband sent me up to see if you're done talking."

Olivia swished her fingers under her eyes and rose. She pushed the chair back into place, then aimed a weak smile at Tom. "Please tell Andrew I'll be down in a minute." As soon as Tom departed, she turned to Suzanne. "May I tell Andrew about Alexa?" She added quickly, "In private — not in front of our girls."

Although Suzanne wanted to deny the request, it was silly to ask Olivia to keep it secret. Eventually everyone would know, and it was better to hear about situations firsthand than through local grapevines, where the story had a tendency to pick up embellishments along the way. "Yes."

Linda sucked in a breath and gripped Suzanne's knee. "Anna-Grace . . . she's your biological daughter?"

Suzanne nodded stiffly.

"But she doesn't know it yet?"

She shook her head. "Her father — Paul Aldrich — and I gave Andrew and Olivia letters to tell her who we were, but she hasn't opened them." When would she finally do it so this tiptoeing on eggshells could end?

Linda leaned in, her eyes sparking with fervency. "Then let Mrs. Braun here tell about Alexa in front of Anna-Grace. Hearing a story about a young girl who was denied the opportunity to raise her own baby and who raised someone else's little girl as her own might give her the courage to find out who gave birth to her and why they didn't keep her."

Suzanne bit down on her lower lip. Alexa's adamant statement — *"She needs to know the truth of who she is, Mom"* — blared through her memory. Somehow Anna-Grace discovering the truth got tangled up with Alexa wanting to discover the truth of her birth, and Suzanne couldn't find the means to agree or disagree with Linda's suggestion.

She sent Olivia a helpless look. "I . . . I

71

can't make that decision for you, Livvy. I don't know Anna-Grace well enough to know how she'd accept it." The realization of how distant she was from the child formed in her womb crushed her. She gulped back tears. "I'll let you decide what to do."

Olivia leaned down and gave Suzanne a hug, squeezing so tight she forced the air from Suzanne's lungs. Then she straightened abruptly, nodded, and scurried out of the room.

Linda bounced her palm off of Suzanne's knee, frowning. "Suzanne Zimmerman, what are you scared of?"

She swallowed a laugh. Linda knew her so well. But she played dumb. "I don't know what you mean."

"Oh, yes, you do." Linda's expression turned grim. "Something's eating at you, but we started talking about Anna-Grace and got you off track. I figure she's part of it, but there's more. So what is it?"

Suzanne pulled in a breath and released it slowly, bringing her raging emotions under control. "What you said about Anna-Grace finding the courage to discover who her birth parents are . . . well, I think Alexa's already gathered her courage."

Linda's brows descended. "She wants to

go looking for her birth parents? She said that?"

"She said" — Suzanne swallowed a knot of anguish — "Anna-Grace needs to know the truth, and she needs to know the truth, too."

Linda slung her arm around Suzanne's shoulders and gave her several comforting pats. "So let her."

Suzanne jerked away and gawked at Linda. "Let her? Didn't you hear how she came to be with me? I didn't adopt her, Linda. I didn't even ask anyone if I could take her. I just did it. As far as the law is concerned, I kidnapped her! Do you think a judge is going to care that I was only seventeen and emotionally distraught? Of course not! If Alexa finds her birth parents, I could end up facing criminal prosecution."

Linda sat staring at Suzanne, her brows low and her lips puckered, for several seconds. Then she pushed to her feet, strode to the door, and bellowed, "Tom! Get up here!" She turned to Suzanne and planted her fists on her hips. "You're gonna tell Tom everything you told me. Every detail of where and how you found that baby girl and how you got your name put on her birth certificate as her mama. Then the three of us are gonna pray together for God's will to be done. Because you and I both know once our Alexa Joy gets her mind set on something, she sees it through. She's gonna go looking for the ones who birthed her and then threw her away. And we need to be ready for the consequences."

CHAPTER 6

Indianapolis
Cynthia

Cynthia hooked the calendar, provided free by the local credit union and bearing scenic photographs of places she'd likely never see in person, on the nail pounded into the wall next to the refrigerator. The heavy pages slanted to the right. She straightened the calendar, then stepped back and stared at the little box indicating the first day of a new year. A new year, a fresh slate . . . What new experiences, blessings, and heartaches awaited in the months ahead?

When she was a girl, she'd hated all holidays and especially New Year's. Another excuse for her mom and most recent stepdad to invite a dozen of their barhopping buddies over and get rip-roaring drunk. Inevitably they ended up fighting. Sometimes with each other, sometimes with their so-called friends, sometimes with her or her brother. Regardless, it was awful. But then she'd met Glenn, and together they'd met Jesus, and her view of a new year changed. It became a time of reflection and renewal.

She pressed her finger to the square representing January 1, where tiny letters spelled out "What's your resolution for this new year?" across the bottom of the box. She shook her head in silent response. She didn't make resolutions. She'd yet to meet someone who kept them. Instead she reflected on the past year, both the good and the not-so-good moments, and prayed for God to reveal things she needed to change to better reflect Him in the days ahead.

The past week since she received the unexpected gift from Glenn, she'd prayed extra hard. When she met her daughter for the first time — because she'd decided to let the investigator start searching — she wanted none of the mars and stains of her past to show.

Only You, dear Lord, let her see only You in me . . .

"Morning, Mom!" Darcy bounced into the room, still in her pajama pants and stretched-out T-shirt, silky brown hair pulled back in a tangled mess of a ponytail that somehow managed to look cute. She flung the refrigerator door open, forcing Cynthia to move aside or be smacked. Carton of milk in one hand and a jar of strawberry jam in the other, Darcy bumped the door closed with her hip and moved to the counter, humming a tune from one of her vast selection of CDs.

Cynthia leaned against the wall and watched Darcy pour a tall glass of milk and then prepare two strawberry jam fold-over sandwiches. Glenn teasingly called Darcy a flibbertigibbet, but Cynthia thought her daughter too graceful for such a clunky term. Her hands moved from jelly jar to bread, her motions seemingly choreographed. Cynthia's heart swelled with love for this lighthearted, flamboyant child, so different from the way she'd been at Darcy's age.

Remorse panged. Would she have been carefree and happy if she'd been raised by parents who loved each other and their children the way she and Glenn chose to love Darcy and Barrett?

One sandwich between her teeth, the other balanced on top of the milk glass, Darcy yanked a paper towel from the holder and scuffed to the little breakfast bar at the end of the counter, leaving a spattering of crumbs, an open bread bag, the jam jar with a knife sticking up out of it, the milk jug sans its lid, and smears of strawberry jam in her wake.

Maybe Darcy was a bit of a flibbertigibbet . . .

Cynthia grabbed the dishrag from the edge of the sink and attacked the disaster zone. But she didn't scold. Her mother's screeching criticisms still rang in her memory. She'd vowed never to be that kind of mother. As she swept crumbs into her hand, she said, "I'm surprised you're up already since you didn't go to bed until after one." They'd enjoyed a family movie night to celebrate the new year. "I figured you'd sleep 'til noon at least."

"Who can sleep when ticket sales open at eight?" Darcy licked jam from her thumb and shot a bright grin across the kitchen. "I gotta be one of the first twenty to call in, or I won't get the bonus fan pack."

Cynthia sent a puzzled look over her shoulder. "Ticket sales? What are you talking about?"

Darcy froze with her milk halfway to her mouth, her jaw hanging slack. Then she clunked the glass onto the counter. Droplets of milk spritzed over the rim and dotted the gray laminate. "You forgot?"

Cynthia blinked twice, searching her memory.

"Mom, you did! You forgot! How could you forget?"

"Instead of getting all worked up, why not just tell me what I've forgotten?"

"Winter Band Blast? At the coliseum — remember?"

The sarcasm coloring Darcy's tone brought back too many memories of other voices from the past. Chills exploded across Cynthia's flesh, and her pulse picked up an extra beat. She dropped the dishrag and moved to the opposite side of the breakfast bar, inwardly praying for calm, calm.

"Darcy, please do not speak to me in that condescending way. It isn't respectful."

"But, Mom, I —"

Cynthia held up one finger and raised her eyebrows. "It's been at least two weeks since anything was mentioned about the Winter Band Blast, and those weeks have been busy ones, pushing the concert to the back burner."

Darcy pulled in a breath and blew it out slowly. Glenn used the same technique to bring his aggravation under control. He set such a good example for the kids — amazing, considering his own volatile upbringing. Resting her elbows on the edge of the

79

counter, Darcy met Cynthia's gaze. "I've been doing a countdown during Christmas break, and I've mentioned Winter Band Blast every day. At supper last night Dad asked if I had enough baby-sitting money saved up to pay for my ticket. I know you worked at the library every afternoon, but you had to have heard me talk about Winter Band Blast at least once during the break. Unless you haven't been paying any attention at all."

Now a hint of hurt feelings crept into Darcy's voice, and Cynthia couldn't blame her. The concert was important enough for her to save her baby-sitting money, count down the days, and pull herself out of bed early when she could have stayed under the covers all day if she'd wanted to. And somehow Cynthia had missed every reference over the past several days.

She reached across the counter and pushed a strand of hair away from her daughter's cheek. "I'm sorry. You're right. I haven't paid attention. I've been . . . distracted."

Darcy tipped her head. "Thinking about the PI?"

Although her thoughts had been centered on how the girl the private investigator was seeking might respond to being found, she nodded.

"Bet you're thinking more about your baby girl, though, right?"

Cynthia swallowed a startled cough. Her daughter was more perceptive than she'd realized. She picked up the dishrag and went to work scrubbing the half-dried smears of strawberry jam on the counter-top.

"Hey, Mom, can I ask you a question?"

Cynthia offered her daughter a wry grin. "Obviously you can. You just did."

Darcy rolled her eyes. "That's something Dad would say."

Cynthia laughed. She moved to the sink to rinse the rag. "What's your question?"

"Why'd you give your baby away?"

The question struck like a stone from a slingshot. Cynthia took her time rinsing, wringing, and draping the rag over the edge of the sink. "What did Daddy tell you?"

"That you were young — like, fifteen. Not old enough to be a mom yet."

Cynthia turned slowly and leaned against the cabinet, needing the sturdy support. Her legs felt weak and rubbery. She folded her arms over her chest and forced a glib tone. "That's about right."

Darcy frowned. "But there's gotta be more to it than that. I mean, yeah, fifteen is pretty

81

young, but I know of at least three girls who are fifteen or even younger who have babies, and they kept 'em. There's even one in my class."

Only a year ago Darcy boxed up her Barbie dolls and asked Glenn to put the box with their other stored belongings above the garage rafters. Cynthia shook her head. "There can't be. You're only in the seventh grade."

Darcy nodded, wide eyed. "It's true. Her name is Charity Webber, and she's gonna have a baby before the end of the school year. She says she's keeping it." Furrows marched across Darcy's girlish forehead. "She's thirteen. Lots younger than you were. So why didn't you keep your baby?"

Ugly images from the past flashed through Cynthia's memory. She'd worked so hard to paint pleasant pictures of family in her children's minds. She didn't want to give Darcy even a tiny peek into the awfulness that had been her childhood. But how to answer honestly without sharing the bleakness and strife of her upbringing?

She prayed for discernment and then formed a careful question. "What do you think you'd need to take care of a baby?"

Darcy shrugged. "A crib, lots of diapers and bottles, burp rags because they spit up a lot. At least the ones I've baby-sat do. Maybe some toys and a little swing. You know, baby stuff."

"Oh, Darcy . . ." Cynthia smiled sadly. "You aren't wrong. All of those things are helpful. But what babies need most of all is love and attention. They aren't a toy you can set aside when you're tired of playing with it. Babies are a twenty-four-hour-a-day, seven-day-a-week, for-the-rest-of-your-life responsibility. And most teenage girls aren't ready for that kind of commitment."

"Then why do so many of them keep their babies?"

Pain stabbed. "Well, maybe the girls you know have someone who is willing to help them. A mom or grandmother or the baby's father — someone to share the responsibility so it isn't so overwhelming."

Understanding bloomed across Darcy's face. "You didn't have help, did you?"

Cynthia shook her head. To her knowledge her mother had gone to her grave without ever knowing she had a granddaughter somewhere in the world. Not that she would have cared, considering how little she'd cared about her son and daughter.

Cynthia's throat went tight, turning her voice into a raspy whisper. "No, I didn't. And I knew I couldn't do it alone. I wanted something more, something better, than what I could offer to my baby. So I gave her away."

Darcy slipped off the stool and rounded the breakfast bar. Without a word she grabbed Cynthia in a stranglehold hug. Gritting her teeth against the threat of tears, Cynthia held tight. After several seconds Darcy released her hold, stepped back, and tipped her head. A loose strand from her ponytail swished across her shoulder and curled up under her chin, giving her an elfin appearance that made Cynthia want to laugh and cry at the same time.

"Can I ask another question?"

Cynthia braced herself, pulled in her breath, and gave a stiff nod.

"Would you call the ticket hot-line number on your phone while I'm calling on mine? It'll double my chances of being one of the first twenty to get through."

Her lungful of air released on a snort of laughter.

"What?" Darcy held her hands outward, her eyes sparkling with mischief. "I really want one of those fan packs. An autographed T-shirt, two backstage passes, a poster, and a stack of CDs all in a custom-designed tote bag to commemorate Winter Band Blast Indianapolis!"

Shaking her head, Cynthia moved toward the wireless phone receiver in its base next to the sink. "What's the number?"

Arborville
Suzanne

Suzanne lifted the coffee mug to her mouth. The rich aroma of the fresh-ground Arabica blend teased her senses. The first sip of the morning was always the best, and she slowly drew in the steaming liquid, allowing it to pool on her tongue briefly before letting it slip down her throat. Wind howled outside the old farmhouse, ringing in the new year in a boisterous manner, but the kitchen was warm, cozy, and — with everyone else still sleeping — solitary.

On the worktable in front of her, the December 30 edition of the *Indianapolis Times* — the most recent edition to arrive via mail — lay unopened. She gave it a lazy glance, both hands cupped around the warm mug. Did she want to read beyond the headline or not? In spite of the gusting wind, her morning felt calm and peaceful. So often events outside of Arborville disturbed her. She took another sip, contemplating. Then she pushed the paper aside. She'd enjoy an hour or two of peacefulness before peeking at the pages.

Floorboards creaked, and Suzanne turned toward the hallway. Linda scuffed around the corner in fuzzy red slippers, her hair standing on end. When her gaze met Suzanne's, she broke into a smile that stretched comically into a yawn.

Suzanne stifled a giggle. "Good morning, sunshine."

Linda snapped her mouth closed and shot a mock scowl across the worktable. "Ha-ha. Where's the coffee I've been smelling? I need a cup. A big cup." She plopped onto the second stool and yawned again.

Suzanne retrieved a mug, filled it, and handed it over with a smile. "Why are you up so early? Your flight doesn't leave until after four o'clock."

"Who can sleep with the aroma of Alexa's special blend of beans wafting up the stairs and tormenting my nose?" She took a deep draw of the mug, smacked her lips, and sighed. "Mm-mm, that's good coffee. You gonna be able to mix it up right when you're the one in charge around here?"

Suzanne's stomach rolled, and she set the cup aside. "I'll do my best."

Linda raised one eyebrow and pinned Suzanne with a steady gaze. "You sure you're okay with all this?"

After praying with Linda and Tom and

giving the situation much thought, she'd agreed to assume responsibility for the bed-and-breakfast so Alexa could travel to Indianapolis and begin a search for her birth mother. Agreeing to it and aligning her heart to it were two completely different things, however. Even so, she smiled to reassure her friend. "As Tom so wisely said, Alexa wanting to investigate her birth during the quietest time in the B and B business and my being here to assume her duties does seem providential. Who am I to question the Lord's leading in her life?"

"Mm-hm." Linda took a sip, her eyebrows high. "You're not fooling me. You don't want her to go."

Suzanne reached for her cup again. The liquid had cooled, but she drank it anyway. It kept her mouth busy so she couldn't voice the multiple concerns rolling through her mind.

Linda shook her head. "Stubborn, stubborn, stubborn. You always have been. But I suppose the Good Lord gave you that trait to keep you plowing forward during hard times. Which is why I know you'll survive letting your girl go traipsing off in search of her past."

"And what if she finds it? What then?" The questions burst out, carried on a note of panic. Suzanne choked back a sob, unable to squelch the tidal wave of worries. "What if her birth mother decides to file kidnapping charges against me for taking Alexa away? I could go to prison!"

Linda grabbed Suzanne's hands and squeezed. "Tom researched it. He says there's a five-year statute of limitations on kidnapping, so you don't need to worry over that."

"Are you sure?"

"Sure I'm sure."

Suzanne clung hard to Linda. Her greatest fear found its way from the recesses of her heart. "But legally Alexa doesn't belong to me. What if her birth parents decide they want her with them? I have no grounds to keep her."

Linda gave a yank that nearly popped Suzanne's wrists. "Gracious sakes, Suzanne, what a thing to say. Alexa's not a little girl who can be forced into something she doesn't want to do. She's a grown woman who can make up her own mind. Do you really believe after twenty years of you being that girl's mama, she's gonna turn her back on you? She loves you. You know that."

Then why couldn't she leave well enough alone and be happy just being Alexa Zimmerman? Suzanne held the bitter query inside. Some things were better left unsaid. She sighed. "I suppose you're right."

"I know I'm right. And you'll figure it out, too, when she comes back here, ready to greet guests and bake rolls and call you Mom, just like always."

Suzanne managed a wobbly smile.

"Now gimme another cup of coffee. And splash some cream in this cup. Heavens to Betsy, that stuff's strong enough to choke a horse."

Laughing, Suzanne rose to do Linda's bidding. As she lifted the percolator, the back porch door opened, and Alexa hurried in on a rush of cold air. She clicked the door closed, shivered, then aimed a bright smile across her mother and Linda. "Oh, you're up, too, Linda! Happy New Year!"

Linda rose and folded Alexa in a hug. "Brr, girl, get some coffee in you and warm up."

Alexa popped open the refrigerator door. "I'll warm up soon enough when I get the stove cranked on. Who wants a mushroom, spinach, and feta omelet?"

Linda took her coffee cup from Suzanne. "You don't have to ask me twice."

Alexa turned to Suzanne. "Mom?"

Gazing into her daughter's gold-flecked brown eyes, Suzanne battled tears. *She's my girl, Lord. Please don't let some woman I don't know take her away.* She swallowed. "Sure, honey. Thanks."

"Comin' right up! And then" — she flashed an impish grin — "I've got to pack." A pinch of uncertainty trembled on her lips. "Will you . . . help me?"

CHAPTER 7

Suzanne

Suzanne pulled in a breath and released it slowly, controlling the urge to cry. She offered a weak smile. "I'd be glad to." Thankfully no lightning bolt came from the sky to strike her dead for lying, but another mighty blast of wind rattled the house. She flicked a wry glance toward the kitchen window. "Assuming of course the cottage doesn't get blown away and all your clothes with it."

Should she hope for such an event? No, of course not. But she couldn't help hoping something might change Alexa's mind about traveling back to Indiana with Linda and Tom and searching for her birth mother.

As Alexa began sautéing the mushrooms and spinach in butter, Tom entered the kitchen. A frown marred his normally placid face.

Linda sent him a worried scowl. "Uh-oh.

91

What's wrong?"

The corners of his lips twitched. "How'd you know something's wrong?"

"When you ain't smilin' first thing, something's wrong. What is it?"

Instead of answering, Tom crossed to the stove and peeked in the pan. He gave Alexa a one-armed hug. "No mushrooms in mine, but some onions would be good if you've got 'em."

Alexa assured him she could modify his omelet, and he returned to the worktable and curled his big hands over Linda's shoulders. "Don't know that you'll see all of it as bad news, but I got a text notice from the airport. All flights've been delayed because of a windstorm moving through. We've been bumped to tomorrow morning at eight."

Suzanne silently cheered — a reprieve, albeit a brief one.

But Linda groaned. "Oh, that means we have to be at the airport by six thirty, so we'll have to be up when even chickens have the good sense to sleep. I hate early morning flights. Call 'em and see if there's an afternoon flight going out tomorrow, would you?"

"Sure thing." Tom planted a kiss on

Linda's mussy hair, then ambled out of the room.

Alexa set the pan aside, pulled an onion from the bin next to the stove, and carried it to the chopping board. She applied the knife with gusto to the vegetable. Droplets of juice arced through the air and landed on Linda's elbow.

Linda pursed her lips and flicked the dots of moisture with her fingers. "Listen here, I'm not wanting to smell like onions all day. Take it easy with that knife."

Alexa grimaced. "Sorry, Linda."

She chuckled. "Oh, now, I was only teasing you. I haven't had my morning shower yet, so no harm done." Then she frowned. "But why're you being so rough on that poor onion? You act like it's an evil that needs to be conquered."

Alexa glanced in Suzanne's direction before answering. "I'm just a little . . . well, frustrated I guess. And I took it out on the onion because there isn't any other good target."

Linda took a sip of her coffee, watching Alexa over the rim of her cup. "You not keen on early morning flights, either?"

Alexa shrugged, scooped the chopped onion into a small bowl, and carried it back to the stove without answering. Linda started to say something to Suzanne, but Mother called from her bedroom.

Suzanne set her coffee aside and rose. "Coming, Mother!" She headed for the hallway.

Alexa scurried over. "Let me get her up and dressed this morning, please?" Moisture glimmered briefly in her eyes. "It'll be a while before I can help her again."

Suzanne nodded. "Want me to finish up the omelets?"

"Absolutely not. You always forget the seasonings." Alexa plopped a quick kiss on Suzanne's cheek and then hurried out of the room, calling, "I'm coming, Grandmother."

The smell of sautéed vegetables was making her stomach roll in eagerness. Suzanne retrieved a bowl and began cracking eggs.

"I thought Alexa said for you to leave that alone."

Suzanne's defenses rose at Linda's droll comment. "I'm not going to cook them, but I can't exactly mess up getting the eggs ready." She grimaced and reached into the gooey mass to pinch out a small triangle of tawny-brown shell.

Linda's rumbling chuckle rolled. "Maybe you better hire a cook while you're in charge out here."

Suzanne scowled at her friend.

Linda pushed to her feet and came at Suzanne with open arms. "C'mere, you." She wrapped Suzanne in her embrace and rocked her from side to side. "No wonder there's shell in that bowl the way you're smacking the poor eggs against the rim. You and Alexa are both taking your frustrations out on innocent produce."

Suzanne couldn't stifle a laugh. Linda always managed to cheer her. She savored the warm, tight hug, finding it as healing as she always had. *Thank You, Lord, for gifting me with this precious friend.*

Linda gave one more extra-tight squeeze and then stepped back. She planted her fists on her hips and pasted a mock scowl on her round face. "And I want you to stop this worrying over Alexa right now. There's no way meeting a new person, even if that person is the one who gave birth to her, is going to erase the last twenty years of loving you've given that girl. You've got no reason to be doing all this stressing."

Suzanne returned to the bowl of eggs and picked one up. She held the cool orb in her hand and stared at the pair of darker speckles on the soft-tan shell. "I know what you're saying is true. In my heart she'll always be my daughter. It is hard to let her go seeking, not knowing what she might find out or what changes it might bring into my relationship with her. But . . ."

Confusion thundered through her. She loved Alexa and didn't want to share her with another mother. Yet at the same time, she longed to develop a relationship with her birth daughter. How selfish to hold Alexa back while still reaching to embrace Anna-Grace. She couldn't make sense of her feelings, let alone find the words to explain them.

The squeak of rubber on hardwood alerted her to Mother's approach. Suzanne swished her hand over her eyes, and Alexa, pushing Mother's wheelchair, entered the kitchen.

"Mom, pour Grandmother some coffee, would you? And if you want, you can toast the bread. I'll get those omelets going. Then let's just eat here in the kitchen where it's warm and cozy, okay?"

Suzanne pushed away from the table as Alexa parked Mother's chair next to Linda and then headed for the stove.

Tom sauntered into the kitchen again. His sheepish expression spoke volumes.

Linda sighed. "We hafta take that early morning flight, don't we?"

Tom sank into the chair Suzanne had

vacated. " 'Fraid so. There just aren't lots of options for flights leaving Wichita."

"It'll be all right, Linda." Alexa spoke cheerfully. Too cheerfully — as if she was eager to make an escape. "You can borrow my earbuds to block out noise and sleep on the plane."

Linda harrumphed, but she didn't decline the offer.

Tom flipped the paper open and began to read while Mother and Linda chatted quietly. Suzanne and Alexa worked in silence, stepping around each other with ease. Suzanne's arms ached to capture her daughter in a hug each time their paths crossed, but Alexa would recognize her desperation and no doubt experience a rush of guilt, so Suzanne stayed focused on preparing breakfast instead.

Even though she was serving family rather than official guests, Alexa took the time to artfully arrange the triangles of toast on either side of the omelets and add a slice of orange, twisted to form a curl, as an embellishment to the plates. Suzanne memorized the appearance of the plate so she could emulate it when she took care of guests in Alexa's absence.

They each grabbed two plates and carried them to the worktable. Alexa gave Tom's shoulder a playful nudge with her elbow. "All right now, put that paper down. It's time to eat."

He aimed a mock scowl at Alexa. "Well, aren't you the bossy one?" He flicked the sheets of newsprint, making them snap, before starting to fold them closed.

Alexa jolted and released a squawk.

Everyone jumped in surprise, and Suzanne nearly dropped the plate she was setting in front of Mother. "Alexa!"

Seemingly unconcerned by the start she'd just given everyone, Alexa plopped the plates onto the table. A piece of toast slid off the edge, but Linda caught it and settled it back in place. She began to scold, but Alexa reached past Tom for the paper, her face alight, and spoke over Linda's protest.

"Grandmother, look!" She gave the pages a quick flip and thrust the folded square in her grandmother's direction.

Mother leaned back in her chair, clapped once, and let out a happy laugh. "Why, look at that! So she's making a name for herself, just like she wanted."

Alexa nodded, her ponytail swishing. "And we'll be able to say we knew her when."

Linda brushed crumbs onto the floor, her scowl deep. "Would you two stop talking in riddles and tell us what's got you all worked up?"

Alexa scurried around the table to Suzanne. "Mom, remember I told you about housing a family whose car broke down? It was last December, remember?" Suzanne recalled the conversation, but before she could answer, Alexa pointed to an article in the middle of the page. "This girl right here in the paper — her name is Nicole Kirkley, but she goes by Nicci K — is the girl who stayed with Grandmother and me! And now she's listed as the opening band for the Winter Band Blast in Indianapolis."

Mother gestured for Alexa to give her the paper. "That agent of hers is sure doing his job, isn't he?" She squinted and held the paper at an angle, scanning the print. Then she burst out laughing and smacked the paper against the edge of the table. "Alexa, guess who wrote this article about Nicci K!"

Alexa laughed, too. "Betcha I know!"

Linda waved both hands. "You're leaving us out again . . ."

Alexa leaned over and gave Linda a one-armed hug. "Sorry, we're just excited." She winked at her grandmother. "It's Briley Forrester, isn't it?"

Mother nodded, her smile wide. "It sure is."

Suzanne had heard that name from both Alexa and Mother. "The Chicago reporter? Why is he writing for the *Indianapolis Times*?"

"He's shadowing Nicci K and chronicling her journey toward becoming a country-western star. I imagine several papers have picked up the serial." Alexa took the paper again and gazed at the article, a sweet smile tipping up the corners of her lips. "That's wonderful for him."

Suzanne sensed there was more to the story than Alexa had shared. She intended to ask her daughter for more details when they were alone, but for now they needed to eat before the food grew cold. She slid into a chair. "Tom, would you ask the blessing?"

Tom gave a short but heartfelt prayer, and they ate with companionable conversation flowing around the table. Midway through the meal, Alexa tapped Linda on the wrist.

"What would you think about going to Band Blast?"

Linda's thick eyebrows descended. "Isn't that a concert for kids?"

Alexa shrugged. "I've never been, but some of my friends went when we were in high school. They said people of all ages attend because the music is everything from country to pop to rock'n'roll."

Linda made a sour face. "Oh, honey, rock'n'roll? That stuff sets my teeth on edge."

"Unless it's the nineteen fifties style." Tom stabbed a chunk of omelet, then used his fork as a pointer. "If they did something from the fifties, I'd be willing to go with you, Alexa."

Alexa grinned. "That'd be fun, but I'm not sure if today's bands play fifties tunes."

He shrugged and went on eating.

Alexa looked down at her plate and toyed with her remaining piece of toast. "Concerts aren't something you want to go to alone."

Her forlorn countenance pierced Suzanne's heart. She wished she could go with Alexa. "Maybe one of your friends from school will want to go with you. You should give some of them a call when you're back in Indiana."

Alexa offered Suzanne a weak smile. "That'd be a good idea if they weren't all away. Most of my crowd went straight to college after high school. I was the lone weirdo."

Linda bopped Alexa on the arm. "You're not a weirdo. You just found something else to do with your life besides going for more schooling. I can't imagine any other nineteen-year-old —"

"Twenty," Alexa and Suzanne chorused.

Linda scowled for a moment, then went on. "Twenty-year-old taking on the responsibility of operating a bed-and-breakfast all by herself. Not to mention all the other baking you do! So don't be calling my favorite girl a weirdo, you hear me?"

Alexa laughed lightly. "Okay, okay, so I'm not a weirdo. But . . ." She bit the corner of her lip. "Briley will probably be at the concert, since Nicci K is playing. It would be nice to see him. He got to be a pretty good friend when he was staying here."

"Oh, all right." Linda pushed her empty plate aside and shook her head. "The things I do for you, girlie. Go ahead and get us a couple of tickets, and you an' me will go jitterbug and she-bop with all the other young uns."

Alexa released a happy squeal and bounced up to give Linda a hug. She grabbed the paper. "I bet the ticket information is in here. They usually start selling seats four weeks in advance."

Suzanne dropped her fork and gawked at Alexa. "Four weeks? You mean you intend to be in Indiana for that long?"

Alexa paused, her smile fading. "Um . . . maybe."

"If you're arranging concert tickets, I'd

say 'certainly.' "

Linda shot Suzanne a frown. "I don't know that we put any time limit on things, but I imagine it'll take a while for Alexa to find the people she's searching for. Bound to be stressful. Planning something fun will be good for her — give her something to look forward to."

As usual, Linda provided the voice of reason. Suzanne reined in her frustration. She didn't want her last day with Alexa to be filled with animosity. But neither did she want to think of a month-long separation. Not when they'd just begun living under the same roof again. "What about Anna-Grace's wedding? Will you be back for that?"

"When is it?"

Mother answered. "The third Thursday in February."

Linda's eyebrows shot skyward. "Thursday? Who gets married on a Thursday?"

Suzanne smiled. "Old Order couples, that's who. It's tradition."

Alexa checked the calendar on her cell phone and gave a decisive nod. "I'll be back before February eighteenth. Even if I haven't located my" — she flicked an apologetic look at Suzanne — "birth mother, I don't want to still be away when

103

spring arrives. Business is bound to pick up then, and I need to be here."

"That's good thinking" — humor glinted in Linda's dark eyes — " 'cause your mama just might run off any potential business with her so-so cookin'."

Everyone offered the expected laugh, but Suzanne noted Alexa's chuckle seemed subdued. Alexa eased around the table and placed her hand on Suzanne's shoulder. "Mom, if taking on the responsibilities of the B and B is too much for you and you really, really don't want me to go, I'll stay."

Assuming Alexa's responsibilities was the least of her concerns. How would she survive if Alexa found and bonded with her birth mother? How would she handle being with Anna-Grace every day yet unable to claim her as her child? She clamped her teeth tight to prevent any worries from spilling out.

"Mom?"

Suzanne pulled in a breath, praying for strength. "You go, do what you need to do, and . . ." Tears threatened, but she blinked and forced a wobbly smile. "Don't worry for one minute about the bed-and-breakfast, your pie-making business, or me. Everything will be completely intact when you return." *Except maybe my heart.*

CHAPTER 8

Indianapolis
Cynthia

After dropping the kids off at school on Monday after New Year's, Cynthia drove straight to the private investigator's office. She'd always hated driving in downtown Indianapolis. The congested streets, the buses blocking her view, the frequent stoplights — and impatient drivers who chose to speed through red lights rather than honor them — left her edgy. She'd stated her apprehensions during breakfast, and Glenn cautioned her not to allow negative thoughts to claim even a tiny portion of her mind. His words rang in her memory.

"Today the search for your daughter begins. This is a day of hope and excitement, the first step toward dreams-come-true. A celebration day, Cyn." She wished she could push aside the deep apprehensions and focus solely on the positive, the way her husband did. But

the fear followed her like a black cloud.

She parked in the second level of a six-story-tall parking garage and walked two blocks to the historic stone-and-plaster building hunkering in the midst of more modern granite or steel-and-glass structures. An icy wind gusted, chilling her frame even through her thick wool coat, and she shivered as she ducked into the tiny half-octagon-shaped alcove that shielded the wide, raised-panel wooden front door.

For a moment she huddled in the alcove, her eyes closed and her heart pounding in a wave of intense nervousness. She pressed both palms to her chest and sent up what had become a familiar prayer in the past week — *Lord, let her forgive me.* The short communication calmed the frayed edges of her nerves. Even though her earthly father had abandoned her long ago, her heavenly Father was always available. She'd lean into His strength for the next several minutes.

She drew in a breath, squared her shoulders, and closed her hand over the elaborately etched brass doorknob. But the knob didn't turn. Old door, cold weather — it was probably just being stubborn. She curled both hands around it and tried again. No, it was locked. She frowned. Had she gotten her day wrong?

She pulled the scrap of paper from her pocket and double-checked the date and time. January fourth, 8:00 a.m. Exactly right. And she was at the right place. Vinyl stick-on letters in a simple block font spelled out OWEN MALLORY, PRIVATE INVESTIGATOR on the door's glass window.

The locked door on the old building, the unpretentious signage, and the fact that part of the retainer was nonrefundable swirled into the other worries she'd carried all morning long. Was this Owen Mallory a con artist, preying on desperate people? Glenn had assured her Mr. Mallory was well respected, a former police officer who'd turned to PI work nearly a decade ago — someone they could trust. So where was he?

Cynthia chewed the inside of her lip. Should she stay or leave? The cold air discouraged her from sticking around very long, but she wanted to get the investigation started before she chickened out. She dug in her purse for her cell phone to retrieve Mr. Mallory's number and give him a call. Before she located him in the phone's memory, someone called her name in a growly voice. She spotted a man across the street, waving his hand over his head. Tall, salt-and-pepper haired, wearing a long leather coat and cowboy boots, he looked like a gunslinger from one of the westerns Glenn watched on late-night television. He hollered, "Are you Mrs. Allgood?"

Shivering, she nodded.

"Be right there."

Instead of moving to the protected crosswalk, he stepped to the curb, glanced right and left, and made a dash between honking cars with his coat flaring out behind him like a cape. She stifled a chortle. A former police officer had just jaywalked?

He crossed the wide sidewalk in two strides, forcing other pedestrians to step aside or be mowed down, and stuck out his hand. "Good morning."

Cynthia placed her hand in his and grimaced when his fingers clamped tightly. For a slender man, he had a powerful grip.

"I'm sorry I kept you waiting." His voice was gruff, as if he had gargled a throat full of gravel. "My car's in the shop, so I had to take the buses this morning. Of course they weren't on schedule." Disgust colored his tone. He released her and jammed a key into the lock, his movements so precise and forceful, Cynthia subconsciously drew back. He swung the door open and held his hand out in a gesture of invitation.

She hesitated. His intensity, as if he

pulsated with nervous energy, intimidated her.

He bobbed his hand. "Well? Are you going to get out of the cold?"

She met his gaze. His eyes, almost as silvery gray as the salt strands in his hair, blazed with passion and purpose. In that moment she decided she could trust him. With a nod she stepped over the threshold.

Arborville
Paul

Paul hurried through the back doorway of his house and closed the door firmly behind him. He shuddered as the warmth of the room touched him. He tossed his coat over the back of a chair and moved to the stove, where he'd left the half-full teakettle sitting. With a snap of his wrist, he lit the burner under the kettle. A second cup of instant cocoa might warm him up again.

As he waited for the water to boil, he listened to the wailing wind. Was there some saying about January coming in like a lion? He didn't think so, but maybe there should be. This year was starting off with a fury. Most of December he'd let Danny walk to school. Only six blocks — not too far for a boy his age to walk. But the outside temperature today was the coldest he could remember. His breath had seemed to turn to ice crystals when he exhaled. Danny might get a frostbitten nose. Maybe it was good he didn't have any big jobs lined up for January — he'd be more available to see to his son.

He frowned, worry nibbling. What had gotten into Danny lately? He'd always been a good boy — curious and rambunctious, yes, but respectful. And cooperative. But his midyear report card from school had included a note from the teacher, Mr. Brungardt, about Danny's failure to complete several assignments and his displaying an attitude of flippancy. As soon as he read it, Paul sat his son down for a stern talking-to and instructions to change his behavior, and Danny had promised to do better. But this morning when he'd dropped Danny off for the first day of school after Christmas break and issued a reminder to keep his focus on his work, the boy scowled and bounced out of the truck without a word.

The kettle whistled, startling Paul out of his musing. He'd enjoy a cup of cocoa, spend some time in prayer — after all, God was better equipped to carry this worry about Danny — and then he'd start drawing the plans for an expansion to the Josts' toolshed. As he emptied a packet of cocoa mix into his mug, the telephone jangled. Still holding the empty packet, he moved to the telephone and plucked up the receiver. "Hello, Aldrich Construction."

"Paul?"

The familiar female voice sent a jolt of re-action through his middle. He dropped the little packet onto the countertop. A puff of cocoa powder burst from the wrapping and dusted the once-clean surface. He turned his back on the mess and gripped the receiver with both hands. "Yes, this is Paul."

"Thank goodness you're home. This is Su-zanne Zimmerman."

His thundering pulse told him he'd already identified her. He swallowed hard and forced a casual tone. "What can I do for you, Suz . . . anne?" It was so hard not to call her Suzy, the way he had all through his growing-up years. The way he had when he'd accompanied her to the barn loft when she was seventeen. The way he continued to think of her.

"I went to our basement to hang a load of wash this morning, and there's water stand-ing an inch deep. I called Clete, but Tanya said he's on his way to Wichita to pick up a part for his truck, and she suggested I call you."

So he wasn't her first choice as a rescuer.

Why did that bother him? He coughed out a short laugh. "I'm not really much of a plumber."

"To be honest, I don't think it's a plumbing problem. I sloshed through the water and checked all the exposed pipes. None of them are wet. So the water has to be coming from something other than a leaky pipe. I'm afraid it's a foundation problem."

Paul pulled the phone away from his ear for a moment, gazing at it in surprise. Then he put it close again. "I'm impressed. I don't know any other woman who would even step into a waterlogged basement to search for the source of the leak."

"I've had so many years of taking care of things on my own, it didn't even occur to me not to check things out."

Sympathy swelled. She'd shown amazing strength to raise a daughter to adulthood by herself and handle all the responsibilities a husband and wife normally shared. He'd only been widowed for three years, and too often he floundered with Danny. How had Suzy managed so successfully?

"Are you available to come out?"

A hint of desperation crept into her voice. So there were some things she couldn't handle on her own. He couldn't resist teasing. "You sound as nervous as the day you found a garter snake in the girls' outhouse at school. At least water isn't slithery and creepy." Funny how he recalled the exact words she'd used to describe the intruder.

A soft laugh carried through the line. "Yes, well, but it is cold and bothersome. And I'm no more eager to deal with it than I was that snake."

So she remembered, too. His heart expanded. "Don't worry. I'll be out as quickly as possible and see what I can do." Concern smote him, and sternness entered his tone. "But don't go into the basement again. Your farmhouse has electricity, and electricity plus standing water can be dangerous."

"Oh." Both contrition and sheepishness colored the simple exclamation. "I didn't think about that. I had my mind on Alexa and —"

He waited, but she didn't finish her thought. He said, "Do you know where the breaker box is located?"

"Yes. Oh! Just a minute, Paul." Her voice became muffled, as if she'd turned the telephone against her shoulder, but he still caught her words. "Anna-Grace, don't go down there. There's standing water in the basement, and Mr. Aldrich says it could be dangerous."

He nearly groaned. Anna-Grace Braun was there, too? Just what he didn't want to do — spend a day under the same roof as Suzy Zimmerman and the daughter they'd conceived but hadn't raised.

A mumbling reply came, and then Suzy's voice, strong again, met his ear. "Sorry about that. The breaker box is in the pantry."

He closed his eyes and wrestled his emotions into submission. "Okay. While you're waiting for me to arrive, go to the box and turn off the breakers for anything in the basement."

"How will I know which are for the basement?"

"They should be marked." Should, but they might not be. Not unless Cecil Zimmerman had taken the time to indicate which breakers went with which rooms. "If they aren't marked, just wait for me, but please don't go downstairs again, all right, Suzy?"

"All right, Paul. And thank you."

The connection ended. Not until Paul settled the receiver back in its cradle did he realize he'd called her Suzy. And she hadn't corrected him.

Indianapolis
Cynthia

"All right, Mrs. Allgood, let's go over the information you gave me and make sure I have it all down correctly."

During their hour together in Mr. Mallory's musty-smelling office with a cold draft chilling her feet and traffic noise constantly intruding, Cynthia had adjusted to the sound of his gravelly voice. She'd even managed to stop staring at the toothpick he poked in and out of the corner of his mouth with his tongue when he was listening intently. But the emotionless tone he employed continued to rankle. She'd poured out details of the most painful time in her life. Couldn't he inject at least a tiny element of warmth in his voice?

He angled his laptop, raised his chin, and squinted at the glowing screen as he began reciting in a near monotone: " 'Baby girl delivered in basement of a friend's home morning of December 3, twenty years ago. Baby never weighed, not taken to hospital, no birth certificate issued. Baby wrapped in towels and left in cardboard box — sturdy liquor box — behind the garage of the

Indianapolis Home for Unwed Mothers on morning of December 4.' "

He glanced at Cynthia, and she was certain she glimpsed condemnation in his steely eyes. She cringed, imagining what he was thinking. *What kind of person leaves a baby that way?* Defensiveness rose as she recalled the fear and desperation that had prompted her choices. One of Glenn's favorite sayings tiptoed through her mind — *"Don't judge until you've walked in that person's shoes."* She started to recite the phrase, but Mr. Mallory went on.

" 'Mother observed woman taking baby from the box into the garage.' "

Despite his flat delivery, Cynthia experienced enough emotions for both of them. If she closed her eyes, she could still see the young woman lean down and peel back the edges of the towel, ribbons from her Amish-style cap trailing down to touch the flaps of the box. Her face had exhibited shock, but after only a moment's pause, she scooped up the wailing baby girl and hurried into the garage with her.

Cynthia had wanted to follow, make sure her baby was okay, but her friend had yanked her to her feet and dragged her away, whispering, *"C'mon. We gotta go. We don't wanna get caught out here."* Numb, weak from childbirth, heartsore, she allowed herself to be tugged up the alley. And she'd never seen her baby again.

She swallowed a knot of sorrow. "Do you think you have enough information to find her?"

Mr. Mallory slapped the laptop closed and rocked in his squeaky chair. "It doesn't seem like much written out that way, but it ought to be enough. You know where the baby was left. You saw her picked up and taken inside. So that gives us a starting point. I'll do some digging at the library in the newspaper archives, see if I can locate an article about an abandoned baby around that time. Lots of times there'll be follow-up articles, too, about the kid finding a home. I might be able to find the names of the adoptive parents just like that." He snapped his fingers.

Cynthia's stomach churned, but she forced a smile. "It . . . it would be nice if it all happened quickly." Then she could bring an end to the wondering and worrying.

He didn't smile in reply. "But you need to remember, just because I find the name doesn't mean we'll automatically find your kid. Some names are so common. There are a dozen Bill Phillips or whatever in town. Takes a while to find the right one.

Sometimes people move out of state and I have to track them down. The name is just the first step. There'll likely be lots of steps before I connect with the folks who raised your girl. Might take a year. Even two."

Two years? How would she survive a two-year wait? The past week had left her battling nausea and sleeplessness.

"Of course, the longer it takes, the more it costs. Your retainer covers twenty hours of billed time. So you'll have to decide if you want me to keep looking once the money's gone."

Cynthia cringed. She and Glenn couldn't offer anything more than they'd already committed. If the retainer were refundable, she'd take the money back right now and pretend Glenn had never given her the gift in the first place. Not proceeding meant squandering the sacrificed dollars. She sighed. "Mr. Mallory, what we gave you is all we can spare. So if you use up the money before you find my daughter, just close the file and be done."

"Whatever you want, Mrs. Allgood."

She left his office, conflicting prayers hovering in the back of her heart. She wished she knew for sure what she wanted concerning her long-lost baby girl.

CHAPTER 9

Arborville
Suzanne

Suzanne perched on the second step from the bottom of the creaky basement staircase. The dampness of the cellar-like space beneath the house always felt cool, but today it was frigid. Paul had used a garden hose to siphon out as much water as possible. The shoebox-sized basement window was still cracked open, the hose dangling toward the floor like an exhausted snake, and chilly wind whistled through the gap. The warmth of the upstairs beckoned, but she crisscrossed her arms, hunched her shoulders, and stayed put.

Only a tiny beam of sunlight penetrated the dusty pane of glass, not nearly enough to expose the entire basement, but she knew Paul was still working. The scuff of his footsteps, an occasional bump as if he had collided with something, and the swing of his flashlight beam proved his busyness even though she couldn't see him in the deep shadows.

And he likely couldn't see her. She should let him know he wasn't alone. She cleared her throat. "Paul?"

The scuffing sounds stopped, and the flashlight beam aimed in her direction. "Yeah?"

"What's the verdict?" She held her breath, half-afraid of the answer. After all the money they'd spent renovating the house to accommodate Mother's wheelchair, their funds were sorely limited. She prayed whatever he'd found wouldn't require a costly fix.

The beam of light grew closer, his frame a dark mass following it. When he reached the stairs, he stretched his hand toward her. "Come with me. I'll show you."

The last time she'd taken his hand and allowed him to lead her, she'd created consequences that still haunted her more than twenty years later. She drew back. "It's okay. I don't need help."

"Under ordinary circumstances I'd agree with you, but the concrete is slippery. I don't want you to fall." His hand inched closer. "Grab hold."

Suzanne gritted her teeth and gingerly placed her hand in his. His fingers closed, the grip strong, sure. And disquieting. She shivered as she stepped onto the uneven floor.

"I've mopped twice." The bright beam of his flashlight bobbed slightly as they moved slowly forward, shifting around her dad's old tool bench and ducking beneath the sagging clothesline. "But it's hard to get things completely dry when it's so cold down here."

"Why n-not close the window?"

"The air will help dry things out." He squeezed her hand. "I'm sorry you're so cold."

To recover from the cold, she just needed to go upstairs. But the effect of being so close to her first love in the dark space with the pressure of his hand around hers and the brush of his warm breath on her cheek — those sensations might linger. A nervous laugh found its way from her throat. "Don't worry. I'll survive. The question is will the foundation survive?"

"Yes."

She released a sigh of relief.

"But it's going to need some repair."

Relief washed away on the tide of worry. "Oh."

"The problem is over here." He guided her to the northwest corner and aimed the flashlight beam at a moist trail zigzagging down the rough concrete wall. "If I remember correctly, your gutters all channel rainwater to this corner of the house. I suspect the flow of water has carved a 'pocket,' so to speak, along the foundation where moisture has accumulated. With temperature changes the water's been freezing and melting for years, putting pressure on the foundation. These concrete walls are as old as the house — more than a century — and like anything else, with time they've eroded."

Suzanne pulled free of his hold, took a short step backward, and hugged herself. Partly because she was chilled clear through, but partly because she needed a little distance. The intimacy of the flashlight's soft beam, the enclosed space, and their solitude was proving very discombobulating to her senses. "Can you repair it?"

Paul grimaced. "Yes. But not until spring, when the ground thaws."

"But we can't have water seeping in here all winter long. We'll end up with mold."

"Well . . ." He scratched his chin, his forehead puckering. "I could do a patch on the inside. It wouldn't be a permanent fix, but it might keep the water out until I can dig down and do the real repair work on the outside." He turned the beam on the wall again and traced the damp crack with his fingertip. "If I also reroute the drain spout so it deposits the water out in the yard instead of so close to the house, it should help prevent more moisture from filling up the channel."

Suzanne nodded. "That would be great. But do you have time? I'm sure you have other jobs lined up, so . . ."

He turned toward her. His face was softly lit on only one side by the flashlight, but she still recognized the upturning of his lips and the gentle sympathy glimmering in his eyes. "I was thinking earlier today that it was a blessing not to have a long list of things to do right now so I can focus more time and attention on Danny. But it also means I'm free to take care of this for you and your mother."

Something in his tone triggered concern. "Is Danny all right?"

Paul gave a little jolt, as if someone had poked him with a pin. "Why do you ask?"

"You just said you were glad to focus more time and attention on him. Is he . . . needy right now?"

To her surprise Paul laughed. Maybe she'd misread something. Embarrassed, she turned to go upstairs.

He caught her arm. "Suzy, I wasn't laughing at you. Please forgive me if I offended you. But your question about him being needy made me remember how I thought maybe he needed a good swat on the seat of his pants this morning."

His explanation surprised her, too. Danny had always been very polite and respectful in her presence. Not that any child was perfect all the time, but she'd never witnessed anything other than obedience from the boy. She gently extracted her arm from his grasp and offered a weak smile. "Maybe you should blame it on the weather. I think it's hard for children — especially boys — to be cooped up during the winter months. It was always hard on Clete when he couldn't get outside to expend his excess energy."

"Maybe." His face pinched into an expression of frustration. "I hope that's all it is, but I'd like to see his attitude change now instead of having to wait for the weather to change. He's . . . he's not been himself lately."

She shouldn't discuss personal topics with Paul Aldrich in the privacy of the basement in the dark. If fellowship members got wind of it, the gossip wheels would churn with fury. But how could she walk away from him when he was clearly in turmoil? "Are you sure you aren't making too much of some simple misbehavior? Children go through different growing stages, and it could be that Danny is just stretching his wings a bit — seeking more independence from you."

Paul's eyes widened. "Do you think so?"

Was he encouraged or discouraged by the thought? She wished she knew for sure. "Alexa went through spells when I felt as though I didn't know her at all. Then, in time, she settled in again. It's part of growing up."

"So you ignore it?" He folded his arms over his chest. The beam from the flashlight, which he held in one fist, painted a bright circle on the floor joists over their heads and highlighted the right side of his face. He seemed genuinely interested in her reply.

Suzanne focused on his right eye — the one she could clearly see — as she answered. "No. You can't ignore a child whose behavior is blatantly disrespectful. But instead of becoming angry or inflicting punishment, perhaps ask Danny what's troubling him. Assure him he can always talk to you. Then follow that up with a reminder of your expectations. Impose consequences if need be. But overreacting will certainly drive a wedge between you.

And those distances aren't easily bridged."

Slowly Paul lowered his arms, bringing the circle of light to the floor. His entire face was shadowed now, but she didn't need to see him to hear the deep contrition in his voice. "I wish I hadn't contributed to creating the distance between you and your family."

"Whoa." She held up both hands, silly since he likely couldn't even see the gesture. "We weren't talking about me. We were discussing you and Danny."

"I know, but your advice made me think of the long separation you had from your family. Maybe if your mother hadn't overreacted, then —"

"Mother and I have mended our differences." She hoped her firm tone would bring an end to the topic. "There's no sense in wallowing in the past."

"Is that what I was doing?"

"I don't know. Maybe." She sighed. "I don't want to talk about it."

They stood in silence with only the sounds of the continuing whistle of wind through the window and the muffled footsteps of Anna-Grace moving around in the kitchen above their heads. Suzanne sent a glance over her shoulder, trying to remember the location of each of the potential stumbling blocks between her and the stairs. She wished she had her own flashlight.

His soft chuckle interrupted her thoughts. "This is pretty funny."

She frowned. "What is?"

"Me holding you captive down here, talking to you about my problems."

Suzanne couldn't find anything amusing about the situation.

He swung his arms slightly, casting the light to and fro. "To be perfectly honest with you, when you called to see if I could come out, I wasn't crazy about the idea. Especially when I heard you talk to Anna-Grace and knew she was here, too. Being with both of you is kind of . . ." He gulped, as if choking back something unpleasant. "Scary."

Interesting choice of words, considering how she'd felt when he reached to take her hand and lead her across the floor. She clamped her jaw and remained silent.

"But here we are, and all of a sudden I was talking to you about Danny, and it seemed kind of right." A hint of puzzlement entered his tone, and he stilled, the circle of light surrounding their feet. "Which tells me we've pretty much mended our differences, too. I mean, I wouldn't be able to talk to you if we were still, the way you put it, wallowing in the past, right?"

Suzanne examined herself. She'd made peace with Paul, and with herself, over the choices they'd made so long ago. So why did his presence create such conflicting emotions? Why did she equally desire to escape him and embrace him? She might not be wallowing in the past, but the past was still impacting her. She had no idea how to answer.

"Have I made you uncomfortable?"

Uncomfortable didn't cover it, but she wouldn't tell him so. "Paul, a cold, damp basement isn't the best place for a long conversation." Goose flesh ran up her arms beneath her sweater, and her body convulsed with a shiver. "Could we go upstairs where it's warm?" He wouldn't want to talk upstairs, not where Mother or Anna-Grace could overhear them. The suggestion was guaranteed to bring an end to the conversation that had taken too much of a turn for her comfort.

"Or maybe we could take it to Wichita. On Saturday."

"W-Wichita?" Had she heard him correctly?

"Yeah." He swung his arm again. The bobbing light made her dizzy. Or was the thought that he'd seemingly just asked her to go out with him responsible for the sensation of spinning? He went on, his words emerging slowly. "If some of Danny's issue is being cooped up, a trip to Wichita might help. And if you came too, you could observe him. Talk to him. Maybe figure out if he's just going through a growing spell, the way you said Alexa did."

So it wasn't a date. Disappointment struck, and Suzanne shook her head, irritated with herself. "I don't know Danny well enough to form any conclusions about why he's not himself."

"So time with him wouldn't help?"

He sounded so disappointed. Her sympathy rose. "Not just an hour or two, no. I understood Alexa's moods because I had a long-term relationship with her. You have the same with Danny. You'll figure it out."

He heaved a sigh. "Boy, I hope so. When I was a kid, my mom was the one more likely to be understanding than my dad was. I think I'm a pretty good dad, but there's no way I can ever be 'mom' to Danny. I miss Karina. I miss her for me, and I miss her for my son." He jerked the flashlight up, sending the beam toward the stairs. "And you're right — we shouldn't be talking this way. C'mon, let's get you out of the cold, and I'll get started on patching that crack."

Upstairs, Paul went directly to the breaker box while Suzanne crossed to the stove. Anna-Grace was nowhere to be seen, but either she or Mother had tucked a baking sheet of biscuits into the oven. Suzanne hunkered near its door, absorbing the warmth. Clicks emerged from the pantry, breaker switches for the basement being pressed to On, and then Paul stepped into the kitchen.

"I'm going to pull the hose, latch the window, and see if I can rig something under the downspout to deflect any water that might come through. After that, I've got to head home for tools. I didn't bring anything strong enough to chip out the concrete. If you want to hang your laundry down there now, it's probably okay."

Suzanne had no desire to go back into that cold space, even if she could turn the lights on. Besides, she'd done a load of personal items. The thought of Paul ducking beneath her slips and underwear made her face fill with fire. "That's all right. I'll hang them in the upstairs bathroom instead. Then nothing will be in your way."

He gave a firm nod. "Probably a wise choice since I might get dust on them when I'm working." He moved toward the back door and then paused with his hand on the doorknob. "Suzy, about you going to Wichita with Danny and me." He licked his lips, his brow furrowing. "Would you think about it? Danny's always with me or with his teacher, Mr. Brungardt, so maybe he just needs a feminine influence in his life."

The heat from the stove was singeing her hip. She moved away a few inches and gathered her courage to answer honestly. "You might be right, but are you sure I'm a wise choice? Considering . . ." She couldn't say more, knowing Anna-Grace might interrupt at any time, but she prayed Paul would hear the unspoken words.

He ducked his head for a moment, then looked her square in the face. "Considering we were once really good friends, maybe you'd be the best choice."

And maybe it would open the door to those old feelings. She held the statement inside, unwilling to let him know how much his presence affected her. Especially since her presence didn't seem to stir anything in his heart. How embarrassing to realize the candle she'd once held for him still contained a small flicker that was all one-sided.

He twisted the doorknob and pulled the door inward, flashing a charmingly crooked grin. "Think about it. Yes or no, you won't offend me. And I hope you'll say a prayer for Danny and me to find our footing together again. See you later, Suzy." He stepped out and closed the door with a snap behind him.

The oven timer began to ding. Suzanne moved to the drawer where the potholders were stored, and as she opened it, Mother wheeled around the corner, the ribbons on her cap floating over her shoulders. She stopped when she spotted Suzanne.

"Oh. I thought you were still downstairs. Did Paul fix the leak?"

Suzanne removed the biscuits from the oven and switched the dial to Off. She carried the baking sheet of steaming biscuits to the worktable, set it down, and finally faced her mother. "He's working on it." She briefly shared his plans for keeping more water from leaking into the basement. "But he said the real repair will have to wait until spring."

"Did he give you any idea how much it will cost?"

She hadn't asked because they'd started talking about Danny. And the past. She shook her head.

Mother shrugged. "Well, if he ends up doing all the work, I won't worry too much. He's good about billing reasonable amounts to members of the fellowship, and if we need to, we can make payments to him. It's nice to have someone we can trust."

Suzanne busied herself removing butter and jam from the refrigerator so she wouldn't have to answer her mother. Odd how Mother claimed to trust him, given their history. Maybe Mother had truly released the past, too. And if Mother trusted him . . . She spun, sending the refrigerator door against the wall.

"Suzy!"

She ignored her mother's startled outburst. "Mother, what would you think about me taking a day trip into Wichita with Paul Aldrich and his son? Just as friends."

Mother rolled near and pushed the refrigerator door closed. Then she angled her head to peer into Suzanne's face. "As friends, you say?"

Suzanne, butter dish in one hand and jam jar in the other, pressed the cold items to the front of her sweater. "Yes."

Mother's brows descended. Slowly she shook her head, causing her cap's black ribbons to sway beneath her chin. "Not possible, Suzy. I've never known of a single man and a single woman who could be 'just friends.' Something — usually an attraction that one party discovers for the other —

interferes. And given your, er, past relationship, I would say it's doubly unlikely the two of you could spend time together as 'just friends.' "

"It's too bad, too."

The intrusion of another voice startled Suzanne so badly she nearly dropped the items in her hands. She jerked her gaze toward the dining room doorway, where Anna-Grace stood framed with an expression of pity on her face.

Mother recovered sooner than Suzanne and spoke first. "What's too bad, Anna-Grace?"

"That Cousin Suzy and Mr. Aldrich can't be friends. Especially since they were once sweet on each other." She grinned sheepishly. "Dad told me you were really close when you were children."

"That was a long time ago." Suzanne wished her pulse would stop its thundering gallop.

Anna-Grace sighed. "I know, but doesn't it seem as though people who were good friends as youngsters ought to be able to remain friends as adults? Sometimes people make things so complicated."

"You don't know the half of it . . . ," Mother mumbled, her head low.

Suzanne sent a warning look in her

mother's direction, but to her relief Anna-Grace gave no indication she'd heard. Instead the girl moved directly to Suzanne and enfolded her in a short, almost-impersonal hug. Then she took the butter and jam and moved to the refrigerator.

"If you don't mind, Cousin Suzy, I'd rather make some sausage gravy to pour over the biscuits. It's really too late for breakfast and too early for lunch, but biscuits and gravy makes a good brunch, don't you think?"

If Anna-Grace wanted to make gravy, she wouldn't stop her. "Sure."

"And why don't you see if Mr. Aldrich would like to join us?" Anna-Grace stepped toward the stove, carrying a carton of milk and a paper-wrapped chunk of ground sausage. "Steven is always telling me I need to get better acquainted with the folks in Arborville, and sitting down to a meal together is a relaxing way to do that. And maybe" — an unexpected spark of mischief brightened her blue eyes — "your old friendship will rejuvenate while you chat over a plate of biscuits and homemade gravy."

Suzanne swallowed a groan. The girl had no idea she was poking a hornet's nest with a stick.

135

CHAPTER 10

Franklin, Indiana
Alexa Zimmerman

Alexa rolled over, yawned, squinted one eye at the alarm clock, then sat up with a startled yelp. Nine thirty? How had she slept so late? Grandmother would be half-starved by now!

She threw the covers aside and bounded out of bed. Halfway across the floor, reality caught up with her and drew her to a halt. She wasn't at the B and B in Arborville. She was in Linda and Tom's guest room. Grandmother wasn't waiting for breakfast, and she didn't need to hurry across the cold grass to the house to get coffee started.

Slumping in relief, she staggered back to the bed and sank down on the mattress. She rubbed her eyes, blinked twice, stretched, and then blew out a noisy breath. Now fully awake and in control of her senses, she understood why she'd slept so late. She,

Tom, and Linda had sat up until well past two in the morning, planning her strategy for seeking her birth parents.

Excitement stirred in her chest. After weeks of protecting Mom's feelings by squelching her own desire to uncover her past, letting everything spill out had been like breaking through a dam — an exhilarating rush. And now that it was Monday — Linda insisted, and Alexa didn't object, on keeping Sunday as a day of rest — she could put the plan into motion.

Eagerness propelled her from the bed. She took a quick shower, forgoing washing her hair so she wouldn't have to spend the time blow-drying it. Dressed and ready to face the day, she headed up the hallway toward the kitchen, where the smell of bacon teased her to hurry her steps. She entered the cheerful room decorated Linda-style, in bright turquoise and cherry red. Tom and Linda, still wearing their bathrobes, sat on opposite sides of the 1950s table in the middle of the red-and-white tile floor, half-empty plates of scrambled eggs, bacon, and toast in front of them.

Alexa plopped into a red vinyl-and-chrome chair. "Good morning! It smells great in here."

Linda grimaced. "We didn't know when

you'd get up, so we didn't fix you anything."

"Oh." A little embarrassed, Alexa rose. "Well, if you don't mind me using your stove, I can —"

"Sit right back down." Tom caught Alexa's hand and gave it a gentle tug. "This place ain't your B and B. I fix the breakfasts here. I'll crisp some bacon in the microwave and scramble up an egg for you while you sit and talk with Linda."

Alexa stood uncertainly next to the chair. "Are you sure? I don't mind taking care of myself." Actually she preferred it. Mom sometimes said she was too independent for her own good.

"I'm sure." Tom planted his hand on her shoulder and gave a little push. Alexa sat. He leaned over and kissed the top of her head. "Salt, pepper, and a little cheddar cheese in those eggs?"

If she were doing the cooking, she'd add sautéed mushrooms, leeks, and red peppers and then sprinkle the eggs with a blend of shredded parmesan and asiago. But Alexa smiled and offered a nod. "That sounds great. Thanks."

Linda pointed to the drip coffee maker and pegged rack of mismatched mugs. "Help yourself. The sugar and powdered creamer are in the cabinet above the pot."

Alexa wrinkled her nose as she spooned powdered creamer into the mug. She liked her coffee white and sweet, but she couldn't imagine the powdered stuff tasting right. Back at the table, she took a sip. Not as bad as she'd expected. Even so, when she was out today, she'd buy some real cream to keep on hand for their morning coffee. She cupped the warm mug between her palms. "Last night after we went up to bed, I started thinking . . ."

Linda's eyes twinkled. "Girlie, you're always thinking."

Tom chimed in from his spot by the stove. "And most of your thinking leads to good ideas." He shook the spatula at her, crunching his brows in a teasing scowl. "Notice I said 'most.' That worm farm idea . . . now, that one was a flop."

Alexa couldn't stifle a laugh. "I was only five!"

Tom grinned. "Point taken." He turned back to the skillet.

Linda tapped Alexa's wrist. "What were you thinking about?"

"Visiting the home where Mom stayed."

Linda rolled her eyes. "Like I told you last night, I can't see any purpose in that. Those people won't know anything about you because your mama didn't take you inside.

As far as they know, you weren't ever there."

Tom crossed to the table and placed a plate of steaming eggs and bacon in front of her. "I gotta agree with Linda on this one. I can't see anything good coming out of you visiting that unwed mothers' home."

Alexa bowed her head to offer grace. When she finished, Tom was standing in front of her, a frown tugging the snow-white whiskers of his mustache downward. Suddenly she was five years old, trying to defend her little Popsicle-stick fences against his lawn mower. She picked up her fork and aimed an innocent look at him. "What?"

He slid into his chair. "Listen, kiddo, your mama isn't in any danger of facing charges for taking you. Like we talked about, the statute of limitations for kidnapping closed a long time ago. But child abandonment? I don't know about that. It's possible your birth mother could find herself in a peck of trouble if the people at the home knew she'd left you out in the cold that way. You don't want to get her in trouble, do you?"

Alexa poked at the fluffy eggs, her appetite gone. "Of course not. I just want . . ." She sighed, seeking the right words. "I want to see the place where my life began. Well, technically, it didn't begin behind the garage at the unwed mothers' home, but that's the first place I know about. I need to see where I was left. See where I met Mom."

For long seconds both Linda and Tom stared at her with their brows furrowed and their lips pursed in indecision. Then, in unison, they shifted to gaze at each other. Although neither spoke, Alexa got the distinct impression much was being communicated. Finally Linda sighed and Tom gave a slight nod.

He placed his thick palm on Alexa's shoulder. "I tell you what. When you're done with breakfast, because you're gonna eat those eggs instead of just playing with 'em, I'll drive you over to the home. You and me will poke around in the alley, let you get your fill of the place." His frown deepened. "But we won't go knock on the front door, agreed?"

Alexa heaved a satisfied sigh. "Agreed."

"Good. Now eat."

She laughingly complied.

Indianapolis
Cynthia

"Why don't you wait here in the car? I'll be back in a few minutes."

Cynthia folded her arms tightly across her chest and peered through Mr. Mallory's windshield at the three-story Victorian

141

home where countless young single mothers had delivered their babies. When the young woman carried Cynthia's baby girl inside, what kind of setting greeted her? Was the home's interior warm and homey or dark and cheerless? She wanted to see for herself. "I'm going in with you."

The investigator huffed out a breath. "Mrs. Allgood, you might've convinced me to bring you along, but I'm not gonna let you intrude on the investigation. No offense, but you're emotionally entangled in all of this. I'm not. So I'm the better one to be asking questions and analyzing the important parts of the answers."

She knew he was right. Especially about the emotionally tangled part. Her stomach felt tied in knots. Her pulse scampered, and a cold sweat dampened her flesh despite the warm air flowing from the car's vents. But she hadn't taken the day off work to sit in the car like an unwelcome dog. "But —"

He held up his hand. "No. I mean it. You'll only prolong things, and the clock's ticking. Just stay put."

The reminder of her limited budget kept her in place when he swung his door open and stepped out. She watched him stride across the cracked sidewalk, his long legs reminding her of a crane's. He trotted up

142

the slanting porch steps. Once on the porch, trellises woven with an overgrowth of brown vines hid him from view, but she envisioned him ringing the doorbell, shifting in place while he waited for a reply, then being ushered inside.

She stared hard at the shadowy spot where he'd disappeared, but her eyes failed to create a solid image. With a sigh she leaned against the seat and tipped her head back. He'd left the engine idling, and warm air continued to seep through the vents. Almost too warm — she was sweating underneath her wool coat. She unbuttoned the coat and then lowered the window a half inch. Cold air whisked in, raising goose flesh, and she shivered. Much the way she had that day she'd hunkered in the bushes, waiting for someone to hear her baby's wails and come to the rescue.

She nibbled her lower lip. Mr. Mallory had told her not to come inside, but what would it hurt for her to go behind the garage, visit the place where she'd last seen her baby girl? The urge gnawed at her, too intense to ignore.

She reached across the console and turned off the ignition. The car wheezed into silence. She slipped the key into her coat pocket — this neighborhood had become run-down over the years, and she wouldn't trust someone not to steal the vehicle — and then stepped onto the street. A cold blast of wind nearly chased her back inside, but with determination she folded the flaps of her coat across her front and headed across the carpet of damp brown leaves.

Windows draped with lace tempted her to sneak a peek inside, but Cynthia aimed her gaze forward and scurried past the side of the house. The garage waited at the far edge of the yard, its single door facing the alley. Back when she'd left her baby, the carriage house had been painted a crisp white with dark-green trim. Over the years the white paint on the lap siding had chipped and peeled, leaving gray patches behind, and the green was now faded to a dusty-moss color. But when she rounded the back corner and stepped onto the crumbling patch of concrete in front of the wide door, remembrance struck with enough force to weaken her knees.

She sagged against the door, barely aware of its complaining creak, and stared at the spot next to the old cinder-block foundation where she'd pushed the whiskey box that had served as her baby's cradle. The garage door was inset, and she'd chosen to place the box at the south edge of the door, reasoning the north wind would be somewhat blocked by the garage wall. Dead leaves had accumulated in that spot, forming a sloping pile of brown and rusty red. An image of the beach towel she'd used to wrap her baby — yellow-and-brown plaid with rusty-looking splotches from the blood she'd cleaned from the baby's head — appeared briefly in her mind's eye and then whisked away, leaving her staring once again at the leaves.

Shifting her gaze to the alley, she located the spot where she'd hidden with her friend — why couldn't she remember the girl's name? — but the lilac bushes were gone now, a toolshed standing there instead. The shed's white metal siding reflected the sun, and Cynthia squinted against the onslaught. Something warm trickled down her cheek. A spider? Panicked, she swatted at the tickle, and her fingertips came away moist.

Not a spider — a tear.

She huddled deep into her coat and bit her lip to stave off further tears. She'd cried the long-ago day she was here, and it hadn't accomplished anything. No amount of tears today would wash away the choice she'd made back then. Crying couldn't bring her baby back. But Owen Mallory's explorations could. Excitement flickered to life inside of her. She jolted upright and turned to head for the car. Just as she rounded the corner, Mr. Mallory stepped into her pathway.

"Thought I might find you out here."

From his flat tone she couldn't determine if he was annoyed or apathetic. She replied tartly, unintentionally injecting defensiveness in her tone. "I needed to . . . visit her."

Not a hint of understanding showed in his expression, but he bobbed his head in a brusque nod. "Gotcha."

She pulled his key from her pocket and held it out to him.

He curled his fist around the key and glanced up and down the alley. "You done now? Because I'm finished here."

Her heart leaped with a hope that both startled and delighted her. "Did you get the names of the couple who adopted my baby?"

"No."

His blunt answer trampled the glimmer of hope. "Did they refuse to tell you?"

"It's cold out here. C'mon." Mr. Mallory caught Cynthia's elbow and guided her to his car. He opened the door for her, then jogged around and climbed behind the wheel. He started the engine, fastened his seat belt, curled his hand over the stick shift, and finally angled a bland look in her direction. "Mrs. Allgood, the director told me the only record they have of someone abandoning a baby here was the year after the home opened — 1964. And it was a boy."

Cynthia shook her head, confused. "That can't be right."

"I checked the books. They've kept meticulous records of every birth — mother's name and home address, baby's gender, weight, height, adoptive family's names . . . But there isn't one reference about an abandoned baby girl."

Cynthia stared at him with her jaw slack.

He snapped the gearshift back and forth from Park to First, the repeated *kerthunk* a jarring sound. "There was another home for unwed mothers run by the Catholic church on the other side of town, but it's closed now. You sure you didn't leave your baby there?"

"I'm sure!" Uncontrollable shudders rattled her frame. She hugged herself. "It was here. Behind this garage. I hid in that alley and watched a woman — an Amish woman — take my baby out of the box and go into the garage with her. I know this is the place." How would she forget where she'd left her baby?

147

He shifted his jaw back and forth and gazed at her through narrowed eyes. "Hmm. Well, you might've left her, but no one from the home found her."

"But I saw the woman take my baby into the garage!" She pressed her fists to her temples and closed her eyes, replaying the memory like an old movie reel. Opening her eyes again, she fixed him with a look of frustration. "If she wasn't part of the home's staff, why would she go into their garage?"

"I dunno." He grabbed the door handle and gave it a yank. Cold air washed into the cab. "But I changed my mind about being done here. I've got one more question to ask before we leave."

Cynthia's chest tightened. "What?"

He grinned — a wry, knowing twist of his lips. "Mrs. Allgood, just sit tight and leave the investigating to me, okay? If the answer gives me anything promising, I'll share it with you. Sit tight."

CHAPTER 11

Indianapolis
Alexa

As Tom drove, Alexa gazed out the window at familiar yet somehow new-to-her businesses and streets. Strange how only a few months in Kansas had changed her view of Indiana. She'd grown up in the Hoosier State and had always considered it her home. How many times had she and Mom driven to Indianapolis to shop at the mall? or bowl at Applegate Lanes? or share a hot fudge sundae at Aunt Betty's Ice Cream Shoppe? More times than she could count. But now the place of her birth, her childhood, her youth seemed foreign. How had her heart so quickly adopted Kansas as home?

She glanced at Tom, who stared ahead with his lips crunched together and his eyebrows pulled into a V. He wasn't happy about her insistence to go to the home where her birth mother had abandoned her. But he was taking her anyway. Affection swelled in her heart. She might have been dumped in an alley, but she landed with good people. Mom, Tom and Linda, the Martens, her church family, and now all of the Zimmermans and the fellowship in Arborville. Her life was richer by knowing them and being loved by them.

"Tom?"

He flicked a look at her out of the corner of his eyes. "Yeah?"

"Thank you for taking me. I love you, you know."

His mustache twitched. "Would you still love me if I flat-out said, 'No, I'm not taking you'?"

She grinned. "Yes. But I'd pout."

He blasted a laugh. "Your mama never put up with you pouting. I can still hear her. 'Alexa Joy, someone's going to think your lip's a stairstep and try to climb on your head.'"

Alexa giggled, remembering her mother's mild scolding.

"But that lower lip sticking out sure got you your way with me when you were little." Tom shook his head, his eyes on the traffic while an indulgent smile played on his lips. "Linda and me prayed and prayed for children, always hoping to be Grandpop and Grammy someday, but never in all my born days would I have suspected I'd grow to love a Kansas Old Order Mennonite unmarried teenager like a daughter and her baby like a granddaughter." He reached across the console and gave her arm a light squeeze. "You and your mama, you've been a blessing to Linda and me."

She cupped her hand over his and offered him a wobbly smile. "No more than you've been to us."

"Well, then, I guess God knew what He was doing when He brought us all together, huh?" He put his hand back on the steering wheel and began to whistle.

Alexa shifted her gaze to the side window to a quiet residential street lined with towering oak and maple trees. The leafless branches stretched outward like gnarled fingers and formed a canopy over the brick pavement. Turn-of-the-century houses, tall and timeworn yet somehow dignified even in their battered state, sat well back from the curb. For reasons she didn't understand, Alexa shivered. Tom's comment echoed in her mind. If God had chosen Mom to be her mother, should she even be trying to find the woman who'd given birth to her?

"Tom, stop!"

He applied the brakes so quickly they both jolted against the restraining seat belts. Tom jammed the car into Park and peered over the hood, searching the street. "What's wrong? Did something run out in front of me?"

"No, nothing's out there." She clutched her hands against the scratchy bodice of her plaid wool peacoat. "All of a sudden I'm not sure what to do."

He glanced in the rearview mirror, shifted into Drive, and eased the car to the curb. He parked and angled himself slightly, his elbow draped over the steering wheel. Concern lined his face. "You mean about snooping around behind the home?"

"Not just that." A lump filled her throat. She swallowed, but it remained. "About snooping at all. Trying to find my biological parents."

His eyebrows shot upward. "You're asking this now? I thought you were all gung-ho about finding your birth mother and maybe even your father."

"I was. I mean, I am. But . . ."

"But what? Either you wanna find them or you don't. Which is it?"

She sucked in a long breath and blew it out. She held her hands wide. "Both!"

Tom burst out laughing.

Alexa considered swatting his arm but decided it wouldn't be respectful. So she glowered at him instead. "It isn't funny."

"Oh yes, it is." His dark eyes twinkled. "You left your mama in charge of the B and B and came all the way back to Indiana so you could maybe find out who left you in the alley behind the unwed mothers' home, and now that you're here and your mama is there, you're waffling."

"I'm not waffling."

"Girlie, in my book, flip-flopping what you want to do is called waffling."

She sighed and hung her head. "I haven't changed what I want to do. I'm just not totally sure it's what I'm supposed to do."

He cupped her chin and lifted her head. The amusement had vacated his expression and only tenderness remained. "What're you worrying about?"

She gathered her thoughts. "Mom's always called me her gift. And you just said God brought us all together."

"Uh-huh."

"So does that mean I shouldn't want to find out where I came from? Should I just be happy where I am, with the family God gave me? I know Mom wants me to leave things alone. What does God want me to do?"

"Oh, honey-girl . . ." He gave her cheek a pat and then lowered his hand to the console. "I don't have the answer to that question, but hearing you ask it sure makes me proud. If you're more concerned about what God wants for you than you are about pleasing yourself, then you're on the way to making the right choice. You're a good girl, Alexa."

Tears stung her eyes. She sniffed. "If I'm a 'good girl,' then it's because I had good teachers." She couldn't imagine a better, more loving mother than Suzanne Zimmerman. Was she being disloyal to try to find her birth mother? Desire to please Mom warred with the curiosity writhing through her. She groaned. "I'm so confused right now."

"Well, you know we don't have to do this today. If you want to go back, talk to Linda some, pray on it, we'll turn around right now."

His kind understanding brought a second sting of tears. "But you drove me all the way over here. It took almost an hour. And you hate driving in Indianapolis traffic."

"You're right about that. Good thing I love you so much, or I wouldn't have done it at all." Teasing glinted in his eyes. "And guess what?"

"What?"

He pointed out the front windshield. "We're here."

Alexa whipped her face forward, her pulse leaping. A sign — weathered, warped, its painted letters faded — stood sentry in front of the house just ahead on the opposite side of the street. She read the sign in a rasping whisper. " 'Indianapolis Home for Unwed Mothers, Established by the North Central Mission Board in 1963.' " She leaned forward as far as the seat belt would allow and stared hard at the house half-hidden by trees.

In its glory days it must have been beautiful, with its corbels and turrets and bay windows and front porch with an attached gazebo. Had the neighbors fussed when needy women began filling the rooms? In 1963 the stigma of being unwed and pregnant would have carried a foul stench. Although much of society had relaxed its stance, in some circles it still held an ugly aroma. Alexa wasn't sure Mom had completely forgiven herself despite the good life she'd carved.

Her gaze drifted upward, absently counting the many windows and trying to estimate the number of bedrooms inside. How many babies had been born within those rooms? How many mothers had — either reluctantly or willingly — handed their children to another set of parents? How many had chosen to keep their children? How many rued the decision later? Had her birth mother regretted the choice she'd made?

"Alexa?"

Tom's quiet voice intruded on her thoughts. She kept her focus on the house as she answered. "Hmm?"

"Do you wanna explore, or should we go back to Franklin?"

The concern etched into his features turned her heart upside down. He might not really be her grandfather, but he loved her. God had surely given her a precious gift when He brought Tom and Linda into Mom's life. "I think I want to talk to Mom." She pulled her cell phone from her purse. "Then I'll decide. Okay?"

"Okay." He folded his arms over his chest and arched his white eyebrows. "But I'm not getting out and giving you privacy. It's cold out there."

She laughed. "It's all right. I don't suppose I have any secrets from you anyway." She pulled up her list of contacts and pressed her finger to the little photo of her mother.

■ ■ ■ ■

Arborville
Suzanne

Suzanne balanced a blueberry pie in one hand and opened the oven door with the other. The task proved unwieldy with the oven set low to accommodate Mother's wheelchair. But by crouching she managed to slide the pie into the hot oven. As she straightened, the cell phone in her apron pocket buzzed.

Anna-Grace glanced over from rolling pie crusts and grinned. "Does that tickle?" She looked impish with flour dusting her cheek and white ribbons trailing along her temples.

Suzanne tried to chuckle, but the sound came out like a strangled cough. Why couldn't she relax around Anna-Grace? In only a few days, the girl had settled in as if she'd always been a member of the household. She was kind and helpful, assisting Suzanne in filling the café's pie orders and doing much of the cooking. Suzanne had prayed repeatedly for God to bring peace to her heart so she wouldn't be on edge around her daughter, but it seemed her prayers got trapped in the attic.

She pulled out her phone and peeked at the screen. Alexa! She snapped it open and pressed it to her ear. "Hi, honey!"

"Hi, Mom."

Alexa sounded subdued. Suzanne's mother-alarm began to ring.

Anna-Grace set the rolling pin aside and inched up to Suzanne. "Is it Alexa?"

Suzanne nodded.

Anna-Grace waggled her fingers at the phone. "Hi, Alexa!"

Suzanne pushed the Speaker button and held the phone outward. Alexa's voice carried through the little speaker. "Is that Anna-Grace? How are you?"

Anna-Grace leaned close and spoke into the cellular device like a microphone. "I'm good. I'm sorry I didn't get to see you before you left for Indiana, but your mom says you'll be back in time for the wedding."

"Yes, I intend to be. Are you making preparations for the ceremony?"

"Not this morning. Your mom and I are baking fruit pies."

Suzanne cringed. Would Alexa think she'd passed her responsibilities to Anna-Grace? She blurted, "It was her idea to help."

Anna-Grace laughed and Suzanne gave a start. She hadn't realized how much Anna-Grace's laughter sounded like hers. She'd need to be careful about laughing unrestrainedly when the girl was in earshot.

Anna-Grace spoke again, her voice louder than it needed to be. "She's right. It was my idea. And I better get back to the crusts. Good-bye, Alexa."

"Good-bye. Thanks for helping Mom."

Anna-Grace bustled back to the worktable, and Suzanne clicked off the speaker before pressing the phone to her ear. "It's good to hear from you. I know you've only been gone a few days, but I miss you."

"I miss you, too, Mom." Melancholy carried in her tone. "It sounds like you and Anna-Grace are busy, but do you have a minute to talk?" She paused then added, "Privately."

Anna-Grace could handle the pies on her own. Suzanne turned to the girl. "I'm going to the front room to talk to Alexa. I'll be back in a few minutes."

"That's fine." Anna-Grace's blue eyes twinkled with mischief. "Be sure to tell her about your date with Mr. Aldrich."

"What?" Alexa's startled exclamation nearly pierced Suzanne's ear.

Suzanne wished she could throttle Anna-Grace. She said firmly, speaking as much to Anna-Grace as Alexa, "It isn't a date. He just wants me to spend some time with Danny and maybe give him some advice on how to handle the adolescent stage the boy has entered." She hurried out of the room before Anna-Grace could say anything else.

Mother was in her rocking chair, knitting bulky pink yarn into a sweater for little Isabella. She nodded at the phone. "Alexa?"

"Yes."

"Let me tell her hi."

Even though she wanted to dive directly into conversation with her daughter, Suzanne obliged Mother, hiding a smile at the ease with which her Old Order mother handled the cell phone. After their short conversation, Suzanne headed for the stairs with the phone cradled against her jaw. "Okay, honey, you've got just me now. What's going on?"

"Honestly, Mom, I'm confused."

So she'd been right — something was troubling Alexa. She entered the 2 Corinthians 9:8 room and settled in the wing chair in the corner. "About what?"

"Whether or not I really should look for my birth mother."

Suzanne's heart caught. She stifled a cry of exultation and forced a calm tone. "Why are you questioning it?"

A heavy sigh carried through the phone.

"If God went to the trouble of making sure you found me and became my mom, does He want me trying to find my real mom?"

The phrase "real mom" was a knife in Suzanne's breast. She closed her eyes.

"Tom and I are sitting right across the street from the home where you had Anna-Grace. All I have to do is get out and walk a few yards, and I'll be where you found me twenty years ago. It'll be the first step toward finding her. But right now I'm not sure I should get out of the car." She paused, her breath puffing as if she'd just run a race. "What should I do, Mom?"

"What should I do, Mom?" Over her years of parenting Alexa, she'd heard the question dozens of times. Alexa asked her opinion on which friends to invite for a sleepover, which dress to wear to a church member's wedding, whether to take art appreciation or home economics for her elective credit, whether to attend the school dances or not. Suzanne had never struggled to offer advice on the little things or the big things in her daughter's life. But at that moment, she didn't know what to say.

If she said yes, go, she'd be pushing her beloved child toward another mother — possibly one who had no more desire to know Alexa now than she had when she wrapped her in a stained towel and left her in a box behind a garage. If she said no, don't go, she'd be giving in to her own self-ish fears. Either way, Alexa risked being hurt.

God, what should I tell her? No answer whispered through her heart.

"Mom?"

Suzanne opened her eyes, and her gaze fell on the embroidered Bible verse Alexa had stitched, framed, and hung on the wall of the guest room. She found herself reading aloud. " 'God is able to make all grace abound toward you; that ye, always having all sufficiency in all things, may abound to every good work.' "

"Huh?"

"It's the verse you chose for this room."

"I know. But why did you quote it to me?"

Suzanne laughed softly. "I'm not sure. I didn't know how to answer you, and the verse was there on the wall, so I read it."

"Oh."

A long pause followed, during which Suzanne listened closely for some guidance from heaven. None came. Eventually Alexa's quiet voice came through the phone.

" 'All sufficiency in all things . . .' Doesn't that kind of mean God can make sure we're ready to do what needs to be done, even when it's hard?"

Suzanne stared at the words. The black stitching began to swim as tears filled her eyes, but she nodded in agreement. "And the beginning — 'God is able' — assures us when we don't have strength, His will be enough."

"So maybe" — Alexa's voice dropped to a halting whisper — "I'm supposed to stop being scared and just do what I came here to do."

Although it pained her, Suzanne nodded again. "If God wants you to meet your birth mother, He will open the doors. But He won't throw you through them. You have to move forward on your own two feet."

A sob hiccupped in Suzanne's ear. "Thanks, Mom. I think I just needed to be sure you were okay with this. That you weren't mad at me."

A hysterical laugh built in Suzanne's throat. Mad? No, that was too calm. She was furious, but not at Alexa. At the circumstances that kept her from claiming one daughter while facing the possibility of losing the other to the woman whose womb had given her life. She swallowed hard and forced a calm tone. "No, sweetheart, I'm not mad at you. Please don't worry."

"I love you, Mom."

Suzanne crushed the phone against her cheek. "I love you, too." She drew in a shuddering breath and stood. "Now I better get downstairs and help Anna-Grace with those pies. Tell Tom and Linda hello for me, and I'll be praying —" Her voice broke. Could she honestly pray for Alexa to find her birth mother? She finished weakly, "I'll be praying for you."

"Thanks, Mom. I'll call you later in the week, okay?"

"Okay. Bye, honey." They disconnected the call, and Suzanne slipped the phone into her pocket. She moved to the staircase and descended slowly, one plodding step after another, as she imagined Alexa crossing the street, examining the spot where she'd been left as an infant, then moving toward the nameless, faceless woman who'd begun to haunt her dreams.

She froze midstep and turned her face to the ceiling. Raising her fist, she uttered a low moan. "Don't let that woman hurt her, God. Do You hear me? Don't You dare let my daughter get hurt."

CHAPTER 12

Indianapolis
Alexa

Tom drove around to the alley and parked behind the garage, leaving the car idling. "Well, this is it."

Alexa tipped her forehead against the cold window and let her gaze drift from the cedar-shake roof of the run-down building to its drooping carriage-style door and then to the cracked cement patch that met the edge of the alley. She'd expected some kind of connection to the place where she'd been abandoned, but nothing stirred through her chest. She didn't break out in goose flesh or even experience a sting of tears. Nothing.

She turned to Tom. "I'm getting out."

"Want me to come with you?"

She considered the question for a moment and then shook her head. "It's okay. As you said, it's cold. Just stay put. I shouldn't be long." She slammed the door behind her and then crossed the short expanse of gravel to the cement pad.

Wind sent a few dry leaves swirling in front of her feet. They danced a do-si-do and joined a cluster of other leaves caught in the narrow inset of the wide door. She moved to the pile and toed it with her shoe. Her breath hung like a little cloud in front of her face, and cold air teased the thin band of exposed flesh on the back of her neck between her coat collar and ponytail. She shivered, recalling Mom saying how cold it had been the day she heard a kitten's mew that wasn't a kitten at all.

She ducked against the door to better block the wind, then looked up and down the alley. Tall bushes, rows of trees, and fences created barriers between the narrow alleyway and the backyards. Other than the wind's whistle and the soft vibration of Tom's car engine, it was quiet, too. No intrusion of traffic or voices or other evidence of people nearby. She shivered again but not from the cold this time. An unexpected rush of anger filled her.

It was so cold out here. And lonely. Not a soul around. What kind of person left a tiny baby in a place like this? Even though it was behind an occupied home, a good fifty feet separated the back of the garage from the back door of the house. In December people wouldn't have been in the yard. If Mom hadn't been leaving that day, if she hadn't gone to the side of the house closest to the garage, Alexa's weak cries might have gone unnoticed. She might have died right out here in this alley.

She gave the leaves a vicious kick that sent them swirling across the hard ground. She'd told Tom she didn't want to get her birth mother in trouble, but at that moment she wished she could call the police, report her own abandonment, and see the unfeeling, irresponsible woman brought to justice. How could she have just thrown Alexa away the way she did?

Tom rolled down the passenger window, leaned across the console, and angled his worried face toward her. "You okay, honey-girl?"

She wasn't okay. She was fighting mad, the last thing she'd expected to be when she talked Tom into bringing her here. She gritted her teeth and shook her head.

"Why don'tcha get back in? No sense freezing yourself clear through."

Her fury created a spark of heat that combated the cold wind. "Not yet." She needed a few more minutes to memorize the dismal, lonely spot where she'd met

Mom. She wanted to remember it so when her path crossed with the woman who'd given birth to her, she could tell her —

"May I help you?"

Alexa leaped away from the garage door as quickly as if she'd been kicked by a mule. A woman — young, sad-looking, with her gaping coat exposing a very swollen belly — stood only a few feet away. She held a filled garbage bag in her hand. Lines of worry — or weariness? — marched across her forehead, giving her an aged appearance despite her round, smooth, youthful cheeks.

Alexa took a hesitant step toward Tom's car. "No. No, I'm —"

"Are you needing to check in? You have to go around to the front."

Heat flamed Alexa's cheeks. "Oh, I'm not here to —"

The woman ducked down a bit and peered at Tom. "Is he your baby-daddy? He can't stay here with you, but they'll let him visit. Especially if you're planning to keep your baby. But you'll have to take classes together. They're real strict about that."

Embarrassment and uncertainty held Alexa's tongue.

The young woman didn't seem to mind carrying on a one-sided conversation, because she continued with hardly a pause.

"Me? I'm not keeping mine." She cupped the underside of her stomach and gazed down at the mound. "I already met the couple who are adopting my baby." She glanced at Alexa, a sad smile curving her chapped lips. "I'm having a girl." She looked down again. "They're real nice, and I know they'll take good care of her. The people here make sure the adoptive parents are good and decent, so if you're gonna give yours up, you don't have to worry."

"I'm not staying here. I'm not having a baby." Alexa finally spit the words out.

"Oh. I was hoping maybe . . ." She seemed so disappointed that Alexa experienced a brief pang of guilt.

Alexa took a step toward her. "You were hoping what?"

"Maybe we could be friends. There's two other girls here, but they, well, bonded with each other. Girls don't do threes very well most times. So I'm pretty much alone. I thought . . ." She shrugged. "Guess it was silly."

"Silly to want a friend?" Alexa shook her head, smiling. "Not hardly. What's your name?"

"Melissa."

Alexa reached to shake Melissa's hand. "I'm Alexa. It's nice to meet you."

"You, too."

Melissa's hand was like ice. With her uncovered head and hands and unbuttoned coat, the winter air would seem much chillier to her. Alexa stepped aside to allow Melissa to pass. "You'd better get rid of that trash and head back inside. You don't want to get sick, especially since you're —" She glanced at Melissa's round stomach.

Melissa stayed put. "This extra weight is like insulation. I'm warm enough." She shifted the trash bag to the other hand. "If you aren't pregnant, why are you here?"

"I'm just kind of . . ." How should she put it? "Nosing around."

"Are you searching for information about an abandoned baby girl, too?"

Alexa's jaw dropped. She summoned Tom with a frantic wave of her hand.

He rounded the car in the space of three heartbeats. "What's the matter, girlie?"

She grabbed his arm with both hands, almost dancing in place. "Tom, this is Melissa. She's a resident here. And she just asked me if I was seeking information about an abandoned baby girl."

Tom aimed a shocked look at Melissa. "How do you know about that?"

Melissa gazed at Tom with wary eyes. Under ordinary circumstances Alexa would have laughed at the young woman's apprehension. Tom, tall and barrel-chested, seemed intimidating, but he was nothing but a big teddy bear. Even so, she hoped his appearance would coax Melissa into answering.

The girl gulped. "I . . . overheard something."

"When?"

"This morning."

Alexa clasped her hands to her throat. "What did you hear? Who was talking?"

Hunching her shoulders, Melissa sidestepped toward the dumpster at the far edge of the garage. "I don't know if I should say. Ms. Reed — she's the director — might not want me talking about it."

"Please, Melissa." Tears pricked Alexa's eyes, and the cold wind chilled the moisture, making her feel as though she blinked ice.

"I —"

"Melissa?" A strident female voice carried from the direction of the house.

Melissa darted to the corner of the garage and peered around its edge. "Yes, ma'am?"

"What are you doing out there?"

Melissa glanced at Alexa and Tom before answering. "Just breathing the cold air. I'll be back in a minute."

"Hurry. The thermometer says it's only

seventeen degrees." A door latch clicked into place.

Melissa scurried to the dumpster. Tom crossed to her in two wide strides. He took the bag, lifted the lid on the dumpster, and tossed the bag inside. Melissa sent him a bashful smile of thanks. She turned toward the house, but he caught her arm.

"I don't want to get you in trouble, but I really would like to know what you heard about the abandoned baby." Tom spoke softly, kindly, convincingly. "She's important to me."

Melissa chewed the inside of her cheek, her face puckered in uncertainty. "I didn't hear much. When Ms. Reed found out I was in the reading room behind her office, she made me go upstairs. I just know a man was here asking about adoptions from twenty years ago. Especially the adoption of a baby who wasn't born in the home but was left here."

Alexa's pulse seemed to double in beat. Might her birth father have sought her out? She gasped a question. "Did you hear his name?"

Melissa shook her head. She clutched at the collar of her coat, her gaze flitting back and forth between Tom and Alexa like a mouse planning its escape from a gang of alley cats. "No. But he said he was a . . . a private investigator."

She hadn't expected that reply. Alexa gawked at Tom, who gawked at Melissa. He sputtered, "Did you say 'private investigator'?"

"He called himself a PI." Melissa made a face. "He had out the record books and asked a lot of questions. So it seemed like he knew what he was doing." She slipped her arm free of Tom's light grasp. "I have to go in or Ms. Reed might come after me. If you want, go around to the front and ask to talk to her about what she told the PI."

Alexa nodded eagerly. "Yes, we can —"

Tom draped his arm over Alexa's shoulders. "Thank you, Melissa. You've been a big help. You get on inside now before this cold air makes you sick."

Melissa nodded and hurried off.

"C'mon, honey-girl. Let's go home."

"But, Tom —"

"Hush now." He hustled Alexa to the car.

In the warm interior Alexa gave him a frustrated frown. "Why don't you want to talk to the director? She could tell us who's searching for me."

He snorted. "I don't need her to tell us." He put the car in gear and headed for the alley's exit. "There can't be more than a

173

dozen PIs in the Indianapolis area. We can research that on our own. Besides, I got the impression Melissa has a hard time staying on the director's good side. If we go ring the front bell, the woman will most likely put two and two together and figure out she's the one who let us know the investigator was there. No sense in stirring up tension between her and the lady she'll be living with for quite a while to come." He eased into the street, shooting her a warning glance. "Besides, that PI might not be searching for you."

Alexa bolted straight up and stared at Tom's profile. "But it has to be me!"

Tom chuckled. "Oh, of course it does. Because you're the only baby girl who was ever abandoned in Indianapolis, right?"

She slumped against the seat. The newspapers gave accounts of abandoned infants several times a year. Even Briley Forrester had been left at a fire station by his mother. Maybe somewhere a parent was abandoning a child right that minute. She bit down on her lower lip.

"Now listen, Alexa. It's possible he is hunting you, but it's just as possible he's hunting some other baby girl. So before you get yourself all worked up and excited the way you like to do, we need to explore some more, okay?"

Alexa, still reeling from the emotional roller coaster of the past half hour, didn't answer.

He nudged her. "Okay?"

She sighed. "Okay."

They left the residential area and encountered downtown, noonday traffic. Tom gripped the steering wheel with both hands and leaned forward slightly, his body tense. "Tell you what. While I'm maneuvering through this mess, why don't you text Linda? Ask her what parts of your find-your-mother plan she got rolling."

"Why can't I call her instead?"

"Because your voice will distract me." He grinned, waggling his brows. "And she needs to practice her texting. She's terrible at it."

Alexa laughed. Somehow Tom always managed to pull her from the doldrums. "All right." She set the keystroke clicks to Silent so the sound wouldn't bother Tom and then typed a short note to Linda. *On our way home. What did u do this morning?*

In only a few seconds, her phone's vibration alerted her to Linda's reply. She lifted her phone and read, *Lost!*

Frowning, Alexa tried to decipher the cryptic message. As she was pondering, a

175

second one popped in.

Lots!

She stifled a snort of amusement and tapped, *Like what?* A series of wavering dots let her know Linda was forming a reply. When it came, it filled the entire square.

I went to the post office and set up a pobox PO. Box for you to get letters. I went to the newspaper office and paiiid for a personal ad asking for information about a baby girl left behind a garage in Indianapapolis. I set up a account an account on social medium media so we can send a message there to lots of people at the same time. How do you backspace on thisthing. I want to fix my err

A second box held the remainder of the message: *Ors.* Alexa swallowed a snicker. Then a third box — containing just the word *Grrr* — popped onto the screen. She forgot about not distracting Tom and burst out laughing.

He grinned at her. "What's funny?"

She held up her phone. "You were right. Linda's terrible at texting."

"Told ya."

"I'm going to put her out of her misery." She applied her thumbs to the lighted letters. *You did get "lost" done! Will show you how to correct err Ors when I get home. Will talk then, too. Love u.*

176

Linda's reply followed quickly. *Haha. Lucky for you I talk better than i type text. Love u 2.*

Tom took the exit for the highway, and his shoulders visibly relaxed as they left the city behind. Alexa waited a few minutes, making sure he was less tense, before speaking.

"Tom? Do you think it would be all right if I went back to see Melissa sometime? You know, to visit her?"

His eyebrows rose. "You wanna do that?"

"Yeah. I think I do." She envisioned the young woman's haunted eyes. Loneliness had seeped from her. "It seems like she could use a friend."

He gave her arm a couple of pats. "That's nice of you, honey-girl. She did remind me a little bit of your mama when I first met her — forlorn and just needing somebody to tell her everything's gonna be okay."

"If she's having a baby on her own and then giving it away, I don't know how she'll be okay." Sadness struck hard. "Mom raised me, but I'm pretty sure she still thought about Anna-Grace a lot."

"And Melissa will think about her baby, too, no doubt." Tom's tone turned thoughtful. "But you know something, Alexa. You just might be the right person to help Melissa be 'okay.' After all, you were raised by a woman who didn't give birth to you but who loved you just as much as any biological mother could love a child. If Melissa sees how you turned out — happy, secure, loved — then it could make her feel better about letting somebody else raise her baby."

Alexa nodded slowly. "You might be right."

"I *might* be right?" Tom laughed. " 'Course, unless you're Linda, you can't always be right."

Alexa laughed, too, then she settled back in the seat and closed her eyes. Maybe God had brought Melissa to the alley when she and Tom were there so she'd be able to befriend the other woman, to offer her comfort and encouragement. Alexa hoped so. Because she wanted something good to come from the visit to that stark, cold place where she might have died twenty years ago, thanks to her birth mother's heartless choice.

CHAPTER 13

Cynthia

Not even during the exhausting infant and toddler days had Cynthia been so eager to send her children to bed. Holding back the information she and Mr. Mallory had uncovered proved torturous during the supper hour when Glenn, as was his custom, asked each of them to share their favorite part of the day. But she didn't want to talk about it in front of Darcy and Barrett. Twice in the past week Darcy had mentioned how "neat" it would be to have a big sister. Even if they located the baby girl she'd given up, it didn't mean the girl would want a relationship with them. She wouldn't plant false hope in her daughter's heart. But she could hardly wait to talk to Glenn.

After supper the children sat at the kitchen breakfast bar and finished their homework while Cynthia washed dishes. Then, as a family, they watched television — two

reruns of Glenn's favorite show, *M*A*S*H* —
before he led them in their short bedtime
devotional. And finally at nine o'clock,
Glenn said, "Okay, gang, sleep."

Cynthia gave each child a hug and kiss,
laughing when Barrett made a horrible face
and wiped his cheek. She didn't care if he
protested. She had never been hugged and
kissed good night, and she would never send
her children to bed without a sweet end to
the day. Barrett would just have to accept
it. Someday he'd look back and appreciate
the affectionate routine.

As soon as the children's bedroom doors
closed, Cynthia plopped down on the sofa
next to Glenn and captured his hand.
"Guess what!"

He smiled. "I think if we take the time for
me to guess, you'll explode. You're sitting
on a powder keg, aren't you?"

What a perfect analogy. She let the keg
blow. "The PI discovered some promising
information this morning about where my
baby girl might be."

Glenn set his Bible aside, his mouth dropping open. "Already? Where?"

"In a Kansas town called Arborville."

"Never heard of it."

Cynthia laughed. "Neither had I. But
when we were at the library, I did some

180

research. It's very small. The last census showed fewer than six hundred people live there. And it was classified as an unincorporated Old Order Amish and Mennonite community, with agriculture as its main source of revenue."

Glenn relaxed against the sofa's backrest, and Cynthia shifted close. He slipped his arm around her, his fingers cupping her hip. "How did he come up with Arborville?"

She wove her fingers through his and tipped her head to gaze into his attentive face. "Remember I told you how I watched an Amish woman pick up my baby and take her into the garage?"

He nodded.

"Well, Mr. Mallory found out that a teenager from Arborville was staying at the home at the same time I left my baby there. So she's probably the one who found my little girl."

Glenn's eyebrows descended into a puzzled frown. "Wait a minute. Are you saying an Amish girl was there having a baby?"

"Apparently."

He whistled a soft *whew.* "I wouldn't have expected that."

"Me neither." Given the Amish's close family ties and religious belief system, it didn't seem likely one of their girls would end up pregnant out of wedlock. But knowing that a girl from a family so different from her own dysfunctional family could find herself in such an unlikely predicament somehow made Cynthia feel a little less guilty. She didn't understand why, but she couldn't deny a small sense of relief in knowing she wasn't alone in making a grievous error of judgment.

"So an Amish girl was there." Glenn tapped his chin with one finger, his expression thoughtful. "She might have found your baby. But why do you think she took your baby?"

Cynthia sat up, eager to divulge everything Mr. Mallory had told her. "First of all, the only record of an abandoned baby at the home is a boy from 1964. That's long before I left my baby there. Mr. Mallory and I explored microfiche, and we couldn't find any newspaper accounts from December twenty years ago about an abandoned baby girl. It's as if I'd never even left my little girl behind that garage, and of course I know I did.

"Plus, according to the home's records, this Amish girl — her name is Suzanne Zimmerman — gave up her baby girl for adoption. It's customary for the adoptive parents' names to be placed on the birth certificate, so there shouldn't be a birth certificate with her name on it as 'mother.' But he found the record of a birth certificate for a baby girl born the day after my little girl, with Suzanne Zimmerman listed as the mother and no one listed as the father."

Wonder bloomed on Glenn's handsome face. "Cyn . . ."

She nodded, her body quivering in excitement. "So Mr. Mallory theorizes this Suzanne Zimmerman didn't hand my baby girl to the home's director, the way I've always assumed. He thinks, instead, she just took my baby as a replacement for the one she gave up."

Glenn shook his head, his jaw slack.

"Tomorrow Mr. Mallory plans to make some telephone calls and see if he can connect with the Zimmermans in Arborville. Oh, Glenn . . ." She tucked herself against his sturdy frame. Her chest heaved as eagerness tried to turn her inside out. "Just think. By tomorrow we might already know whether or not my little girl wants to meet me."

Glenn's arms wrapped around her and held tight. He rested his chin against her hair. "That would be an answer to prayer."

She sighed, closing her eyes. "Yes." She tried to picture her daughter the way she might appear now, but somehow the only image she could conjure was of Darcy. She opened her eyes again and peered up at Glenn. "If my baby girl was raised Amish, do you think she'll have any interest at all in meeting me? Do you think she's ever been told she wasn't born to her mother?" She jerked free of Glenn's hold. "What if she hasn't been told? What if my contacting her completely pulls the . . . the rug of security from under her feet? What if —"

"Shh, Cyn." He captured her shoulders and pulled her close again. "You're getting ahead of yourself. We don't even know for sure that Suzanne Zimmerman has your baby girl. There isn't any sense in worrying about what-ifs until Mr. Mallory's theory is proven."

She took several calming breaths. Glenn was always logical. Sometimes his penchant for logic frustrated her — couldn't he get emotionally worked up once in a while? — but she realized the truth of his statement. Worrying accomplished nothing. And even though circumstantially it seemed as though they were on the right route to finding her baby, it was possible this would turn out to be a false lead.

She needed to keep her emotions under control. But she'd waited twenty years to hold her little girl again. Now that the opportunity hovered just beyond her fingertips, all fear had fled, and only desire filled her.

"I know you're right," she whispered against his shirt front, appreciating the strength of his arms, his comforting presence. "But I want to find her so badly. Mr. Mallory has enough money for a certain number of hours. He used up at least eight of them today."

Glenn pressed his lips to her temple. "If this is God's will, Cyn, we'll find her. Leave it in His hands instead of Mr. Mallory's, okay?"

"Okay." She turned a hopeful look upward. "Can we pray about it together? Now?"

His sweet smile provided approval. He slipped from the couch, and she joined him in kneeling with their elbows on the scarred coffee table where Barrett had carved his initials when he was five and Darcy had spilled lemonade, leaving a faded circular patch. Glenn had offered to replace the table with a newer one, but she loved the evidence of family life this old one reflected.

She folded her hands, closed her eyes, and listened as Glenn prayed aloud.

"God, Cyn's little girl is out there

somewhere. All these years that she's been missing her baby, You've kept Your watchful eye on her. Thank You for caring for Cyn, for me, for all our children."

Her heart caught at his choice of the word *our.*

"If it's Your will for Cyn and her baby to be together again, please lead us to her."

Cynthia scrunched her eyes so tight that pinpoints of light exploded behind her closed lids. Her heart begged, *Please, please, please let it be Your will for me to find her. Oh, God, please.*

"If finding her would be too hurtful for the girl, then I ask You to comfort and strengthen Cyn. Either way, we trust You to do what is best for both Cyn and her daughter." Glenn paused, as if giving Cynthia an opportunity to add her petitions, and after a few silent seconds finished with "Amen."

Cynthia echoed, "Amen."

Over the next few days, Cynthia nearly chewed her fingernails to the quick — an old nervous habit she thought she'd abandoned — waiting for the telephone to ring. Mr. Mallory had instructed her to wait for his call rather than to try to contact him. He'd promised to let her know when he had something of value to share. But why was it taking so long?

Impatience made her snappish with Darcy and Barrett, and when Glenn gently reprimanded her, she informed him, in a tone much like the one her mother had often used, that she had every right to be on edge and maybe he should try being a little more understanding.

Immediately after her harsh retort, she apologized, and Glenn said he forgave her, but he kept his distance for a few hours, reigniting her frustration. Why couldn't he realize how hard this was and cut her some slack?

Friday morning after dropping the kids off at school with a distracted farewell, she drove to the library and parked in the small lot for employees. With the car idling, she pulled out her cell phone and scrolled to Mr. Mallory's number. She'd waited long enough for him to contact her. She needed to know what he'd been doing all week, or she might climb out of her skin.

She jabbed her finger against his number and then pressed the phone to her ear. It went straight to voice mail. Gritting her teeth against a groan, she disconnected the call and tossed her phone into her purse. Over the course of the day, she called him five times, each time getting his voice mail instead of the investigator himself. The last time she left a curt message. "This is Cynthia Allgood. Call me."

But he didn't call on Friday. Or on Saturday morning. Saturday noon, after several hours of tension, Glenn followed her into the kitchen and suggested they grab hamburgers at a fast-food restaurant. "Afterward we can take in a matinee at the multiplex. They have eight different theaters. I'm sure we'll find something good."

Cynthia turned from the refrigerator. "You and me?"

"All of us." He offered a wide grin. "We'll make it a family event."

His words stabbed like a knife. The hole carved in her heart the moment she had abandoned her baby girl had grown larger and larger over these past days, the longing to reconnect becoming more and more intense. In her mind "family" included her first child, and if she couldn't have time with all of them, she didn't want time with any of them. She recognized the ridiculousness of her feelings, yet her emotions raged unrestrained.

She grabbed a package of slivered ham and the mayonnaise jar and gave the fridge door a shove. "No, thank you."

He trailed her to the counter. "Why not?

The kids would love it."

She frowned at him over her shoulder. "I'm not in the mood. Besides, I'd have to leave my cell phone off in the theater. Mr. Mallory might call, and —"

Glenn blew out a huff and muttered, "Mallory again."

She leaned against the counter and folded her arms over her chest. "What is that supposed to mean?"

"It means I'm tired of that man controlling our household." He flicked a frown toward the living room, where Darcy and Barrett played a board game, their voices rising in a playful squabble. "Settle down out there!"

The noise immediately ceased.

Cynthia hissed, "Don't take your frustration with me out on them."

He raised his eyebrows. "You mean the way you haven't been doing all week?"

She yanked the loaf of bread from the cupboard and plopped it onto the countertop. When she opened the drawer for a butter knife, Glenn caught her wrist. She glared up at him, but he didn't let go.

"I've had it, Cyn. All week the three of us have tiptoed around, trying our best to stay out of your way." He spoke quietly, almost kindly, but his blue eyes glinted with irritation. "I know you're uptight, and I get the reason why. But we can't all just put our lives on hold while we're waiting to see if you're going to meet your daughter."

She wrenched her hand free. "So don't. Go do what you want to do. I'm not holding you back."

He stared at her for several seconds, his mouth set in an unsmiling line and indecision playing in his expression.

Her heart pounded as she waited for him to reach for her, pull her close, whisper sweetly that he was wrong to expect her to leave the house when she was waiting for such an important call, that of course he'd stay here with her.

"All right then." He turned and strode through the living room to the front entry closet. "Hey, buckaroos, grab your coats."

Cynthia hurried to the wide doorway as the pair jolted to their feet. Barrett said, "Where are we going?"

"To get some burgers and then go see a movie."

Barrett released a whoop and galloped to his dad.

Darcy sent a puzzled look from Glenn to Cynthia. "Aren't you coming, Mom?"

Glenn tossed Darcy her coat. "She doesn't want to go. So it's just you guys and your old dad. C'mon."

Very slowly Darcy pushed her arms into the sleeves of her coat. Her gaze on Cynthia, she inched toward Barrett and Glenn. For a moment it seemed Darcy would refuse to go, but then she said, "Bye, Mom."

Barrett waved at Cynthia, almost dancing in place. "Bye, Mom! Dad, what movie are we gonna see?"

"I don't know yet, buck—" The door closed on the last of Glenn's reply.

Cynthia stood in the doorway and stared at the front door. Sadness and hurt and anger swirled through her, stealing her appetite. She returned to the kitchen and put away the food, then slid onto one of the kitchen stools and lowered her head to her hand. She'd always believed reconnecting with her baby girl would complete her family. Instead, would seeking her daughter tear her family apart?

CHAPTER 14

Arborville
Paul

Maybe this wasn't such a great idea after all. Paul gripped the truck's steering wheel with both hands and glanced past Danny's head to Suzy. She gazed out the window, seeming to examine the snow-dusted fields where winter wheat lay dormant.

He gritted his teeth. All week he'd anticipated driving to Wichita to eat at Danny's favorite fast-food chicken restaurant. Each day while on break from working in the Zimmermans' basement, he'd caught a few minutes with Suzy to tell her more about Danny. She listened intently, seeming to memorize the details. His chest pinched in an odd way. Those short conversations had made him feel more and more at ease with her. He'd been sure this evening would be relaxing, would be beneficial to his relationship with his son.

But tension filled the truck's cab. They'd just turned onto the highway, and Suzy sat quiet on the opposite side of the seat, apparently having already given up on trying to coax the boy into talking to her. Although the temptation to give Danny a solid jab with his elbow played through his mind, he stiffened his muscles and resisted. But the minute they arrived at the restaurant, he planned to haul his son into the men's room for a stern talking-to about being rude to a friend.

A friend . . . He glanced again at Suzy. With her hair swept back into a bun and her face angled away, he was able to admire her pleasing profile. Back in the days when they ran barefooted along the creek, she'd had long yellow braids that flopped against her shoulder blades. No matter how tightly Abigail Zimmerman wove those braids, a few tendrils of hair always worked loose to form little squiggles at her temples and at the nape of her neck. A smile tugged his lips as he took note of a wavy strand tucked behind her ear. Some things didn't change.

He jerked his gaze forward. And other things changed a lot. Like being able to have a friendship with Suzy. They weren't ten years old anymore. And she wasn't a part of their fellowship any longer. She attended worship services with her mother every Sunday, but she hadn't approached the deacons to renew her membership. She still wore English clothing, although modest, and her head was uncovered.

An uncomfortable feeling wiggled through his gut. He hadn't asked the deacons about spending the evening with Suzy away from Arborville. Would he be reprimanded? The silence in the cab combined with his concerns. Almost reflexively, he applied the brakes, signaled, and pulled onto the shoulder.

Both Danny and Suzy turned puzzled faces in his direction. Suzy said, "Is there something wrong with your truck?"

Paul hit the emergency flashers, then sent her a look he hoped would communicate his confusion. "No, the truck's fine." He pulled in a big breath and let it out with a whoosh. "But I wonder if we should go back."

"Why?" Danny blasted the question.

"Because neither of you is talking. It doesn't seem like you're having much fun." Although he answered Danny, he kept his gaze fixed on Suzy.

Pink stained her cheeks. "I'm sorry. I was kind of . . . lost in thought."

Paul wished Danny wasn't sitting between

them so he could ask her what she'd been thinking about. Was she worried about the deacons' reaction to their excursion, too? Why hadn't he considered the ramifications of taking Suzy Zimmerman on what the community would surely consider an act of courting?

Danny folded his arms over his chest. "I don't want to go back. Auntie Ann's Chicken is my favorite place to eat. I want chicken fingers for supper."

Paul finally met his son's gaze. He tempered his tone, but he let his expression speak to his disappointment in Danny's behavior. "And I want you to answer Miss Zimmerman with more than a yes or no when she asks you questions, because it's the polite thing to do. Right now neither of us is getting what we want, are we?"

Danny scowled and ducked low. "I didn't know what to say."

A silly excuse. Danny had never been short on words.

Suzy touched Danny's arm. "Maybe it's hard to answer questions when you don't know the person who's doing the asking."

Paul almost snorted. Until now, Danny had never met a stranger. And he couldn't call Suzy a stranger after being in and out of the farmhouse dozens of times since she returned. The boy was just being obstinate, and he started to say so. But Suzy went on.

"What if for the next ten miles you ask me questions? Then you might feel as if you know me a little better, and it will be easier to talk to me."

To Paul's surprise, Danny sat upright so quickly it seemed someone had caught him by the collar and given a yank. "Okay."

Suzy sent Paul a hesitant smile. "Is that all right with you?"

She was asking a little too late since she'd already gained Danny's cooperation. Still worrying about the deacons' reaction to their trip to Wichita, he said, "Are you sure you wouldn't rather . . . go back?" *Go back to Arborville? Go back to when you were a part of the fellowship? Go back to before we climbed into the barn loft and made the biggest mistake of our lives?*

"Yes, I'm sure."

For a moment her reply seemed to apply to the questions rolling in his mind, and he gave a start. Then he gathered his senses and nodded. He turned off the emergency flashers and glanced in the rearview mirror. "Okay then. We'll go on." And hopefully there wouldn't be a big uproar when the fellowship got wind of what they'd done. Now or back then.

■ ■ ■ ■

Suzanne

As soon as Paul pulled onto the highway, Suzanne offered Danny an encouraging smile. "All right. You can ask me anything except my age or my weight." She stifled a laugh when Paul chuckled.

Danny pursed his face, seemingly deep in thought. Suzanne glimpsed so much of Paul in him, despite his sullen behavior. Warm affection trickled through her chest. Looking at Danny sent her backward in time to happy, carefree days. Kind of a nice distraction, considering the places her thoughts had been carrying her only a few minutes ago.

"You used to live in Arborville, right?" Danny's boyish voice carried above the engine's growl and the grating of rubber tires on wet pavement. "How come you moved away?"

Paul jerked a warning frown in her direction. She nodded, hoping he would read assurance in the gesture, and formed a careful reply. "Well, at first it was my mother's idea for me to visit Indiana. But once I got there, I met some nice people who helped me finish high school and then train to be a nurse.

I started working at a hospital, and I liked it so much I decided to make Indiana my home."

Paul's shoulders appeared to wilt a bit with her honest, albeit incomplete, answer.

"My friend Jay — you know, your nephew — says you and my dad courted a long time ago."

Paul stiffened again, and Suzanne wished she'd placed a few more restrictions on Danny's line of questioning. She managed to smile. "That's true. Your dad and I were very good friends for a long time." The warmth of affection that had begun to flicker when she gazed at Danny increased as she lifted her attention to Paul. "I think we're still friends."

He aimed a quick, lopsided grin at her before returning his attention to the road.

"But you're not courting?"

Suzanne shook her head, shifting her full attention to Danny. "No, Danny. We're not courting."

The boy lapsed into silence, staring ahead.

Suzanne waited a bit before giving him a light poke with her elbow. "Hey. You've got some more miles of question time waiting. Don't waste it."

Danny sat frozen for a few more seconds and then tipped his face to her. "What's your favorite color? Do you like chicken fingers? How come you don't wear a cap like the other ladies in Arborville? Do you know how to hit a baseball? When is Alexa coming back?"

Suzanne pursed her lips and pretended to give his questions great consideration. Then she answered in a rush. "Purple. Yes. Because the church I attended in Indiana didn't require me to. Yes, I do. And I'm not sure."

Danny's eyes widened. "You know how to hit a baseball?"

She swallowed a laugh. Of course he would focus on that topic, given his love for the sport. "Mm-hm. I actually was a pretty good batter when I was a girl. I was a decent pitcher, too."

If his eyes grew any bigger, they'd pop from his skull.

She added, "But that was a long time ago. I'm not sure I'd be very good at it today."

Danny spun to face his father. "Is that true, Dad? Was she good at baseball?"

A grin teased at the corners of Paul's lips. "Miss Zimmerman wouldn't lie about such a serious thing. One time, when we were your age, she threw three strikes in a row and got me out."

"You let a girl throw you out?"

Suzanne burst out laughing at the derision in Danny's tone, and Paul joined her. Paul said, "Hey now, don't hold it against me. Back then she was known as Sizzlin' Suzy on the playground, so we're not talking just any girl. Suzy was special."

Something changed in his voice. Something indiscernible, yet she experienced a shiver of awareness. She needed to change the subject. Quickly. She nudged Danny. "What position do you play?"

For the next several miles Danny regaled Suzanne with story after story about his favorite plays. Then he moved from playing baseball to fishing, and Paul once again chimed in about how good Miss Zimmerman was at baiting a hook and snagging fish. His compliments were probably meant to build her up in Danny's eyes, to make the boy willing to open up to her, but the words had a deeper effect. When Paul spoke glowingly of her, something in her chest seemed to expand and tingle. A feeling she hadn't experienced since she was seventeen years old and recklessly in love with eighteen-year-old Paul Aldrich.

She should have told Paul to turn around when she had the chance.

They eased into the town of Goddard,

which melded into Wichita with nothing more than a sign to alert people they were leaving one city for another. Things had changed so much since Suzanne lived in Arborville and visited Wichita for occasional shopping expeditions. Although she'd driven Mother to doctor appointments since her return, she hadn't been everywhere in the city, and she examined the businesses as Paul drove them to the strip mall that housed Danny's favorite eatery.

Paul parked as close to the restaurant's door as possible. "Button up, Danny, and put your hood on, too."

A hint of belligerence appeared in the set of Danny's mouth, but he yanked the hood into place and even jammed on his mittens without being told. Suzanne followed the boy's example. Even on a short walk, the January wind could cut through a person.

Paul trotted around to her side of the pickup and opened the door for her. She hadn't expected the gentlemanly gesture, and her movements turned clumsy as she slid out. Cold air smacked her, and she angled her face to the wind in the hope Paul would blame her flushed cheeks on something other than embarrassment.

Danny dashed ahead and held the door for them. Suzanne thanked him. He shrugged. Paul poked him on the shoulder, and the boy said, "You're welcome." He pushed his hood back, leaving his hair standing on end, and without conscious thought Suzanne reached out and smoothed her hand over the thick brown strands. Danny jolted as if she'd scorched him with her touch.

She pushed her hand into her pocket and pretended she hadn't noticed his reaction, but his leap from friendly to frosty stung. She was beginning to understand Paul's concerns. Danny reminded her of a chameleon walking through a flower garden, changing with each new plant it encountered, unrecognizable from one moment to the next.

The firm set of Paul's lips indicated his displeasure with his son's behavior, so she wasn't surprised that as soon as they placed their orders, Paul ushered Danny to the hallway leading to the bathrooms. By the time their order was ready, they still hadn't returned, so she carried the tray to a table and sat down to wait. The aromas rising from the little paper boxes and grease-stained bags made her stomach twist. If the chicken fingers and onion rings tasted as good as they smelled, she'd bring Alexa here when she returned from Indiana. Alexa loved onion rings, and she always proclaimed the greasier they were, the better. She hoped Paul and Danny would hurry up before the food grew cold. The thought of eating cold, greasy onion rings didn't appeal.

Someone tapped her shoulder. She turned to find Danny behind her chair with Paul standing guard over him. The boy's red face and watery eyes told a story, and it took great self-control not to pull him into her arms for a comforting hug.

"Miss Zimmerman, you didn't hurt me, and it was impolite for me to pull away from you." His voice wavered, and he flicked a look at his dad before meeting Suzanne's gaze again. "I'm sorry."

Her heart melted. She gripped her hands together to keep from reaching for him. "You know what? I'm sorry, too, Danny. You're not a little boy, and I kind of treated you like one." She tipped her head. "Is that why you pulled away from me?"

He stared at the floor, shifting from foot to foot. "Sort of."

Paul gave his son's shoulder a little shake. "Stand still and look at Miss Zimmerman when you talk to her."

His voice wasn't harsh, but Suzanne still cringed. The restaurant was crowded, and the patrons sitting on both sides of their table watched their exchange with interest. Suzanne whispered, "Maybe we should talk about this later." She deliberately glanced right and left, praying Paul would take the hint.

He did. He cupped his hand around the back of Danny's neck and guided him to a chair. Danny plopped down and shrugged out of his coat. Paul sat next to him, opposite Suzanne, and lowered his voice to a whisper. "Let's pray and eat, and then we'll talk more in the truck."

CHAPTER 15

Indianapolis
Cynthia

Cynthia sat in the living room, television off, book open in her lap but unread, cell phone at her hip, and waited for Glenn and the kids' return. The front door didn't open until the supper hour. She looked over her shoulder at the trio, noting their flushed, happy faces, but she didn't greet them. And they didn't greet her, either.

The moment after they'd hung their coats in the closet, Glenn said, "Okay, buckaroos, go hang out in your rooms and study your Sunday school lessons. I need to talk to your mom."

Cynthia's stomach seemed to roll over. Hunger or apprehension? She hadn't eaten anything since breakfast nine hours ago, but she was pretty sure the reaction was apprehension. She rose. "What about supper?" Anything to put off an argument.

"We had popcorn and Cokes at the movie," Darcy said.

"And Hot Tamales and Skittles," Barrett added.

Cynthia gawked at them. "You ate all that on top of burgers?" Glenn must have spent a fortune. Theater food was always overpriced. With all that junk in their stomachs, they wouldn't be hungry again until next Tuesday.

"Yep." Barrett patted his tummy as he bounded past her. "Best day ever. Sorry you missed it, Mom." He disappeared around the bend into the hallway.

Darcy followed her brother. As she rounded the corner, she glanced back and offered a sheepish grimace. But she didn't say anything.

Cynthia sank back onto the sofa. Glenn perched next to her, almost sitting on her cell phone. She snatched it up, scooted over a few inches, and rammed her hip against the armrest.

He frowned. "Aren't you tired of being alone yet?"

Of course she was. She'd hated every minute of the house's silence while her family was away. But she hated arguing even more. She'd rather pretend the earlier disagreement had never occurred. "I was just giving you some extra space."

Glenn's gaze narrowed. "Mm-hm." He stretched his arm across the sofa back, his fingertips brushing her shoulder. "When have I ever wanted extra space?"

She looked away. Her church friends often expressed envy about her closeness with Glenn. Although they'd been married more than fifteen years, they still behaved like newlyweds — holding hands when they walked, sneaking a kiss when no one was looking, sitting close with his arm around her. After a childhood of no affection, she relished Glenn's demonstrative nature and also relished reciprocating. Their behavior embarrassed their children, but they'd never cared. They loved each other and weren't averse to showing it.

So why had she moved away when he sat down next to her? She wished she understood her tumultuous emotions.

"Cyn?"

She angled her head so she could peek at him out of the corner of her eye. The disappointment on his face pierced her. She averted her gaze.

"This afternoon was awful. Being out with the kids but without you . . . I felt like something was missing."

"Something was missing." His statement

described the way she'd felt her entire life. First she missed the nurture of loving parents, then she missed the precious baby girl she gave away. She thought Glenn understood because he'd grown up in the same kind of household she had. They'd compared notes when they met in the class designed for family members of alcoholics and had found so many similarities between their childhoods. Those shared experiences had initially drawn them together, and when love blossomed between them, the remembered hurts from their past had led them to commit to never inflict that kind of harm on each other or their children. They'd honored it, too. Until now.

She forced a reply past the knot in her throat. "I know."

"I don't want another day like this one. With you holding yourself away from the rest of us."

Tears both of deep hurt and great frustration stung behind her nose. He'd left her alone all day, not the other way around. She swallowed the words that would surely lead to a quarrel.

"Darcy, Barrett, and I are your family. They need your attention, and I do, too. Putting your whole focus on finding your baby girl isn't fair to me, and it's especially unfair to —"

Her cell phone rang. Owen Mallory's name and number appeared on the screen. With a cry of elation, she leaped from the couch and tapped the Accept button. "Hello?"

"Mrs. Allgood, hello. Owen Mallory here."

"Yes." Her breath released in short puffs, and her hand shook so badly she feared she'd drop the phone. She gripped it two-handed and pressed it tight to her ear. "What did you find out?"

Glenn pushed off the couch and left the room.

Arborville
Paul

Only six fifteen and already dark. Paul had never liked the short days of winter. And he especially disliked it this evening. The black-ness outside the vehicle matched the dark mood inside. Although Danny had relaxed and chatted a little bit while they ate, once they left the restaurant, his surly attitude returned. He sat in the middle of the seat with his shoulders hunched and his arms folded tight across his chest.

Suzy seemed tense, too, sitting stiffly with her linked hands gripped in her lap. The pale light from the dashboard highlighted her tight lips and furrowed brow. Her uncomfortable pose unsettled him. Or maybe the greasy onion rings were responsible for the roiling in his stomach. Either way, he wished the miles would pass quickly. This evening hadn't gone the way he'd hoped.

With the city behind them and a quieter stretch of highway to travel, he placed his hand on Danny's knee and gave a little squeeze. "Okay, Son. You can finish your apology now."

Danny sent a pleading look at Paul. "Do I have to?"

For one moment Paul considered relenting. He was weary of battling his son, weary of feeling like the bad guy. Being the sole provider he could handle. He'd even pretty well settled into being the sole caretaker. But the sole disciplinarian? That wore him down. Only the biblical admonition about training up a child in the way he should go prompted him to speak firmly. "Yes, Son, you do. Because when you've wronged someone, you need to set things right."

Suzy suddenly shifted to face him. "Paul, maybe Danny has reasons he'd rather not share with a stranger."

"You aren't a stranger. You and I are —" Paul clamped his mouth closed. They were . . . what? Employer and employee? Friends? Old lovers? The last thought put a bitter taste in his mouth. He shouldn't lecture Danny about setting things right when he'd failed miserably to do so in his own life. He fisted the cold plastic steering wheel and glared ahead.

"You wanna know why I pulled away?" Danny hunkered so low it appeared half his head was swallowed by his coat. The quilted nylon muffled his voice. "It's 'cause only a mom should fix a boy's hair. Like Jeremy's mom does to him, and Jay's mom does. I let you comb my hair sometimes, Dad, because you're my dad and . . . and I don't have a mom to do it. But nobody else should."

Sympathy pursed Suzanne's face, proving Danny's statement tugged at her heart, but Paul wasn't so easily moved. A woman touching his hair shouldn't create so much resentment. There had to be more to his son's behavior than that. And his explanation didn't address the way he'd flip-flopped from cooperative to contrary at school. Would Danny next accuse the teacher, Mr. Brungardt, of acting like his mother?

Paul said, "Well, I think —"

Suzy turned her gentle smile on Danny. "Thank you for explaining why it bothered

211

you for me to touch your hair. Now may I tell you why I did it?"

Danny, still half-hidden within the folds of his collar, angled his face toward Suzy. "Yeah. I guess."

"You see, I'm a mom. And moms are funny people. When they see a mess, they want to clean it up. When they see an unmade bed, they want to make it. When they see a dirty face, they want to lick their finger and wipe it clean."

Danny snickered. Paul bit the insides of his cheeks to hold back his smile.

"So when they see somebody's hair going in directions it shouldn't, they want to put it back where it belongs." She leaned down and lowered her voice. "Want to hear a secret?"

Danny popped out of his coat and said, "What?" Then he hunkered in again.

"One time when your dad was working at my mother's house, his hair got all messed up because he had sawdust in it and he'd rubbed his hand over his head to get rid of the sawdust. And when I saw how messed up it was, I almost fixed it."

Paul's stomach jumped straight into his chest — one big leap. He struggled to breathe.

Danny emerged slowly, like a timid turtle

from its shell. "You did?"

She nodded. "See? It's not just you. It's everybody, and it's because I'm a mom. Moms are just" — she held her hands outward in a gesture of defeat — "weird."

A grin grew on Danny's face. He giggled, glanced at Paul, and giggled again. "That's really funny how you wanted to fix Dad's hair."

Paul tried to ignore both of them as he turned off the highway onto the dirt road leading to Arborville. But it was hard. He sensed Suzy's gaze on him as she spoke again.

"I know. I have to watch myself. This being a mom thing . . . It can get you in trouble if you aren't careful."

Did she know how his pulse was pounding, thinking about her running her fingers through his hair? He wouldn't pull away like Danny had. In fact, he might return the favor and weave his fingers through her thick, wavy locks. Even twenty years after he'd last touched her silky tresses, he remembered how they felt. Downy soft and —

"Paul?"

He jerked the steering wheel. "What?"

"You just drove right past the lane to my farmhouse."

Heat blazed his face. "Oh. Sorry." He slowed the truck and brought it to a halt. Then, berating himself for getting so lost in the past, he performed a three-point turn and reversed his direction. When he pulled up to the house, he put the gearshift into Park and set the emergency brake.

"Danny, stay put. I'm going to walk Su— Miss Zimmerman to the door."

"Okay. Put your hood up."

Paul cleared his throat. "Don't be smart."

His son had the audacity to snicker. And Suzy grinned. Were the two of them now in cahoots against him? He slammed out of the truck and rounded the hood to open the door for Suzy. As he did so, the dome light's glow flowed over her and Danny, and he caught Danny whispering something in Suzy's ear.

She must have found whatever he said pleasing, because a smile broke across her face.

"I'll see what I can do. Good night now, Danny."

Paul helped her out of the truck and then offered his elbow. The porch light didn't reach all the way across the steppingstones. Small solar lanterns lined the pathway, but their multicolored globes offered minimal illumination. Deep shadows made the crossing less secure. No gentleman would let a lady stumble. Even if the lady's presence was making his stomach twirl like leaves in a tornado.

With the sun's descent, the wind had calmed, but the air was still cold. So he didn't dally as he led her to the porch. They reached the steps and Suzy released his arm. "I'm fine now. You don't need to walk me to the door."

"Oh. All right." Why did it disappoint him that she wanted him to leave her there at the base of the steps? He shoved his hands into his coat pockets. "Thanks for going with us. Even though you and Danny didn't talk a lot, I might have picked up a few clues to his change in behavior."

A tender look crept across her face. "Paul, to be honest, I think he's just realizing how his family is different from his friends', and he's struggling with it. Don't be too hard on him."

He drew back slightly. "Do you think I'm too hard on him?"

"I don't know." She pushed her hands into her pockets and pressed her elbows tight to her sides. "What happened in the bathroom?"

"What happened in the truck right before you got out?"

Her fine eyebrows pulled down. "What?"

"Danny and you were talking. What did he tell you?"

"Oh, Paul." She laughed, her breath forming a cloud that breezed past his cheek. "That wasn't anything to worry about."

He planted his feet wide. "I'll be the judge of that."

She sighed, creating another little puff of condensation. "He just asked if baking was a mom-thing, too, and if so, could I bake him one of Alexa's chocolate cakes."

Paul dropped his jaw. "He asked you to bake him a cake after he —" He shook his head. "That boy. As brazen as the prodigal son demanding his early inheritance."

"You never told me what happened in the bathroom."

He borrowed her statement. "That wasn't anything to worry about."

"In other words, mind my own business, huh?" Not even a hint of rancor colored her tone.

He couldn't resist a grin. "Sort of."

She bounced in place. "Fair enough. But —"

"Suzy, you're cold." Why was he protective of her? The feeling didn't make sense, but he couldn't deny it. "You need to go in."

"In a minute. Listen to me, please." She placed her hand on his forearm, the touch light but enough to seal him in place. "Alexa went through spells when she longed for a father. During those times she was moody and unpredictable. Sometimes children know they're sad, but they don't understand why, so they react the only way they know how — with frustration. Not frustration at you, although it can feel that way, but frustration with the situation. My getting angry at Alexa never helped her deal with her desire to have a daddy, and your getting angry at Danny won't help him, either, if he's longing for his mom."

Paul pulled in a breath. "So I shouldn't have given him a swat when I took him to the bathroom?"

She smiled, and he suspected she'd already guessed what took place in there. "Not necessarily. If you really believe his behavior was deliberately disrespectful, then punishment is appropriate. But . . ." Her fingers closed around his arm. "Don't punish him for missing his mom. He lost someone he loved, and he's bound to mourn."

"But it's been more than three years." Long enough for both Danny and him to move on. To another relationship, perhaps?

He shoved that thought aside. "Shouldn't his mourning be done?"

Sadness pinched her features. "You can't put an expiration stamp on mourning. Time doesn't matter nearly as much as the heart. Danny might mourn more intensely now because he's old enough to understand better what he lost."

Paul hadn't considered that. Didn't he go through spells when he missed Karina more than at other times? Why shouldn't Danny suffer the same waves of stronger mourning? He put his hand over hers and pressed hard. "Thank you, Suzy. That makes sense."

"No problem."

He forced a short laugh. "How'd you get so smart, anyway?"

She seemed to drift away for a moment, her expression dreamy. "I was lucky to have two very wise people mentoring me while I raised Alexa. Their advice was always prayed over and carefully given. I'm just passing a little bit of it along to you."

"Are you talking about the couple who took Alexa to Indiana with them?" Some people in town had questioned her wisdom in allowing Alexa to travel with the pair.

"Yes. They kept me from overreacting to my two-year-old's temper tantrums and my twelve-year-old's bids for independence. I d-don't know what I w-would have d-done without them."

"You're shivering so hard you can't even talk. Time to go in."

"But I wanted t-to tell y-you —"

"In, Suzy." He grabbed her elbow and propelled her up the steps. He opened the front door and discovered Anna-Grace standing on the other side of the threshold in the dark foyer.

The girl backed up, her cheeks blooming with bold pink. "I — I heard someone talking, and I came to see if some unexpected guests had arrived at the B and B."

Suzy eased free of Paul's grasp. "It's just us."

She shot an inquisitive look from one to the other, settling her gaze on Suzy. "Did you enjoy your evening?"

Paul stepped inside and pulled the storm door closed to block the cold air. "Yeah. Yeah, we . . . did." He hated how tongue-tied he got around Anna-Grace. How could he relax around the child who didn't know she belonged to him?

Suzy began unbuttoning her coat. "How was your evening, Anna-Grace?"

The girl's smile quavered. She wasn't completely comfortable, either. He hated that, too. "Quiet. Aunt Abigail and her night nurse have been playing Scrabble. Steven was going to come over, but he said the English essays were taking longer to grade than he expected, so he cancelled."

Impishness glinted in her Zimmerman-blue eyes. "Maybe if you go to Wichita next Saturday, I'll go along, too, and keep Danny company. Or he could stay here with me. That is" — she glanced from Paul to Suzy and back to Paul — "if you have plans to take Cousin Suzy out another time."

Paul smiled — a quick, wavering upturn of his lips. "We'll see. Good night, Suzy. Thanks again for spending time with Danny." Without waiting for her to reply, he scooted out of the house. Not until he pulled into Arborville did he remember Suzy had wanted to tell him something and he'd escaped before she said it. He turned onto the gravel driveway of his house and killed the engine. Then he sat for a moment, his tight fists gripping the steering wheel and his gaze aimed unseeingly ahead as he tried to imagine what she'd intended to say.

Danny bumped his elbow. "Dad? Aren't we gettin' out?"

"Oh. Yeah." Paul trailed Danny across the dark yard to the house. To discover what she wanted him to know, he'd have to spend some one-on-one time with her. His pulse stuttered. But then again maybe he shouldn't. No sense in stirring up the fellowship.

CHAPTER 16

Indianapolis
Cynthia

Cynthia entered the bedroom and found Glenn reclining on all four bed pillows, watching a news station on their tiny, secondhand television. He picked up the remote control from the nightstand and punched a button. The volume dropped by several decibels.

She crossed to their shared dresser. "You don't have to turn it down on my account."

Glenn bounced the remote against his thigh. "Thought you might want to . . . talk."

She yanked open the middle drawer and rummaged for a pair of pajamas. Her oldest ones, faded and stretched out from her pregnancy belly. Ratty looking. She rarely wore them anymore, but tonight they would give a signal that she wasn't in the mood for any romancing. Pajamas clutched against her front, she faced Glenn. "I didn't think you wanted to talk. After all, you took off and didn't come back." Oh, how she wanted to tell him what Mr. Mallory had said, but not unless he asked.

His expression hardened. "I was trying to talk to you, but you weren't paying attention."

Seriously? She plunked her fist on her hip. "Glenn, my phone rang!" Would he ask now about her call from the PI?

"That's what I mean — you weren't paying attention."

With a huff she whirled and stormed up the short hallway to the bathroom. The door was closed, so she banged on the doorjamb. "Who's in there?"

"It's me, Mom." Darcy. Probably playing with her hair in front of the big mirror. If she didn't attend cosmetology school when she graduated from high school, Cynthia would be shocked.

"Hurry up, please."

"Okay. Just gimme a sec."

Cynthia waited, her body tense, and listened to a series of dull thuds and bumps that spoke of items being dropped into drawers. Then silence fell but the door didn't open. She leaned close. "Darcy?"

"I'm coming, I'm coming." Finally the

bathroom door swung inward, and Darcy stood framed in the opening, a wide grin on her face. She held her open hands beside her cheeks like a pair of sunbursts. "I wanted to fluff it more before I showed you. What'cha think?"

Cynthia flicked a glance over the curls cascading from the ponytail situated on the top of her daughter's head. "I think you spend too much time in front of the mirror."

Darcy's smile faded. She lowered her hands. "You don't like it? I was gonna wear it this way to Band Blast."

"It's fine. Now please move out of the way so I can get in there."

Darcy's gaze dropped to the pajamas wadded in Cynthia's hands. "You're changing in here?"

Heat exploded in Cynthia's face. Darcy was old enough to understand the subtle meaning behind her mother choosing not to change clothes in front of her father. Embarrassment brought a rush of defensiveness. "That's none of your business, Darcy. Now scoot."

Darcy inched around Cynthia, both hurt and anger glimmering in her eyes. She stomped down the hallway. "Why is everybody so grouchy around here?"

"Be respectful, young lady," Glenn warned from the bedroom.

Darcy slammed her door.

Cynthia did the same with the bathroom door. Then she dropped the pajamas onto the counter and sank down on the edge of the tub. She caught a glimpse of herself in the mirror and gave a start. A deep V pinched between her eyebrows, and the corners of her lips pulled downward. Stress, anger, and so much sadness was etched into her features. Tears pooled in her eyes, making her reflection waver.

She stared at her wide, watery eyes and whispered the news she longed to tell Glenn. "Mr. Mallory found out the Zimmermans have a bed-and-breakfast in Arborville, and a woman named Suzanne Zimmerman answered the phone when he called. So he decided it would be best for him to continue his investigation in Arborville. He's heading there on Monday. He said he won't even charge for the travel hours because he's going there to satisfy his curiosity as much as to find information about my daughter. And he said we could work out the financial details later if his services exceed our deposit. Isn't it wonderful? I'm so happy."

One tear slipped free of her lashes and

spilled down her cheek. But she knew very well it wasn't a tear of joy.

Arborville
Suzanne

"Suzy, you know what the Bible says about the Sabbath. You're meant to rest, not work."

Suzanne cringed. Couldn't Mother have waited until they were home to reprimand her? Why bring it up in Shelley's dining room, where the entire family had gathered for Sunday lunch? Fortunately, Shelley had set up a table in the kitchen for the children, and Anna-Grace and her broad-shouldered, blond-haired beau had volunteered to supervise the group of rowdy youngsters. So she was spared their witnessing her mother scold her like a misbehaving child.

She set aside her fork and aimed an apologetic look across the table at her mother. She honored the fourth commandment whenever she could, but sometimes life interfered. This was one of those times. She hoped her sisters, brother, and their spouses would understand and not take offense. "I have to get the 2 Corinthians 9:8 room ready for the guest checking in tomorrow. I'd do it tomorrow morning if I didn't have six dozen cookies to bake then." Keep-

226

ing up with Alexa's baking orders might be her ruination. If Anna-Grace weren't so willing to help, Suzanne would tell the customers to find someone else to bake for them until Alexa returned.

Shelley frowned. "Did Mother say he's coming from Indiana?"

Suzanne used her fork to rearrange the lima beans on her plate. Shelley served lima beans more often than anyone else she knew. "That's right."

"Is he bringing his wife?"

Considering the way he'd laughed when she asked if his wife was accompanying him, she assumed he was divorced. Divorce was as alien as out-of-wedlock pregnancies in Arborville. "Um, no. He said he's coming alone."

Clete's wife, Tanya, looked up with interest. "Is he someone you know, Suzy?"

Suzanne recognized the glint in her sister-in-law's eyes. If Shelley was the most structured of their family and Sandra the sunniest, then they'd have to brand Tanya the most romantic. She consistently tried to steer Suzanne toward one of the single men in the area. But Suzanne wasn't interested. Except in one. And she couldn't possibly pursue that one. She laughed lightly. "I lived in Franklin. He's from Indianapolis."

"So?"

"Indianapolis is a very large city. Think two and half Wichitas."

Tanya's brown eyes grew round. "Oh, my . . ."

"Exactly. So no, I've never met this man before."

Clete pushed his empty plate aside and folded his arms on the edge of the table. "What brings a man from Indianapolis to Arborville?"

Suzanne shrugged. "When I asked, he said 'business,' but he didn't expound on it, and I didn't push the subject."

"Strange . . ." Clete puckered his forehead.

Sandra's husband, Derek, shot a worried scowl at Clete. "You don't think he's one of those big-city fellows who try to buy up land to build cookie-cutter houses or cheap apartment buildings, do you? All the farmland around here would seem awfully tempting to someone like that."

Tanya turned to Clete, too. "We don't want cheap apartments in Arborville."

Clete shook his head. "The people around here wouldn't sell to somebody they didn't know. If he even tried, he wouldn't get very far. I don't think we need to worry about that." He quirked his eyebrow and fixed Suzanne with an unsmiling gaze. "I'm not too keen on having some big-city single man staying in the house out there with you, Mother, and Anna-Grace."

Sandra chided, "Now, Clete, they've already had a single man staying out there. Remember? The Chicago reporter who was here last fall. That worked out all right."

"But he stayed in the summer kitchen, not in the house. Suzy's putting him in the house. And Anna-Grace is there, too, on the same floor. That just don't seem right to me."

Suzanne reached over and squeezed Clete's arm. Although she thought his fears unfounded, she appreciated his concern. "Alexa put sturdy locks on all the bedroom doors, and Mother's nurse stays awake all night. If this man attempts any shenanigans, Marjorie will take care of him. She's a no-nonsense kind of person."

"That's true." Sandra nodded, her expression innocent. "Marjorie Wells went running across the yard with a frying pan when she thought Briley Forrester might be bothering Alexa."

Shelley dropped her fork and gawked at Sandra. "Are you serious?"

"Mm-hm. Alexa told me about it. As Suzy said, the nurse will make him toe the line."

Shelley shifted her aghast gaze to Suzanne. "What kind of a place are you running out there that Mother's nurse needs to use a frying pan to defend people?"

Suzanne didn't mean to laugh. But she couldn't help it. Shelley's overreaction tickled her. Her laughter deepened her sister's glare, so she quickly apologized and then added, "She only thought she needed to defend Alexa. As it was, Pepper, our border collie, was the one jumping on her. The guest was actually trying to help. It was all a misunderstanding."

"That time." Shelley turned to Mother. "I agree with Clete. If a married couple was coming, then fine. But how can you approve a single man staying in your upstairs with Anna-Grace right next door?"

Suzanne spoke before Mother could. "She's in the Ruth 2:10. Another bedroom and the bathroom separate her room from the 2 Corinthians 9:8."

Shelley whisked her attention to Suzanne. "What does that matter? Next door, across the hall — either way it isn't a good situation. Anna-Grace's parents would have a fit if they knew, and rightly so! You shouldn't even be taking reservations from people like that."

Had Shelley forgotten she was speaking to one of Anna-Grace's parents? Suzanne would never knowingly put her daughter in a dangerous position. She pressed her palms to the tabletop and battled remaining in her seat. "Shelley, we haven't even met this man, and you're already classifying him as a troublemaker. And only because he isn't married and comes from a big city. That's hardly fair. Believe it or not, there are trustworthy people who live outside of Arborville."

Shelley folded her arms over her chest and turned aside.

Suzanne gentled her voice. "I've got enough sense to determine if it's unsafe to let him stay with us. If I have any concerns at all after I've met him, I'll —"

Shelley snapped, "Send him to Pratt or Wichita?"

Alexa needed the income guests could provide. Not unless he was an ax murderer would Suzanne send him elsewhere. "I'll have Anna-Grace stay in the cottage with me for the length of his stay. Now, if you'll excuse me, I have a room to ready."

"What about Mother? How will she get back to the farm?" Shelley snapped the questions, her voice as sharp as if Suzanne never gave their mother any consideration.

She picked up her plate and silverware. "Would you like to come with me now,

Mother?"

Mother shook her head. "I'm not done visiting."

Clete's pickup sat so high it was hard to get Mother in and out of it, so she turned to Sandra and Derek. "Would you mind bringing Mother out when you're finished?"

Sandra beamed a bright smile. "Of course not, Suzy."

Derek added teasingly, "Thanks for giving us a chance to take a car ride. That'll put Ian and Isabella to sleep for sure."

Suzanne grinned a thank-you and hurried into the kitchen. She started for the sink, but then she froze just inside the door, captured by the scene in the room. Anna-Grace sat at one end of the table, Steven at the other, with the children lining the sides. She might have been looking through a window at her daughter's future — a home-cooked meal shared in a cozy kitchen, an attentive husband, a quiverful of happy, beautiful children. Would they invite her for a meal sometimes, the way Shelley, Sandra, and Clete invited Mother?

"Anna-Grace?" The word came out raspy and low, but Anna-Grace looked up.

"Yes, Cousin Suzy?"

Cousin Suzy. Sorrow swelled, creating a knot in her throat. Anna-Grace's children

232

would never call Suzanne "Grandmother." She scurried across the floor and deposited her dishes in the sink. "I'm heading back to the farm. Do you want to come with me, or would you rather have Steven bring you later?"

Steven spoke up. "I'll bring her later. I'm not ready to let her out of my sight just yet."

Anna-Grace hunched her shoulders and giggled, her rosy cheeks bright against the white ribbons trailing from her cap.

Exactly what Suzanne had expected. Way back when, she and Paul had wanted every possible chance to be together, too. The knot of sadness grew. Suzanne cleared her throat. "All right. I'll see you later. Enjoy the rest of your afternoon."

She drove the familiar road from town to the farm and pulled in next to the barn. As she made her way along the walkway to the porch, her head low to block the wind, she went over the careful instructions Alexa had given her for making sure the rooms were ready for guests. Fresh sheets on the bed, fresh towels in the bathroom, washcloth accordion-folded on the edge of the sink, a fluffy bathrobe hung on a hook inside the door, and two truffles — store-bought since Suzanne didn't make truffles — on the nightstand.

As she stretched clean sheets over the mattress, she sent up a prayer. *Let this man be honorable and trustworthy, Lord, so Anna-Grace won't have to stay out in Alexa's cottage with me.* A selfish prayer? Absolutely. But also necessary to preserve her heart.

CHAPTER 17

Arborville
Paul

Monday morning was overcast and chilly but calm — mild enough for Danny to walk to school. Paul drove him anyway. Mostly to make sure he didn't sample anything from his lunchbox on the way. Lately he'd become a bottomless pit, and Paul couldn't keep enough food in the cupboards to satisfy him. Had Anna-Grace ever gone through an eat-everything-in-sight stage? He gave himself a mental shake, putting his focus back on Danny. The stuffed lunchbox was for lunch, not a post-breakfast snack. Besides, he'd hidden something inside, and he didn't want the boy discovering it until the middle of the day.

He glanced at his son, who fiddled with the lunchbox's plastic handle. Head low, bottom lip slightly extended, forehead pinched. What was he thinking about? Along with the excessive hunger had come a new restraint unlike the Danny that Paul had always known. There'd been times in the past he wished he could put a cork in Danny's mouth to stop his endless flow of words. Now he'd give almost anything to see his son's boundless exuberance return.

Paul pulled up in front of the plain red-brick building, applied the brakes, and shifted into Park. "Okay, here you go."

Danny reached for the door handle.

Paul caught his arm. "Hold up there. Stay out of your lunchbox until your noon break. You had plenty of breakfast." *Plenty* was an understatement. The boy had consumed two eggs, two pieces of toast with jam, a bowl of cereal, and a banana. Enough to hold a grown man until lunchtime.

Danny scowled but nodded.

"Is your homework in your backpack?"

"Yes, Dad."

"Both math and social studies?"

"Yes."

"You're sure you got everything done?" Twice last week Danny had chosen to finish some work but not all. Paul felt a bit like the Gestapo, quizzing his son, and Suzy's advice not to be too hard on him tickled the back of his mind, but he couldn't let Danny get by with laziness.

"Yeah."

"Good. Remember to turn it in."

Danny huffed. "I will."

Paul leaned sideways, aiming a kiss for his son's cheek. Danny ducked, and Paul ended up brushing the crown of his head instead.

"Dad!" The boy glanced out the window, his movements jerky, almost panicky, then turned a sour look on Paul. "I'm not a baby anymore." He yanked his hood into place.

Paul couldn't decide if he was more sad or angry about the boy's reaction. Would a little girl have allowed his good-bye kisses each morning? An unexpected question spilled out. "If I were your mother, would you let me kiss you good-bye?"

Danny's jaw dropped and he stared at Paul. "I . . . I . . ."

Suzy's advice whispered through his mind. "Danny, it's hard for me sometimes not having a wife." *Or my daughter.* "So I know it's hard for you not to have a mom. If you're sad or even mad about your mom being gone, you can tell me, all right?"

Danny didn't say anything.

Paul sought a means of offering comfort and settled on a tactic he'd been using when the desire to reach out and claim Anna-Grace overwhelmed him. "When you start feeling sad, think about the people who are important and available in your life. There's me. There's your neighbor, Mrs. Lapp. And your teacher, Mr. Brungardt."

"He's not the same as Miss Kroeker." Danny almost spat the comment.

Paul nodded slowly, understanding dawning. Apparently Danny missed the womanly influence a female teacher had provided. In a similar way, no matter how much he loved his son, Danny could never take the place of Anna-Grace. He sent up a quick, silent prayer for guidance before forming a calm reply. "No, Danny, he isn't the same as Miss Kroeker, but he does care about you. And even though my kissing you isn't the same as a mom giving you a kiss, I still want to kiss you good-bye. You'll never be too big for me to give you hugs and kisses. Because I love you."

Love — for his son, for his daughter — roared up with such intensity it nearly strangled him. He reached to tug Danny close, the way he had when Danny was little and frightened by a bad dream or had scuffed his knee or was disappointed or upset or sad. The way he'd never been able to embrace his daughter. Paul needed to hold his child.

Danny flung the door open. "I gotta go in. Bye, Dad." He slammed the door and trotted off without a backward glance.

Paul watched until Danny joined a group of other youngsters and the entire throng disappeared behind the schoolhouse door. Then he sat a little longer, pondering. Should he retrieve Danny's lunchbox from the shelf in the school's front entry and take out the note he'd placed between the peanut-butter sandwiches and the foil-wrapped chunk of chocolate cake Suzy had baked? When he'd tucked it in the box, it seemed like a good idea — something he remembered his mom doing when he was a boy. But now he wasn't sure how Danny would respond.

It was weird to be so disconnected from his child. He'd often wondered how he'd feel when Danny grew up and left home. But he hadn't expected to experience loneliness while the boy still resided beneath his roof. The school bell rang. Two last stragglers — one boy, one girl — raced across the brown grass and darted into the building. Paul sat for a few more minutes, debating with himself about getting that note. He repeated the words in his mind: *Baseballs are white, ball mitts are brown, a smile is always better than a frown.* Childish. Stupid. A big mistake. And yet . . .

He remembered finding little notes in his

lunchbox, jamming them into his pocket, acting embarrassed but inwardly smiling and puffing up with importance because his mom had done something extra for him the other kids' moms hadn't. He put his truck in Drive and pulled away. He'd risk leaving it there. It sure couldn't make things worse. And maybe it would open the door to talking more about the hole Karina's death had left in the middle of their lives. But of course, he wouldn't talk about Anna-Grace. Not to Danny.

Indianapolis
Alexa

How could a week be so busy and yet so unproductive? Every day since her arrival in Indianapolis, she — with either Tom or Linda, depending on who wanted to make the drive — had gone to the library to scan newspaper articles from around the time of her birth for possible clues to her parentage. Despite hours of searching, they found nothing helpful. The ad Linda put in the Indianapolis paper resulted in a spattering of letters, and Alexa followed up on each one, but none led her to her mother or father. Linda's Facebook post asking for information showed that more than ten thousand people had seen it thanks to multiple shares, but instead of leads she received encouragement to keep searching or good-luck wishes. Alexa's frustration level rose with every day. With all the social media and instant access, shouldn't it be easier to find someone?

Monday at breakfast Linda peered at Alexa over the rim of her coffee cup and raised one thick eyebrow. "All right, what are you wantin' to do today? We still haven't drove the neighborhood where you were left to see if anybody knew of a girl who was pregnant but never showed up carrying a baby in her arms."

The door-to-door search had been Tom's idea. He perked up. "Why, sure, we could do that. I still think it seems likely your birth mama lived close to the home in Indianapolis. Might be somebody saw something that didn't mean much at the time but could be helpful to us."

Alexa sighed. "Would you think I was awful if I said I didn't want to do any searching today?"

Neither showed a hint of disappointment or surprise. Linda squeezed Alexa's hand. "Of course not, girlie. You've been going at it like a house afire since you got here. I wanted you just to sit around and regroup yesterday, as you recall."

Alexa grimaced at the hint of scolding. Linda hadn't been happy about her spending Sunday afternoon at the library. But she'd gone anyway. Alexa sighed. "I know."

"Taking a day off to let things simmer just might be the best idea yet."

Alexa planned how to word her next request. Linda might not be any happier about it than she'd been about Sunday's library excursion. She shifted to face Tom. "Instead of just sitting around, though, I'd like to run a special errand."

Tom picked up another Alexa-baked apple-walnut muffin from the plate in the middle of the table and peeled back the wrapper. "Where to?"

"Indianapolis. The home."

He nodded. "You wanna go see Melissa."

"Uh-huh. But it means I'd need to borrow your car." Although she'd thought about and prayed for the young woman every day since encountering her in the alley a week ago, she hadn't visited her. "I could take her the rest of the muffins and maybe a box of candy. Or some flowers if I can find a bouquet. Something to cheer her up."

Linda frowned as Tom reached for yet another muffin. "How many of those things are you gonna eat? If you don't quit, Alexa won't have any to take to that girl."

Alexa hid a smile. Linda had just given her approval for the day's plan.

Tom laughed and put the muffin back on the plate. "All right. I guess Melissa is eating for two. She needs it more than me."

Linda aimed a knowing look at Tom's middle. "Mm-hm."

They all laughed, Tom the most boisterously.

Alexa retrieved a paper plate and transferred the remaining muffins. "It seems funny not to take her any baby things, you know? That's what you usually take to somebody who's expecting. But since she isn't planning to keep her baby, it wouldn't be appropriate."

Linda's expression turned thoughtful. "Maybe you could get a nice nightgown and robe for her to wear after the baby is born. Something to make her feel pretty."

"Oh, and fun socks!"

Both Tom and Linda drew back.

Alexa couldn't help laughing at their expressions. "C'mon, you have to admit, it makes you feel happy all over to wear a pair of bright purple-and-orange socks." She held up her leg to show off her colorful kneesocks.

Tom screwed his face into a grimace. "I

don't know, Alexa. Seems to me wearing socks like that is a good way to get a man kicked out of the bowling league."

She grinned. "Well, I like them, and I bet Melissa would, too. So when I shop, I'll see if I can find some funky socks." She turned to Linda. "And a nice sleep set. I think that's a great idea."

"Just don't get too carried away on your spending spree." Linda brushed crumbs from the table into her hand. "Remember you don't have an endless income right now. Gotta exercise some caution."

Alexa nodded. She'd brought a prepaid debit card with her, but she'd already dipped into it to buy Band Blast tickets, a few groceries so she could bake some of her special pastries, and gas for Tom's car. She'd go through at least half a tank today running errands. "I'll be careful."

"I know you will, honey. Your mama raised you to be frugal."

Alexa started to clear the table, but Linda shooed her away. "You've got shopping to do before you head to Indianapolis. You'll want plenty of visiting time with that girl at the home, so go on now. I can clean this up."

Alexa paused midtask. So far the Dennings had only allowed her to wash her own bedding and clothes and do a little baking. She wasn't accustomed to someone else cleaning up behind her, and she didn't want to get used to it. "I have time to do both."

Linda scowled, but her eyes twinkled. "Are you gonna argue with me? You won't win. Just ask Tom."

He gave an exaggerated nod. "She's right. You might as well just scoot."

Alexa backed away from the table, holding up her hands in surrender. "All right, all right, the cleanup is yours." She darted over and hugged first Linda and then Tom. "Thank you."

Tom patted her back and set her aside. "You're welcome. Just plan your morning so you aren't in rush-hour traffic, all right? No sense in getting yourself all stressed out."

She offered a mock salute. "No stress today. I promise."

CHAPTER 18

Indianapolis
Alexa

As Alexa browsed the sleepwear department in one of Indianapolis's many discount supercenters, she found the week's tension slowly melting. Doing something for somebody besides herself felt good. Really good. And after-Christmas sales meant she could stay within budget — another plus. She examined the contents of every rack, determined to find the perfect pajamas that would bring a smile to Melissa's sad, seeking face.

She liked a flannel pants-and-top set in bright lime green with little flamingos printed all over. Who could possibly be sad wearing something so bright and cheerful? But uncertainty about size sent her to the gowns, which would be a bit more forgiving than something with an elastic waist or buttons. After a bit of contemplation, she decided on a sunshine-colored long T-shirt with a rainbow embroidered across the bodice. Not as flashy as the flamingos but still a happy pattern. And it was one-size-fits-most — no worries about it not fitting. Then she located a fleecy robe in rainbow stripes and, on a whim, tossed a pair of fuzzy yellow scuffs into the cart.

From the sleepwear area she headed toward the displays of socks. She passed a discount bin and paused to peek inside. She and Mom had never been able to ignore bargain bins. Not that they always bought, but browsing was fun. Sock multipacks filled the bin. She hissed happily, "Yessss!" and dug through the display. She scored a six-pack of bright-colored animal-print socks for only two dollars and fifty cents. She smiled as she plopped the socks onto the bulky robe. She wanted some for herself, but she exercised self-control and pushed the cart onward.

She'd intended to buy candy or flowers, but she decided the cart was full enough. She did stop in the card aisle, however, and picked up a "thinking of you" card along with a large sky-blue gift bag and tissue paper with little rainbows printed all over so she could wrap the gift nicely. After checking out she hustled across the cold parking lot to Tom's car and pulled up the GPS on her phone. No sense getting lost in the unfamiliar neighborhoods.

Less than twenty minutes later she parked in front of the home for unwed mothers and turned off the car's engine. Her phone's time readout showed ten forty-five — creeping up on noon. Based on what little Melissa had said about the home's strict policies, she assumed they would enforce a set lunchtime, and in all likelihood she wouldn't be welcome to stay. She'd do whatever the director said — no sense in getting Melissa in trouble. Worry struck. Were unscheduled guests allowed? If not, she'd just leave the package and go. But she sure hoped she'd get to visit with Melissa for a little while at least.

She hooked the bag's handles over her wrist and balanced the plate of muffins on her palm and then stepped carefully across the cracked sidewalk beneath a canopy of drooping, leafless tree branches. The cloud cover made it seem more like early evening than midday, and Alexa shivered. She stepped onto the porch, giving a furtive glance left and right. All the overgrowth on the many trellises — why didn't they trim those vines back for the winter? — gave the shadowy porch an almost sinister feel. The cluster of covered porch chairs pushed into the corner became slumbering beasts waiting to awaken and pounce. Childishly imaginative? Yes, but she couldn't deny a fierce desire to escape the surroundings. She pushed the doorbell with one emphatic jab.

Within moments the inside door opened, giving her a view of a wood-paneled entry bathed in soft light from an antique tin chandelier hanging on a long chain. A middle-aged woman peered through the storm door's screen at Alexa. "May I help you?" Not unfriendly, but not welcoming, either.

Alexa remained in place although she really wanted to leap over the threshold from the cold, dark porch into the warm, lighted entry. "Yes, ma'am. I'm here to visit Melissa. May I come in?"

"Your name?"

"Alexa Zimmerman."

The woman's brows descended slightly, and she looked Alexa up and down, seeming to take stock of her. "Are you family?"

Couldn't they have this cross-examination inside? Alexa forced a polite tone. "No, ma'am. Just a friend." She held up her bag. "I brought her a gift. May I bring it in?"

After a moment's pause the woman unlatched the screen door, and Alexa eagerly stepped past her. Another shiver convulsed her as the warmth of the small entry room touched her. She smiled — a genuine smile. But her smile wavered when the woman turned a suspicious frown on her.

"I'll need to examine the contents of the bag."

Alexa subconsciously drew back. She'd gone to great care fluffing the tissue just so. If they took everything out and put it back again, the tissue would get rumpled. She wanted the gift to be pretty for Melissa. "It's just a nightgown, robe, and socks. A little something . . . cheery."

Now that she was inside, she realized how stark and cheerless the interior was despite the bright chandelier. No pictures on the walls, no rugs on the wood floor, nothing to make the space feel like a home. No wonder Melissa had seemed so sad. Alexa didn't want this unsmiling woman to ruin the appearance of the gift.

"If you'd like, you can watch Melissa open it. Then you'll see what's inside." Alexa held her breath, hoping the woman would accept the compromise.

"Our policy is to examine every item that comes in from the outside." The woman spoke briskly but not unkindly. "Some of our girls come to us battling habits that aren't healthy for them or the babies they carry. The policy isn't meant to be intrusive but protective."

Alexa's breath eased out. "It's just . . ." Would the woman understand? "The bag is so pretty right now, and if we rummage through it, the tissue will get ruined. I promise you can examine everything that comes out of it. But can Melissa be the one to open the gift?" She paused, then added, "Please?"

Finally the first hint of a smile creased the woman's face. "All right. Follow me."

Alexa trailed her from the entry, past what had probably been a grand parlor in the house's heyday but now was a sad-looking room with faded wallpaper and outdated, mismatched furniture, to a small room tucked beneath the winding staircase. Despite the room's lack of windows, the beautifully ornate chandelier hanging from the middle of the recessed ceiling fully il-luminated the walls lined with overflowing bookshelves and highlighted a large wood table surrounded by slat-backed chairs. Melissa and two other young women sat at the table, open books in front of them. All three looked up. The unfamiliar pair just stared, but Melissa's face lit with surprise.

Alexa waved, smiling. "Hi again."

Melissa rose awkwardly and took two steps toward Alexa. "Hello! You came to see me?"

The genuine astonishment in her voice made tears prick in Alexa's eyes. She bounced her hand holding the bag and plate. "Yes. And I brought presents." The other two eyed the items with interest. Thank goodness she'd brought the muffins. "A little treat for you to share, and then something just for you, Melissa." She hoped the other two wouldn't be offended. Why hadn't the woman called Melissa out of the room instead of parading Alexa in front of all the residents?

Melissa reached eagerly for the muffins and turned toward the others. "Don't they look good?" Then shyness seemed to attack her. She held the plate hesitantly toward the woman. "Is it all right if we have some, Ms. Reed?"

The director plucked the plate from Melissa's hands. "After the cook examines them for foreign substances. If they're safe, we'll put them on the lunch table."

Alexa couldn't decide if she wanted to slink away in embarrassment or rise up in indignation. Did the director really believe she'd put something dangerous in the muffins? "They're apple-walnut with oats and lots of cinnamon and nutmeg and a touch of clove. I hope you'll like them."

The director set the plate on a little stand next to the door and pointed to the bag hanging from Alexa's wrist. "Go ahead and open that, Melissa."

Melissa released a nervous giggle, but she sat and placed the bag on the floor between her widespread feet. Ms. Reed stood watch, arms folded over her chest, while Melissa carefully removed the fluffed bursts of tissue and placed them on the table in a neat pile. She peeked into the bag and let out a gasp. "Rainbows! I love rainbows!"

The other two girls exchanged glances and snickered. Melissa's excitement faltered.

Alexa stepped closer, trying to block the pair from Melissa's line of vision. She pulled the folded robe from the bag and shook it out. "I'm glad you like the colors. I love rainbows, too. They're so cheerful. God hung the first rainbow in the sky as a promise to Noah never to flood the entire earth again. So every time I see a rainbow, I see it as a promise of better things to come."

Melissa's face bloomed with wonder. She took the robe and crushed it close. "I like that thought. Better things to come."

Ms. Reed took the robe. "See what else is in there, Melissa." She explored the robe's pockets while Melissa obeyed her command.

A huge smile expressed Melissa's delight with the nightgown and the socks, and she didn't even seem to mind when Ms. Reed took them for a thorough examination. Still sitting, she turned a look of puzzlement on Alexa. "Thank you. But why did you bring me these things?"

Alexa slid into the remaining chair and leaned close, hoping the others wouldn't overhear her answer. "Everybody needs something new now and then to make them feel pretty and special. I hope that's how you feel right now."

Tears flooded the girl's eyes. She nodded.

Alexa smiled. "Good."

Ms. Reed plopped the gown and socks, which she'd pulled from their paper wrapper and separated, into Melissa's lap. Two socks slid to the floor. Alexa reached for them as the woman spoke. "Melissa, take your things to your room and put them away. Then you may visit with your friend in the front room until lunch." She faced Alexa. "We serve lunch promptly at noon. Our routine is very important here. It gives our girls security and structure."

Alexa squirmed. Ms. Reed seemed to forget the others were even in the room.

Grandmother always complained loudly when people talked about her as if she weren't there. But none of the girls protested.

"Since this isn't Melissa's day to set the table, she can visit with you until eleven fifty-five. But then she'll need to go up and wash for lunch."

Melissa jammed the socks, gown, and robe back into the bag. Unfolded, they made the seams bulge, and Alexa hoped the bag wouldn't burst. Melissa pinched the tissue into one plump bunch and stood. She gave Alexa a hopeful look. "It'll only take me a minute or two to put these things away. I'll meet you in the front room, okay?"

Alexa understood the unspoken question — *Will you still be here when I come down?* She looked directly into Melissa's pleading eyes. "Don't rush. I'll be here."

Arborville
Suzanne

The doorbell rang, and butterflies immediately danced in Suzanne's stomach. She hoped she hadn't made a mistake by reserving a room for the Indiana businessman. Her siblings' concerns rolled through her mind as she hurried to the foyer and opened the door.

A tall, slender man wearing a long, unbuttoned leather coat over jeans and a faded blue-and-white-plaid flannel shirt stood on the porch. His silvery hair was wind tossed, and a spattering of salt-and-pepper whiskers dotted his cheeks. Suzanne tried not to frown — she shouldn't greet a guest with anything except graciousness — but he didn't look like any businessman she'd seen before.

A battered briefcase hung from his clenched hand. Maybe he was a down-and-out traveling salesman rather than her expected guest. Their Old Order community, known for being nonconfrontational, attracted lots of people selling wares. Mostly frivolous items. "May I help you?"

He beamed a broad smile, but somehow it didn't quite reach his eyes. Or maybe his gray irises were too pale to light up. "You sure can. I made a reservation at Grace Notes B and B. If this is the place, you can let me in. If this isn't the place, you can direct me on."

For a brief moment Suzanne considered directing him on to Wichita or Pratt. Alexa hadn't put up a sign stating their right to refuse service to anyone, but something about this man left her edgy.

He shifted in place, his coat flaps waving.

"Ma'am?"

Suzanne gave herself a little shake. If Clete and Shelley hadn't raised such a fuss yesterday, she probably wouldn't think twice about welcoming him. She stepped aside and gestured to him. "You've found Grace Notes. Please come in."

One long-legged stride brought him over the threshold. He seemed to sizzle with pent-up energy, and Suzanne instinctively moved aside and let him pass through the foyer. She closed the door and trailed behind him, observing him jerk his gaze from one corner of the room to another, seemingly fascinated with his surroundings. Then, unexpectedly, he spun around and stuck out his hand.

"I'm Owen Mallory. And you're . . ."

She gave his hand a quick squeeze and then slipped her hands behind her back. "I'm Suzanne Zimmerman. It's nice to meet you, Mr. Mallory."

He stared at her, unblinking, for several seconds. She stood beneath his penetrating gaze, battling the urge to fidget. Or escape. Before she could do either, Mother rolled her wheelchair into the front room and captured the man's attention.

Questions flashed in Mother's blue eyes. "Is this our guest, Suzy?"

Suzanne nodded. "Yes, Mother. Please meet Owen Mallory. Mr. Mallory, this is my mother, Abigail Zimmerman."

Mr. Mallory politely shook hands with Mother. He shot a glance between the two women. "I hope you won't think I'm rude, but I'm curious. You" — he bobbed his head at Mother — "have a cap, but you don't." He faced Suzanne, his brow furrowing. "Aren't you Amish, too?"

Suzanne forced a light laugh. "Neither of us is Amish, Mr. Mallory, although you aren't the only one to suffer confusion. Mother belongs to the Old Order Mennonite fellowship here in Arborville. I attend their services, but my membership is with a Mennonite Brethren church in Franklin, Indiana."

"Ah. I see." Interest flickered in his pale eyes. "So you are a native of Indiana?"

There wasn't a good answer to his question. Suzanne smiled. "Yes and no. But I'm here for now, giving my daughter some help in operating the bed-and-breakfast. She's the actual owner of Grace Notes."

Mr. Mallory appeared ready to speak, but a rustle intruded. Anna-Grace stepped into the front room. Her cheeks were flushed from the stove's heat, and a few blond wisps of hair clung to her temples. She moved

258

behind Mother's wheelchair and offered Mr. Mallory a shy smile.

He stared at Anna-Grace for several seconds, then zipped his gaze to Suzanne and frowned at her for an equal amount of time. Something — disappointment? — briefly sagged his features, but then he seemed to paste on a smile. He held out his hand to Anna-Grace. "I'm Owen Mallory, and you must be Suzanne's daughter, the owner of Grace Notes."

CHAPTER 19

Much to Alexa's shock, Ms. Reed asked if she'd like to stay and eat lunch with Melissa. She started to refuse. Her conversation with Melissa had been stilted, as if she was afraid she'd say something wrong, and Alexa had nearly decided coming here had been a mistake despite the girl's initial happy reaction. But the pleading in Melissa's eyes changed her mind. She quickly called Tom and Linda, secured their approval to keep the car longer, and then joined Melissa, Ms. Reed, and the other two girls, Polly and Lennah, in the dining room.

The food was already on the table. Simple fare, from the looks of things — baked chicken tenders, buttered noodles, steamed broccoli, and store-bought wheat bread with margarine — but it smelled good. She eased into her chair and bowed her head, expecting someone to offer grace. Instead a spoon clinked on the side of a serving bowl.

She lifted her head in time to grab the bowl of broccoli, which Lennah handed to her. Too surprised to do otherwise, she spooned a few chunky florets onto her plate. They passed the bowls around the table without speaking, so unlike Alexa and Mom's habit of dinnertime chatter or even the Zimmerman family meals. Were they always this quiet, or was her presence putting everyone on edge? She wished she knew.

Once their plates were filled, they picked up their forks and began eating, their focus on the food rather than on each other. Everything was well seasoned — Alexa didn't think she could have done better herself with the chicken — but she still had trouble swallowing. Such tension. No wonder Melissa seemed so strained and tired. Alexa had only endured a few minutes of Ms. Reed's "structure." After several months she'd probably be half-crazy.

Alexa cleared her throat. The three girls jumped, and Ms. Reed sent her a frown. Alexa released a nervous titter, then yanked up her water glass and drowned the sound. She ate a couple more bites, her tongue picking up the savory flavors of basil and garlic on the noodles, but the silence was too stifling. Somebody needed to say . . . something.

She jabbed a piece of broccoli and sent a smile across the group. "This is a pretty room."

Everyone froze and stared at her, forks held halfway between plates.

Alexa glanced around the large space. "Yes, very pretty. It has so much character with the stained-glass windows and built-in cupboard. I've always loved old houses because of their character. Are the parquet floors and the wood moldings original?"

Ms. Reed frowned again. "I assume so. I've never asked."

"Oh."

Ms. Reed returned to eating, and the others followed her example.

Alexa poked at her food, but she couldn't take a bite. The silence was making her skin crawl. She tried another question, one that might encourage lengthier answers. "So . . . where are all of you from? Indianapolis?"

The three girls, in unison, stared at Ms. Reed. The director set her fork beside her plate and dabbed her mouth with her napkin. "Lennah is from Minnesota, Polly's family lives nearby, and Melissa came to us from Kansas."

"Seriously?" Alexa laughed, hardly able to believe what she'd just heard. "Melissa, you're from Kansas?"

Very hesitantly, Melissa nodded.

"What a coincidence! I moved to Arborville, Kansas, last May from Franklin. How long have you been in Indiana?"

Melissa shot a quick look at Ms. Reed before answering. "Since late August."

"Then we kind of traded places, didn't we? I operate a bed-and-breakfast in my grandparents' farmhouse. It has a lot of character, too, but not nearly as much as this house." Although Grandmother's farmhouse seemed much cozier and homelike. Amazing what a little elbow grease and some fresh paint could do for an old house. A hopeful thought filled her mind and spilled out of her mouth in a rush. "Maybe you can visit me there sometime."

Melissa hung her head. "Maybe." She picked at her chicken.

Ms. Reed lifted her fork and speared two noodles. "Melissa isn't yet sure she will return to Kansas. Regardless, it will be at least three months before she's released. She'll do her convalescence here after the baby is born. The midwife recommends four to six weeks before our girls are released for lengthy travel." A tight smile pulled up the corners of her lips. "So you'll need to put your plans on hold." She used her knife to cut a small bite of chicken. "If your home is now in Kansas, what brings you to Indianapolis?"

Alexa came very close to sharing her search for her birth mother. But something in Ms. Reed's expression — distrust, disdain, or maybe just disinterest, as if she was only making polite small talk and really didn't care about her reasons — brought a different response. "Tying up some loose ends." She shrugged. "It's kind of personal."

Ms. Reed sent a warning look at the girls, and they all dug into their plates. Alexa decided to clean her plate, too. The sooner she finished, the sooner she could get out of here. The place, in spite of its gracious character, was starting to give her the heebie-jeebies.

When they'd finished, Lennah rose and began clearing the table. "I'll bring in our dessert." She glanced at Alexa. "The cook cut up the muffins you brought, but she said they'd go good with ice cream."

Ice cream in January. A cold dessert to accompany a cold atmosphere. Alexa gave an involuntary shiver and then forced a smile. "I hadn't thought of serving them with ice cream, but cake and ice cream are a good combination, so she's probably right."

Lennah left the room, balancing her load, and the others sat quietly with their hands in their laps until she returned. She placed a tray on the table. When Alexa peeked into the bowls, she couldn't hold back a gasp. The cook hadn't cut the muffins in halves or even quarters, the way Alexa had envisioned. Instead she'd obliterated them into nothing more than crumbs. If it wasn't for the chunks of dried apples and walnuts and evidence of oats, she wouldn't even have recognized the topping on the scoops of vanilla ice cream.

"Why'd she chop them up that way?" She hadn't meant to ask out loud. Her question hung in the room like an unwelcome stench.

Ms. Reed's face puckered. "She needed to know for sure what was in them." She touched Lennah's wrist. "Serve the dessert, please, or you might still be washing dishes when Mr. Ramirez arrives for your relationship class." She faced Melissa and added sternly, "Your guest will need to leave as soon as we've finished eating. You can't miss today's class."

"Yes, ma'am."

Alexa gritted her teeth as waves of fury crashed through her. They'd chopped her muffins to bits because they were afraid she'd put something in them that would be harmful. The director had snatched away Melissa's gifts and pawed over them out of fear. These girls sat around a table in tense silence instead of enjoying a relaxed meal. Was this how Mom had been treated when she stayed here twenty years ago, like a prisoner? Just because these girls had become pregnant out of wedlock didn't make them criminals.

"Are you going to eat your dessert, Alexa?" Ms. Reed's tart voice cut into Alexa's thoughts. "We need to finish so the girls have time to clean up before their one thirty class."

She didn't want the dessert. She wanted out. "Actually I —" Alexa's gaze collided with Melissa's. The young woman had said very little during Alexa's time at the home, but her eyes spoke volumes. She wanted Alexa to stay. So she tamped down her negative retort. "I'm eager to see how my muffins taste as an ice cream topping."

She dipped her spoon. As she ate, she vowed to find out the official visiting hours and come back as often as she could. She didn't know why this young woman with the swollen belly had become so important to her. She only knew she felt drawn to her. Mom would probably say God had placed

Melissa on Alexa's heart. It made sense, given how strongly she felt connected to someone she'd just met.

Melissa's time at the home was nearing its end, and Alexa's time in Indianapolis would end as soon as she located her birth mother. This couldn't be a long-term friendship unless they found a way to stay in touch once they were both back in Kansas. Even if their friendship was temporary, she'd do her best to make Melissa feel as though someone cared. She'd also try as hard as she could to talk Melissa out of giving up her baby for adoption. Because in Alexa's opinion, getting pregnant wasn't the girl's biggest mistake. Getting rid of her baby would be.

Arborville
Paul

After lunch Paul drove out to the Zimmerman farm. Even though no one had asked him to check the trough he'd constructed to channel water away from the corner of the house, he felt obligated to make sure his work was holding up okay. A houseful of women — even though Clete came and went out there — didn't need to deal with water in the basement. And the last thing he wanted was to get mold growing. Then Alexa would have to close her inn. He couldn't stand to think of all her hard work being destroyed by something as avoidable as mold spores.

He parked beside the barn and shut off the ignition. When he stepped out of the truck, the Zimmermans' border collie, Pepper, trotted up to him and whined. He rubbed his hand over her black-and-white ears. "Hey, girl, aren't you cold? Let's put you in the barn, huh?" The dog pawed at Paul's leg, released a little yip, and dashed for the barn.

Paul chuckled. Sometimes he thought that furry beast understood English. He pulled his new shovel from the back of the truck, propped it over his shoulder, and headed across the yard. Carving out cold ground wasn't much fun, but if he could shave off a few inches to encourage water to run away from the house instead of pooling next to it, it would help until spring arrived and he could officially repair the foundation.

As he neared the barn, a strange sound — not a moan, not a scream, but something in-between — met his ears. He stopped, tipping his head. What was that? It rose again, wavering before dropping low. Pepper stood on her hind legs and dug at the door, adding her whine to the mournful sounds emerging from inside. Paul's pulse pounded.

Someone was in great distress. He dropped the shovel and jogged to the door.

"Hush, Pepper." One hand on the dog's head, he leaned close to the inch-wide gap between the barn's solid wall and the door. "Who's in there? Are you all right?"

The sound abruptly stopped. After a few seconds someone rasped, "P-Paul?"

Recognition made his knees go weak. He yanked the door, causing it to shriek on its rails, and moved it just far enough for him to slip through. Pepper darted between Paul's feet. Deep shadows shrouded the interior, but Pepper ran a straight course to the middle of the barn and sat. Then she lifted one paw to the woman standing close to her dad's old tractor with her arms folded over her waist and her face damp and chalky.

His heart lurched. "Suzy . . ." He crossed the hard ground in less than half a dozen strides and took hold of her shoulders. "What is it? What's wrong?"

Her face crumpled. She sagged against him, and he had little choice but to hold her. She clung to his shirt front, her face buried in his chest, and sobbed with such force his entire body trembled along with hers. Pepper dropped flat on her belly with her head on her paws and added her low whines to Suzy's cries. Fear turned his mouth to cotton. Someone must have died. He couldn't imagine anything else that would cause such an intense expression of grief.

Very gently he cupped her face and tipped it upward. Red nose, red eyes, red-blotched cheeks, damp, straggly hair clinging to her temples — she'd been crying for quite some time. When Karina cried, which wasn't often, he'd kissed her to give her comfort. But he couldn't kiss Suzy. He didn't know what to do.

He swallowed. "Suzy, what happened? Who —"

She pulled in a ragged breath and wailed a name. "Anna-Grace."

Paul thought his heart stopped beating. Pain roared through his chest, and his legs wobbled. He released Suzy and sank onto the closest tractor tire. She covered her face with her hands and continued crying in harsh, hiccuping sobs. Pepper army-crawled into the space between Paul's feet and the tire and hunkered there. He sat in stunned disbelief, hardly aware of the dog bumping his leg, and stared at Suzy's convulsing form. Anna-Grace . . . . Had there been an accident? Had she suddenly fallen ill? He'd seen her just yesterday in service, and she'd seemed fine. Quiet, the way she always was around him, but fine.

Unable to hold his questions inside, he caught her elbows and pulled her hands down. "When? How? Tell me."

"This morning." Suzy gasped the answer, her chest heaving. "Right before lunch. I — She — Oh, Paul . . ."

Still holding her elbows, he forced his quivering legs to support him and rose. Pepper whined and slunk to the corner, where she watched the two of them with sad eyes. He slid his hands to Suzy's shoulders and massaged her collarbone with his thumbs. "Please tell me. How did she . . ." He couldn't say the word *die.*

She grabbed his shirt again, her fists pulling the fabric taut, and peered up at him in agony. "I thought she'd see it, but she didn't. I thought she would finally know. Mr. Mallory — he saw. He's a stranger, but he saw. Why couldn't she? I'm so tired of pretending, Paul. I can't do it anymore. I want her to know."

Paul shook his head. "Suzy, you're not making any sense. Was Anna-Grace in an accident? What happened to her?"

She sucked in a sharp breath and held it, her eyes wide. "An accident? No."

"She isn't hurt?"

"No. She's fine. She's just . . ." Fresh tears rolled down her cheeks. She lurched free of his grasp and staggered to the tractor. She collapsed onto the tire he'd vacated and hung her head low. "Every morning we eat breakfast across the table from each other. Then we bake together. At noon we sit down and eat together. In the afternoon I help her with wedding details. We're together for hours every day. Every day she looks at me and doesn't see. And every day I die a little more inside, wanting to call her 'Daughter' instead of 'Cousin.' I want to hear her call me 'Mother,' not 'Cousin Suzy.' " Defeat laced her tone, but the deep grief seemed to have faded.

Still confused, Paul bent down on one knee and took her hands. "What happened this morning?"

She raised her head slightly to meet his gaze. "A guest — Mr. Mallory — arrived. He and I were talking, and Anna-Grace came into the room. He took one look at her and said . . ." Her voice quavered. "He said, 'You must be Suzanne's daughter.' " A sob broke. She crushed one fist to her mouth. "Do you know what she did?"

He shook his head slowly, careful not to turn away from her pain-filled eyes.

"She laughed, Paul. She laughed. And

then she said, 'No, Suzy is my dad's cousin. She's not my mother.' " Suzy lowered her fist to her chest and pressed it tight, as though she needed to hold her heart together. "Not her mother." Tears welled again, turning her eyes into pools of misery. "I checked Mr. Mallory in. I showed him to his room. I sat at the table and ate lunch with Mother and m-my daughter. And when we were done, I came out here and threw up. And then I started crying." Twin tears slipped down her pale cheeks, following the pathway of so many tears before. "She doesn't see, Paul, because she doesn't want to. She doesn't w-want us."

A band seemed to wrap around Paul's chest and tighten. He groaned, "You don't know that."

"Yes, I do. If she wanted to know, she'd see it. She couldn't help but see. She could open her letters and confirm it for herself. People in town are starting to speculate. I see how they stare at Anna-Grace and me when we're out together. She's not a stupid girl, Paul. She looks in a mirror every day, and she looks at me every day. She's choosing not to see because she doesn't want —"

Paul couldn't take the hurt squeezing his chest anymore. He needed comfort. He couldn't take the pain in Suzy's expression or voice anymore. He needed to comfort her. With a strangled moan, he lurched forward, swept her into his arms, and captured her moist lips in a salty kiss.

CHAPTER 20

Arborville
Suzanne

Suzanne, her eyes closed, eased against Paul's sturdy frame. The last time a man had kissed her, years ago before she'd given up dating entirely, she'd been repulsed by his groping hands and eager mouth. She'd wanted to escape. But this kiss — Paul's kiss — stirred a wild flutter of pleasant emotion. His arms were her haven, his lips her joy, his cinnamon-scented breath her blessed consolation. Tears ran in warm rivulets down her cheeks, tears of sweet homecoming. She wanted the kiss never to end.

She slipped her hands along his ribs and up his back, then gripped his shoulders from behind and curved her spine to fit more snugly in his embrace. When she tipped her head, giving him better access to her lips, his hands tightened on her waist, pulling her close. But then he abruptly stepped away from her.

She staggered. The backs of her knees connected with the tractor tire, and she sat, grateful for the support. She gazed up at him in confusion. "Paul?"

He turned his back on her and ran his hand through his hair. A growl left his throat. He drew in several deep breaths, released each in audible heaves, then he angled his body to face her again. Regret pinched his features. "I'm sorry. I shouldn't have done that."

Still reeling from the wave of unfamiliar yet oh-so-wondrous feelings his kiss had awakened, she couldn't speak.

"It's just that you were crying. And I didn't know what else to do."

The meaning behind his statement trampled her. Suzanne shrank low, abashed. She'd melted against him in complete surrender. The kiss had been her deliverance, but it was only impulse for him. How could she have behaved with such shamelessness?

He took a step toward her. "Suzy?"

Humiliation writhed through her. She leaped up and stumbled for the door. A black-and-white blur of fur raced into her pathway, and she had to stop or trip over the old dog. The moment she halted, Paul's hand wrapped around her upper arm and held her in place. She wriggled. "Paul, let me go." She needed to cry again, but she didn't want to do it under his watchful gaze.

"Not yet."

"Please . . ." She whispered the entreaty, her aching throat resisting the release of words.

Paul turned a stern gaze on Pepper. "Pepper, go lie down." He waited until the border collie moved a few feet away and plopped onto the straw-covered ground. Then he looked at her.

The remorse in his brown eyes stabbed her. She lowered her gaze and prayed for God to swoop in and give her the strength to flee. She should have uttered that prayer before Paul kissed her.

"Let me explain."

She gritted her teeth, holding back moans of anguish. "It's not necessary. I understand." Hurt tangled her vocal cords into knots, and her voice came out tight and shrill. "You were just . . . comforting me." *And bringing me to life.* "It wasn't anything." *To you. To me it was everything.* How could a simple kiss incite such a reaction?

Paul's fingers tightened on her arm. "No, Suzy, it was more than your comfort. It was my comfort, too. But it was selfish of me. That's why I'm sorry." Still gripping her, he moved in front of her and curved his other hand along her jaw. "Please look at me."

Her face was raised. She had no choice with his strong palm cupping her cheek, but she kept her eyes averted.

He sighed. "Can I tell you what I want?"

Her gaze still angled away from him, her face held captive by his large, warm, rough palm, she managed a tiny nod.

"I want Anna-Grace to know, too. I want Danny to know. I want everyone to know. I want us to be at peace with her. And with each other. I thought we were. At peace, I mean. But now . . ." He gulped, a loud, anguished swallow.

Her traitorous eyes shifted and met his gaze. The sorrow glimmering in his brown eyes completely derailed her determination to remain aloof. She instinctively lifted her hand to cup his, pressing it more firmly against her cheek. "I'm not angry at you, Paul." She was furious with herself for allowing her emotions to run rampant and take the simple gesture of comfort beyond its intention. "I can't even honestly say I wish you hadn't kissed me. I . . . I needed it." For comfort, but also to bring dormant parts of her heart to life again. "I was selfish, too." More than he knew.

A weak smile quavered on the lips that

had ignited her senses so thoroughly only minutes ago. "Thank you. For not being mad. For understanding." He released her, took a small step backward, and slipped his hands into his jacket pockets. "I think maybe part of the reason I needed comfort from you is because Danny wouldn't let me kiss him good-bye this morning. He wouldn't let me hug him, either, and when I told him I loved him, he didn't say it back, the way he always used to. I didn't expect to be at odds with him until he was a teenager. I'm not ready for it."

An unexpected chuckle formed in Suzanne's chest and found its way up her throat.

He frowned, his eyebrows crunching together. "Is something funny?"

"No. Not at all. Just ironic."

"What?"

She sought the best way to explain her thoughts. "Both of us have a child who's at a distance right now — Alexa physically and Danny emotionally. And both of us have a child we can't claim — Anna-Grace."

Paul nodded, his expression thoughtful. "I see what you mean. Kind of gives us common ground, doesn't it?"

"I guess so. Maybe we both needed that

kiss for more reasons than either of us realized."

"Maybe . . ."

They stood in silence for several seconds, the breeze whispering through the cracked barn door and stirring up the musky scents of hay and animals and old wood. Those same scents had filled her nose two decades ago when Paul had led her to the barn loft. Did the aromas carry him back to that night, too?

He pinned her with a serious expression. "Suzy, I'm glad you came back. Even though it's hard, being so close to Anna-Grace and having to keep our secret from her, at least neither of us has to deal with it alone. We can support each other." His cheeks turned ruddy. He toed the barn floor the way he had years ago when embarrassment took hold of him. "What I'm saying is, anytime you need to talk about Anna-Grace, you can come to me. You don't have to hide in the barn and cry. Okay?"

She wanted to ask if he'd kiss her every time she cried. But she only nodded. "Okay." She touched his arm. "And you can come to me, too. As you said, we can support each other."

"Yeah. That's what friends do, right?"

She smiled. "That's what friends do."

The corners of his eyes crinkled with his warm smile. He stood motionless for a few more seconds, seemingly as uncertain how to proceed as she was. Then he yanked his fist from his pocket and jammed his thumb toward the door. "I came out to check that trough — make sure it's working right. I'd better go do it before your mom or Anna-Grace sees the truck and comes hunting for me."

She forced herself to speak with a casualness she didn't feel. "It must be working. We haven't had any more water in the basement."

"That's good." He backed up, his heels scraping along the barn floor. "Now remember, if you need to talk, you know where to find me."

She nodded. "I know. Thank you, Paul."

He snapped his fingers at Pepper. "C'mon, girl. You can keep me company while I dig." With a final smile and nod to Suzanne, he strode outside with Pepper bouncing along at his heels.

Suzanne crossed to the slight opening and watched him move in sure strides across the yard. He paused, scooped up a shovel from the hard ground in a smooth motion, and continued on. That's what friends do, she'd told him. Months ago Mother had said there was too much history between them for mere friendship to be possible. She'd inwardly argued at the time. But now she touched her lips with her trembling fingers and replayed her fluttering response to his kiss. She confessed to the empty yard, "Mother was right."

Indianapolis
Cynthia

In the middle of supper, Cynthia's cell phone rang. Her pulse leaped into overdrive, and she pressed her palms on the tabletop, ready to leave her chair. Glenn shot her a low-browed frown from across the table. She knew what the look meant — their family rule had always been no phone calls during mealtimes. She should let the call go to voice mail.

She stood, hoping he read the apology in her face. "Just let me see who it is." She snatched the phone from the end of the counter. Owen Mallory's name and number showed on the screen. She hit the Accept button and scuttled for the living room. "Hello?"

"Mrs. Allgood, I'm in Kansas. At the B and B I told you about."

Her heart pounded so hard she could hardly breathe, let alone talk. "And?"

"It's not much of a town. Doesn't even have paved streets." He snorted. "Can't imagine why people want to live like this."

Cynthia didn't care about the town. "What about Suzanne Zimmerman?"

"I've met her."

His gravelly voice sounded as unemotional as always. How could such a flat delivery raise such excitement in her? "Is she the one?"

"I'm not sure."

The simple sentence deflated her. She sat on the sofa's armrest, her legs refusing to hold her upright. "Why?"

"Well, for one thing she isn't Amish. None of them are. Her family is Mennonite. She says she's Mennonite, too, but she doesn't wear a cap, and she dresses differently than the others. Also, she said she lives in Indiana and is only in Kansas to help her daughter for a little while."

Cynthia gasped. "Her daughter?"

"That's right. I haven't met her because apparently she's out of town. I haven't found out where yet. And it may not matter because I might not have the right Suzanne Zimmerman. *Zimmerman* is a pretty common name, and *Suzanne* sounds old-fashioned enough to attach itself to lots of Old Order women."

Cynthia forced herself to think. The woman she'd seen pick up her baby was young — maybe still a teenager. "How old is this Suzanne Zimmerman?" She held her breath while she waited for the answer.

He chuckled, a dry sound. "I'm not the best at judging a woman's age, but I'd say early to midforties, only because she's got a daughter old enough to run a B and B."

Too old, then, to be the girl she'd seen so long ago. Cynthia's shoulders sagged. "Oh."

"I'm gonna stick around a couple of days, try to meet all the Zimmermans in town, see if I can dig up anything of use. I'll give you a call if I find out something worthwhile."

She disconnected the call, then sat with the phone cradled in her palms and stared unseeingly at the wall. She'd been so certain the investigator would find her baby girl living in the little Kansas town. The disappointment bowed her shoulders and put an ache in the center of her chest.

"Cyn?" Glenn stood in the doorway between the kitchen and living room. "Your food's getting cold."

Apparently so was the trail. She blinked to hold back tears.

"Come eat."

He didn't ask about the telephone call.

He didn't ask why she was sad. He acted as if nothing was wrong, as if nothing of importance had happened. She lifted her chin in a stubborn gesture. "I'm not hungry."

He gazed at her for several seconds, his lips in a grim line. Then he shook his head and sighed. "All right then. Suit yourself." He turned.

She bounded upright and balled her fists on her hips. "Glenn!"

He paused, sighed, then crossed to her. "What?"

"Owen Mallory just called. Don't you want to know what he said?"

"I assume he didn't find anything or you wouldn't have lost your appetite."

She glared at him. "And don't you care?"

He glanced over his shoulder as if making sure the kids weren't peeking around the corner. Then he leaned close and lowered his voice to a husky whisper. "Of course I care, Cyn. If I didn't want you to find your daughter, I wouldn't have hired Mallory in the first place. But I also care about the two kids sitting in there at the supper table. They feel like they're losing their mother to some girl they've never met."

His statement stung, bringing a rise of fierce defensiveness. "That's ridiculous."

He raised one sandy eyebrow. "Is it?"

"Of course it is!"

Glenn aimed his gaze toward the ceiling and drew in a long breath and then slowly released it. She stood with her arms folded across her chest and her teeth clamped together so tightly her jaw ached. Seconds ticked by.

Finally he faced her again. "I'm not saying I'm sorry I contacted a PI. But I wish I'd known how it would change things around here. I wish I'd better prepared myself and the kids for those changes." He paused. "Cyn?" One tiny, hope-filled word.

Mired in anger and disappointment and even guilt, she couldn't look at him.

Glenn sighed. "I hope Mallory finds your daughter soon. Then maybe we can get back to normal." He returned to the kitchen.

A flutter of voices carried from around the corner — Glenn, Darcy, and Barrett enjoying their time together. She wanted to join them. She wanted to laugh and talk and tease with them. She took a step toward the kitchen. Laughter blasted from the table, a burst more joyful than any she'd heard in days. Her chest exploded with hurt. A hurt she couldn't even explain. She changed direction and hurried to her bedroom instead.

CHAPTER 21

Arborville
Suzanne

Monday evening after supper Suzanne instructed Anna-Grace to gather her necessities and take them to Alexa's cottage. Although Mr. Mallory struck her as more eccentric than dangerous, she decided Anna-Grace's parents wouldn't appreciate her sharing the upper floor with a strange man. She'd do the motherly thing and have the girl bunk with her for the duration of his stay.

"What about the dishes?" Anna-Grace gestured to the table.

Suzanne smiled. Andrew and Olivia had brought up Anna-Grace well. She possessed a servant's heart. "I'll take care of them. Just go ahead."

While Anna-Grace was upstairs collecting her things, Mother followed Suzanne into the kitchen. "Are you sure you wouldn't rather have Anna-Grace stay with Sandra and Derek? It would only be for a couple of days. And it would probably be easier for . . . you."

Suzanne stacked the dirty dishes on the edge of the sink. "Yes, it probably would." She hoped she wouldn't dissolve into another crying jag. Both Mother and Anna-Grace had questioned the reason for her red nose and eyes when she'd returned to the house earlier that afternoon, and she wasn't sure they'd completely accepted her excuse that the barn was cold. If she broke down in front of Anna-Grace, she'd have to spin a wild fib or confess the truth. She didn't want to do either.

"But it wouldn't be easier for Anna-Grace. All her wedding preparation items are here. She has a list of things to accomplish each day. She wouldn't be able to get much done at Sandra's with Ian underfoot, and if she skips a few days of working on the wedding, she'll feel rushed at the end." Suzanne sighed. "It's better to have her stay with me."

"If you say so." Mother didn't sound convinced.

"I do." Suzanne bent down and placed her hand on Mother's bony shoulder. "But you know what? I appreciate your concern.

Thank you for caring about my heart."

"Gracious sakes, Suzy." Mother's cheeks blazed pink. "As if I wouldn't care about my own daughter." She winked, chuckled, and then angled her chair for the doorway. "I'll get the rest of those dishes."

When Mother's night nurse arrived, Suzanne took the woman aside and informed her about the single male guest in the 2 Corinthians 9:8 room. "I doubt he'll cause any trouble, but it's kind of . . ." She searched for an appropriate word.

"Awkward?" Marjorie supplied.

Suzanne nodded. "Yes, awkward to leave you and Mother in the house with a man we don't know. I'll keep my cell phone close, Clete's number is on the refrigerator, and Steven Brungardt — you've met him, Anna-Grace's beau — also said he'd be available if you need to call for help. Since Steven lives less than a mile away, he's probably your best contact. I put his number under Clete's."

Marjorie's eyebrows pulled together and her eyes gleamed. "Oh, don't you worry. I grew up with four older brothers, and I know how to hold my own. One good smack with a frying pan to the side of his head, and he won't have the ability to cause any commotion."

Suzanne laughed. "Just make sure you don't dent the pan. Alexa would be upset with both of us if we ruined her good cast-iron frying pan."

Marjorie grinned as if relishing the thought of giving a troublesome man a headache. She headed to the dining room, where Mother had set up the board for their nightly Scrabble match, and Suzanne trudged across the dark yard to the cottage.

She paused halfway between the house and the old summer kitchen. Stars twinkled in a black sky. Cold, crisp air nipped her cheeks. From the barn Pepper barked — one sharp yip of greeting and then silence. Such peacefulness out here in the open. She shifted her gaze from the winking stars to the glowing cottage windows. Anna-Grace must have switched on every lamp in the room. She shivered.

When she entered those walls, she would be alone — completely alone — with her daughter for the first time. She closed her eyes and tried to pray. *Lord* . . . No words would form. She shivered again, her entire body shuddering. She needed to go inside, get out of the cold. Squaring her shoulders, she took a forward step. She would have to trust God to understand and give her what she needed to survive being in such proximity to her child.

She entered the cottage and blinked against the onslaught of light. A shimmer of gold caught her attention, and she squinted, bringing Anna-Grace's form into focus. She sat on the edge of the bed in a long, flowered nightgown, brushing out her hair. Long, wavy, as shiny as spun gold. Exactly like Suzanne's hair when she was that age. Paul hadn't been able to keep from running his hands through it that night in the barn loft.

Anna-Grace smiled. "There you are. I hope you don't mind. I took my bath early so I wouldn't be in your way if you needed the bathroom. I wasn't sure about your routine." She ran the brush down the length of her hair, making it crackle.

"N-no problem." Suzanne dragged her gaze away from Anna-Grace's flowing hair and the memories it stirred. She moved to the coatrack in the corner and clumsily snagged her coat on a hook. "I worked the night shift for years and got into the habit of showering when I awakened late in the afternoon. Even though I sleep nights now instead of days, I still like to shower when I get up."

Anna-Grace set the hairbrush aside and slipped under the covers. "We ought to be good roommates then — not stepping on each other in the bathroom."

Suzanne forced a laugh. "Yes." She didn't know what to do with herself. If she were alone, she'd read a book or work on the needlepoint sampler kit Alexa had given her for Christmas. But Anna-Grace was already in bed at not yet nine o'clock. Should she put on her pajamas and go to bed, too? She stood rooted in the middle of the floor, uncertain.

"Cousin Suzy?"

Suzanne whipped her gaze in Anna-Grace's direction. The girl had pulled up her knees under the quilt and sat with her arms draped loosely around her legs. Her blond hair spilled across her shoulders, and her wide blue eyes gazed at Suzanne in complete openness. How young, how beautiful, how innocent she appeared. Mother-love swelled, filling her so completely she wanted to wail with both delight and agony. She swallowed. "Yes?"

"I don't think I've thanked you for letting me stay with you."

Suzanne waved her hand. "You don't have to thank me for that."

The girl nodded empathically. "Oh yes, I do. I know it's an intrusion to have me here. I appreciate your hospitality. I also appreciate the help you've given me in getting ready for my wedding. Mom was so worried I'd have to do it all on my own. When I told her how much you were helping, she cried. That's how thankful she was."

Suzanne's chest constricted. Drawing a breath proved difficult. She managed a weak chuckle. "It's nothing. Really."

Anna-Grace's eyes grew round. "It's a lot, Cousin Suzy." She angled her head slightly, the lamplight glistening on her hair and highlighting her delicate features. "Dad told me you were his favorite cousin on his mother's side when he was growing up. I think I understand why. You're a very nice person. I'm glad we've had the chance to get to know each other."

Tears stung, and Suzanne quickly looked away. "Well, now, that's a very nice thing to say. Thank you." She balled her hands into fists and rubbed her eyes, feigning a yawn. With her eyes wiped clean of tears, she turned a smile on Anna-Grace. "I think I might take a bath after all — relax and unwind. All right?"

"Of course." Anna-Grace picked up a book from the nightstand and opened it across her knees. "Enjoy your bath."

Suzanne closed herself in the bathroom. *"You're a very nice person."* She squeaked both spigots on high. *"I'm glad we've had the chance to get to know each other."* She buried her face in her hands and prayed the spatter of water against the hard porcelain muffled the sounds of her weeping.

At breakfast Wednesday, Mr. Mallory paused in shoveling scrambled eggs into his mouth. "Ms. Zimmerman, I know my reservation was only for two nights, but would it be all right if I stayed one more?"

Mother spoke before Suzanne could answer. "Haven't you finished your business?" Her gaze narrowed. "You never said exactly what kind of business you're conducting in Arborville."

He grinned at her. "No. I suppose I didn't." He looked at Suzanne. "Well?"

Suzanne set her coffee cup aside. Truthfully, she wanted him gone. Not because he'd been any trouble. She only saw him at breakfast and for a few minutes in the evening before he closed himself in his room. But being with Anna-Grace both day and night was taking its toll on her. She needed some separation. If not for escaping to the barn and calling Paul on her cell phone to release her pent-up frustration, she might have combusted by now.

She offered what she hoped was a convincing smile. "There isn't anyone scheduled for your room tonight, so it's fine if you need to stay another day."

"Good." He drank the last of his coffee, tipping the cup nearly upside down to catch every drop, then clunked it onto the edge of the table. "Could I get a refill?" He dug into his eggs again.

Suzanne started to rise, but Anna-Grace touched her wrist. "I'll get the pot." She scurried out.

Mother stared at their guest for several seconds, indecision playing on her mouth. Suzanne tried to catch her eye, to give her a pleading look. She didn't want her outspoken mother scaring off a paying guest. But Mother wouldn't shift her gaze from the man. She cleared her throat. "Mr. Mallory?"

He swiped his napkin across his mouth and gave her a glance. "Yes?"

"My daughter Sandra called yesterday afternoon and said you'd stopped by her house."

He nodded. "I sure did." Anna-Grace came in with the coffeepot. He watched her round the table and fill his cup. "Thank you, Miss Braun." He bounced a smile at her and raised the cup to his mouth. After taking a loud slurp, he smacked his lips. "Mm, that's good coffee. You ladies have figured out the way to a man's heart, that's for sure." He waggled his thick eyebrows.

Mother's frown didn't fade. "Not an hour after Sandra called, I heard from my daughter-in-law, Tanya. She also had a visit from you."

Mr. Mallory gripped his mug between both palms. "So did your daughter Shelley. But you probably already knew that."

"Yes, I did." Mother leaned sideways and rested her elbow on the wheelchair's armrest. The ribbon falling from her cap crumpled against her forearm, the black stark against the robin's-egg blue of her dress. "All three of them said you asked some unusual questions. So I'm curious what your business is here in Arborville. Is my family involved somehow?"

The man lined up his fork, knife, and spoon on his empty plate, his movements slow and deliberate. He lifted his napkin to his mouth and rubbed it back and forth, then wadded it up and laid it over the silverware. Using his fingertips, he pushed the plate toward the middle of the table and finally stacked his arms on the table's edge. He craned his neck to look directly into Mother's face. "My business might involve your family. And then again, it might not."

Mother huffed. "The way you tiptoe

around a question makes me think you'd be a good court lawyer, Mr. Mallory."

He burst out laughing. "No, no, ma'am, I could never be a lawyer. You see, policemen and lawyers are too often at odds."

Anna-Grace had sat silently watching their exchange, occasionally flicking a puzzled glance at Suzanne. "How so?"

Mr. Mallory rubbed his nose and grimaced. "Policemen arrest the bad guys. Lawyers find ways to let them go."

"Are you a police officer? You don't wear a uniform."

He grinned at Anna-Grace. "I gave up my uniform a few years back. But I'm still in the business of . . . rounding up people."

Suzanne went cold all over. She dropped her fork and it clanked against her plate. Their guest looked at her, his expression searching. She picked up her fork with trembling fingers and used it to chop a bite-sized chunk of now-cold eggs. Slowly he shifted his attention to Mother again, but Suzanne sensed he was observing her from the corner of his eye.

"You just might be able to help me, Mrs. Zimmerman. Can I ask you the same questions I asked your kin?"

Mother raised her chin. "You can ask. But I might not answer."

His low chuckle rumbled again. "Fair enough." He slid back his chair, putting himself at eye level with Mother. "Do you have any children besides Suzanne, Cletus, Shelley, and Sandra?"

Mother scowled, shaking her head. "No."

"Did you give birth to all your children?"

"Well, I didn't find them under a cabbage leaf."

He threw back his head and laughed. The sound bounced off the high ceiling and filled the room. He brought himself under control and grinned at her. "Does that mean yes?"

"Of course it means yes." Mother rolled her eyes. "How else would I get my children?"

"Through adoption." His voice lost its almost-teasing quality and barked out crisply. He leaned in. "Do you have any children through adoption, Mrs. Zimmerman?"

"No, I do not." Mother answered as tartly as he'd asked.

Without warning he spun and pinned Suzanne with an intense stare. "What about you, Ms. Zimmerman. You said you have a daughter. Is she natural born or adopted?"

Images of Alexa and Anna-Grace alternately flashed in her mind. Dizziness struck, and she gripped the edge of the table. She opened her mouth, but nothing came out.

Mother snapped, "She gave birth. Why does it matter? And why are you interrogating her?"

He eased against the chair's tall back, his gaze never wavering from Suzanne's. His face relaxed into its formerly friendly expression. "Was I interrogating you, Ms. Zimmerman? I apologize." He flipped his hand as if shooing away an insect. "Sometimes I get a little carried away. I didn't mean any offense."

Suzanne lowered her head and finally found her voice. "Don't worry about it. No offense taken."

Anna-Grace's sweet voice rang. "Mr. Mallory, I don't know if it would help you or not, but I was adopted."

CHAPTER 22

Arborville
Suzanne

A roaring filled Suzanne's ears — a freight train racing directly toward her stalled car. If she didn't do something, say something, she'd be demolished. She jumped up. "Anna-Grace, would you help me clear the table, please? I believe everyone is done." Her voice came out shrill, unnatural, but Anna-Grace rose without a moment's pause.

"Now hold on a minute." Mr. Mallory stuck his palm in the air like a traffic cop. "Miss Braun?" His steel-gray gaze roved over Anna-Grace's mesh cap and trailing ribbons. "Have you always been Mennonite?"

"Yes, sir. My parents, grandparents, and great-grandparents — all are part of the Old Order fellowship." A proud smile graced her face. "I come from a long line of faithful saints."

The man's eyes narrowed. "But you were adopted into the family, not born to it — isn't that what you said?"

Anna-Grace's smile wavered. Hurt glistened in her eyes. "Well, yes, but I . . ."

Protectiveness swelled up in Suzanne, and she spoke without thinking. "I really don't think that matters much to Anna-Grace. She's been Andrew and Olivia Braun's daughter her entire life — more than twenty years. Birth isn't nearly as important as heart."

She sensed Mother gawking at her, and she couldn't blame her. Had she really just stated that out loud? Of course she meant it where Alexa was concerned, but her heart ached with desire to claim Anna-Grace. She shot Mother a sharp look — *Don't you dare ask me any questions right now!* — and busied herself stacking dishes. Anna-Grace followed her example.

Mr. Mallory draped his elbow over the chair's back and examined the two of them for several seconds, his lips twitching. As Anna-Grace turned toward the kitchen with her load of dishes, he barked out, "Miss Braun, did you grow up in Arborville?"

She paused and gazed at him uncertainly

301

over her shoulder. "N-No, sir."

Mother waved at Anna-Grace, and the girl scurried out the door. Mother glared at Mr. Mallory. "I don't appreciate you bothering my great-niece. Anna-Grace is a timid girl, and you're scaring her. Don't ask her any more questions."

"Then how about I ask you instead." A grin creased his face. "You're not timid. Not by a long shot."

Her glower darkened, but Mr. Mallory only kept grinning that relaxed, cocky grin. Mother folded her arms over her chest. "I'm not altogether sure I want to answer your questions, either. You are an infuriating man, Mr. Mallory."

"I've been told that before." He shifted around and braced his elbows on the table. "No more inquisitions. Just one two-part, easy-to-answer question, all right?"

Suzanne wanted to flee the room. But her legs had turned to stone, her muscles so stiff she couldn't move. Her ears rang, but Mr. Mallory's throaty voice carried over the piercing blare.

"When's Anna-Grace's birthday, and where's home for her?"

Mother curled her hands over the wheelchair's tire grips and pushed away from the table. She rolled the chair toward

Suzanne, her mouth set in a firm line of determination. "Suzy, for goodness' sake, take those dishes to the kitchen before the food is so dried on we'll need a chisel to get those plates clean."

Suzanne's legs automatically carried her forward in jerky strides. She passed through the short hallway between the dining room and kitchen, Mother's and Mr. Mallory's voices following her.

"Anna-Grace's age and hometown are none of your business, Mr. Mallory."

"None of my business? I'm not so sure about that, Mrs. Zimmerman." A wry chuckle rasped, sending a chill down Suzanne's spine. "I suppose time will tell."

Indianapolis
Alexa

After they'd finished lunch Wednesday, Tom drove Alexa to Indianapolis. She'd wanted to go yesterday afternoon, but sneet — she loved the funny word describing the cross between snow and sleet — had fallen, and Linda proclaimed they'd catch pneumonia if they trooped around in the cold and wet. Since Linda was always right, Tom said they needed to wait a day. So Alexa had waited. Begrudgingly, but without argument.

The roads were still a little slick in places

from yesterday's moisture and last night's freezing temperatures, so she sat in silence rather than distracting Tom. She fiddled with the notebook where she'd recorded every tiny bit of information they'd managed to uncover. The notes were disappointingly short and unhelpful. Even Tom's calls to every private investigation agency in town hadn't yielded anything of value. Two hadn't bothered to respond to his voicemail queries, and the ones he spoke to directly weren't willing to divulge information without a retainer. Tom refused to pay for answers, and Alexa didn't have the funds. So what she'd thought would be a solid lead toward locating her birth mother turned out to be a dead end.

God, let today's venture uncover something I can use. I want to find her. I want to tell her — She ended the prayer abruptly. What she wanted to tell the woman who'd given birth to her and then dumped her in an alley wasn't very Christlike. God wouldn't be pleased.

She opened the notebook to a fresh page and wrote across the top: "January 13 — Door-to-Door Info Seeking." She drew little curlicues on both sides of the title and then put a swoopy line underneath. The embellishments didn't make the page seem any less stark. She smacked the book closed.

Tom, his eyes on the road, reached over and tweaked her ponytail. "Don't give up before we start."

She swallowed a snicker. He knew her so well. As well as any birth grandfather could. Maybe even better than some. "Okay, okay," she teasingly groused.

His grin rounded his full cheek. "We'll be there soon. Just relax."

She tried to relax but it wasn't easy. Mom had called last night, all stressed out about a man — a former police officer, she said — running around town asking questions. Alexa thought it curious, but after hosting Briley Forrester, someone asking questions didn't make her as suspicious as she once might have been. She hoped her assurances helped Mom feel better about the guest. The man planned to leave soon, anyway, so Mom wouldn't have to deal with him much longer.

She spun on Tom, forgetting her plan to stay quiet. "How much longer do you think it will take to get some information we can actually use? I need to get back to Kansas. I promised to make special cookies for the grade school kids' Valentine's Day party. Mom won't know how I want them decorated. Then I've got to get the rooms

305

ready for the two couples staying Saturday the thirteenth for Valentine's Day. And Anna-Grace's wedding is February 18. Family will stay with us that night. After that —"

"Whoa, girlie, slow down." Tom chuckled. "That wedding and the Big Heart Day are almost a month away yet. No sense in getting yourself all worked up over it. You young people these days, thinking everything has to happen right now. I blame it on microwaves."

Alexa burst out laughing. "Microwaves?"

"Uh-huh." He took the exit for Indianapolis. He eased off the ramp into the flow of traffic and then went on as if there'd been no interruption. "Used to be if you wanted hot soup for dinner, you spent an hour chopping vegetables and boiling meat to make the broth. Then you waited another hour or so for everything to cook up. Nobody fussed about the time it took until microwaves came along and you could heat up a can of soup in two minutes." He shook his head, his lips pursed into a rueful grimace. "Now nobody wants to wait for something good. They want to snap their fingers and get it right now."

"So you think I'm being too impatient?"

"Aw, honey-girl . . ." Tom's smile turned

tender. "I think you're eager for answers, and I can't say that I blame you. But not everything can be microwaved. Some things take time." He winked at her. "If you're supposed to find your birth mama, it'll happen. God'll open the door when the time is right. Can't you trust that?"

She sighed. "I'm trying to."

"I know you are."

She sighed again. "I'll try to be satisfied to let things slow simmer instead of getting zapped, okay?"

He laughed. "Now you're talkin'."

Alexa's determination flagged as the afternoon wore on. Her nose dripped and her toes froze as she and Tom trudged from house to house in the neighborhood surrounding the unwed mothers' home, ringing doorbells or knocking on doorjambs. Most of the time nobody answered at all. Of those who did answer, the majority said they hadn't been living there twenty years ago, so they couldn't help at all. The three who had lived in the area way back then claimed they hadn't noticed any pregnant girl except the ones from the home itself. One of those three didn't even try to hide his disdain for the home and its occupants. The snooty attitude made Alexa sad for Mom and for Melissa, Lennah, and Polly.

Why couldn't people love like Jesus loved instead of condemning people for making mistakes?

The reflection jolted her. Wasn't she on a mission to condemn someone, too? She pushed the thought aside. Her situation was different. She'd been directly affected by her mother's heartlessness. These neighborhood people had no connection to the girls at the home and therefore had no business judging them. Those people had reason to be ashamed. She didn't.

She stomped her feet hard against the concrete sidewalk to put some feeling back in her toes and trailed Tom to the car. Once inside, he started the engine and put the heater on high. Cold air blasted from the vents.

Alexa hugged herself and shivered. "Is it okay to wish the heater was like a microwave — instantly hot?"

"I'm with you on that wish." His breath hung in front of him. "I'm chilled clear through. You couldn't have got the idea to hunt for your birth mom in June or July?"

"You were the one who said January was a good time to go hunting since not much was happening at the B and B."

He grimaced. "Guilty." He heaved a huge sigh, fiddling with the heater knobs. "Well, I think we both need to get something warm inside us or Linda's prediction about us catching pneumonia just might come true. Then there'll be no living with her."

Alexa glanced at her cell phone's clock. Three thirty-five. "Tom! Three thirty to five are the open hours for the girls at the home. Could we go see Melissa? I bet Ms. Reed would give us a cup of hot tea or cocoa if we asked."

He shifted into Drive. "The home's a lot closer than a downtown coffee shop. And even if she doesn't have anything hot to drink, the house oughta be warm. All right. We'll drop in on your friend and see how she's doing."

Ms. Reed insisted on Alexa leaving her purse beside the door, and she searched through the pockets of their coats before hanging them on ornate hooks above a built-in bench next to the staircase. Tom didn't act insulted by the woman's actions, but Alexa had a hard time not seething.

Just as she had the last time, Melissa lit with pleasure when she spotted Alexa. But her smile turned shy when her gaze fell on Tom. They sat, at Ms. Reed's direction, around the table in the library. "You're less likely to be disturbed in there," she said in a tone as chilly as the outside air. She departed, but she left the door wide open, and they could hear her rustling around in her office on the other side of the wall.

Melissa kept her head low, picking at a hangnail on her thumb and sending nervous sideways glances at Tom. He leaned back, propped his ankle on his knee, and chatted as if the girl wasn't scared spitless of him. Within minutes she came out of her turtle-like pose and began offering stilted and then open responses to his questions.

Alexa sat back and observed the pair's exchanges. She marveled at Tom's innate kindness. Linda was kind, too, but crusty. Sometimes her brusqueness put people off until they really got to know her and figured out how soft she was underneath. But Tom was so personable, so sincerely pleasant. Mom always said he could make friends with a hungry grizzly bear, and Alexa believed it. She watched Melissa blossom under his warm attention, losing her inhibitions and finally sharing a bit of her past.

"Maybe if Mom hadn't died, Dad wouldn't be so . . ." The girl cringed. "I guess . . . bitter. It's probably not easy for a man to raise three kids on his own. Anyway, when I turned up pregnant, he got madder than I'd ever seen him. Called me all kinds of names." Her face glowed pink, and she ducked her head again, her chin quivering. "He gave me money for an abortion, but I'd waited too long to tell him a baby was coming. The clinic wouldn't do it. That made him mad, too."

Alexa had to bite the tip of her tongue to keep from saying what she thought about Melissa's father. So heartless and cruel! He'd be a good match for her birth mother.

Melissa fiddled with a strand of her lank brown hair. "Anyway, he said there was no way he was going to raise another kid so I'd better find some way to get rid of it."

Alexa said, "Wouldn't your boyfriend help you?"

A sad smile appeared on Melissa's sheepish face. "You mean my baby-daddy?"

Heat filled Alexa's cheeks. The term sounded so impersonal and almost vulgar. "I guess so."

"He's not my boyfriend. He's just a guy from school. I met him at a party, and we . . ." She licked her lips and angled her face away. "We were both pretty drunk. He says he can't even remember doing anything with me. So . . ." She shrugged.

Alexa gave Tom a can-you-believe-this look and turned on Melissa. "Whether he can remember it or not, he's responsible for this baby, too. After it's born, you can have

311

a DNA test and prove he's the one. Then you can —"

"I don't want anything from him." Melissa's eyes sparked. "I know what it's like to have a daddy who doesn't want you around. I wouldn't wish that on an enemy. I'm sure not gonna wish it on this baby. She deserves better than that."

Tom placed his hand on Alexa's arm, the gentle pressure stilling her planned retort. He said softly, "How'd you end up here in Indiana, Melissa? It's a long ways from Kansas."

Melissa shrugged. "Long story short? My dad was ragging on me at work, about how stupid I'd been and how he couldn't stand to look at me, and one of his coworkers told him he ought to ship me off someplace. So Dad Googled 'homes for unwed mothers' " — she made air quotes with her fingers — "and started calling different places. This one took his insurance, so here I am." She closed her eyes, cupped her round belly, and sighed. "I'll be glad when this is all over."

Alexa remembered the director saying Melissa wasn't certain where she'd go after the baby was born. She started to ask Melissa about her plans, but the click of heels on hardwood intruded.

Ms. Reed stepped into the room and

pointed at the keyhole-shaped Regulator clock tick-tocking on the wall. "Four fifty-five, Melissa. Time to tell your guests good-bye."

Alexa shifted in her chair to face the director. "May I come back tomorrow at visiting time, please?" Belatedly she faced Tom. "If I can borrow the car."

Tom pushed up from the table. "It's fine with me if the weather isn't too bad. I don't like the idea of you driving on ice." He looked at Ms. Reed. "So I guess it's up to you, Ms. Reed."

The woman offered a tight smile. "Melissa seems to enjoy your company. As long as you don't prevent her from completing her assignments, it's fine for you to visit during our free hours."

Melissa awkwardly stood, one hand pressed on the small of her back. "We have free hours in the evening, too, Alexa. Seven thirty to nine."

Tom shook his head. "It's dark by then. I don't want Alexa driving this neighborhood at night." He gave Ms. Reed an apologetic grin. "Not to be derogatory, ma'am."

Ms. Reed sighed. "I'm aware that the crime-infested areas of any major city tend to broaden over time, and this neighborhood has fallen prey in the past years. That's why we're so cautious about what comes into the house. We want this to be a safe haven for our girls and the babies they're bringing into the world."

Alexa examined the director's weary face. Maybe she didn't mean to come across like an army sergeant. Maybe she was just overly protective. In that moment Alexa decided she liked Ms. Reed after all. She smiled. "Thank you. I promise not to get in the way, but I would like to spend more time with Melissa."

"That's fine." Ms. Reed's forehead pinched into a frown. "You said your name is Zimmerman. Is that correct?"

Alexa nodded.

She tapped her mouth. "I've heard that name somewhere else recently . . ." She seemed to think deeply for a few seconds. Then she held out her hands. "Ah well, it will come to me eventually. But for now, we need to begin our dinner preparations. We'll see you tomorrow, Alexa. Have a safe drive home."

CHAPTER 23

Indianapolis
Cynthia

When Glenn and Cynthia joined the Southern Baptist church shortly after their marriage, they'd made a promise to be in the church whenever the doors were open. Over the years they'd faithfully attended Sunday school, morning worship, discipleship classes, evening worship on Sundays, and the combined Bible study and corporate prayer time on Wednesday evenings.

Of all the services, Cynthia liked the Wednesday Bible-study time best. A smaller crowd attended, and the minister, known to the congregation as Brother Gary, spoke to them from a metal music stand placed between the front two pews instead of from the pulpit. Only adults filled the benches because the children attended their own evening classes, so people openly shared. The informal setting encouraged a give-

and-take of ideas, and Cynthia often thought she learned more during the twenty-minute Wednesday Bible study than the two hours of Sunday morning study and worship. She also loved the prayer time — believers coming together in one accord to lift their praises and petitions to God.

During the winter months, attendance dropped off for all but the Sunday morning worship, and at times either she or Glenn had sheepishly suggested they stay in rather than drag the children through the cold. After all, a person could worship God anywhere, right? But somehow when one of them wanted to stay in, the other always wanted to go, and the entire family bundled up to head out the door. Afterward, she'd always been glad they'd made the effort.

Until this evening.

After they'd dropped Darcy and Barrett at an ice-skating rink with the other young people from church, she begged Glenn to turn around and go home. When he refused, she pleaded, "Please don't tell them." She even cried. But he turned stubborn and said, "We need their support, Cyn. That's what churches do for their members. They support them. I'm asking for prayer tonight and that's that."

So now she sat beside Glenn on their

regular fifth-from-the-front, right-side-of-the-aisle pew. Her Bible lay open in her lap to one of her favorite passages in the book of James. She stared at the words, but they didn't reach her the way they always had before. Her pulse thudded worse than a herd of stampeding cattle, drowning out the minister's voice. Cold sweat formed on her back. Her muscles trembled. Glenn slid his arm across the back of the pew and draped his hand over her shoulder. A familiar gesture, one she'd always responded to by either twining her fingers through his or pressing more snugly beneath his arm. Tonight the light weight of his hand seemed cloying. She shrugged, and he moved it.

She glanced at her cell phone, which she'd placed on top of her purse on the pew beside her. She'd turned the volume off. No matter how eager she was to communicate with Mr. Mallory, she wouldn't let it intrude on Bible study or prayer. But its glowing face showed the time. In a few more minutes the Bible study portion of the evening would end and the minister would ask about the prayer needs of the congregation. Her stomach writhed. What would her church family think of her once they heard Glenn's request?

Years ago, as a newly married couple,

they'd shared their testimonies with this congregation. Their stories were so similar — growing up in angry, dysfunctional homes, battling feelings of worthlessness, attending classes for relatives of alcoholics, and meeting a Savior who loved them and wanted to give them a better future. The church people had clapped, accepted them into membership, and afterward had come up and congratulated them for choosing not to follow in their parents' footsteps.

Back then she hadn't confessed to giving birth to an out-of-wedlock child. Not once had she mentioned it to her pastor, her Sunday school teacher, a deacon, or any of the friends they'd made. Only Glenn had known. But now — because Glenn insisted they needed their church family's support — everyone would know. Would they clap and congratulate her, or would they gape at her in shock and disappointment?

"The wisdom in James's letter to the twelve tribes is applicable to us today." Brother Gary was closing the study.

She pressed her hands to her stomach. Nausea rolled through her middle. She hoped she wouldn't throw up.

"As we move into our prayer time, let's remember verses five and six of chapter one. Asking God's will for a situation is the same as asking for wisdom. Let's believe God's way is best and not doubt that He will provide guidance when we ask." The pastor laid his Bible aside. "What requests do we need to lift to our all-knowing God this evening?"

Glenn raised his hand.

"Yes, Glenn." Brother Gary aimed a bright smile in their direction.

Glenn grabbed the back of the pew in front of them and pulled himself upright. Cynthia clutched her hands together. Would her heart leave her chest? She'd never felt such an intense booming beneath her breastbone. She wanted to grab her husband, yank him down, laugh, and tell everyone that he'd only been kidding, that they didn't need anything. But her trembling limbs refused to cooperate.

"This might surprise a few people, but a long time ago, when Cyn was still a teenager, she gave up a baby for adoption."

A few stifled gasps came from behind her. Cynthia bowed her head, awash in shame.

"Her daughter is twenty years old now, and Cyn would like to find her. So we're asking for prayer. For us to know for sure if it's God's will for Cyn and her daughter to reunite." He paused, his nostrils flaring with a slow intake of breath. "The search has been" — he blew out the air — "stressful. So we need prayer for us, too." He sat so hard it appeared his legs had given out.

Brother Gary crossed to their pew and shook their hands by turn. Not an ounce of condemnation showed in his expression, but the murmurs rolling at the back of the church increased the disgrace-induced fire in her cheeks.

The minister faced the congregation. "It took a great deal of courage for Glenn and Cynthia to share this burden with us. We didn't get to verse twenty-six of James chapter one this evening, but I would encourage each of you to read it tonight and let it remind you of your obligation to this brother and sister in Christ. We'll be tempted to speak among ourselves, maybe find fault with the decision Cynthia made. Because we're human." He cast a brief, tender smile on Cynthia. "But instead of judging, let's choose words of encouragement. I suspect our sister has suffered enough censure already. Now . . ." He moved back to the front. "Who else has a request?"

Others raised their hands, and Brother Gary wrote the needs on slips of paper. He passed them out, and people gathered in small groups to pray over the stated requests. Cynthia and Glenn joined two other couples, Jim and Judy McCoy and Dean and Jill Harrison. A lump filled her throat when Jim asked God to bring Cynthia and her daughter together and also to give her and Glenn peace as they waited to meet her daughter. Their group hadn't even taken the slip with Cynthia's request on it, but still he prayed over them. She was deeply touched by the gesture, and she told him so when they'd finished and the group separated.

He gave her a couple of awkward pats on the shoulder. "You're welcome." A worried frown pinched his face. "Can I tell you something?"

He seemed so serious, she started to refuse.

"It might make you feel better."

After a moment's hesitation she nodded. She followed Jim out of the sanctuary, where people still milled in small groups and chatted quietly, across the reception area, and into the small alcove beneath the stairs leading to the balcony.

He leaned against the wall and began talking without preamble. "My sister Terri couldn't have kids, so she adopted a little girl through the foster-care system. Katie was three when she joined the family, and she's twenty-one — no, twenty-two — now. Her birth mother, Erica, came looking for her shortly after she turned eighteen. At first we weren't too sure if it would be a good idea for Katie to get to know her birth mom. After all, the state had taken Katie and her siblings away from Erica for good reasons. Plus, by then my sister had pretty much forgotten that Katie had ever been anybody's daughter but hers, and she wasn't at all happy about some other mom stepping on her toes.

"I won't lie to you. It was tough for a while. Lots of tension and conflict. Especially between Terri and her husband, because they didn't agree at all about what should be done. But it turned out to be a blessing. Katie got to know her birth brother and sister and their families. She and Erica became friends, and my sister is even friends with Erica now." He paused, his brow crinkling. "Even though Katie's still our family, she's their family, too. It's worked out all right." He squeezed her shoulder, then lowered his hand. "I'll pray it turns out all right for you, Glenn, your kids, and your daughter's adopted family."

Tears flooded Cynthia's eyes. His kindness soothed her more than she could explain. "Thank you, Jim."

He smiled and moved off. Two more church members approached and assured her of their intentions to pray for God's will over her "situation." Their choice of words made her stiffen, but she thanked the pair anyway, choosing to believe discomfort rather than disparagement colored their tone. She scanned the wide reception area for Glenn, eager to tell him what Jim had said. Apparently stress and tension were a normal part of these kinds of searches. Knowing that another family had survived it might encourage him.

He wasn't at either end of the reception hallway, so she peeked into the sanctuary. She spotted him down front, sitting on one of the prayer benches with Brother Gary. Their backs were to the doors, and they both bent forward, their heads close together. Were they praying? If so, she wanted to join them. She and Glenn needed to pray together if they were going to weather these stormy seas.

Moving quietly so she wouldn't disturb them, she made her way up the middle aisle and started to slip into the pew behind them. But she picked up on Glenn's words, and they stopped her cold.

"I should've thought it all the way through before I started this. Cyn's . . . obsessed. If

I could take back that Christmas gift, I would."

He wasn't praying. He was complaining. About her. A spear of betrayal pierced the center of her chest. The pain was so sharp she lost her grip on her Bible, and it fell to the carpeted floor with a muffled thud. Both men sat upright and looked at her. Glenn's face reflected horror and Brother Gary's showed great compassion.

The minister stood and extended his hand toward her. "Cynthia, come here. Let's talk."

She bent over clumsily and snatched up her Bible. Clutching it to her aching chest, she shook her head. "No. I don't have anything to say." She glared at Glenn. "How dare you? How dare you stand up in . . . in God's house and ask for prayer for us like you're my support and then turn around and say something like that? You're a hypocrite, Glenn."

He propped his elbows on his knees and buried his face in his hands.

Brother Gary took a step toward Cynthia. "I understand it was hurtful to hear what Glenn just said. He was speaking privately to me. It wasn't meant for your ears."

She laughed. She'd never been rude to a minister — not even before she became a churchgoer — but if she didn't laugh, she'd dissolve into tears that might never end. So she let the humorless laughter roll for several seconds and then growled out, "No, I'm sure it wasn't. But I'm glad I heard it. I'm glad I know just how much he doesn't want me to find my baby girl. It's better for me to know the truth because now . . . now . . ." Now what? She didn't know.

She turned and ran up the aisle, out of the sanctuary, and straight to the women's rest room. She locked herself inside and removed her cell phone from her purse with shaky hands. She wouldn't go home. Not with the man who had so callously deceived and betrayed her. But who could she call?

She scanned her list of contacts. Most of the people saved in her phone were mutual friends. If she called them, they'd be placed in the uncomfortable position of choosing sides. She didn't want to be the cause of dissension between another husband and wife. Why would she want her friends to hurt the way she was hurting? She snapped the phone closed and pressed it to her forehead. Who did she know that had no connection to Glenn? A series of faces paraded behind her closed eyelids.

Relief burst through her. Lindsey. Her coworker at the library. Cynthia wouldn't consider Lindsey a close friend. After all, the woman was half a dozen years younger, twice divorced, childless, and something of a party girl. But based on some of the comments she'd made about men and their inability to commit, she wouldn't think twice about giving Cynthia temporary sanctuary from Glenn.

Locked in the bathroom stall, she pulled up Lindsey's number and prayed the woman would answer. After only one ring Lindsey's chirpy voice blasted Cynthia's ear. "Hello! Start talking!" Loud music — rock or rap or something too fast and noisy — blared in the background.

Cynthia cringed. "Lindsey, this is Cynthia Allgood. You know, from the library?"

Her laughter rang. "Of course I know. What's up?"

"Um, I . . ." What was she doing? Hadn't she promised to be better than her mother, who flitted from one failed relationship to another, never committing to stand firm through the rough times? She and Glenn had vowed to weather every storm together, as a team.

Glenn's voice swooped through her mind. *"If I could take back that Christmas gift, I would."*

Anger swelled, driven by a tide of deep

326

hurt. "I hope you won't think I've lost my mind, but I have a huge favor to ask . . ."

CHAPTER 24

Indianapolis
Cynthia

Even though she didn't ask her to, Lindsey stood guard at the head of the hallway while Cynthia packed enough clothes to last several days and gathered her essentials from the bathroom. Glenn and the kids sat in the front room, television off, quiet as a trio of foxes hiding from a hound. Apparently Lindsey had been correct when she said Glenn wouldn't cause a fuss if there was a witness. Or maybe he was only trying to protect the kids from seeing their parents in a knock-down-drag-out fight. They'd always promised not to quarrel in front of Darcy and Barrett.

For as much as promises were worth these days . . .

She zipped the duffel bag closed, heaved it over her shoulder, and clomped up behind Lindsey. The woman shot her a look that asked, *Ready?* Cynthia nodded, and Lindsey moved toward the front door, her unsmiling gaze aimed at Glenn. Cynthia tried not to look at her husband or children, but some invisible cord pulled her attention in their direction anyway. Glenn remained stoic, no hint of emotion in his expression. However, confusion and hurt glistened in Barrett's eyes. Darcy kept her back to her mother, but anger and hurt pulsated from her stiff form.

Cynthia paused.

Lindsey curled her hand over the doorknob. "Cynthia, you coming?"

Barrett knelt on the sofa, gripping the tall back and staring at his mother. His blue eyes begged her not to go.

Cynthia dropped the bag and crossed to the sofa. She placed one hand on Barrett's cheek and the other on Darcy's shoulder. Her daughter still didn't turn around. "I'm sorry I can't take you with me. There isn't room in Lindsey's apartment. But I'll come over tomorrow morning and drive you to school. I'll pick you up after school like I always do and take you home. I'll still see you every day, okay?"

Darcy shrugged out from beneath Cynthia's hand and stormed to her bedroom. The slamming of the door rattled the walls.

Cynthia sighed. She smoothed Barrett's hair. "Don't worry. Everything will be all right."

Her son's chin quivered. "No, it won't."

With her expression Cynthia silently begged Glenn to step in, offer assurances, form a united front, the way they always had. He held eye contact with her, but his lips remained pressed in a grim line. Shaking her head in both resignation and frustration, she closed her eyes for a moment and gathered her courage. Then she faced Barrett and forced her wobbly lips into a smile.

"I'll see you tomorrow morning, okay?"

Barrett — her eleven-year-old boy who had sworn off hugs — launched himself into her arms. "Don't go, Mom. Please? Don't go."

She struggled to support his weight. She struggled to support the weight of her guilt. "Barrett, honey, I . . ." She gulped. Why didn't Glenn say something? Apologize? Tell her he'd been wrong to want her to give up the search for her daughter?

She pressed kisses on Barrett's tear-dampened cheek and rocked him from side to side. "I love you very much. I'm not leaving because of anything you or Darcy did. But I need . . ." Oh, her throat ached. Talking was torture. "I need a little time away to think. That's all. Okay?"

Barrett's grip loosened. He slid from her arms and stood for a moment, glaring up at her with such betrayal she thought she might wilt beneath his gaze. Then he flopped over the back of the sofa in a way she'd never allowed and buried his face in the cushions.

Glenn finally spoke. Quietly. With great restraint. A complete contrast to the fury glimmering in his eyes. "Are you sure this is what you want to do, Cyn?"

Want to do? Of course not. What she wanted was to have her family — all of her family — under one roof, happy together and loving each other. But she couldn't have what she wanted. So she'd have to settle for second best.

"I have my cell if something comes up with the kids. Like I told them, I'll take them back and forth to school so you won't have to change your routine. I can even fix supper for you all when I drop them off if it will help."

"It will. Otherwise all they'll get is epicurean delight and golden deliciousness."

She wanted to smile at his pet names for sliced hot dogs in beans and macaroni and cheese, the only two dishes Glenn knew how to fix. They'd always joked about his limited prowess in the kitchen, such a contrast to the wonderful dishes she concocted. But his voice was as emotionless as Owen Mallory's, no hint of humor. She swallowed. "All right. Bye, then."

She turned toward the hallway. Hope fluttered in her chest. She called, "Good-bye, Darcy. I'll see you tomorrow." She waited, but no reply came. So she reached over the sofa and ruffled her son's hair. "Sleep well, Barrett. See you in the morning."

He dug deeper into the cushions and didn't say anything.

It hurt to breathe. She had to get out of there. Cynthia slung her purse over her shoulder, grabbed the duffel, and fisted her car keys so tightly the jagged edges dug into her palm. "I'm ready." *Liar.* She followed Lindsey out the door.

Indianapolis
Alexa

Alexa followed Melissa up the winding staircase to the second floor. Ms. Reed had left to run errands — her usual Friday morning routine, Melissa said — and the cook, a grandmotherly woman named Eileen, granted permission for the two to visit in Melissa's room, so they would have complete privacy. Alexa silently celebrated the turn of events. She hadn't wanted to bring up Melissa's intention to give away her baby girl in front of the others. Now she'd have a captive audience. And she intended to take full advantage of the situation.

The floorboards in the dim hallway creaked beneath the faded carpet runner. Doors lined both sides of the long hall, all of them open. Alexa couldn't resist peeking inside. Every room was the same. White painted walls, simple curtains, bare wood floors, a pair of twin beds draped with navy-blue spreads, two dressers, and a desk. Impersonal. Utilitarian. The creative side of her longed to bring the rooms to life.

Melissa's room was the last on the left, and she moved back to let Alexa go in first. As she stepped over the threshold, a small burst of color captured her attention. She crossed directly to the dresser and gingerly fingered the crumpled, rainbow-patterned tissue she'd put in Melissa's gift bag. The paper bouquet, jammed into a yellow paper cup and centered proudly on the dresser's scarred top, made her want to cry.

Melissa came up behind her, one hand curved protectively beneath her tummy's swell. Her pink T-shirt stretched taut over the round shape. With the little pucker of her belly button poking out, her shirt resembled an inflated balloon. She smiled shyly and nodded at the bouquet. "Kinda silly, huh?"

Alexa sniffed hard and fluffed the paper, expanding the makeshift bloom. "No. Not really." She sent a glance around the room. "It's the nicest decoration in here."

Melissa laughed softly and eased onto one of the beds, still holding her stomach. "They don't encourage us to decorate the rooms. I guess they don't want us to feel too much at home since our time is limited."

Alexa retrieved the wooden chair from the desk, dragged it over, and sat close to Melissa. "How much longer 'til your baby comes?"

"She's due February 25, but the midwife thinks I might go early. I'm already starting to dilate."

Unease tiptoed up Alexa's spine. "Doesn't it make you kind of nervous, having your baby here with only a midwife instead of being in a hospital?"

Melissa laughed, a light trickle of self-conscious amusement. "I don't think it would matter where I had her. I'd still be nervous." Her hands rubbed slightly up and down on the fullest part of her belly, the movement seemingly reflexive rather than intentional. "Just the thought of having a baby scares me." She sighed. "I'll be glad when it's all over."

Alexa leaped on her comment. "Are you sure?"

Melissa's fine reddish-gold brows pulled into a frown. "What do you mean?"

"Are you sure you're ready to be done? With pregnancy. Because once she's born, you won't be able to do what you're doing anymore."

"What am I doing?"

Alexa pointed. "Melissa, you're constantly caressing your stomach."

Melissa's hands froze. Her startled gaze dropped to her stomach and then met Alexa's again.

"Why do you do that?"

Very slowly Melissa rubbed her tummy again. "I don't really know. It's just . . ."

"Natural?"

"Yeah, I guess so."

Alexa leaned forward, bracing her hands on her knees. The thick corduroy of her skirt felt scratchy under her palms. Probably a lot different than Melissa's T-shirt. "Want to know why I think you do it?"

Melissa shrugged, her expression wary.

"I think you're really caressing your baby.

Because you love her."

Tears flooded the girl's eyes. She ducked her head.

Alexa moved to sit beside her. "Melissa, I know you love your baby. I can tell by the way you constantly hold your hands around her. I see it when you say 'her' and 'she' instead of 'it,' the way a lot of people talk about unborn babies. I bet you've even picked out a name that you call her in your head, haven't you?"

A tear slid down Melissa's cheek and plopped on her T-shirt next to her belly-button bump. "Kind of."

"What is it?"

"Evelyn. After my mom."

"It's a beautiful name."

"It's kind of old-fashioned, but I've always liked it. My grandma called her Evvie. I always liked that, too."

"Evvie . . ." Alexa sampled it. She nodded. "I can see why you like it." Hesitantly she touched Melissa's arm. "So if you love Evvie, why are you giving her away?"

Melissa angled an anguished look at Alexa. "It's because I love her that I'm giving her away."

Alexa frowned. "That doesn't make sense."

Melissa pushed upright and moved behind

the chair. She clutched the slatted top on the backrest and glared at Alexa. "Yes, it does. When you really, really love someone, you can't be selfish and do what you want. You have to do what's best." She thumped her fist on the chair's thick slat with the emphasized words, as if pounding nails in a coffin. "What's best for them, not for you. Don't you see?"

Alexa stood and held her hands wide. "No, Melissa, I don't see. How can it be best to give the baby you've carried in your belly for nine months — a baby you've grown to love — to strangers? You'll regret it. I know you will."

Melissa swiped away the tears staining her cheeks. "How do you know?"

"Because of my mom. She gave the baby girl she delivered right here in this home to someone else. And she never forgot. She never got over it. Even though she had me, she always wished she had her baby, too." Funny how much it stung to say all that out loud. "When you love somebody that much, you can't be completely happy without them."

"When you love somebody that much, you don't think about your own happiness. You think about theirs!" The veins in Melissa's neck stood out. Her face glowed red, and her entire body trembled. She gripped the chair so tightly her knuckles turned white. "That's how much I love my baby. Enough not to care about me but to care only about her. Of course I love her. I can't help it. I feel her move inside of me, and I know she's alive and real, and I want to cry because I love her so much. But I'm not ready to be a mom. I don't know how to do it by myself. I can't give her a nice house and nice clothes or a dad. But the people who want to adopt her can."

She'd started out nearly yelling, her frame stiff, but the longer she talked, the more her body drooped, and the softer her voice became. She sagged against the chair and whispered, "That's why I'm giving Evvie up. So she can have everything I can't give her."

Alexa stared at Melissa for long seconds, thinking about all she'd said. It all sounded so noble, so selfless. But there was something more Melissa needed to know. She took the girl by the elbow and guided her to the bed. Melissa sat, automatically cupping her stomach again. Alexa perched on the edge of the chair and held her stomach, too. Her insides jumped with nervousness, but she'd say all she'd planned.

"When Evvie finds out she was adopted,

she'll think you didn't want her."

Her jaw slack, Melissa gawked at Alexa. "No!"

Alexa nodded somberly. "Yes. She will. Ask me how I know."

Melissa closed her mouth and sat in silence.

Alexa pretended she'd asked. "I know because my mom isn't my birth mom. I was . . . adopted." Not officially, but she didn't know how else to explain it without going into all the details.

Melissa's face went white.

"My mom never got over giving away her baby girl, and I won't ever get over being abandoned by the woman who gave birth to me." She bit down on her lower lip for a moment, forming a serious question. "Is that what you want for yourself and for Evvie?"

Melissa looked away. Her throat muscles convulsed. "I think you should go, Alexa. I'm tired." She rolled onto her side and pulled up her knees, balling her fists beneath her chin.

Alexa grabbed the afghan from the end of the bed and draped it over Melissa's form. "Think about what I said, okay? Make sure you aren't doing something you'll regret later on."

Melissa crunched her eyes closed and didn't answer.

With a sigh Alexa left the room. She descended the stairs slowly, skimming her hand on the railing. Years ago Mom had gone up and down these stairs. She tried to imagine her mother with a round belly like Melissa's, sticking out so far it hid her feet. Did Mom grip the rail so she wouldn't fall and hurt the child she carried? Probably. Alexa's hand tightened as she came down the final risers.

A twinge of guilt attacked along with the thought of Mom. She should've told Melissa the whole story — how much Mom loved Alexa even though she wasn't her biological child, how she'd raised her without a husband's help, and how Alexa had always felt secure and happy. Tom had even suggested she should. But she left it out because she hadn't wanted Melissa to think an adoptive mother would do a better job of raising Evvie than Melissa could. Had she shortchanged Mom by only telling the bad parts?

She pictured Melissa curled on the bed, her pose reflecting inner torment. The guilt pressed harder. She'd wanted to encourage Melissa, not destroy her. If Melissa knew how well Mom had done on her own, maybe it would help her believe she could raise a baby on her own, too. She changed direction and started back up the stairs.

Ms. Reed stepped from her office and glanced in Alexa's direction. Her face lit, and she hurried across the floor to the staircase. "Alexa, I'm glad to see you. I finally remembered where I'd heard the name Zimmerman."

Alexa stood with one foot on a higher riser, eager to return to Melissa before the visiting hours ended. "Yes, ma'am?"

"Right after the first of the year, a private investigator — What was his name? Malcolm, Mallon, something like that . . ."

Alexa blurted the name of the man staying at her B and B. "Mallory?"

Ms. Reed nodded. "Yes, that's it. Mallory. He came here to gather information about an abandoned baby." She shrugged. "I couldn't help him much. For one thing, I wasn't in charge twenty years ago. For another, the record books didn't show any evidence of a baby being left. But while he was here, he also went through and examined the names of the girls who resided at the home during that time. One of the girls had the last name Zimmerman." Ms. Reed smiled. The first genuine smile Alexa had seen her offer. "Isn't that a coincidence?"

A man named Mallory had snooped around here at the home, and now a man named Mallory was snooping around Arborville. It had to be more than coincidence. Alexa forced a calm tone. "Yes, it sure is." She stepped off the stairs and inched toward the coat hooks. "Ms. Reed, will you tell Melissa I'll try to visit her next week — maybe Monday?"

"Of course, Alexa. Drive safely now."

"I will." She grabbed her coat and bag and hurried out the door, with the bag bouncing on her shoulder and the coat draped over her arm. As she ran, she rummaged in her purse for her phone. She needed to call Mom.

CHAPTER 25

Arborville
Suzanne

Suzanne placed the last pie in the plastic carrier and blew out a sigh of relief. Another morning of baking completed and just in time to deliver the pies to the café for the lunch crowd. She'd always liked pie, but after two weeks of baking a dozen pies five mornings out of seven, she wasn't sure she'd ever eat a slice again. She was — as Mother had teasingly called it yesterday — "pied out."

Anna-Grace slipped on her coat. "If you don't mind, I'll ride along to town with you. I'd like to mail the wedding invitations, but I prefer some prettier stamps than what the post office had the last time I was there. The postmistress said they would have heart ones closer to Valentine's Day. I hope they're in by now."

Truthfully, Suzanne did mind. She'd only

moved Anna-Grace back to the house last night with Mr. Mallory's departure. Her emotions were still running amuck. "Would you like me to pick up the stamps for you? That way your aunt Abigail isn't left here alone." Mother would survive being alone for the length of time it would take Suzanne to run two errands, but she couldn't think of any other excuses.

The girl shrugged, smiling. "That's fine. Thank you. But since I'm already bundled, I'll help you carry these out to the car."

Suzanne trailed behind Anna-Grace, balancing two of the three pie containers in her arms. If her arms weren't occupied, they might pull her daughter into a hug. Anna-Grace's consistently cheerful spirit and sweet nature were impossible to resist. They placed the containers in a row in the backseat of the car, and Anna-Grace turned toward the house. Before she'd taken a step, the phone in Suzanne's pocket rang with "My Girl" — Alexa's ringtone.

Anna-Grace aimed a grin over her shoulder. "Tell Alexa hello from me, please."

Suzanne nodded and slipped behind the steering wheel. She slammed the door, sealing herself inside with the smell of fruit and pastry, and answered the phone. "Hi, sweetheart."

"Hi, Mom. Are you busy?"

Suzanne poked the key into the ignition. "Just getting ready to take the pies to town. But we can talk while I drive."

"You might not want to be driving when you hear what I have to say."

Suzanne's hand froze. "What's that?"

"That man you said was staying at the B and B — Mr. Mallory? I guess you were right to wonder about him. Ms. Reed, the director of the unwed mothers' home, just told me Mr. Mallory had been here asking questions about an abandoned baby, and he found your name in the record book. That's probably why he came to Arborville." Excitement threaded Alexa's tone, but the statement stole Suzanne's ability to breathe.

Alexa went on, unaware of her mother's panicked reaction. "I bet he's looking for me. He has to be looking for me, doesn't he, Mom? It's more than circumstantial that he'd be here and then go to Arborville, right?"

Right. Nothing else made sense. But Suzanne couldn't draw enough air to answer.

"Mom?"

She forced herself to suck in a shuddering breath. "I . . . I'm sure you're right, honey. It sounds like . . . like your birth family wants . . . wants to find you." This was what

Alexa wanted. Suzanne should be happy. But only fear gripped her.

"Now I have to decide what to do. What do you think? Should I go visit this Mr. Mallory and tell him I was left behind the home? See if I'm actually the one he's trying to find?"

Suzanne's heart thudded against her ribs. *Tell her yes.* But when she opened her mouth, something else came out. "Are you sure that's what you want to do?"

The other end of the connection fell silent.

Suzanne closed her eyes. She'd disappointed Alexa. She pushed aside her selfish wants and focused on her daughter's need. "I'm sorry, sweetheart. I shouldn't have asked that. It wasn't for you. It was for me. Of course you should find out whether he is seeking you. I'd be very surprised at this point if he wasn't."

"Yeah. That's what I was thinking."

Alexa's voice came through subdued rather than eager. Remorse struck Suzanne hard. "Don't let my reaction steal your excitement, honey. It's just hard for me to think of you belonging to any other mother than me. Okay?"

"I don't belong to any other mother." A hard note crept into Alexa's tone — an undercurrent of anger that chilled Suzanne even more than Alexa's earlier excitement had. "And I can't wait to tell the woman who's trying to find me exactly that."

Suzanne started to question her daughter, but Alexa rushed on.

"I'm gonna get off the phone now. You need to get those pies delivered, and I want to drive back to Franklin. Tom and Linda will flip when they hear what I found out from Ms. Reed. Bye, Mom. Love you."

The connection went dead. Suzanne sat staring at the blank screen for several seconds, her heart continuing to thump hard and fast. Alexa didn't want a relationship with her birth mother. She only wanted to let the woman know she wasn't wanted or needed in her life. She should celebrate Alexa's attitude. But instead of elation, sympathy for the unknown woman flooded Suzanne and brought a sting of tears.

If this woman had hired someone to locate Alexa, then she wanted her daughter. Just as Suzanne wanted to claim Anna-Grace. She bowed her head and whispered, "Lord, my emotions are such a muddle. And so are Alexa's, it seems. I don't know how to advise my precious girl, so I'm asking You to guide her. Open her to what You deem best for her even if . . . even if . . ." Could she actually say the words? She swallowed tears and rasped, "Even if it means she forms a relationship with the woman who gave birth to her."

She waited for peace to descend, the peace that always came when she yielded her will to the Father's. But tension stiffened her muscles and made her temples throb. She sighed. As Alexa had said, she needed to deliver the pies. So she started the engine and headed for town.

Paul

Paul hopped out of his pickup and aimed himself for the post office. He hadn't bothered to button his coat — it was plenty warm in the truck cab with the heater blasting — and the chill air slapped against his stomach. He hurried to the door and wrenched the knob, eager to step inside where Mrs. Bartel always had the furnace set high enough to melt chocolate.

As he pulled on the knob, someone from inside pushed, and the door nearly clipped him on the side of the head. He leaped backward as Suzy stepped out of the post office. Memories from their last time together swooped in with as much force as the swinging door and clopped his heart. His gaze zeroed in on her mouth, then bounced to her bright-blue eyes, which seemed to be focused on his lips.

He no longer needed the heat from Mrs. Bartel's furnace. He scuffed another few inches in reverse, putting her out of reach. "H-hi, Suzy."

"Oh . . . Paul."

She seemed so relieved to see him, concern struck. "You okay?"

She shook her head.

He tipped toward her, keeping his hands in his pockets, and lowered his voice to a near whisper. "Is it Anna-Grace?"

She shook her head again.

The little beret-style knitted cap she'd tugged over her head slipped, uncovering one delicate earlobe. Without thinking, he reached up and pulled the nubby blue cap back into place. Color flooded her cheeks, and he jammed his hand into his pocket again. "Then what is it?"

She glanced left and right. He didn't blame her. He hoped nobody saw him make such an intimate gesture. The tongues would start wagging for sure. She lifted her pink-stained face to him. "I can't really talk about it out here. In the open."

"Want to meet someplace? Talk?" He was bound and determined to grease the Arborville gossip wheels. But he cared about her. Hadn't they decided to be friends? So he couldn't just ignore her when she was in distress. Of course he couldn't. He waited while indecision played in her eyes. She wanted to talk to him — confide in him — but she was probably worried about what townsfolk would say. "Tomorrow's Saturday. If you don't have guests at the inn, we could go to Wichita again. Just us this time. No Danny."

The pink in her cheeks changed to splashes of red. "Is that wise?"

Her caution both pleased and aggravated him. "Probably not. But the offer still stands."

She chewed the inside of her cheek, once more searching the street as if expecting someone to rescue her from having to tell him yes or no. The cold must have kept her rescuer at home. She sighed. "Paul, I really would like to talk to someone. I'm confused, and it would probably help to get your opinion on the situation. But if we go to Wichita by ourselves, people will think we're . . ." She dipped her head. "Courting. And that could get you in trouble."

"Because you aren't a member of the fellowship anymore? Or because you showed back up here with a daughter and no husband?"

She flicked a look at him before lowering

her head again. "Both."

He brushed the sole of his boot back and forth on the cold sidewalk, the soft *whish-whish* keeping time with his scampering pulse. He planted his boot. "Suzy." He waited until she lifted her gaze. "Have you given any thought to rejoining the fellowship?" Standing on the post office porch with a January breeze chilling both of them wasn't the best place for this conversation, but maybe there wasn't any good place for it. The whole topic was hard and uncomfortable. No matter how she answered, it would affect him.

"Sure I've thought about it."

"And?"

She shrugged. "I don't know. So much depends on whether I choose to stay here . . . or not."

"You're thinking about going somewhere else?" The question snapped out more sharply than he'd intended. He softened the impact of his words with a hesitant smile.

"My severance package won't last forever. I'll have to find a job eventually. If not here, then somewhere. Nothing's opened up for me within driving distance, but Linda told me I could probably get a job at any hospital in the Franklin area, given my good work record there." Suzy lifted her shoulders in another shrug and held the position. "So I really don't know."

"But would you like to stay — if you can find a job?"

She gazed at his face. The fuzzy collar of her coat framed her jaw and softened the worry lines creasing her forehead. "My daughter . . . both of my daughters . . . are here. My mother and my brother and sisters are here."

I am here, he wanted to add. But he didn't.

"So, yes, I'd like to stay. If God opens a door for me to support myself."

Sadness and maybe even a hint of resentment pricked Paul. Had her years of raising Alexa without a partner stolen her desire to ever share her life with someone? Did she have to be so independent? He pushed those questions aside. "What about the fellowship? If you find a job around here, will you ask to join again?" He swept a deliberate gaze from the top of her covered head — he knew without seeing it that she'd coiled her hair into a bun under that hat — along her coat and skirt and up again. "I still see quite a bit of the Old Order in you."

She finally relaxed her shoulders, releasing a light laugh with the motion. "I suppose one never completely loses the foundation of faith to which she was born."

His pulse gave a hopeful leap. "Then does that mean yes?"

She sighed, her breath hovering in a little cloud. "Paul, if I had to be completely honest, a part of me wants to be a member of the fellowship again. Even though everyone has been kind, it isn't the same to sit in the pew beside Mother and know that my name isn't listed on the membership roster. But if I ask to have my membership reinstated, I'll have to give an account to the deacons of the years I spent away. I'll have to tell . . . everything."

He understood exactly what she meant. He gritted his teeth. The damp breeze had nearly frozen his ears. He needed to get out of the cold. He needed to send her out of the cold. But he wasn't ready to let their conversation end. Talking with Suzy, even when they discussed hard things like telling the fellowship leaders how badly he'd erred when he was an eighteen-year-old youth, revived something inside him that had lain dormant for too long. He wanted her in the fellowship again so he could openly pursue a relationship with her. They had a history together. They could've spent the last twenty years together. Was it too late to build what could have been?

She spoke softly, her expression seeking.

"If I rejoin, are you prepared for the fallout? Because there will be fallout . . ."

"Fallout? Yes. There will be." He leaned close, gazing directly into her wide eyes of sky blue — the eyes that had captured his heart two dozen years ago. "But there could also be restoration. Are you prepared for that?"

CHAPTER 26

Indianapolis
Cynthia

Cynthia stretched and rolled over on the lumpy mattress, cringing when the box springs creaked. Lindsey had warned her the bed was secondhand and would probably be uncomfortable. Lindsey was right. Cynthia rubbed her eyes and then squinted at the plastic digital alarm clock. Almost nine o'clock? How strange to sleep so late. Especially on a Sunday morning.

She sat on the edge of the bed and stared at the spot of floor between her feet. The multicolored speckles on the gray carpet danced as tears flooded her eyes. Right now Glenn and the kids were loading up for the drive to church. Barrett was probably pestering Darcy, and Darcy was probably complaining to Glenn. And Glenn was probably being diplomatic and patient, the way he always was with the kids. Or was his anger at her spilling over on them? She rubbed her eyes again and sniffed hard.

Only four days away and she was so homesick her chest ached. She could hardly eat. Sleep? She couldn't call the short dozes between long hours of tense wakefulness anything resembling sleep. She collapsed on her back with her feet still dangling over the edge of the bed and stared at the popcorn ceiling. What was she doing here?

The apartment was completely quiet. Finally. Lindsey's music had blared until well past two that morning, covering the sounds of whatever she and her three guests had been doing in the combined living and dining room. Based on the random bursts of laughter and slurred voices raised in off-key singing, Cynthia speculated lots of liquor had been included. So different from the Saturday evenings at home with Glenn, playing board games with the kids or watching a DVD and eating milk-drenched popcorn with a spoon.

She missed them. All of them. And the kids missed her. They'd both said so yesterday when she took them home after their day at the mall — Barrett pleadingly and Darcy with more than a hint of anger. They wanted her to come home again. But even though she stood in the little foyer of their house for nearly fifteen minutes talking with the kids about their homework, Glenn had stayed somewhere else in the house. He hadn't said a word to her about coming back.

She pulled up her legs and coiled into a ball on top of the rumpled bedspread. When she'd found her baby girl, she would swallow her pride and ask Glenn if she could come home. But if she asked now, he might expect her to give up the search. She couldn't do it. Not when they were so close.

Owen Mallory's call on Friday had sounded so promising. His final statement reverberated in her memory: *"I'll be shocked if the girl named Anna-Grace Braun isn't really your daughter, hauled to Kansas by Suzanne Zimmerman and given to her relatives to raise."* He'd traveled from Arborville to another little Mennonite town called Sommerfeld and talked to Anna-Grace's adoptive parents. Even though they hadn't told him much, their very secretiveness served to deepen his suppositions. By tomorrow he should be back from Kansas with a spoon he'd pilfered because Anna-Grace had used it. With it he intended to compare her DNA to Cynthia's.

Her entire body trembled, nervousness and anticipation warring for victory. She spoke to the empty room. "Anna-Grace . . ." An old-fashioned name. Nothing like Darcy or Barrett. Or even Cynthia. She'd never allowed herself to attach a name to her baby, and it felt good to have something to call her. It made her more real.

As soon as the DNA results came back, as soon as she knew for sure Anna-Grace really was the baby girl she'd left behind the garage, as soon as she'd made contact with Anna-Grace and secured her daughter's forgiveness, then she would go home. It shouldn't be much longer now. Not much longer at all.

Franklin, Indiana
Alexa

After church Tom and Linda took Alexa to their favorite pizza restaurant for the Sunday buffet. The restaurant was crowded, families with kids in tow swarming the salad and pizza bars. Alexa would have preferred going to the house and baking her own pizza, but she kept her opinion to herself. Tom loved busy places where lots of people gathered. He claimed he stored up energy from being around noisy, rambunctious crowds. Alexa used to be the same way. But lately, bustling places seemed to drain the life from her. By the time she slid into their booth, she was ready for a nap.

Linda took one look at her and started to laugh.

Alexa glanced over her shoulder, half expecting a clown to lurk there. "What?"

"Your face, that's what! You look like you'd rather be anywhere than here — even in a dentist chair."

Alexa sighed. "At least I'd be the only one in the chair." She scanned the noisy room. "Half the population of Franklin is here, don'tcha think?"

Tom chuckled. "Probably more like a third. This, the Chinese buffet, and the fried chicken place always do a booming business on Sundays." He grinned, lifting his head and pulling in a deep breath. "Ahhh, the sound of family. I can't get enough of it."

Alexa hung her head. So that's why he liked crowds. At home it was only him and Linda. How much they'd missed by not raising a big, boisterous brood of their own. She gave Tom a sympathetic look. "I'm sorry I complained."

He reached across the table and took her hand, his smile intact. "No worries, honey-girl. Your mind's a little cluttered right now, so all this disorder is bound to seem overwhelming to you. Let's pray, huh? Then we'll eat and skedaddle on out of here."

While Tom asked a blessing for their meal, Alexa vowed to eat slowly so Tom could enjoy the ruckus as long as he wanted to.

"Amen." He picked up a piece of greasy pepperoni. "Mm-mm, I can feel my arteries clogging already, but it's gonna be worth it." He took a mighty chomp.

Linda rolled her eyes, shaking her head. "You're worse than a kid."

He waggled his eyebrows at her.

While witnessing their antics, Alexa's sour mood faded. She picked up a slice of mushroom and ham thin-crust pizza and tried to take as large a bite as Tom had. She ended up with tomato sauce all over her cheeks, which made Tom and Linda both laugh, and the remainder of her doldrums disappeared. She swiped her face clean with a napkin and asked the question that had rolled in the back of her mind and stolen her focus during the morning sermon. "Do you think the private investigator will call me on a Sunday? I left my cell phone on the dresser in my room."

"If he does," Linda said staunchly, "he'll leave a message, and you can call him back tomorrow. One more day of waiting isn't going to kill you."

Alexa huffed, but she smiled afterward so Linda would know she was teasing. "I never thought I'd die from waiting. But I'm surprised he didn't call right away when he got my message. After all, if he's hunting for the baby that was left behind the home, I'd think he'd be glad to get a call from the very person he's trying to find."

"Could be he hasn't got the message yet." Tom pointed his half-eaten pizza slice at her. "Or maybe he's working more than one case. Has to focus on something else for a little while first."

If he'd traveled all the way to Arborville, it seemed to Alexa he was pursuing her with his whole attention. But what did she know about private investigating? Maybe he was juggling several cases at once. "If he hasn't called me back by tomorrow, I'll call and leave another message."

"You do that." Linda chopped her pizza into chunks with her fork. "And we'll keep checking Facebook and the mailbox, too. Even if he doesn't respond, something'll eventually turn up. All the praying we've done won't be for naught."

"Not to change the subject, but . . ." Tom pointed to a table where a man, woman, and four kids ranging in age from maybe four to sixteen chowed down on pizza and breadsticks. "Look at that bunch. Betcha that's a newly formed stepfamily. Or maybe two single parents having lunch together."

Linda gazed at the table for a few minutes, then turned to Tom. "Why do you think that?"

"See how the two younger kids look like each other and the two older ones look alike? The little ones are gravitating to Mom, and the older two are kinda keeping their distance from her — like they aren't too sure they really like her yet. And the man, he's ignoring the younger ones' lack of manners, but I saw him correct the boy sitting next to him. Makes me think that one belongs to him but the little ones don't." He nodded, his expression smug. "Yep. Blended family."

Alexa sipped her soda while furtively watching the family.

Tom went on thoughtfully. "It's gotta be a little awkward at first, taking care of somebody else's kids or letting some new mom or dad come into your life. People do it every day, what with the divorce rate being as high as it is. But I can't imagine it's easy to bring two families together and make 'em into one. It's hard enough just for a man and woman to handle it when they marry up. Then throw a handful of kids into the mix? That'd be a real challenge."

He jerked his attention to Alexa, his

eyebrows rising. "I just thought of something. Our Suzanne never married, so she didn't have any other kids after you. But maybe your birth mom did things different. Maybe she's got a husband and children. If that's the case, when you meet her, you might get to meet some brothers or sisters, too."

The soda soured in Alexa's stomach. She set the cup aside.

Tom kept grinning, wonder lighting his dark eyes. "That'd sure be something."

It would be something, all right. Hadn't she always wanted younger siblings? She'd begged Mom to have another baby until she understood where babies came from. Then she'd quit asking. But she kept praying for a brother or sister until she hit her high school years. By then she figured Mom was too old to want another child and gave up. But she never stopped wishing for a whole family.

Linda snorted. "You're just now thinkin' of that? I considered it from the time Alexa said she wanted to start hunting her mama. I think it's a lot more likely Alexa does have half-siblings than doesn't." She turned a smile on Alexa. "So whaddaya think of the idea, Alexa? Think you'd like being a big sister?"

Alexa swallowed a lump of agony. "I'd . . .

I'd love it, I think."

Tom beamed. " 'Course you would! You'd be a good big sister, too. A good role model, good listener, good advisor, good —"

"Gracious sakes, Tom, look at the girl's face. You're scaring her to death, telling her all the things she'll have to be all at once." Linda patted Alexa's hand. "Don't you worry one bit, girlie. If we find out your mama had other kids, you won't have to dive into a relationship with them any more than you'll have to dive into one with your mama. You can ease in, okay?"

Alexa managed a shaky nod.

Linda sat back and gestured toward Alexa's plate. "Now go ahead and finish eating. The noise in here is about to give me a headache. I'm ready for some peace and quiet."

"Not 'til I've had my fill of dessert pizza," Tom announced. "Lemme out, Linda. They just brought out a fresh cherry one, and I want some before it all gets snatched up."

Linda wriggled out of the booth and stood aside while Tom departed. Then she slid back in. She shot a frown at Alexa's plate. "Why aren't you eating?"

Alexa grimaced. "I kind of lost my appetite, I guess."

" 'Cause of what Tom said about you having brothers or sisters?"

"Uh-huh."

Sympathy creased Linda's round face. "Oh, honey, you don't need to worry about that."

Yes, she did.

Linda leaned over her plate, bringing her face closer to Alexa's. "Lemme tell you something. You already know I come from a big family."

Alexa nodded. "Fourteen brothers and sisters in all." She'd often tried to imagine that many children around a dinner table, but the image wouldn't gel.

"That's right. But there's something you don't know. Only six of us were born to my mama and daddy." Linda nodded when Alexa gasped. "That's right. The other eight were my cousins — children from two of my daddy's brothers. Their mamas just dropped them off with us, and my parents raised 'em." Her face took on a dreamy expression, as if she'd drifted into her past. "Sometimes my daddy did special things for me and my sister and brothers — gave us presents, took us places — that he didn't do for the nieces and nephews. Even though he gave them a place to stay and a decent upbringing, sometimes I thought he felt burdened by all those extra children."

She gave a little jolt, as if coming awake. "But you know what? My mama never played favorites among us. Not ever. She loved each one of us — her born children and her took-in children — just as much as the next."

A tender expression crept through Linda's eyes. "You see, God did something extra special when He crafted a mother's heart. He made it expandable, so no matter how many children came along, she'd have enough love to cover all of them. If your birth mama does have other children, she'll still have love left over for you. She's probably saved a little part of her heart just for you, for the day when she'd meet up with you again." She nodded, giving Alexa a big smile. "It'll all work out. You just wait and see."

Alexa thanked Linda and took a nibble of her pizza to assure her she'd set her worries aside. But she couldn't bring herself to share the real source of worry. If her birth mother had other children, Alexa would want to know them. She'd want to be their big sister and claim them as her siblings.

But how could she have them unless she allowed her birth mother into her life?

CHAPTER 27

Arborville
Suzanne

Suzanne loved Sandra. Becoming re-acquainted with her good-natured sister was one of the best things about returning to Arborville. But on this Sunday afternoon, she had to repeatedly remind herself how much she loved her youngest sister to keep from growling at her. What was Sandra thinking, inviting Paul and Danny to Sunday dinner and then putting Suzanne right beside Paul at the table? Actually, Suzanne knew what Sandra was thinking — and she'd need to set her sister straight as soon as everybody cleared out. Not that it seemed it would be anytime soon.

The children's happy voices carried from the living room, where they built towers with Ian's massive set of homemade wooden blocks. Since they were having such a good time, the adults lingered over dessert and

coffee. Multiple conversations took place —
Shelley and Harper with Mother, Derek
with Tanya, Steven holding Clete's attention, and Paul commending Sandra on the
wonderful meal. The meal itself, a beef-and-
noodle casserole layered with basil and cottage cheese, had probably been fairly easy
to prepare. But Suzanne couldn't imagine
how Sandra had found time to bake dozens
of little pecan pie tarts and bite-sized apple
turnovers when she had an active three-
year-old and a learning-to-crawl baby
underfoot. Given her sister's accomplish-
ments, Suzanne needed to quit complaining
about baking pies five mornings a week. At
least she had a helper rather than two little
hindrances.

Suzanne gazed toward the opposite end of
the table at her helper. Anna-Grace sat smiling up into Steven's face as he explained his
desire to update the math curriculum at the
Arborville school. A lump filled Suzanne's
throat. Anna-Grace's pride in her soon-
to-be husband beamed in her expression.
Each time Steven glanced at her, tenderness glowed in his eyes. They'd weathered a
major storm and emerged on the other side
even more in love with each other. She
couldn't ask for anything better for her child
than to love and be loved by a solid,

hardworking, Christian man. She prayed Alexa would find similar happiness someday.

"You're staring."

The whispered voice in her ear made her jump. She jerked her head and found Paul leaning close, a secretive grin on his face. She licked her lips. "W-what?"

"At Anna-Grace." He flicked a look across the table, then returned his brown-sugar gaze to her. "It's hard not to, I know. I struggle with it myself. She's a beautiful girl. You can just see happiness on her." His eyes took on a sheen of moisture, but he blinked and it disappeared.

Suzanne blinked rapidly, too. "I'm glad she's happy. I was just thinking that I couldn't ask for anything better for her than to marry a good Christian man like Steven. But I can't help wishing . . ."

"That you could be part of her life, too?"

She nodded.

"At least you can be Cousin Suzy to her. I'm just Mr. Aldrich, the man who renovated her house." Pain laced his quiet voice.

"Oh, Paul . . ." Once again she berated herself for her attitude. When had she become so self-centered? First complaints about baking the pies and now about having to deny her true relationship with Anna-Grace. Paul was right. She at least had time with their daughter on a daily basis. Even though it hurt to be near her and unable to claim her, she and Anna-Grace had become friends. She touched his arm. "I'm sorry. I wish —"

He shook his head. "No more wishing, okay? It only leads to dissatisfaction."

He was right about that, too. All the wishing in the world couldn't change their situation. She needed to focus on the positives of now rather than wallowing in what could have been.

He added, "We've been blessed in spite of it all." The clatter of blocks followed by Danny's exultant "Woo-hoo!" and a burst of children's laughter exploded from the front room. Paul whisked a grin in the children's direction and then aimed it at Suzanne. "Probably more than we deserve."

She started to agree with him, but Shelley interrupted.

"Suzy, pass the apple turnovers this way, would you? Mother wants another one."

Reluctantly Suzanne turned her attention from Paul to the half-empty platter.

Mother grimaced. "I shouldn't have more. I've already had two little pies and three turnovers, but something about the cold weather increases my appetite. I can't seem to get enough."

"Please finish them off," Sandra said. "If you don't, I will, and I don't need any more sweets." She patted her stomach, twisting her lips into a scowl. "I can't seem to lose my baby fat this time." She looked forlornly at Derek. "It came off faster with Ian, didn't it?"

He shrugged sheepishly. "I don't know. You always look the same to me."

Sandra frowned.

"Beautiful." He delivered a quick peck on her lips that erased the scowl.

Sandra laughed. "Well, I'd like my dresses to fit more comfortably. As soon as this cold weather clears, I'll start walking. That should help."

Anna-Grace turned to Sandra. "Oh, Cousin Sandra, I wish Steven's house —"

"Our house," he corrected.

She giggled. "Our house was closer to town. I'd walk with you every day. I love getting out, and it would be so fun to walk with you, Isabella, and Ian. Little ones turn the simplest events into an adventure." Her cheerful expression clouded. "I miss Mom and Dad, but I think I miss Sunny the most. Even though she's fourteen years younger than me, we had so much fun together."

Shelley said, "Do your folks let her call you? As little as she is, she might forget you if she doesn't stay in contact."

Suzanne swallowed a gasp. Did Shelley have any idea how tactless her statement was? And painful. Shelley and Sandra had been so young when she left home. How close might they be if she'd stayed in Arborville during her sisters' growing-up years?

Anna-Grace turned a wide-eyed look at Shelley. "Sunny won't forget me! We talk on Saturday afternoons when Mom calls, and I write her letters twice a week. She sends me pictures in return, and across the bottom she always writes, 'I love you, Sissy.' "

Shelley's husband, Harper, leaned forward, blocking Shelley from Suzanne's view. "You and Sunny will stay close. You and your folks will make sure of it. Don't worry."

Anna-Grace's stiff shoulders relaxed. A weak smile curved her lips.

Harper turned to Steven. "Just curious about something, if you don't mind me asking. Since Sommerfeld is really home to both of you, do you think about going back there to live? There are two schools where Steven could teach if a position opened up."

Beside Suzanne, Paul pulled in a short

breath. She understood. Her pulse sped. If she stayed in Arborville, would it make her life easier or harder if Anna-Grace moved back to Sommerfeld?

Steven and Anna-Grace exchanged warm glances. Steven said, "We've talked about it some. Both of our families are there, and especially when we have kids —"

Pain stabbed Suzanne's heart while a pretty blush stole over Anna-Grace's face.

"— it'd be nice to be close to the grandparents."

Paul's hand rested on the edge of the table. His fingers curled into a fist. Suzanne battled the temptation to place her hand over his, share the anguish she knew he was suffering. *Our grandchildren,* her heart cried.

"But that's a ways in the future. I haven't even finished my first year of teaching here yet, and who knows if one of the Sommerfeld teachers plans to leave anytime soon. So we'll just have to wait and see what the Lord has in store for us."

Steven's answer seemed to satisfy everyone else around the table, but Suzanne couldn't focus on the continued conversation. Her mind flooded with fuzzy images of Steven and Anna-Grace's children. Blond-haired and blue-eyed, for sure, given the parents' features. Little ones who would call Paul

"Mr. Aldrich" and her "Cousin Suzy." If the title stabbed each time Anna-Grace used it, how would her heart survive hearing her grandbabies refer to her that way?

She leaped up, banging her chair's legs against the floor. Everyone stopped talking and looked at her. Considering the racket in the next room, she couldn't believe they'd heard the thud of the legs. Instead, her abrupt movement had probably captured their attention. It must have seemed as though she'd been fired from a cannon. She tamped down a hysterical giggle.

"Sandra —" Her voice sounded shrill. Unnatural. She took a steadying breath. "Let me help you clear the table, and then I think I'll head home. I'd like to give Alexa a call and see how . . . how she's doing."

Shelley frowned at Suzanne. "When exactly is she coming back? I understand wanting a vacation. Gracious sakes, she worked so hard getting that farmhouse fixed up and then opening a business. But she's been gone more than two weeks already. I can't imagine being away from home for that long."

Suzanne forced a light laugh. "I'm sure Tom and Linda are having so much fun with her they aren't ready to send her back yet. She'll be here in time for Anna-Grace's wedding, though."

Anna-Grace released a dramatic sigh. "That's good. Because she promised to bake the cakes." She grinned at Steven. "Carrot cake for you, and white cake with raspberry filling for me, right?"

"Right." The pair locked gazes, seeming to forget anyone else was in the room.

Mother glanced at the two young people and cleared her throat, her lips twitching with a compressed smile. "Well, Suzy, if you're leaving, I guess that means I have to go, too. So let's get this mess cleared, and we'll all scoot out of Sandra and Derek's way. They'd probably like to get their little ones down for a nap soon anyway."

Suzanne hadn't intended to break up the gathering, and she said so.

Sandra offered her an impish grin. "It's okay, Suzy. I'm about ready for a nap myself. For some reason Isabella woke up around two and wanted to play. She was so cute I couldn't deny her, but it made for a short night."

The women collected the used items from the table and carried everything to the kitchen. With six of them helping, they brought it all in one trip, then bumped into each other trying to get it organized for washing.

Sandra laughingly waved her hands at the crowd. "Everybody, go home! Derek and I will get this."

Anna-Grace gawked at Sandra. "Derek helps with dishes?"

Sandra giggled. "Yep. He always has." She glanced toward the kitchen doorway as if making sure nobody listened in, then lowered her voice to a raspy whisper. "He helps with laundry, sweeps the floors for me, and changes Isabella's diapers, too. The only things he won't do are cook and dust."

Shelley snorted, scraping food scraps into the trash bin. "Personally, I think it's shameful. He has his job and you have yours. Do you go to the Feed and Seed and help him during the day? Of course not. So why do you expect him to take over your work at home?"

Hurt flickered in Sandra's eyes, but she answered kindly. "I don't expect it of him, Shelley. He just does it." Shelley rolled her eyes. Sandra turned to Anna-Grace. "We like doing dishes together because we talk while we work. Him helping with housework probably isn't traditional, but who says everything has to be done the way it always has been? Not every new idea is bad."

Tanya nodded. "I agree. And why shouldn't men know how to clean house and cook meals? Sometimes they end up alone. Like Paul Aldrich. I bet being a widower and having to take care of everything himself would have been a lot easier for him if he'd already spent some time helping Karina with household chores. Clete isn't one to help me on a regular basis, but if something happened to me, I know he'd at least be able to keep the house clean, the kids fed, and laundry done. I've made sure of it."

Shelley clapped the last plate onto the counter. "Well, I haven't asked Harper to lift one finger with either the housework or the children. He has his job and I have mine. If something happens to me, Ruby and Pearl will see to the chores for their father. They're learning to be wives and mothers from me." She folded her arms over her chest and bounced an imperative smirk over the circle of women. "I happen to like the traditional way of doing things."

Mother muttered, "You just enjoy being able to complain about your heavy workload."

Shelley stomped out of the kitchen.

Mother patted Sandra's arm. "The Bible says woman is meant to be man's helpmeet, but I don't see anything barring a man from being the woman's helpmeet, too. When your father and I were first married, he helped me with the dishes for the same reason you just said. It gave us a chance to talk and catch up on the day's events. Of course, when Suzy got big enough to take on chores, she started doing the dishes. Then Clete helped her."

Tanya's eyes widened. "My Clete did dishes?"

Mother chuckled. "He sure did. And folded laundry and scrubbed baseboards."

Tanya's jaw dropped, and she stared toward the dining room, where the rumble of men's voices continued to roll. "That stinker! He always acts so helpless when it comes to housework." Her gaze narrowed, a cunning look entering her eyes. "Well, he's been exposed. Guess who's going to dry dishes for me tomorrow?"

The women all laughed. Suzanne joined in, but her laugh was more restrained than the others'. Sandra shooed them all from the kitchen, and as Suzanne passed through the dining room, she found herself focusing on Paul. He'd been alone for more than three years now, and clearly he and Danny had managed on their own. They were both well fed, clean, and well dressed. She'd never seen the inside of his house, but since he and Danny were so neat looking, it stood to reason the house was clean, too.

Paul, do you no longer have the need for a helpmeet? Oh, how she wanted him to need someone. To need her. Pressure built in her chest, and she hurried back to the kitchen and pulled Sandra away from the stack of dirty dishes. "Sandra . . ."

Her sister turned, and immediately concern etched lines in her forehead. "What's wrong?"

How intuitive she was. Suzanne blinked several times to bring her tears under control and forced her lips into a quavering smile. "I need you to help me with something."

Sandra gripped Suzanne's hands. "Anything."

"I need you to help distance me from Paul Aldrich." She ignored Sandra's startled intake of breath and hurried on, determined to say everything before she lost her nerve. "He and I . . . we agreed to be friends, but I fear Mother is right that friendship between a single man and a single lady doesn't work very well. One person's feelings will run deeper than the other, and someone . . ." She gulped. "Someone inevitably gets hurt. So, please, when our families are together, will you be the barrier between us?"

"Oh, Suzy . . ." Sympathy laced Sandra's tone, and fresh tears pricked Suzanne's eyes. Her sister, her little sister — two inches shorter and a dozen years younger — pulled her into a snug embrace. Suzanne clung, absorbing the comfort Sandra offered. Sandra whispered against her cheek, "Your feelings are running deep, aren't they?"

Suzanne managed a brief nod. She whispered, her breath stirring the black ribbon on her sister's cap, "But I can't let them. I have to stop thinking of Paul as anything more than a friend. He doesn't want more. I lost him once. I can't go through that again."

Sandra squeezed tight, then released Suzanne. She peered into Suzanne's face, her brow furrowed. "I'll do what you've asked, but are you sure it will help? Once I started loving Derek, I don't think anything could have changed my heart. You can't turn love off like a faucet, Suzy."

"Well, I have to." She drew in a determined breath. If she couldn't stifle the flow of emotion coursing through her for Paul, she'd have to leave Arborville again. This time for good.

CHAPTER 28

Indianapolis
Cynthia

On Monday morning Cynthia pulled up in front of her house and beeped the horn. Glenn should already be gone. He liked to be in his classroom a good half hour before the buzzer rang. But just in case he'd changed his routine to accommodate the kids being home alone, she didn't want to go up and ring the bell. Moments later the front door popped open, and Barrett and Darcy stepped out. Barrett remained on the stoop while Darcy secured the door, and then the two of them ambled across the dry grass together, their shoulders occasionally bumping.

Watching their cheerless progress, Cynthia battled tears. What had happened to her boy who galloped to the car, her girl who disdained walking beside her little brother? The two of them had changed so much in the few days she'd been away from them. *Lord, let Mr. Mallory find my baby girl so I can come home.* The plea twisted her heart. Would Glenn and the kids get used to not having her around and decide it was okay to go on without her? It had never taken her mom long to get over one lost boyfriend and replace him with another.

Darcy slid into the passenger seat and Barrett flopped into the back. They slammed the car doors in unison. Hard. Rocking the vehicle. Ordinarily Cynthia would caution them. Glenn said slamming car doors loosened the fittings. But instead of scolding she smiled. "Ready to go?"

Neither smiled in reply, but Darcy said, "Yeah."

Cynthia waited until they snapped their seat belts into place, then she pulled into the street. She drove to the end of the block and turned onto Center Street. Other mothers were pulling out of driveways, making the morning run to school. Glances in those vehicles showed bouncing children, mothers' mouths moving either in reprimand or instruction. Cynthia could imagine the racket within those interiors. But in her car, things were quiet. Deathly so. Unnerving. She gripped the steering wheel with both hands and counted the seconds, waiting for one of the kids to say something. But they didn't.

She cleared her throat and forced a cheerful tone. "Did you guys have breakfast, or do we need to hit a drive-through?" She glanced at Barrett in the rearview mirror, anticipating his eager grin. Even if he'd already eaten, he wouldn't turn down a sausage biscuit.

Barrett stared out the side window. He acted as if he hadn't heard the question.

Darcy fiddled with her backpack straps. "We ate."

"What did you have?"

"Cereal and toast."

Cynthia sneaked another peek at Barrett. "Are you sure you don't want something more?"

Her son didn't respond.

Still hopeful, she said, "We have time. We can stop."

Darcy angled a derisive look at her mother. "Give it up, Mom. We aren't little kids. You can't buy us off with Happy Meals."

Cynthia wanted to argue that wasn't what she was trying to do, but she couldn't bring herself to lie. If only the kids would relax, laugh, talk the way they always had together on the drive to school. The cloying silence made her want to shriek in agony. She tightened her grip on the steering wheel and gritted her teeth for a moment. Then she braved a question. "What'll it take then?"

Out of her peripheral vision, she watched Darcy pucker her lips in and out, her intense gaze fixed on Cynthia's profile, as if plotting something wild and extravagant. Cynthia waited, anticipating an imaginative, clever, teasing response from her flamboyant daughter.

"You already know."

The flat response deflated her. Yes, she supposed she did. Cynthia sighed. "Darcy, do you think I like being away from you and Barrett?"

"And Daddy!" Barrett barked the words, suddenly coming to life.

"And Daddy," Cynthia echoed. She shook her head. "I hate it. It's hard. Harder than anything, ever." And she'd lived a hundred hard lives before she married Glenn.

"Harder than giving away your baby?" How snide Darcy sounded.

Cynthia swallowed. "Even harder than that. Because I gave her away to save her. It was the best thing to do at the time. But this . . ." Tears distorted her vision. She blinked rapidly. She needed to focus to drive.

"But this isn't for us. It's for you. Is that what you were going to say?"

Cynthia couldn't look at Darcy. Her daughter's words — too true and too wise for her young years — pierced her.

Darcy sighed and turned her gaze forward. "Can't see how it's so all-blamed hard to be selfish."

Cynthia should reprimand Darcy for her attitude and her choice of words. Glenn didn't tolerate disrespectfulness, and he'd never allowed cursing, not even in mild forms. He said people who resorted to curse words were taking the lazy way out instead of expressing themselves in a civilized way. But she didn't have the energy to argue. Especially because Darcy was right.

She pulled up to the junior high, and Darcy unsnapped her seat belt. She threw the door open and shot a glance into the backseat. "Bye, Barrett. Have a good day." Then she bounced out and gave the door a solid whack that slammed it into its casing.

Cynthia hit the Down button on the passenger window and called, "Bye, Darcy!" Darcy, her sleek brown ponytail swishing wildly over her shoulders, didn't even pause. With a sigh Cynthia raised the window and then aimed a sad smile at her son. "Okay, buckaroo, your turn."

Barrett scowled. "Dad calls us buckaroo."

Cynthia snapped, "Well, excuse me. I didn't realize he held exclusive rights to the nickname."

Barrett hunkered low and stared out the window again.

Cynthia eased back into traffic, inwardly berating herself. She might not like the kids' attitudes, but she understood them. Their world had been turned upside down, and she was the one who'd flipped it. She'd never wanted to be like her mother, who constantly stole her children's sense of security, but she'd ended up like Mom after all.

The grade school was only three blocks from Darcy's junior high, and they reached it within minutes. She pulled into line behind other cars waiting to unload students. Barrett reached for the door handle, and she said, "Wait. It's cold. We'll be at the door soon." He slunk back against the seat with his arms folded over his chest.

The tension in the car was awful. Cynthia found herself eager to let her son out so she could breathe again. Then she inwardly kicked herself for once again being selfish. They inched forward as other cars departed, and finally they were two car lengths from the school's front doors. "Almost there," she said, choosing a light tone that contrasted with the tightness in her chest.

Her phone rang. She reached into her purse and pulled it out. Mr. Mallory's number glared up at her. She clicked On and pressed it to her ear. "Hello?"

"Mrs. Allgood, do you have time this morning to come by my office? I need a mouth swab from you, and I also want you to listen to a message on my machine."

Cynthia needed to be at the library by nine, but if she hurried, she could make it. "Yes, I can do that. So you're back from Kansas?"

"Yep. Front door's unlocked. Just let yourself in. I'll give you a full report of my time in Kansas while you're here. I think you'll be pleased."

She cringed. "How many hours did you rack up?"

A laugh blasted her ear. "Lots. But don't worry about that. Just get over here."

Her pulse leaped, both worry and anticipation battling within her. "Okay, thanks. I'll see you soon." She dropped her phone and twisted around to send a smile into the backseat. "Barrett, guess what? Mr. Mallory —" Her voice stilled. The backseat was empty.

Barrett had slipped out, and she hadn't

even realized it.

Franklin
Alexa

Alexa tucked a pan of cinnamon rolls in the oven and set the timer. She was getting too used to these lazy mornings. Neither Linda nor Tom, who operated on what Tom called their "retirement clock," wandered out of their bedroom before eight. She presumed the smell of rolls and coffee would rouse them soon enough, though, so she poured herself a cup of rich black coffee and sat at the table to wait for them.

As she lifted the cup to her mouth, her cell phone rang. She glanced at the clock, frowning. Who would call her so early? The number seemed vaguely familiar, but she couldn't place it. She flicked the phone on and offered a hesitant greeting. "Hello?"

A gruff male voice boomed, "Is this Alexa Zimmerman?"

"Yes. Who is this?"

"Ms. Zimmerman, Owen Mallory here."

The PI! Alexa automatically jolted to her feet. She bumped the table, and coffee splashed over the edge of the cup. She gripped the phone with both hands and rasped, "Y-yes, Mr. Mallory. You must have gotten my message."

"I did. And I'd like to talk to you. But not on the phone. In person. Can you come to my office today?"

Her heart set up a thrum stronger than any bass drum. "What time?"

"What time suits you?"

She scrambled for a reply. Tom and Linda were still in bed, the rolls were in the oven, she hadn't brushed her hair yet, it was at least a thirty-minute commute to downtown Indianapolis . . . "Maybe, um, tenish?"

"Let's say ten thirty. Will that work?"

Alexa hoped Tom wouldn't mind. "Yes."

"All right. See you then." The line went dead.

Alexa hugged the phone to her chest, her breath puffing out worse than after she'd run the hurdles in high school track. Ten thirty. Two and a half hours. How would she last that long? She raced up the hallway to Tom and Linda's room and banged on their door.

"What — Who's out there?" Linda didn't sound at all pleased.

Alexa pressed her face close to the door. "It's me, Linda. You guys have to get up. You have to get up now."

"Is the house on fire?"

"No."

"Are you bleeding?"

Alexa danced in place. "No!"

"Then what's so important?"

"I have to go to Indianapolis. The private investigator called and he wants to see me." She pressed her ear to the door. Scuffling noises came from behind the wood along with muffled whispers.

The doorknob turned and Alexa stepped back. Tom, decked out in his Christmas plaid bathrobe, grinned at her from the other side of the opening. "He wants to see you, huh?"

She nodded eagerly, her entire frame trembling. "Yes. At ten thirty."

Tom squinted at the little clock on the dresser, then looked at Linda, who sat up in bed with her hair all askew. "What'cha think? Do we send her by herself, or do we go with her?"

Linda flung the covers aside and hooked her heels on the edge of the bed, pulling herself out. "You must've lost every bit of sense the Good Lord gave you if you'd even consider sending her off to some strange man's office all by herself." She waved at Alexa while she marched toward the door of their attached private bathroom. "Pour me a big cup of coffee, girlie. I'll be out after I've dunked my head in cold water and woken myself up."

Alexa laughed and Tom joined her. He winked. "Ditto on that coffee." He chucked her under the chin with his knuckles. "Settle yourself down now. We'll be ready soon."

Alexa headed for the kitchen. She borrowed one of Linda's favorite phrases and called over her shoulder, "Don't dally now. Time's a-wastin'."

Tom laughed and closed the door.

Alexa tapped her phone and pulled up her mother's number. One more tap of her finger, and the call connected. She waited for Mom's hello and then blurted, "Mom, guess what!"

Indianapolis
Cynthia

Cynthia sat forward, tense and attentive, in the hard plastic chair in Mr. Mallory's office and listened to the voice-mail recording. *"My name is Alexa Zimmerman. I was abandoned behind the Indianapolis Home for Unwed Mothers in December twenty years ago. Ms. Reed from the home told me you'd been there asking about records. I thought you might want to talk to me. Please return my call at —"*

Mr. Mallory pushed the button to silence the machine. He rocked in his chair and squinted across his desk at Cynthia. "That voice sound at all familiar to you?"

Cynthia eased into the chair, frowning. "Should it?"

He shrugged. "Dunno. That's why I'm asking."

"Play it again." He did, and she listened intently. She shook her head. "No. It isn't familiar."

"Okay. Well, I'll be talking to her. Interrogating her, actually, just to make sure this isn't some stunt."

Cynthia jolted. "A stunt? Why would somebody pretend to have been abandoned?"

He chuckled. "Mrs. Allgood, there are all sorts of people in the world, and attention getters make up a strong percentage of the population. You wouldn't believe how many people crawl out of the woodwork when rewards are posted or a plea's made for the public's help in apprehending a criminal."

"I haven't offered any reward."

"Didn't say you had. But some people's reward is just getting noticed — feeling like they're important. This girl might be one of that kind. Especially considering I've already got a strong lead on where your baby ended up." He bounced his fist lightly off the envelope of samples. "The DNA will prove or disprove my theory soon enough."

Cynthia gripped her hands. "How long 'til you get the results?"

A sly grin climbed his cheek. "A week at most. One nice thing about having connections with the police department is getting access to the crime lab. Got a buddy there who helps me out now and then. He'll run the swabs in between his other duties and let me know."

Cynthia pulled in a big breath and let it out slowly. "A week . . ."

"Yep. I'll swab the girl who left the message, too, after I've talked to her." He laughed. "That'll make her feel important. Then if the first swab I took doesn't match yours, we'll run hers. Fair enough?"

"Fair enough." Worry struck hard. She bit her lower lip for a moment, gathering courage. "Mr. Mallory, I'm sure you've already used up our retainer. How much more am I going to owe you before this search is complete?"

He flopped a notebook open and ran his finger down a column, his eyebrows pinching so close they formed one bushy line above his gray eyes. "I wrote off my travel hours and only clocked the ones I actually used for research while I was in Kansas. Right now you've got two hours left on the clock."

"Will that . . . be enough, do you think?"

He closed the book and shrugged. "Hard to say. Let's worry about that bridge when it comes time to cross it. In the meantime lay low and wait for me to call." He grinned again. "If all goes the way I think it will, you'll have an answer by the beginning of next week."

CHAPTER 29

Arborville
Suzanne

Thank goodness it was Monday. The café was closed, so she didn't need to bake pies. Suzanne's hands were shaking so badly that if she tried to peel and slice apples she'd probably cut off her own thumb. She could hide out in the cottage instead and pray the morning away.

She stared at her phone, which lay on the table and blinked off the seconds. Alexa's voice rang in her mind. *"Just think, Mom, by the end of today I could call you with the name of the woman who left me to freeze in the alley."* Alexa had sounded excited, but there was also a hard edge to her tone. A resentment so unlike her normally kind, forgiving daughter. But Suzanne hadn't tried to correct her or advise her. She'd just promised to be in prayer.

Now she needed to figure out how to pray.

She paced the floor, her stocking-covered feet echoing dully on the hardwood floors. Should she go to the house and ask Mother to pray with her? No, Anna-Grace was in there. They couldn't risk her overhearing. Maybe she should drive to town — ask for Tanya or Sandra to join her in prayer. She shook her head. How could they focus with toddlers underfoot? Besides that, Mother always said, "Little pitchers have big ears." Clete and Tanya's Jana and Derek and Sandra's Ian had big ears and the ability to repeat whatever they heard. She couldn't go to either of their houses. Shelley would be alone. Suzanne almost laughed. Had she really considered going to Shelley? She shuddered, imagining Shelley's reaction if she showed up unannounced on her doorstep.

If Linda wasn't with Alexa, she'd call her longtime mentor and ask her how best to help Alexa through the conflict. Linda would have advice ready, and she'd pray with Suzanne without even being asked. But she couldn't pull Linda away from Alexa now. Alexa needed her even more than Suzanne did.

Her feet slowed to a stop, and she stared unseeingly out the window at the empty cornfield behind the house. The barren field seemed a reflection of the hollowness in her chest. "If only I had a friend here in Arborville . . ."

Another voice rose in her memory and whispered through her mind. *"What I'm saying is, anytime you need to talk about Anna-Grace, you can come to me. You don't have to hide in the barn and cry. Okay?"* Twice already she'd called Paul and unburdened herself about Anna-Grace. He'd proven his willingness to be her friend and listener. Would he still be as willing if she needed to talk about Alexa? If she needed him to pray with her?

"I just need a friend." She groaned the statement to the empty room. Quickly, before she could talk herself out of it, she marched to the table, snatched up her phone, and punched his number.

Paul

Paul, coat buttoned to the collar and baseball cap secure over his hair, reached for the front door. As he closed his hand on the doorknob, the telephone on the kitchen wall blared. Eagerness to hop in the truck and make his trip to Wichita pulled hard. Surely whoever it was could wait until he got back. He listened to the rings — five in a row. Then six. And seven. He grimaced.

The call must be important or they would've hung up by now.

He trotted to the kitchen and snatched up the receiver in the middle of the ninth ring. "Aldrich Construction."

"Hello, Paul."

Boy, was he glad he'd answered the phone. He leaned against the wall, his muscles turning liquid. "Hi, Suzy."

"Are you busy?"

He was. He had an order of twelve-foot Sheetrock waiting in Wichita, and he'd promised to be there before noon to retrieve it. "Not particularly."

"Do you have time to talk?"

A grin yanked at his lips. He'd thought about her all day Saturday, wishing he'd been able to convince her to drive to Wichita with him. Then sitting beside her Sunday at Derek and Sandra's place had stirred all kinds of old feelings. He wanted time with her. He wanted more than just time. "Sure we can. But —" He glanced at the wall clock. He really needed to go, but he didn't want to put her off. An idea struck. He straightened and let his words race from his mouth. "I need to make a run to Wichita. Wanna ride along? We can talk all the way up, maybe grab some lunch in town, then talk all the way back." A whole day with

Suzy. He couldn't imagine anything better.

"Well . . ."

"Otherwise it'll be this afternoon before I'm free. And I'll have Danny with me. If you need privacy, then . . ." He let the offer dangle, holding his breath while he waited for her to make up her mind.

She must have been holding her breath, too, because a whoosh sounded in his ear. "All right."

He let his breath rush out.

"Do you want me to drive in and meet you?"

He tapped his chin, trying to decide what would be best. "How about we meet at the filling station north of town? You can leave your car there until we get back." Would she think they were being sneaky? Honestly, it was the perfect meeting spot — smack between his house and Abigail Zimmerman's farm. "I know it's on the highway, but nobody will bother it. The attendant on duty will make sure of it. I meet Amish folks there when I give them a ride to town for appointments or shopping."

"All right. Give me fifteen minutes or so, okay?"

"Okay." They disconnected the call, and he darted for the front door with an even greater eagerness than before. Just before leaving he paused, whipped his coat open, and sniffed his armpit. Being in the warm house while trussed up like a turkey had made him sweat. Or maybe talking to Suzy Zimmerman had made him sweat. Either way, he needed another splash of something.

He zipped to the bathroom, doused his armpits with his sandalwood aftershave, and even patted another few drops onto his smooth cheeks just to be sure it would cover any hint of perspiration. Satisfied he wouldn't offend her nose, he left his coat flapping and jogged to his truck.

Suzanne

When Suzanne pulled into the parking area of the gas station and saw Paul's truck waiting, she almost changed her mind about going with him. Mother's uncertain expression haunted her. She hadn't forbidden Suzanne from going, but she'd warned, "You're playing with fire, Daughter." The sight of him revved her pulse into overdrive, and she was afraid Mother was right.

But she couldn't just turn around and leave. She'd at least need to tell him she couldn't go after all. She parked next to his truck where she could roll down her window and shout a message to him. But shouldn't she be more polite about it? She shut off the ignition and climbed out. At the same time he hopped out of his idling truck and rounded the hood, a huge smile of welcome on his face. "Hi, Suzy. Are you ready to go?"

"Actually, I —" A spicy scent came with him. The essence, so masculine and intoxicating, filled her senses and chased away her determination to stay behind. "I'm ready." She hit the lock on her car door and gave it a shove. The slam sealed her fate.

He opened the passenger door for her. His pickup stood much higher than her car, and she had a little trouble climbing in with her narrow corduroy skirt. Embarrassment heated her face. She must seem a clumsy clod. But if he thought so, he hid it well. He offered another grin before he closed her door and trotted around to slip behind the steering wheel. His long legs — and the freedom trousers offered — made it look easy to get into the cab.

They both buckled in, and he put the truck in Reverse. As he pulled onto the highway, he sent a short apologetic grin at her. "This is a business trip. That's why I'm dressed in my work clothes."

He wasn't all business minded, though, no matter what he said. She couldn't recall him smelling this wonderful when he came over to rebuild cabinets or fix the basement wall. If he'd applied the cologne to please her, he'd succeeded. She forced a smile. "It's fine. I appreciate you taking time for me. I'm" — she chose her next words carefully — "a little lost and in need of a friend."

For a few seconds disappointment seemed to pinch his face, but another warm smile cleared the expression. "I'm glad you thought of me. What's going on?"

The truck's engine rumbled and the tires hummed against the pavement, creating an oddly soothing background tune. "It's Alexa." She filled him in as best she could, detailing Owen Mallory's visit to the B and B and Alexa discovering he'd also visited the home in Indianapolis. She finished by telling him Alexa was on her way to the man's office right now to tell him she'd been left behind the home.

Paul listened intently, but he didn't ask any questions while she talked.

She finished by saying, "I told Alexa I would pray for her this morning, but to be honest, I don't know what to pray. Part of me wants to pray that whoever sent Mr. Mallory is not Alexa's mother — that it's all a big misunderstanding. And the other part of me wants to pray that this person is Alexa's mother because Alexa is very angry with the woman and intends to tell her to stay away."

"Either of those scenarios end the same — with Alexa remaining your daughter, and yours only."

She nodded. "I know. So why am I so hesitant? Either way, I win."

He drove in silence for several miles, his gaze aimed ahead and his focus seemingly on the road. Suzanne was beginning to wonder if he'd forgotten what they were talking about when he suddenly glanced at her and said, "You win, yes, but are you afraid Alexa will lose?"

How had he summed up the root of her fear? She loved her daughter. She wanted the very best for her always and in all things. If Alexa rejected her birth mother without taking the chance to really get to know her, she might be denying herself the opportunity for a loving, positive relationship. If she never found her birth mother, she might always feel as if a part of her was missing. Suzanne didn't want her precious child living with regrets.

Without thinking, she reached across the center of the seat and placed her hand on his arm. "I've spent twenty years hauling around a boatload of wish-I-hads. I want so much more for Alexa. I don't want her to look back someday and say, 'I wish I had . . .' "

Paul moved his arm, dislodging her hand. He popped his turn signal on and eased onto the shoulder.

Suzanne stared at him, confused, as he put the truck in Park and pushed the button for the emergency blinkers. "What are you doing?"

A soft smile lifted the corners of his lips. "I'm going to pray." He offered her his hands, and she took hold. His strong fingers, warm and callused, closed comfortingly around hers. He shut his eyes. "Our loving heavenly Father . . ."

Suzanne sat transfixed, eyes open, gaze pinned on his face as he spoke to God. Paul's ease in praying aloud, the expression of complete trust on his face, touched her as deeply as the words he lifted on her behalf.

"In Your Word You've given many promises. You promise never to leave nor forsake us. You promise to give us wisdom when we ask. You promise that when we repent of our sins, You are faithful to forgive them and cleanse us of all unrighteousness. You promise that our sins are cast away the moment they're uttered. Therefore I know I can come to You holy, clean, forgiven, Your beloved child." His fingers tightened on hers. "And so can Suzy, both of us forgiven of our 'wish-I-hads.' "

He had wish-I-hads, too? Suzanne swallowed tears and closed her eyes, the reverence of the moment overtaking her.

"Suzy's daughter is Your child, too. You want the best for her, which means living a life devoid of despair and remorse. Guide her right now, our Father. Whisper Your will to her ears and let her heed Your voice only. Erase any chance of choosing unwisely, which would lead to deep regrets, and let her walk forward on a pathway that brings only peace. We place Alexa . . . and ourselves . . . in Your capable, caring hands and trust You to bring beauty for ashes, the oil of joy for mourning, the garment of praise for the spirit of heaviness . . ."

Suzanne added her voice to his as he quoted the scripture from Isaiah. "That You might be glorified."

Paul squeezed her hands. "Amen."

She opened her eyes and released a squeal of shock.

Paul jolted. "What?"

She pointed at his driver's-side window. A police officer peered in at them.

Paul quickly rolled down the window. "Yes, sir?"

The officer peered past Paul to Suzanne.

"Are you all right?"

Suzanne nodded. "Yes. Just fine."

He turned to Paul, his face still set in a stern frown. "What are you doing?"

Paul cleared his throat, rubbing his finger beneath his nose as if trying to hold back a sneeze. "I was praying."

He stared blankly at Paul. "Praying?"

Suzanne coughed into her hand to keep from laughing. Likely the officer had never heard that excuse before.

"Yes, sir," Paul said. "I figured it was better to pull off since I always close my eyes when I pray."

The officer jerked his gaze away, pinched his chin for a moment, and then looked into the cab again. Although his lips were set in a grim line, suppressed humor brightened his eyes. "Well, since you're all right, I'll leave you to . . . pray. Have a good day, folks." He strode off.

Paul rolled up the window, leaned back with his eyes closed, and released a heavy sigh.

The bubble of laughter she'd forced down found its way from her throat.

Paul shot a startled look at her. "You think it's funny?"

She nodded, unable to squelch the chortles shaking her shoulders. "Yes, I do.

The expression on his face when you said you were praying . . ." She held her stomach and laughed freely.

Within a few seconds Paul joined her. He pointed at her. "I wish you could've seen your face when you opened your eyes and saw him outside the window. Your mouth dropped so wide I saw your tonsils."

They laughed even harder, relief no doubt adding to the levity. After several minutes of uncontrolled mirth, they took a few breaths that brought their chortles under control.

Paul grinned at her, his eyes sparkling. "You feel better now?"

Suzanne smiled broadly. "I do. Thank you, Paul."

"You're welcome. Let's move on now before the officer comes back." He put the truck in gear and pulled into the traffic.

Suzanne leaned into the seat and basked in the wonderful feelings coursing through her. Paul's prayer had soothed her and given her an element of hopefulness that Alexa would make the right choice concerning her birth mother. And the shared laughter had revived her. She looked at Paul, who drove with one wrist draped over the steering wheel and a relaxed smile curving his lips.

He glanced at her and caught her looking. "What?"

She didn't turn away. "Nothing. I'm just . . . happy."

He reached over and took her hand. "Me, too." They drove on in companionable silence with their fingers linked. The way "just friends" didn't.

CHAPTER 30

Indianapolis
Alexa

She couldn't say what she'd been expecting, but Mr. Mallory's office took Alexa by surprise. Although housed in a historic building, the character of its past had long since been stripped away, leaving a soulless shell behind. Dull gray painted walls, gray-speckled tile on the floor, two gray file cabinets standing sentry in one corner . . . Alexa shivered. Maybe the gray surroundings had also colored the man. He greeted her when she came in and even shook her hand, but he spoke with such a flat, emotionless voice, she hadn't felt welcomed. Not one bit.

He turned his steel-gray gaze on Tom and Linda. "Are these your parents?"

Alexa gestured her friends forward. "No. This is Tom and Linda Denning. They're friends of the family."

He didn't bother shaking their hands. He headed for a massive desk, made of gray metal, that stretched nearly from one wall to the other in the narrow space. He angled himself sideways to get behind it and then plopped into his chair — one of those tall, etched-wood ones with a leather seat like bankers used a hundred years ago. The antique chair offered the only touch of charm in the entire room.

Mr. Mallory held his hands toward the two chairs facing his desk. "Come in. Sit. Let's talk."

Alexa wrinkled her nose. The chairs had hard plastic seats shaped like a snow shovel's scoop. "I'll just stand. Tom and Linda can sit."

Tom, ever the gentleman, took her elbow and guided her to one of the chairs. "You sit, honey-girl. I don't mind standing." He moved behind her and placed his warm hands over her shoulders. Linda perched in the second chair, grimacing when its metal frame squawked. As soon as they were all settled, Mr. Mallory leaned forward and pinned Alexa with an intense look she suspected he hoped would intimidate her.

"All right, young lady, suppose you tell me how you came to leave me that message."

Alexa opted for the basic facts and told him about her adoptive family in Arborville mentioning his visit and then Ms. Reed indicating he'd also visited the home seeking information.

He nodded, seeming to accept her answer. "All right. But what makes you think I'm searching for you?"

She took a deep breath and offered the explanation she'd practiced on the drive over. "My adoptive mother told me she found me behind the garage of the home." She shivered, partly because the stark surroundings left her cold inside and partly because the image of the cracked concrete and age-worn garage flashed in her memory. "She took me to the hospital to make sure I was all right" — something her birth mother hadn't bothered to do — "and then she gave me a loving home."

"Where?"

Alexa blinked. "Where . . . what?"

"Where was your home?"

"At first we lived in Indianapolis, and then we moved to Franklin when I was six years old."

"You didn't live in Kansas?"

His narrowed, steely gaze made her want to fidget. If it wasn't for Tom's strong hands on her shoulders, she might wriggle out of

411

the uncomfortable seat. "No, not when I was growing up. I do live there now, though, in the B and B you visited."

"So Suzanne Zimmerman is your adoptive mother." A statement, not a question.

Alexa nodded anyway. "Yes."

He leaned closer, his eyes glinting. "What about Anna-Grace Braun?"

She thought for a moment, trying to decide the best way to answer. Then she shook her head. "She doesn't have anything to do with me and my birth family. Don't worry about her."

Very slowly he leaned back until he'd angled the chair into a semireclined position. Its springs released a long, low whine, sending another chill up Alexa's spine. The way he eyeballed her through barely opened eyelids reminded her of a snake waiting to strike. She reached up and slid her hand underneath Tom's, gaining comfort from his stalwart presence.

Mr. Mallory gently rocked the chair, a steady *squeak-squeak* from the springs accompanying the movement. "You realize it's very simple for me to prove you aren't the person I'm seeking with a DNA swab. DNA doesn't lie."

Alexa looked directly into his hard gaze. "Neither do I."

To her surprise he burst out laughing. He rose in one smooth movement and approached the closest file cabinet. "All right then, Alexa Zimmerman. Let's see if you are who you say you are." He rummaged in the top drawer and returned with a plastic-wrapped cotton-topped stick in hand. "Open wide."

Arborville
Suzanne

Paul parked next to Suzanne's car and left his truck idling while he jogged around the hood and opened the door for her. As she turned to climb out, she looked into his eyes — his brown-sugar eyes — and impulsive words left her lips. "Why don't you and Danny join Mother, Anna-Grace, and me for supper tonight?" What was she doing? Hadn't she instructed Sandra to act as a buffer between them? Yet here she was, bold as a peacock, inviting him to supper. But she owed him. A home-cooked meal could be her thank-you for him buying her lunch, praying with her, and cheering her up.

He drew back, uncertainty replacing the tenderness his eyes had held only moments earlier. "Are you sure? It's not Sunday, our fellowship's regular visiting day. People might . . . talk."

Mother would have plenty to say, but at that moment Suzanne didn't care. She was tired of worrying about what people would think, about might-have-beens and wish-I-hads. She couldn't change the years that had passed, but she owned today. And today she wanted to enjoy a meal with Paul and Danny. She smiled. "Good. If they're talking about me, they won't be gossiping about somebody else."

He laughed. "All right then. What time?"

"Six?"

"Perfect." He took the keys from her hand and unlocked her car door, then opened it for her. When he placed her keys in her palm, his fingers brushed the tender place at the base of her thumb, sending a tingle all the way to her shoulder. "We'll see you then, Suzy."

She drove straight to the little grocery store in Arborville and bought two pounds of fresh chicken breasts, a bag of baby spinach, and a small container of feta cheese. She was pretty sure Alexa used a mix of asiago and goat cheese for the recipe she intended to make tonight, but the store didn't have asiago or goat cheese. She hoped feta would do.

To her surprise when she arrived home, she found Mother in the kitchen peeling potatoes. She lowered the grocery sack to the counter. "Where's Anna-Grace?"

Mother continued flicking brown peelings into the waste can. "She borrowed the car and drove into town. She said something about decorating bulletin boards at the school. Then she and Steven plan to grab pizza at the convenience store with another young couple from the fellowship."

Warmth eased through Suzanne's frame as she thought about her daughter finding her place of belonging in Arborville. "It's nice she and Steven are already settling in and making friends."

"Mm-hm." Mother peered at Suzanne over the top of her glasses. "I told her to go because I thought we might need to talk."

Suzanne chuckled. She crossed to the worktable and picked up a potato. "What are you making over here?"

"Potato soup. I've been craving it for days."

"Oh. Well . . ."

Mother lowered the paring knife and half-peeled potato to her apron-covered skirt. "What?"

"I sort of invited someone to supper."

"Sort of? How do you sort of invite someone?"

Suzanne sighed. "I flat-out invited

415

someone to supper, and I was going to make one of Alexa's recipes — chicken and spinach pinwheels in cream sauce."

Mother didn't blink. "Paul?"

Suzanne nodded.

"And Danny's coming, too, then?"

She nodded again.

Mother plopped the potato and knife in the bowl with the other peeled potatoes and pushed the bowl aside. "I can wait another day for potato soup. Make your chicken pinwheels. And after supper" — she jabbed one finger in Suzanne's direction — "we are going to talk."

Alexa's recipe came out perfect, and Suzanne couldn't help feeling a burst of pride as she carried the platter of pinwheels drizzled with a buttery cream sauce to the table.

Paul's eyebrows rose. "That looks amazing, Suzy. Almost too pretty to eat."

Danny licked his lips. "I'll eat it. We were just gonna have potato soup. That looks lots better."

Mother burst out laughing. "Sit, Suzy, before this better-than-potato-soup dish grows cold. Paul, will you do us the honor of offering the blessing?"

"Of course."

Suzanne listened for the second time that day to Paul speaking to his Lord. Her heart swelled. Back when they were teenagers, she'd sometimes worried that Paul viewed his relationship with God too casually, almost flippantly. But in his prayers she recognized a depth of spirituality. He'd grown and matured in more ways than physically in the past years. Today's Paul was even more appealing than the eighteen-year-old one had been.

"Amen."

They passed the platter of chicken as well as the bowl of home-canned green beans and Mother's yeast rolls. Both Paul and Danny loaded their plates, and Suzanne couldn't help smiling when they dug in and proclaimed the food delicious. Well, Paul said "delicious." Danny just grinned and said, "Mmm, Miss Zimmerman, you're a good cook." His sincere compliment went straight to her heart.

Danny seemed less tense than he'd been the last time they were together. He contributed little to the conversation around the table, but that was typical of an Old Order child, who was taught to remain silent in the presence of adults unless someone addressed him. But he didn't sit in sullen silence. His bright eyes followed

417

the speakers the way spectators follow a tennis ball back and forth on the court, and occasionally he grinned at someone's comment. Quiet, yes, but still involved. She'd been praying for him to settle down, and it pleased her to think her prayers had been answered.

The four of them went through the entire two pounds of chicken breasts as well as a dozen rolls and an entire jar of beans. Suzanne had inwardly bemoaned not having a dessert to offer, but after watching Paul and Danny consume two full servings each, she decided maybe it was all right. Surely they didn't have room for anything else.

Danny drained his milk glass, swiped away his milk mustache with the back of his hand, and leaned back in his chair with a big sigh.

Paul nudged his shoulder. "What do you say to Mrs. Zimmerman and Miss Zimmerman?"

Danny sat up straight. "Did you make dessert, too?"

Paul lightly thumped the back of his son's head.

"Sorry." The boy hung his head and mumbled, "Thank you for supper."

Suzanne laughed. "To be honest, Danny, I was just thinking about dessert. After you ate such a big supper, I didn't think you'd have room in your tummy for dessert."

Danny peeked at her from beneath his heavy fringe of eyelashes, his expression serious. "Miss Zimmerman, you need to know something about boys."

She swallowed her amusement and matched his serious tone. "What's that?"

"Boys always have room for dessert."

Mother chuckled. "You're absolutely right, Danny. I could never keep enough cookies in the cookie jar to satisfy my son, Clete, when he was your age. And I seem to recall" — her eyes became dreamy — "your father ate his fair share of cookies from my old jar, too."

Danny zipped a quick look at Paul, whose cheeks bore a slight red streak, then turned to Mother again. "Are there cookies in your jar right now, Mrs. Zimmerman?"

She pretended to think deeply for a few seconds, then she smiled. "I believe there are. Anna-Grace baked a batch of oatmeal cookies with butterscotch chips and pecans."

Paul glanced left and right. "I just realized . . . Where is Anna-Grace?"

Suzanne said, "She's with her beau and some other Arborville young people this evening."

A slow smile grew on his lips. "So . . . she's settling in."

Suzanne smiled her reply. She read in his eyes the same mix of happiness and sadness she always experienced when thinking of the daughter she couldn't claim as her own.

Mother cleared her throat. "Well, Danny, do oatmeal cookies appeal to you?"

He shrugged. "A cookie's a cookie. Dunk them in milk, and it doesn't matter what kind they are."

Paul gawked at his son. "Danny!"

Danny looked up at him innocently. "What?"

Mother's laughter rang. She pushed her chair away from the table. "You come with me, young man. We'll put some cookies on a plate and grab the milk pitcher." She rolled her chair through the butler's pantry, and Danny bounded after her like an eager puppy.

Paul watched his son until he turned the corner to the kitchen. "I'm sorry. I really have taught him manners."

Suzanne smiled. "He's fine, Paul. Earlier I was thinking he seems to be more relaxed and sunny again. I'm glad to see the change."

Paul laid his napkin on the table, then fiddled with the scalloped edge. "We still have our moments, but I'm trying, as you said, to be patient with him. I have managed to get him talking a little bit, and you were right about him missing his mom. I think he finds it especially upsetting that he can't remember a great deal about her. He said it makes him feel like he never even had a mother. He's been asking lots of questions, and I always answer, even when it's hard. Hopefully, eventually, he'll once again be okay with it being just him and me."

His final words stabbed, and she lowered her head.

"Suzy? Are you all right?"

He'd said he was patient with Danny and answered even his hard questions. Would he give her the same treatment if she asked a bold question? She met his gaze. "Karina's been gone a long time now."

He nodded solemnly. "Coming up on four years."

She gathered her courage. "Don't you ever want to marry again so it isn't just you and Danny alone?"

His fingers stilled on the napkin edge. He stared at her, his brown eyes registering surprise and something else she couldn't quite interpret. He licked his lips, then drew a breath that expanded his chest. "Suzy, I —"

"Here we are!" Mother's cheerful voice intruded. She wheeled into the dining room with a plate of cookies balanced in her lap. Danny followed, carrying the milk pitcher with both hands. Mother put the cookies on the table, then reached for the milk. As she turned with the glass pitcher, her gaze drifted across the two of them, and her eyebrows crunched together. "What's wrong?"

Paul took the pitcher from her and set it gently on the tablecloth. He patted the chair Danny had vacated and waited until his son sat. Then he looked at Mother. A half smile curved his lips. "Nothing's wrong, Mrs. Zimmerman, but your daughter just asked me a question, and I intend to answer it. When I'm done, I'd really like to hear what you think."

CHAPTER 31

Arborville

Paul

Paul sent up a quick, silent prayer for God to render him incapable of speech if he was rushing things. When he turned to Danny and spoke his son's name, his voice came out strong and sure. *Thank You, Lord.*

"What, Dad?" Danny's expression held both curiosity and apprehension.

"Son, I'm going to talk to Mrs. Zimmerman and Miss Zimmerman. I want you to listen, though, because what I say will affect you, too. When we go home, we'll talk about it again, so right now you're just to listen. Do you understand?"

Danny nodded, solemn and wide eyed.

Paul shifted his attention to the mother and daughter sitting side by side across the table. Two pairs of blue eyes peered back at him, and he saw the same emotions he'd glimpsed in Danny's face. He hoped his

423

answer to Suzy's question wouldn't increase their apprehension.

"Mrs. Zimmerman, Suzy asked if I ever intended to marry again. I've been asked that a lot in the last couple of years. I suppose it's to be expected, seeing how I have a son to raise and no wife to help me." He angled his gaze to Suzy. "Truthfully, I've thought about it. I love my son, but I get lonely. I miss having someone to talk to and laugh with and share my concerns with. I'm sure you know what I mean. You raised a daughter all on your own."

Suzy nodded, the movement slight. The understanding glowing in her eyes encouraged him to continue.

"Even though I've thought about marrying again, not until lately have I considered doing more than just think about it. Not until you came back to town."

She sucked in a little breath, but Mrs. Zimmerman didn't give a start. In fact, a knowing smile creased her wrinkled cheeks. He resisted the urge to fidget and focused on Suzy.

"There's a whole lot standing in the way. There's Anna-Grace." Thank goodness she wasn't at the table listening, too. Having his son's unwavering gaze boring into the side of his face was enough. "There's the fellowship. And there's our . . . history."

"The history doesn't matter." Suzy almost blurted the statement. Her cheeks flooded with pink. She added, more hesitantly, "That is, we've forgiven each other. The . . . past . . . can remain in the past."

He read the meaning behind her words and gave a grateful nod. "Still, there's Anna-Grace. And the fellowship. Even if we've let it go, the members will be concerned about our past."

"Yes . . ." Lines of concern marched across Suzy's forehead. He longed to run his thumb along them, smooth them out, soothe her.

Mrs. Zimmerman rested her arms on the table's edge. "Paul, may I ask a question?"

"Of course."

Her gaze narrowed. "Do you love my daughter?"

He didn't need to hesitate. "I've loved Suzy since she was a pigtailed ten-year-old running barefoot along the creek bank in pursuit of frogs."

"I mean today. Not from before, but now."

He looked at Suzy. At her golden hair combed neatly into a braided twist. At her modest blouse and sweater vest. Her Old Order trappings were gone, her youthful face replaced by a maturity that spoke of growth and change and strength. He smiled. "I love today's Suzy." Her face bloomed bold crimson, and tears winked in her eyes.

Mrs. Zimmerman turned her pointed gaze on her daughter. "Suzy, what about you? Do you love Paul? Not the Paul who banged in and out of my back door but the one sitting across the table right now?"

Suzy's lips quavered, but when they parted, a simple answer wheezed out. "Yes."

Paul's heart rolled over in his chest. If there hadn't been a four-foot-wide table between them, he'd have her in his arms, and it wouldn't matter one bit if they had witnesses.

"Well then," Mrs. Zimmerman said in her typical straightforward manner, "I don't think you need to concern yourselves about Anna-Grace. That situation is part of the past you said you could leave behind. But the fellowship . . ." She shook her head. "I won't sugarcoat things. Setting things to right with them will take some doing." She looked from Paul to Suzy, her eyes glowing with confidence. "But if you really love each other, you'll find a way."

Danny didn't say a word all the way home, but Paul could tell by the way his son's face remained pinched in a scowl of concentra-

426

tion, questions were rolling in his mind. They entered the house together, hung up their coats and hats, and kicked off their boots. And with the thud of their boots on the floor, Danny's dam burst.

"You really love Miss Zimmerman? The way you loved my mom? Are you gonna marry her? Why's the fellowship a problem? And why's Anna-Grace a problem? And what do you mean when you talk about 'the past'?"

"Whoa, Son, one subject at a time, okay?"

Paul curved his hand around the back of Danny's neck and guided him to their couch. They sat, angling themselves so their knees bumped. He looked into his son's upturned face and a knot of love nearly choked him. These past weeks he'd felt less like Danny's hero and more like his enemy. When he'd finished talking, he might have totally lost his hero status in his son's eyes. If only the past had no effect on today.

"First of all, 'the past' is the life I lived before you came along. In my past, as you already know, I loved Suzy Zimmerman and I wanted to marry her."

Danny crunched his face. "Then how come you didn't?"

This was the part of the past he wished he could erase. "Well, Son, I sinned. You know what sin is — breaking one of God's laws. The Bible tells us that physical intimacy is meant to be between a husband and wife only. But Miss Zimmerman and I were intimate." Would Danny understand? He was growing up, but he was still so young. "We came together in a way that created a baby."

His son's mouth dropped open. "You did?"

Paul nodded. He wanted to shift his gaze to the ceiling, the floor, the sofa — anywhere but into his son's shocked face — but he made himself maintain eye contact. "Yes. A baby girl. Having a baby when you aren't married goes against the Bible, and it goes against the teachings in our fellowship. Miss Zimmerman's mother was very upset, so she sent Miss Zimmerman away and I didn't see her again. Not until she came back to Arborville."

Danny sat in stunned silence for several seconds, his jaw hanging slack. Then his face lit. "The baby you had . . . is it Alexa? Is she my sister, Dad? Huh?"

The two of them could be related, given their mutual tendency to be, as Alexa termed it, gung-ho. Paul caught Danny by the shoulders. "No, Danny, Alexa is not your sister."

Confusion crinkled his brow again. "Then where is my sister?"

Paul didn't dare tell him. Not until Anna-Grace chose to know. His chest ached, and he searched for an answer that would protect Anna-Grace and still be truthful. "Another family adopted her."

"So she's not my sister?"

Paul shook his head, giving Danny's shoulders a gentle squeeze. "In the eyes of the law, no. She isn't part of our family at all."

"So I don't have a mom, and I don't have a sister." A hard edge crept into Danny's voice. Disappointment flickered in his eyes.

Paul thought his heart might break. Seeing his precious boy hurt by the consequences of his actions was worse than suffering them himself. He pushed an apology past his aching throat. "I'm sorry, Son."

"Me, too." Danny sat with his head low, picking at a small tear in the knee of his school pants. "Sure would've been fun to have a sister." Then he bounced his chin upward, his gaze colliding with Paul's. "But I could get a mom again, right? You said you love Miss Zimmerman. If you marry her, then —"

"Danny, Danny, please slow down. Listen to me." He waited until Danny stopped his wriggling. "Yes, I love Miss Zimmerman. And if it were up to just me, I'd ask her to marry me. I think she'd be a good mom for you, and I know she'd be a good wife to me. But before I can marry anyone, before I can even court anyone, I have to ask the deacons for their approval."

Danny threw his hands wide. "So ask 'em."

Paul closed his eyes and stifled a groan. If only it were that simple. He looked at Danny again. "The deacons won't say yes unless the woman I want to court is part of an Old Order fellowship."

Danny's puzzled expression didn't clear.

"Miss Zimmerman goes to our fellowship, but she isn't a member."

"Oh . . ." He chewed his lip for a moment. He shrugged. "Then she can join."

Paul laughed — one short, mirthless huff. "It's not quite that easy, Danny. Before she could become a member of our fellowship, Miss Zimmerman would have to confess her sins to the Deacon Council."

"So she'd have to say that you and her had a baby girl together without being married?"

Stated so baldly, it stung. Paul nodded.

"And she doesn't want to tell?"

How could she tell? The deacons weren't

stupid. They might as well put up a billboard: Suzy and Paul begat Anna-Grace. "She isn't ready," he said gently.

Danny bolted upright and blew out a mighty breath. "So I guess that means I'll never get another mom."

Paul grabbed him and pulled him into a hug, and for once Danny didn't pull away. He buried his head in the curve of Paul's neck and let Paul hold tight. He whispered into his son's ear, "Remember what the Bible says? 'With God all things are possible.' If I'm supposed to marry Miss Zimmerman, if she's supposed to be your new mom, then it will happen. And if it doesn't . . ." He kissed Danny's temple. "Then we'll know God has something else planned for us. Okay?"

Danny didn't answer.

Indianapolis
Cynthia

Lindsey tossed her coat over the back of the sofa on her way through the little front room, bopping Cynthia in the back of the head with one of the coat's toggle buttons. Her scarf dropped from her hand midway across the floor. "Hey, Cyn, what're your plans for dinner?"

Over the past week Cynthia had learned

that Lindsey left a trail wherever she went. She'd also taken to shortening Cynthia's name. Cynthia never minded when Glenn called her Cyn. It felt affectionate and intimate. But when Lindsey did it, it seemed like another way to be lazy — as if it took too much effort to say all three syllables. Maybe she'd start calling Lindsey "Lin" and see how she liked it. Then again, maybe she wouldn't. She couldn't risk getting tossed out. Where would she go?

She peered into the kitchen, where Lindsey was opening and closing cabinet doors. "I hadn't given it much thought yet." She hadn't had an appetite in a week. "Did you have something in mind?"

Lindsey banged another door closed and leaned on the counter, her arms folded over her chest. "Yeah. I met this guy named Zane a couple of weeks ago. He claimed he was a gourmet cook and offered to come over and cook a four-course candlelit dinner anytime I asked. Since there's nothing here to fix, I was thinking about taking him up on it. But the point of a candlelit dinner is to be alone, if you catch my drift."

Cynthia caught the drift. She also couldn't help being concerned. "Where did you say you met him?"

Lindsey began investigating the contents

of the refrigerator. "At Basker's — you know, the bar."

Cynthia was blissfully ignorant of Basker's and every other bar in town. But she feared Lindsey knew them all. She crossed to the kitchen. "Do you think it's wise to invite some man you met in a bar to your apartment?"

Lindsey gawked at Cynthia over the top of the refrigerator door. "What are you now, my mother?"

"Of course not. I just think —"

"Well, I hope you aren't giving me relationship advice. That would be pretty ironic, considering your situation at the moment."

The sarcastic arrow found its mark. Cynthia backed up.

Lindsey grinned. "Uh-huh. Thought so." She gave the door a swat that closed it. "Look, I said you were welcome to stay for as long as you needed to, and I'm not going back on my word, but it's been a full week already. Don't you think it's time to start searching for your own place?" She grimaced. "Not to be rude or anything, but I'm not used to answering to anybody. It's a little . . . awkward." Lindsey flounced past Cynthia, her short, dyed-red curls bouncing. "As for tonight, if you could just make

433

yourself scarce for a couple of hours, maybe three, I'd really appreciate it. Zane is a real hottie, and I don't much want to share him with you." She disappeared into her bedroom.

Cynthia wandered into the small second bedroom and closed the door. She sat on the edge of the bed and stared at the movie poster hanging on the opposite wall. She could stay in the room all evening, out of Lindsey's way, but the idea didn't hold any appeal. The walls were paper thin, and she'd hear everything. She was already weary of Lindsey's idea of a fun evening.

Glenn and the kids were probably, right now, sitting down to eat the Crockpot meal she'd left for them. Her mouth watered as she thought about the tender pork chops cooked in cranberry sauce with slices of peppers and onions. Had Glenn remembered to make a batch of brown rice and maybe a vegetable to go with it? She hoped so. The kids needed a balanced meal.

She stood and paced the small room, restlessness driving her around the space while images of her family paraded through her mind. When they finished eating, they'd load the dishwasher — Barrett putting things in the wrong places and Darcy fixing it — and then they'd grab their coats and drive to church for the Wednesday evening services.

Her heart caught. They'd be out all evening. A perfect opportunity for her to go over, throw in a load of wash, and gather a few more things. No one would bother her over there, and she wouldn't be intruding on Lindsey's evening with Zane. She hesitated. It would be — she borrowed Lindsey's word — *awkward* to be in her house when she no longer officially lived there. Then she squared her shoulders. It was still her house. Her name was on the mortgage alongside Glenn's. Her children were there. She had every right to go in and out as she pleased. And right now, she pleased to go in.

She grabbed her coat from the closet, snatched up her purse, and headed out the door.

CHAPTER 32

Indianapolis
Cynthia
Cynthia waited at the end of the block until Glenn's minivan pulled out of the driveway and rounded the corner. Then she pulled up to the curb and parked. For a moment she sat staring at the simple brick ranch-style house that had been her first real home. Only brick and mortar, but so much more to a girl whose childhood was spent moving from one seedy apartment or small rental house to another. This house had become her safe harbor. She missed her family, but she missed her home, too.

She got out and pulled her bag of laundry from the backseat. Glenn had left the porch light on, the way he always did during the evening and nighttime hours, so she stepped into a warm yellow glow as she mounted the porch steps. Her key turned the lock and she entered the house. The smell of the pork chops still hung heavily in the room, adding to the sense of "home." She stood on the tiny square of linoleum that served as their foyer and inhaled deeply, savoring the aroma, and then gave herself a little push. She needed to wash her clothes and get out of there before Glenn and the kids returned. A little over two hours — that was all she'd have.

After tossing her coat over the back of the couch the way Lindsey did, she headed for the small utility room behind the kitchen, her bag of clothes in hand. Normally she'd separate her clothes into three piles — whites, lights, and darks — but tonight she needed to hurry the process, so she tossed the whites and lights together. Once the washing machine was filling, she headed to Glenn's and her bedroom to collect a few more clothes.

She snapped on the hall light and moved to the first doorway on the right. The door stood open, giving her a glimpse of the dark room. She reached around and hit the light switch, then remained with her toes touching the 1970s army-green carpet and her heels planted on the hallway's tan carpet. She examined the room by increments, noting the neatly made bed, the uncluttered floor and dresser top, and Glenn's school shoes — lace-up brown oxfords — placed beside the chair in the corner. Everything looked exactly the way it had when she left. An odd feeling wiggled through her middle.

She took a step into the bedroom, reminding herself she was not an intruder, no matter how her stomach churned in discomfort. She went to the dresser first and pulled out several pairs of underwear and socks, which she laid on the dresser's uncluttered top. Then she moved to the closet and slid the door open. It moved soundlessly on its well-oiled rails. They might not live in a brand-new house, but Glenn took pride in keeping everything they owned in working order, even closet door fittings.

Sadness — a sadness she couldn't even define — struck. She crushed a half-dozen sweaters together between her palms and unhooked their hangers from the rod, then shifted to place them with her other items.

A shadow moved across the floor toward her. A man-shaped shadow. She shrieked, threw the clothes in the direction of the intruder, and dove into the closet. Her palms slid along the smooth wood as she scrambled to close the door behind her. Why didn't the inside have some sort of handle? Her frantic motions stilled when she heard a familiar male voice say, "Cyn, what are you doing?"

She peeked out, her heart still pounding. Glenn stood a few feet away, his face pinched in puzzlement. She also couldn't help noticing he looked very, very tired. Guilt and sympathy tried to push aside the fear she'd just experienced, but she drew on anger instead. What was he doing here? "I was escaping what I thought was a burglar."

He emitted a brief huff of half laughter, half derision. "That's not what I meant."

She knew what he meant. "I needed some more clothes, and I didn't think anyone would be here." She inched out of the closet but stayed well away from him. "Why aren't you at Bible study?"

"Want to know the truth?"

Hesitantly, she nodded.

"Because I couldn't make myself go in alone. It didn't feel right."

His answer stole her manufactured anger. She crouched and began collecting her tossed sweaters. He knelt and put the pink fuzzy one — the one he'd bought her last year during the after–Valentine's Day sales — back on its plastic hanger. They rose at the same time, and he held the hanger out to her.

She swallowed a knot of sorrow and took it. "Thanks."

They stood in silence for several seconds, Glenn looking somewhere beyond her shoulder and her trying to look anywhere except at him. Her gaze landed on the bed. The shams rested at an angle against the headboard and the throw pillows were fluffed and centered on the bed. Words slipped from her mouth without effort. "You did a good job on the bed."

"No, you did."

She frowned in confusion.

A sad smile curved his lips. "I haven't slept in it since you left."

Something in her chest fluttered. "Y-you haven't?"

Furrows etched his forehead. Deep grooves formed a line from the sides of his nose to the corners of his mouth. Dark circles smudged under his eyes. "Nope."

"Where have you been sleeping?"

"On the couch."

Little wonder he looked so worn-out. The lumpy, old couch was at least six inches too short for his frame. She clicked her tongue on her teeth, shaking her head. "Glenn, you can't get a decent night's rest out there. Sleep in the bed for heaven's sake."

"I can't."

"Why not?"

"For the same reason I couldn't sit in the

church pew tonight. Because you aren't in it."

His words took the strength from her legs. She sank down on the bed, the armful of sweaters flopping across her lap. "Oh, Glenn . . ."

He stood still as a statue for several seconds, then his body jerked into motion. One wide stride brought him to the bed, and he sat, smashing one of the pink sweater's sleeves. "When I saw you at the closet, I hoped you were putting things away, not taking things out." Pain laced his tone. Pain and disappointment and a hint of resentment.

Cynthia hung her head.

"When are you going to come home, Cyn?"

She glared at him, her chin quivering. "Do you really want me to?"

His brows crunched together. Anger glinted in his eyes. "I didn't tell you to go."

"No, but you didn't ask me to stay."

He propped his elbows on his knees and stared downward.

"And you told Brother Gary you wished you hadn't hired the PI to find my daughter." The hurt returned with such force she pressed her feet firmly on the floor to keep from toppling. "How could you tell him something like that?"

Glenn angled a weary look at her. "You didn't hear everything. You missed me saying I wished I had spent time in prayer with you before I hired the PI. I wanted to surprise you with the gift. But instead the kids and I got the surprise. We got pushed to the side while your entire focus turned to this girl none of us know." The lines in his forehead deepened. "That hurt, Cyn. It hurt a lot."

Defensiveness seared her insides. She snapped, "It hurt that you couldn't be excited with me — that you couldn't want her as much as I do."

He sat up abruptly and let his head sag back. He spoke toward the ceiling. "I do want her. For your sake, I want her." He slowly lowered his head and met her gaze. "But I don't want to lose you to her."

She huffed. "That isn't going to happen."

Glenn raised one brow. "You have to admit, ever since you opened that gift, your whole focus has been on finding your daughter. When the search went well, you were happy. When it went poorly, you were impatient with the kids and snappish to me. The search" — he crunched his lips closed for a moment as if seeking the right words — "consumed you and changed you, and there wasn't anything left of the mother and wife Darcy, Barrett, and I have always known. We felt like we lost you before you walked out the door."

"I wouldn't have left if I hadn't felt like I'd lost you." Her voice rose, taking on a childish whine.

Glenn returned to his low-slung pose. Silence descended, each second rife with tension and unsaid words. The washing machine buzzed, announcing the end of the cycle.

Cynthia rose and set the sweaters aside. "I need to transfer my clothes to the dryer." She waited, but he didn't say anything. She sighed and headed for the door.

Feet pounded behind her. Arms closed on her shoulders and spun her around. He cupped her jaw in his hands and lifted her face the way she'd seen a hero do in one of the late-night classic movies. She sucked in her breath, expecting Glenn to kiss her. But he only stared at her with his blue eyes blazing.

Frozen within his light hold, she whimpered, "G-Glenn?"

"Do you love me, Cyn?"

She did. Or it wouldn't hurt so much to be away from him. "Yes." She swallowed, tears clouding her vision. "Yes, Glenn, I do."

"Then don't run off again. Stay here with the kids and me."

Oh, how she wanted to stay. But she couldn't go back to the way it had been — with her on one side and him and the kids on the opposing side. She needed them to be a family, one united team again. She gripped his wrists. "Will you support my search instead of resenting it?"

"Will you keep it in perspective, remembering Darcy, Barrett, and I need you, too?"

She blinked, clearing her vision so she could see him clearly. No bitterness lingered in his expression, only longing. Her heart swelled with love for him, for their children, for her baby girl, making her chest go tight. "I'll try."

"And we'll try, too." He lowered his face and pressed his lips to hers in a sweet kiss of reconciliation that melted her remaining frost of resentment. Then he stepped aside. "Go transfer your wet clothes. I'll put these things away" — he waved at the stacks on the bed — "and then we'll go pick up the kids together, okay?"

Cynthia cringed. "Will they be mad to see me?"

"Probably. At first." He spoke gently, but his words still pained her. "They're mad because it hurt them when you left. But they're good kids, and they love you. They'll forgive you."

She nodded and headed for the laundry room. Her feet plodded as if she dragged a heavy load behind her. She and Glenn had chosen to make up, but she wouldn't be completely free of her burdens until she'd also made things right with her children. Glenn had said they'd forgive her, and she believed him. Hadn't she always forgiven her mother when Mom broke down and sobbed about how sorry she was for hitting Cynthia, pushing her, ignoring her, bringing yet another worthless man into her life? Of course she had, because it was her mom, and despite everything, she loved her. So she forgave her. But Cynthia never forgot the hurtful things.

Darcy and Barrett might forgive her, but she'd walked out on them. They'd never forget. She prayed she hadn't permanently cracked the foundation of her children's security. Because if she had, she would never be able to forgive herself.

Franklin
Alexa
Alexa awoke with a start, wide eyed and fully alert. The room was still dark. Her

alarm clock's glowing numbers showed 5:37. Why was she so awake this early? Especially considering she hadn't turned in until almost midnight. She and Mom had talked until her cell phone battery died, filling each other in on the past day's events. Alexa could hardly believe Mom spent a whole day with Paul Aldrich, most of it away from Arborville, and then admitted she loved him. Alexa chuckled, bouncing the mattress. Wow, leave for two weeks and see what happened? Maybe she should've left Mom in charge of the B and B a long time ago.

She lay on the bed, hands linked over her stomach beneath the puffy comforter, and stared at the gray-shadowed ceiling. One small part of her conversation with Mom replayed in her mind.

"Would you be able to forgive me, honey, if I married now?"

Such an odd question. Why would Mom need forgiveness? Alexa already liked Paul and Danny Aldrich. If Mom got married to her long-ago sweetheart, that meant Alexa would gain an instant dad and a little brother. Those were both good things in her opinion. Unless . . . She frowned. Surely Mom didn't intend to form a new family that didn't include Alexa.

She shook her head, tangling her hair against the pillowcase. No, Mom wouldn't do that. So there must be some other reason she thought she needed Alexa's forgiveness. When she talked to Mom next, she'd ask. But for now she should sleep. She rolled to her side and closed her eyes, but her tense body refused to relax. Maybe she'd just get up.

Grabbing the edge of the comforter, she prepared to toss it aside. But then she groaned and pulled it tight beneath her chin again. She didn't dare get up. She might disturb Tom and Linda. They'd stayed up late last night, too, going out for pie and coffee after Bible study with some friends from church and then listening to Alexa's report on Mom's love life. If she knew Linda, she'd kept Tom up even after they'd gone to their room, talking about Mom. Mom would probably get a call from Linda today with more questions than Mom could possibly answer.

"Would you be able to forgive me, honey, if I married now?"

When everybody was awake and Linda was starting her second cup of coffee — it wasn't smart to pester her with questions before then — she'd get Tom's and Linda's opinion on Mom's strange statement. No matter what Mom meant, Alexa would forgive her. She'd never withhold forgiveness from Mom. But from her birth mother? That was a completely different situation.

CHAPTER 33

Arborville
Suzanne

"If you tell him no, you're crazier than a pet raccoon."

Suzanne burst out laughing. She cradled the cell phone against her cheek and closed her eyes, imagining Linda's impish grin. "Oh, Linda, you are priceless."

"You think I'm kidding?" Humor laced Linda's tone despite her tart words. "I'm as serious as a courtroom judge. After all these years of being alone, you deserve the love of a good man, and from what Alexa tells us, Mr. Paul Aldrich is a very good man."

Suzanne gently rocked in the padded chair Alexa had purchased at a garage sale and reupholstered in a crisp yellow-and-white plaid. She could stay here all day and be content. The cottage was quiet, and being away from the house allowed her to speak freely. A smile pulled at her lips. "Alexa's right. Paul is one of the best men I've ever known. Loving him and being loved by him is a gift beyond description."

A soft sigh drifted from the phone. "I'm so happy for you, girlie."

She was happy, too, but she — and Alexa and Linda — had to be realistic. "We're getting ahead of ourselves. Yes, Paul said he loves me, but he hasn't officially asked me to marry him. We can't even court, not with us belonging to different churches."

Linda huffed. "I'm sorry, Suzanne, but that's a ridiculous rule in my opinion. You're both Christians, saved by grace, aren't you? You're both adults, capable of making wise decisions, right? So why does church membership have to bungle things up? Love is love, and that's all that should matter."

"And in most places you'd be right. But this is Arborville." Suzanne cringed, considering everything she would have to give up for Paul to openly court her — her membership with the Franklin Mennonite Brethren church, her cell phone, wardrobe, and non-fellowship-approved vehicle . . . and her secrets. That was the hardest — the secrets. She sighed. "Maybe it's too late for us. After all, we're both closing in on our fortieth birthdays, and —"

"And you think you're too old for love?"

Linda's snort blasted in Suzanne's ear. "Girlie, you ain't too old for love until they lay you in a grave. If the Good Lord saw fit to reawaken the feelings you two once shared, then it'd be plain sinful to ignore 'em, and that's all I'm gonna say about that."

Suzanne smiled. She was fairly certain, given time, Linda would say plenty more on the subject. "Well, as I said, it's too early to speculate on what will happen. Paul and I have asked for a meeting with the deacons." Her throat tightened and a stone of worry settled in her stomach. "Depending on their reaction and advice, we'll decide our next step. But I'm preparing myself to give up on the idea of becoming Mrs. Paul Aldrich just in case." The stone rolled over and she grimaced.

"And I'm telling you right now, Tom and I are gonna be praying our hearts out that those deacons look past their silly rules to the precious gift of love rekindling between you two. I'd start singing that song Diana Ross used to belt out about ain't no mountain high enough, but I'd probably pickle whatever you ate for breakfast."

"Toast and jam," Suzanne said. "I cooked this morning."

Linda tsk-tsked. "You can't be just throwing toast at a husband, you know, so start practicing some of Alexa's recipes. Because, girlie, unless God didn't make little green apples, you an' Paul Aldrich are gonna be husband and wife someday. Now . . ." She pulled in a breath and whooshed it out in Suzanne's ear. "Before I start breaking into some other song from the late, great sixties, I better let you go. I need to take a shower and gussy myself up for a trip to town. That girl of yours is wantin' to go into Indianapolis and visit her friend at the home again this afternoon, and she asked me to go along. Alexa's got some idea I can maybe talk sense into the little gal, although where she got that idea, I'll never know."

Fondness welled in Suzanne's chest. "Alexa can talk you into anything, can't she?"

"Yes, she can, even taking her to that crazy concert that's creeping up on us. I'm still hoping one of those bands will actually play something I know so I can sing along and embarrass the soup out of her."

Suzanne's laughter rolled. She shook her head, hugging the phone in lieu of hugging her friend. "Linda, what would we do without you?"

"I don't know, so let's hope we never have to find out."

■ ■ ■ ■

Indianapolis
Alexa

Ms. Reed let Alexa and Linda in, then performed her customary check of their coats and purses. Alexa was used to it already even if it bugged her, but Linda glowered at the woman. She muttered in Alexa's ear, "Do I look like some sort of druggie to you?"

Alexa whispered back, "Rules are rules. She does it to everybody."

Linda huffed, but she didn't grab her belongings and storm out.

Ms. Reed finished her inspection and turned a weary smile on Alexa. "Melissa was afraid you weren't going to visit her anymore. It's been a full week since you were here last."

Alexa cringed. She'd been busy, but she should have at least called. "I'm sorry. I hope she's free to visit today."

"She is. She's in the library, but the other girls are there, too. How about I send her to the front room? The three of you can visit there."

Alexa had hoped they could go to Melissa's room again. The old parlor wasn't

453

exactly private with its wide doorway opening into the large foyer, but if they kept their voices low, they might be able to have some semblance of privacy. She smiled. "That sounds great."

Alexa led Linda to the parlor. Linda's wide brown eyes scanned the room. She didn't hide her dismay. "My heavens, what a sad place. Looks like none of the furnishings have been changed in the past thirty years."

Alexa sat in one of the mismatched chairs. "I doubt they have the money to fix things up. Places like this are probably moving toward extinction. These days, people hardly blink when a girl turns up pregnant out of wedlock. Not like it was when Mom got pregnant."

Linda sighed and plopped onto the longer of the two sofas. "In some ways maybe that's good — that we don't trundle people off in disgrace. But on the other hand, there doesn't seem to be much shame at all anymore. People do whatever they want to without a thought for the consequences. Seems like there oughta be a balance somewhere."

A movement caught Alexa's attention, and she jumped up as Melissa entered the parlor. She rushed toward the girl, smiling, but Melissa didn't smile in return. Her large eyes looked sad, and her hands lay listlessly on top of her round belly. The girl had never been openly gregarious, but it appeared something inside of her had withered in the past days.

Alexa found herself faltering. "H-hi, Melissa. I'm sorry it's been so long between visits. I had a lot to do. But it's good to see you again, and I brought someone to meet you. You remember Tom?" She gestured to Linda. "This is his wife, Mrs. Denning. She's one of my dearest friends, and I know you'll love her as much as I do."

Linda chuckled as she crossed the faded area rug. She took hold of Melissa's limp hands and gave them a squeeze. "Hi there, sugar. You call me Linda, the same way Alexa does, okay? It's awfully nice to meet you in person."

A small smile briefly played on Melissa's lips. She withdrew her hands from Linda's and shuffled to the short sofa in front of the bay window. She sat on the edge of the sofa, her palms braced on the firm cushions as if prepared to launch herself off at any minute.

Linda shot a questioning scowl at Alexa and moved back to her previous seat. Alexa chose to join Melissa, though. The girl scooted over a bit, then sat looking at the floor, unspeaking.

The tension ate at Alexa, making her fidgety. She'd hoped Melissa would bring up their last conversation so she wouldn't have to, but minutes were ticking by, and Melissa showed no interest in saying anything. Linda made a now-what face. If Linda was at a loss for words, they were in trouble.

She cleared her throat and dove in. "Melissa, I brought Linda because —"

Melissa's head bounced up. "I thought about what you said, about how Evvie would think I didn't want her if I gave her up. I talked to Ms. Reed about it, too."

Alexa gave a start. She couldn't imagine taking anything of a personal nature to the stoic woman. "What did she say?"

"She said it could be true. That some adopted kids do feel like they were unwanted. But that other adopted kids are too happy with their new parents to worry about it. They're wanted by their adopted parents and that's enough. She said Evvie stood just as good a chance of being fine as not."

Alexa said softly, "Ms. Reed is in the business of placing babies with hopeful parents, so her opinion might be skewed."

Linda tromped over, her face set in a

frown. "Ms. Reed's opinion might not be the only one that's skewed. Scoot out of there, Alexa, and let me talk to Melissa."

Alexa shifted to a chair and Linda settled herself beside Melissa. She picked up Melissa's hand and cradled it between her palms. "Lemme see if I'm understanding all this right. You're planning to give your baby girl up for adoption, but Alexa doesn't think it's the best thing to do."

Melissa nodded. She flashed a resentful look at Alexa. "She said I'll regret it forever if I give my baby away." Her expression pleading, she turned to Linda. "But I don't think that's true. Why would I regret giving her to parents who really want her and will love her?"

"Maybe Alexa's just afraid you'll change your mind someday and it'll be too late to get your baby back. Giving up a baby isn't like lending a toy to a friend. It's for keeps. It's a big, big decision. I think she wants to make certain you're very, very sure."

Melissa's lips twisted into a grimace of pain. "I was very, very sure until she came along. Then she got me all mixed up."

Linda patted Melissa's hand and then stroked it the way someone would pet a puppy's head. "Okay, let's go back to before Alexa got you mixed up. Why did you decide to put your baby up for adoption?"

Misery tinged Melissa's features, but she shared how she got pregnant, her father's reaction, her sad home life. Her lower lip quivered. "Dad won't help me, and I don't have anybody else. Even if he would help me, I'm not ready to be a mom. It wouldn't be right for me to keep this baby. I love her. I love her a lot. I love her too much not to give her up." She tipped her head and gazed at Linda with tears swimming in her eyes. "Does that make sense?"

"Oh, darlin' . . ." Linda pulled Melissa into her embrace. She held the girl close, smiling over Melissa's head at Alexa. "Do you know what you've tapped in to?" Within Linda's arms Melissa shook her head. "You've tapped in to a love so deep it reminds me of the love God had for His Son."

Melissa drew back, puzzlement creasing her face. "What do you mean?"

Alexa leaned in, confused by Linda's statement, too.

"Did you know God gave up His Son, Jesus, for the sake of mankind? It's true. God loved His Son, but He also loved the world, and He knew the only way the world could be saved was for Jesus to take on the sins of all men and die for them." Linda stroked Melissa's hair as she spoke, her voice as tender as Alexa had ever heard it. "So as much as God loved Jesus, He gave Him up — His beloved Son. It must've broke God's heart to give Jesus over, but He did it because He knew, in the long run, it would be best." She smiled, using her thumb to brush away a tear that ran down Melissa's cheek. "And that's how you're loving your baby girl right now — enough to give her up because you know down in your heart of hearts it would be best."

Alexa charged over. "But —"

Linda held up her hand. "Alexa, you can't decide for Melissa. There are some decisions that are purely our own. Accepting the gift of salvation Jesus gave by submitting to the Cross is one of those. And the one Melissa is making is another." She slipped her arm around Alexa's waist and drew her close. "Honey-girl, I know why you feel the way you do. But you can't put your feelings on Melissa or on any other girl who's found herself in this kind of situation."

She kept hold of Alexa and turned to face Melissa. "Girlie, in this world there isn't a whole lot of unselfishness left. But what you're doing — thinking of your baby first — is pure unselfishness. It won't be easy for you. After your womb is empty and your baby's gone to her new home, your arms and your heart are gonna ache."

Tears welled in Melissa's eyes, and Alexa's vision swam.

"But you console yourself by remembering how much you love her and how much you want for her. You remember you did what you did for all the right reasons. Don't you beat yourself up, do you hear me? And don't you wallow in regret." Linda chuckled her deep, rumbling chuckle that always made Alexa smile, no matter how sad she felt. "I opened a fortune cookie one time and found this message — 'To err is human; to remain in error is stupid.'"

Melissa gave a tiny giggle, ducking her head.

"Having a baby before you're ready for it is certainly an error in judgment. But doing the responsible, unselfish thing and letting that baby be raised by people who are ready and willing? That's not even close to an error. All right?"

Melissa nodded, tears streaming down her face. "All right. Thank you, Linda."

"You're welcome, darlin'." She released Alexa to give Melissa another long hug, then she reached for Alexa again. Alexa sank down on her other side, and she pulled both girls close, rocking them gently to and fro. "Oh, you young ones . . . Someday you'll be as wise as me, but until then it sure is nice to be needed."

CHAPTER 34

Arborville
Paul

Paul walked Danny to the neighbor's house Friday after supper. The sun had already slunk below the horizon, taking the wind with it, so the evening was calm. Except for Paul's insides. A dozen bats, not of the baseball variety, flapped in his belly, and his flesh prickled with sweat despite the chilly temperatures.

Danny tromped intentionally hard as they crossed the Lapps' yard, breaking the crusty coating on the snow that had fallen last night. He lifted his foot extra high and must have thrown himself off balance because he slipped. Paul caught him before he lost his footing, and Danny sent his father a sheepish grin before stomping onward. Danny's near mishap increased the apprehension writhing through Paul's middle. Were the roads slick? He wouldn't want Suzy sliding into a ditch.

He knocked on the Lapps' door and it opened promptly. Mrs. Lapp had probably been watching for them. She loved doting on Danny. Before sending Danny over the threshold, Paul leaned down and whispered in his ear, "Remember, what we talk about at home is for us only. No yapping."

Danny nodded. "Okay, Dad."

Mrs. Lapp shook her finger at Paul. "I hope you weren't telling him not to ask for a snack. I have fresh gingerbread in the oven, and I picked up a tub of that premade whipped cream from the grocery store. I just don't have the strength to whip my own cream anymore, but the store-bought's not half bad."

Paul forced a chuckle. "Danny's at an age when he wants to eat twenty-four hours a day. Even though he had a good dinner, he'll be hungry again soon. Thank you for treating him."

"Oh, I enjoy it. I'll set aside a big piece for you, too. You can have it when you get back from . . . wherever you're going."

Paul hid a grin at the hint. "Thank you. That sounds great. I shouldn't be too late."

The elderly woman's smile remained intact. "Have a good evening now, and don't worry one bit about Danny. He and I will have a good time." Mrs. Lapp closed the door.

Paul trotted to his truck and climbed in, eager to get the evening over with while at the same time wishing he could postpone it. His father always said not to put off for tomorrow what could be done today, but he wasn't sure Dad was talking about attending a meeting with the Deacon Council.

The streets were dark and deserted, thick clouds hanging low. The fog became writhing ghosts in the headlights' beams. The sight unnerved him, and he wasn't one to be bothered by thoughts of ghosts and goblins. Maybe he should have walked. Only four blocks. He and Danny walked to church more often than they drove. If he'd walked, no one would see his truck parked with the deacons' vehicles and wonder about his reason for the private meeting. But that would be cowardly.

He pulled onto the churchyard. The floodlight mounted on the building's front lit the hoods of four vehicles. He recognized John Kreider's newer blue truck, Oral Bergen's old green truck, Girard Epp's sedan, and Sylvan Muller's panel van. Suzy hadn't arrived yet. Her compact car, which didn't meet the fellowship's restrictions, was missing. He parked beside the Muller van, leaving space for Suzy's car. Her little car could hide between the larger ones, but his vehicle would be prominently displayed. He might be a lot of things, but he didn't want to be branded a coward.

That's why he was coming tonight. The deacons had said they only needed to meet with Suzy. It would be easy to sit back, let her take full responsibility the way he had twenty years ago, but Paul was done with easy. Suzy was worth fighting for, and he'd let her know by standing at her side this evening.

Headlights broke through the fog — low, skimming the gravel road. His pulse skipped. Suzy's car . . . He waited until she pulled into the slice of space he'd left, then he hopped out and jogged around to the driver's side.

Her eyes widened in surprise when he opened the door for her. "You waited for me?"

"Yeah, but I just got here, too, so I didn't wait long." He moved aside as she stepped from the vehicle, then gave her door a push. "I was afraid the roads might be slick since the snow melted and then froze again. Did you have trouble?"

"None at all." She stood hugging herself, her wary gaze aimed at the church doors.

She released a self-conscious laugh. "Although sliding into a ditch might be preferable to what's waiting for me in there."

Paul couldn't find any words of assurance, so he just offered his elbow, and she took hold. They walked together across the hard ground, he tempering his stride to match hers. She'd worn a midcalf-length straight skirt — brown, he thought, although it was hard to tell with the shadow of her coat falling over it — and the little slit in the back seam didn't allow for wide steps. He didn't mind slowing down, though. It meant a few more seconds of time alone with her before they faced the firing squad.

Stop it! Hadn't Abigail Zimmerman told them they were meeting with Christian brothers who had their best interests at heart? Hadn't they prayed, first together and then individually, for God's will? Of course they had. He led Suzy up the front steps, his confidence increasing with each step. He wouldn't be a bit surprised if, right now, Abigail was covering the meeting with prayer. He needed to trust more and worry less.

He reached for the doorknob, aiming a wobbly smile at Suzy.

"Ready?" She bobbed her chin in a brief, emphatic nod. "Let's go."

■ ■ ■ ■

Suzanne

Suzanne crossed the damp, creaky boards to the women's door while Paul entered through the men's door. A wall separated the pair of cloakrooms, and during those brief seconds when he was out of sight, fear tried to take hold of her. *Lord, let me lean on You, not on Paul.*

Revived, she hung her coat on a hook, tugged her sweater hem over her hips, then smoothed her hand over her hair. She hoped her attire and hairstyle, although different from the other women in the fellowship, would be satisfactory. She'd done all she could to prepare. Now it was time to share.

Taking a deep breath, she stepped from the cloakroom into the worship room. Paul had already made his way to the front and was sitting on the first bench on the men's side. The four deacons — she knew all but one of them — sat on old wooden folding chairs lined up along the front edge of the preaching dais. For a moment her feet refused to move. The row of men looked so somber and forbidding. She sent up another short prayer for strength and moved up the center aisle.

She reached the front, and the eldest deacon, Girard Epp, stood and stepped down from the dais. He held out his hand, and Suzanne took hold, grateful for the small touch. Without a word he guided her to the front women's bench and gestured for her to sit. She sank down and folded her hands in her lap. She wanted to look at Paul, but she kept her gaze fixed on Deacon Epp as he returned to his chair, sat, and then sent a serious glance down the line of deacons.

Deacon Epp said, "I think we should start with prayer. Brother Bergen, would you speak to the Lord, please?"

The one man Suzy hadn't recognized stood, bowed his head, and asked God to guide them and give them discernment. Suzanne found herself echoing some of his words in her heart — especially the request for God's perfect will to prevail. The man ended with a solemn "amen," and he sat.

Deacon Epp turned to Paul. "Brother Aldrich, you're welcome to speak first, if you like."

Paul rose. Color streaked his neck and cheeks, but he stood with squared shoulders, widespread feet, and hands linked behind his back — a formal pose, yet somehow at ease, too. "I'm here mostly to support Suz— Miss Zimmerman. As you, Brother Kreider, and Brother Muller might remember, when we were still young, she and I were very good friends. More than friends. I wanted to court her."

The three deacons he'd addressed nodded.

"She left Arborville, and I married Karina Kornelson, but as you also know, Karina went to her heavenly reward when our son was very young."

Understanding spread across Deacon Epp's face. "Brother Paul, do you intend to ask permission to court Suzy Zimmerman?"

Paul turned a soft look on her. It lasted only a few seconds, but it lit something deep within her that continued to blaze even after he shifted to face the row of deacons again. "That's my intention."

Deacon Epp faced Suzanne. "Then should we assume you're here to ask to be reinstated as a member of the Arborville fellowship?"

Suzanne stood. "Before I make that request, there's something you need to know."

Deacon Muller waved his hand. "Miss Zimmerman, it's common knowledge that you bore a daughter out of wedlock."

Suzanne could imagine the talk that had

traveled through town. But they hadn't arrived at the whole truth yet. "Yes, I think everyone in Arborville knows I have a daughter, but they don't know who my daughter truly is or who her father is." While the deacons sat silent and attentive, she shared about being sent away as a seventeen-year-old, giving birth to a child and giving her up for adoption, then raising someone else's child as her own. "Because my baby's father lived here in Arborville, I never planned to return. I knew my return would raise questions, and I thought it was better if he never knew about our baby. But God had other plans."

She risked a glance at Paul and discovered him watching her with such a look of admiration her knees trembled. She wished she could stand beside him, hold his hand. *Lord, let me lean on You . . .* Facing the deacons again, she continued in a strong voice that hid her inner quaking. "God brought me back to Arborville, and He allowed love to" — she remembered Linda's choice of words — "rekindle between us despite the grave error we made in our youth."

Four pairs of eyes widened. Deacon Muller's jaw dropped open. He spluttered, "Are you telling us the father of your baby

470

is . . ." In unison the four men gawked at Paul.

Paul didn't flinch. "Yes. I fathered Suzy's baby. We've asked God's forgiveness, and in His mercy, He granted it. We've also forgiven each other."

Suzanne said, "So now I'm seeking the forgiveness of my family's fellowship leaders in the hope I can once again be a part of this body of believers."

She and Paul stood with a wide aisle separating them, yet she felt his support from the distance. He wasn't holding her hand, but she felt as though he held her heart. If the deacons denied her request, Paul wouldn't be given approval to court her. If they wanted a life together, he'd have to leave the fellowship. She prayed he wouldn't be forced to make such an excruciating choice. He loved the people in this community, and they loved him. She didn't want him to be forced to choose between her and his fellowship.

Deacon Epp pressed his palms to his knees and pushed himself upright. "Brother Aldrich, Miss Zimmerman, thank you for your honesty. I'm sure this wasn't easy for either of you." He shot a look at the other three deacons. "It wasn't easy for us to hear. The Zimmerman family has always had an

471

excellent reputation in this fellowship. Your father, Cecil, was a dear friend of mine and a trusted leader in our church. We'll want to move forward carefully so we don't sully his memory within the community."

Suzanne asked once again for courage from the Lord, and then she spoke softly. "Deacon Epp, the mistakes I made were mine, not my father's or my mother's or my siblings'. I, and I alone, am responsible for the choices I made. If you decide there should be any kind of corporate discipline, it needs to involve only me."

Paul stepped forward. "And me."

Deacon Epp gazed at Suzanne for several tense seconds, and then he nodded. He gestured to the deacons. "Gentlemen, let's go to the cloakroom, pray together, and make a decision concerning Miss Zimmerman's return to membership." The four of them filed across the front and along the side of the men's row of benches. They entered the cloakroom, and low mumbles could be heard coming from the small room.

Suzanne and Paul stayed on their benches, occasionally glancing at each other, offering encouraging smiles when their gazes met, but not speaking. Her back began to ache from sitting so stiffly, and the board beneath her seemed to grow harder with each minute that passed. She sat on these benches for worship, but during worship the congregation rose to sing or pray, and someone spoke from the dais, taking her attention away from the uncomfortable seat. She longed to get up, pace the room, stretch her stiff legs. But afraid of being caught, she sat as still as possible and waited for the deacons to make their decision.

Finally, when her feet were starting to tingle from lack of blood flow, footsteps alerted them to the leaders' return. Both she and Paul watched the men's progress. She searched their faces for some sign of what they might say, but their expressions hadn't changed from before. Three of the men halted along the wall when they reached the front, but Deacon Epp walked slowly and seemingly with great effort across the stained wood floor and stopped between Paul and Suzanne.

His hands linked behind his back, he looked first full into Paul's face and then into Suzanne's. "Brother Aldrich and Miss Zimmerman, we don't want to punish you for something that happened long ago, something you've already brought to the Lord and received His forgiveness for. So please understand we don't stand in judgment on you."

Suzanne's heart began to pound, and she noticed the muscles in Paul's jaw twitching.

Deacon Epp continued in a low, throaty voice. "You've been forgiven, yes, but your choices back then could impact the young people of our fellowship. If we let this go — simply sweep it under the rug, as they say — what kind of message are we giving to our youth? This is a dilemma the four of us don't feel qualified to handle on our own. We need to seek the entire fellowship's guidance.

"So, Miss Zimmerman, on Sunday after worship we'll release all the children and young people who are not yet published. Then we will call a special meeting of the membership. I'll ask you to confess to them what you shared with the council this evening, and then we will put your membership to a corporate vote."

CHAPTER 35

Indianapolis
Cynthia

Waking in Glenn's arms was sweeter than ever after their time apart. Curled on her side with Glenn's warm frame folded against her back and his arm draped over her waist, Cynthia kept her eyes closed and lay perfectly still, listening to his steady breathing. *Thank You, Lord, for bringing me home.*

Her heart panged when she remembered fleeing, not taking the time to seek God's guidance before acting in anger. She'd set a terrible example for Lindsey, which hindered her Christian witness. And her selfish choice had left bruises on her children's souls. Just as Glenn said, they offered their forgiveness when she asked, but they held themselves cautiously aloof, as if fearful she might choose to leave again. She lay in the circle of Glenn's arms and prayed for God to heal the wounds she'd inflicted on Darcy and Barrett and to somehow correct the poor impression she'd given Lindsey.

Glenn snuffled, his muscles twitching. Cynthia eased onto her back, careful not to dislodge his arm, and planted a kiss on the underside of his jaw. He made a horrible face and batted at his cheek. She stifled a giggle and kissed him again, this time closer to his mouth. His eyes popped open. He blinked twice, his forehead pinched in confusion, then his gaze settled on hers. A lazy smile bloomed.

"G'morning." He opened only one corner of his lips, aiming the words at the ceiling. He always wanted to spare her his morning breath.

Cynthia snuggled in, speaking with her face pressed against his bare chest. "Good morning to you."

"Ready to get up?"

She rolled sideways and burrowed her face into his neck. "Not really. It's Saturday. Do we have to get up?"

He chafed her spine with his palm, his breath warm against her temple. "I can't think of any reason why we'd need to."

The sound of running feet accompanied by a pair of angry voices erupted in the hallway.

"I'm gonna tell!" Barrett's voice.

"I'll tell 'em myself, Batwit, if you'll get out of my way!" Darcy sounded mad enough to spit.

Glenn groaned. "Well, there is that reason . . ." He scooted from the bed, leaving Cynthia warm beneath the covers. He snagged a T-shirt to pull on over his pajama pants as he crossed to the door and yanked it open. Darcy, her fists upraised, nearly fell through the opening.

Barrett dove past her and pressed his palms to Glenn's stomach. "Dad, Darcy was on the computer. I saw her on Facebook! And she didn't ask first!"

Darcy stomped her foot, glaring at her brother. "I said I'd tell them! Tattletale! Snitch! Narc!"

"All right, that's enough." Glenn planted his fists on his hips. "Barrett, go to your room."

"But, Dad, she —"

"Now, Barrett."

With a mighty expulsion of breath, Barrett whirled and stomped out of the room.

Glenn turned his attention to Darcy. "What are you doing on the computer without permission? You know the rules."

"You guys were sleeping. I peeked in, and you looked so" — pink flooded her face —

"cute together, I didn't want to bother you. My friend Jenna texted and said Emily from church posted some pictures from the youth ice-skating party, and there was a really good one of her and me skating couples with Connor and Ethan. I wanted to see it." Darcy raised her shoulders in a sheepish shrug. "Are you really mad?"

Glenn didn't relax his pose. "Yes, I am. It doesn't matter how cute you thought your mother and I were." He glanced at Cynthia, and she pulled the covers over her mouth to hide her smile. He cleared his throat and went on. "You should have asked first. You have no business being on the computer when one of us isn't there to supervise."

Barrett's muffled voice carried from behind his closed bedroom door. "That's what I told her!"

Glenn stuck his head into the hallway and called, "Enough, Barrett." He turned to Darcy again. "No computer for a week. Got it, buckaroo?"

Darcy poked out her lips in a pout and lowered her head. "Got it." She jerked upright, giving Glenn a pleading look. "But before I shut it down, can I show you and Mom something?"

Glenn's lips quirked into a half grin. "The photo of you skating with Connor?"

"Jenna skated with Connor. I skated with Ethan." Her uncombed hair flopped across her forehead, hiding her right eye. She pushed the brown strands aside and then tweaked her finger at them. "Come here. Tell me what you think." Darcy trotted out of the room.

Cynthia shrugged into her robe and followed Glenn to the desk in the corner of the living room where the computer monitor sent out a bluish glow.

Darcy slid into the chair and pointed to a photograph on the screen. "Look, Mom. This popped up on Jenna's newsfeed. Do you think maybe this girl could be your daughter? The dates are right."

Cynthia leaned close and examined the image. A young woman with long dark hair pulled back into a sleek ponytail held up a poster bearing a simple message: "My name is Alexa. I turned 20 in December of last year. I am looking for my birth mother, who left me behind an Indianapolis garage when I was a newborn. If you have information about my birth parents, please send me a message at PO Box 1464, Franklin, IN."

A girl named Alexa had left the message on Mr. Mallory's voice mail. Could this be the same Alexa? Cynthia held her hand to her throat, her pulse leaping worse than frog legs in a hot skillet. "I . . . I don't know. Maybe . . ."

Glenn, too, leaned in and frowned at the photo. "It does seem pretty coincidental, doesn't it, that the time and place you left her match up. I don't really see much resemblance between her and you, though, except for her hair color." He zipped an impish grin in her direction. "When you leave yours natural."

She self-consciously touched her blond highlights as she squinted at the screen. "Can you make the picture bigger, Darcy?"

"I can try." She punched some buttons on the keyboard, and with each click the picture increased in size. Six clicks, and then she smiled up at Cynthia. "Is that better?"

Cynthia nodded. Now she could clearly make out the girl's features. Her heart leaped. "Glenn! Is that a birthmark on her upper lip?"

Glenn frowned. "You mean that big freckle?" His jaw dropped open. He looked at Cynthia's face and then Darcy's. He shook his head, his eyes widening in disbelief. "I'm so used to those brown spots on your mouth and Darcy's, I don't even notice them anymore. But you're right, she has one, too, almost in the same place as both of yours."

Cynthia yanked open the desk drawer and fumbled around for a pen and paper. Her eager hands were clumsy, but she latched on to what she needed and bumped the drawer closed with her hip. She thrust the notepad and pen at Darcy. "Here, write down the box number. My hands are shaking so much I won't be able to read it later."

Darcy grinned and took the items from her.

Cynthia reached for Glenn, and he pulled her close. She coiled her arms around his waist and beamed up at him. "If this is my daughter, we won't need to bother Mr. Mallory anymore."

Glenn's expression turned wary. "Now, let's wait and see how that DNA test comes out, okay? He seemed pretty sure your daughter is living in Kansas. Besides, Indianapolis is a big city. It's possible this girl is actually someone else's daughter."

Cynthia tried to smother her excitement, but it refused to die. "Darcy, print the picture for me, would you?"

She shot a startled look at Cynthia. "In color?"

Cynthia laughed. They preserved their color ink cartridge for really special things. But this was special. Her first photo of her firstborn child . . . "Yes, in color."

"Okay. And . . ." Hopefulness glistened in Darcy's blue eyes. "Does this mean I'm not grounded from the computer anymore?"

Glenn lightly bopped the top of her head. "No. When you're done printing the picture for Mom, shut it down and stay away from it." Then he bent down and kissed her rumpled hair. "But thank you for finding this."

Darcy sighed and turned her attention to the computer. Cynthia stood beside the printer, waiting for the image to emerge. Her stomach jumped when the machine buzzed to life. She clutched her hands beneath her chin, watching the image appear by tiny jerks, one row of color at a time. First the poster, with a tiny peek at her daughter's fingers — because they had to be her daughter's fingers — wrapped around the edges, finally her daughter's chin, then her mouth with the telltale birthmark, her nose and eyes and the top of her head. The printer belched the finished picture into Cynthia's waiting hands, and she held it aloft.

She burst out laughing — a joyful explosion. "Glenn! She has brown eyes! Just like me!"

Glenn smiled and gave her a one-armed hug.

She sighed, staring at the grainy image with Glenn's arm snug around her shoulders and her heart thudding in happy double beats. When her hands decided to stop shaking, she'd sit down and write a letter. A long letter. Typing would go faster, but she wanted her daughter to have a handwritten letter, something more personal than words printed on a computer, something of herself. She'd tuck in a family photo, too — the one they'd done a year ago when the church updated its directory. She had a couple of extra three-by-fives around somewhere.

The words she'd longed to say to her child filled her head, and her fingers tingled, eager to release her thoughts onto a page. Her daughter. She'd found her daughter.

Arborville
Suzanne

If Mother wasn't holding her hand, she just might flee the chapel. From behind the simple wood stand on the speaking dais, Deacon Kreider delivered a message based on verses twelve through sixteen in chapter one of James. Verses about the importance of standing firm against temptation. Had he chosen the passage before or after the meeting last night?

" 'Do not err, my beloved brethren,' " he quoted, his face somber and his tone dire.

Suzanne inwardly squirmed. The man was setting her up for rejection. She shifted her gaze slightly to Paul's bench. Was the message making his stomach quake, too? If so, he hid it well. He sat straight on the backless bench, his shoulders square, face aimed toward the speaker.

Last night after the meeting, they'd stood between their vehicles and talked. He'd promised to stand beside her today even though the deacons hadn't said it was necessary. He also said he would speak in her defense during the members' discussion and vote if someone expressed concern about letting her return to the fellowship.

"And I'll tell you something else, Suzy. If they vote you out, they've voted me out, too. We made a baby together, and we'll take the consequences together." When she'd started to argue, he held up his hand. "I mean it. If you go, I go." His expression, bathed by the light flowing from the church's large lamp, turned tender. "There are other fellowships, even other Mennonite denominations. We'll find a new church family, and we'll worship there together — you, me, Danny, and Alexa. Okay?"

Even as she'd agreed, she realized if they

left, Alexa wouldn't be with them. How she prayed they wouldn't be forced into such a painful choice.

"Please rise and sing."

At the announcement Suzanne jerked back to the present. Her hand still within Mother's firm grasp, she stood and joined her voice with the others in the chosen hymn. *What can wash away my sin? Nothing but the blood of Jesus . . .* A smile — the first one of the morning — teased the corners of her lips. Jesus's blood had washed away her sins. God was for her, so what could mere men do to her? Peace descended, and she sang while joy exploded in her soul.

The hymn ended, and the leader instructed them to kneel for prayer. Suzanne bowed low over the bench, sending up prayers of gratitude for God's amazing ability to forgive even the vilest offender. *Your will, Father. Let Your will prevail today . . .* Somehow she knew Paul was offering the same petition.

At the leader's "amen," everyone rose and turned toward the front. Instead of the typical blessing to go in peace, Deacon Kreider said, "Please, everyone, sit back down."

Confused mutters rolled around the room. As Suzanne sat, Mother reached for her hand again, and she clung. Not because she needed Mother's comfort — she'd found her place of peace — but because she sensed Mother needed assurance.

Once everyone was settled, the deacon instructed all children ages three years old to fifteen years old to go to the basement with his wife so the grown-ups could have a special meeting. More mutters rumbled, and confused young people gathered the smaller ones and followed Mrs. Kreider around the corner. The pounding of their feet on the wooden stairs thundered briefly and then faded away. When silence fell, Deacon Epp stepped to the front, and Deacon Kreider moved aside.

Deacon Epp swept a tight smile across the room. "Thank you for your patience. I know you have dinners waiting at home and this meeting comes as a surprise, but we need to conduct some family business this morning. A long-ago member of our fellowship has returned to Arborville. Most of you know her — Suzy Zimmerman, daughter of Cecil, who is now departed, and Abigail Zimmerman."

Several people craned their heads and looked at Suzanne, Anna-Grace included. Most smiled, some boldly, others more shyly. Sandra and Anna-Grace both beamed. Shelley didn't turn around. Nervousness tried to take hold of Suzanne again.

"She's asked to be reinstated, but there are unique circumstances. The Deacon Council and I wanted her to speak to the body first." Deacon Epp made eye contact with Suzanne and held out his hand in invitation. "Come, please, Miss Zimmerman."

Suzanne made her way up the aisle, aware of every pair of eyes in the room following her progress. As she passed Paul's bench, he rose and accompanied her for the last few yards. Together they faced the congregation, and Deacon Epp joined Deacon Kreider off to the side, where they stood with serious gazes pinned on her.

Suzanne sent up one more quick prayer for God's will and then offered a nervous "Good morning." Several people returned her greeting, which warmed her. Under their curious, attentive gazes, she began the careful explanation she'd planned last night — telling the truth while trying to protect Anna-Grace wouldn't be easy. "As you already know, I recently returned from Indiana, where I'd been working as a nurse for the past several years. Coming here was . . . coming home. I grew up in Arborville, in this fellowship. My family is here" — she glanced at her sisters and at Clete, then let her gaze linger on Mother — "and I would like to be a part of their church fellowship again. The deacons thought it best for me to explain the reason I left Arborville almost twenty-one years ago."

Someone on the women's side released a gasp. Suzanne glanced at her sister, and Shelley's horrified expression stole her ability to speak for a few seconds. Suzanne swallowed, gathering courage once more. "When I'm finished, they'll allow you to decide whether or not to grant me membership. I only ask you vote as the Lord leads you, because I want God's will more than my own."

With Paul at her side and Mother's warm smile encouraging her from the back of the room, Suzanne shared her story. People drew back in surprise at her confession of becoming pregnant when she was seventeen. Mouths opened in shock when she told about giving her baby away for adoption. Admitting she'd raised a baby abandoned behind the home for unwed mothers proved the most difficult as memories of that confusing time of both intense pain and unspeakable joy rolled through her. Tears swam in some eyes as she confided her reasons for not returning to her family.

She finished, "God led me back to Arbor-ville so I could make things right again with my mother, my siblings, and my baby's father. I stand forgiven in God's eyes, and I now seek your forgiveness for misleading you. Thank you."

Deacon Epp stepped close. "Brother Aldrich, do you have anything to add?"

"Yes." Paul gave Suzy a brief look that communicated his complete support and deep love for her before facing the congregation. "I fathered Suzy's child. Therefore, I'm equally at fault for Suzy leaving Arbor-ville and being separated from her family all these years. If there is judgment, it belongs on my shoulders, too."

Deacon Epp cleared his throat. "Thank you, Brother Aldrich and Miss Zimmerman. You may return to your seats." He stood in silence while Paul escorted Suzanne to her bench and then made his way to his own bench on the men's side. The deacon clasped his hands over the flaps of his suit coat. "Before we make a vote, would anyone like to speak?"

Shelley stood so quickly the ribbons on her cap bounced. "I would."

Suzanne's heart seemed to lodge in her throat, cutting off her breath.

Deacon Epp nodded. "All right, Sister Unruh."

"I've been mad at my sister for years. Mad at her for leaving. Mad at her for not coming back. Then mad at her because she did come back."

Suzanne shrank at Shelley's harsh tone. She closed her eyes and reached blindly for Mother's hand, and warm, strong fingers curled around hers, offering comfort.

"Everything inside of me wants to say no, she can't rejoin this fellowship the way she's rejoined the family — as if she's never been away. But after today's message . . . about resisting temptation . . . I can't. If I said no, it would be for me, not for her. It would be my will, not God's will."

Suzanne popped her eyes open and stared disbelievingly at the back of her sister's stiff form.

"I don't want to err, so I won't be voting this morning." She sat as abruptly as she'd risen. Sandra laid her head on Shelley's shoulder, and Shelley rested her temple on the top of Sandra's cap for a moment. The simple, silent communication between the two of them brought a sting of tears to Suzanne's eyes.

Deacon Epp scanned the room. "Anyone else?" Heads turned, people glancing around, but no one rose. He gave a brusque nod. "All right then. Miss Zimmerman, would you please step into the cloakroom while we cast our votes?"

Suzanne removed her hand from Mother's grip and scurried around the corner. She leaned against the wall, her heart seeming to beg with every beat, *Your will, God. Your will . . .*

Deacon Epp's voice boomed. "All who wish to welcome Suzy Zimmerman into membership with our fellowship, indicate so by raising your right hand."

CHAPTER 36

Franklin
Alexa

Alexa dropped her cell phone on her bed and clattered across the hall to Linda and Tom's closed bedroom door. They'd gone in nearly an hour ago for their regular Sunday afternoon nap. She hoped they'd rested enough because she couldn't wait one more minute to share Mom's news.

She gave the door three hard thumps with her fist. "Tom! Linda! Can I come in?"

Linda's croaky voice answered. "Yes, but use the doorknob. Don't break the door down."

Giggling, Alexa darted into the room and plopped down on the end of the bed. She pinched Linda's toes through the afghan covering her. "Sorry I interrupted your nap, but you have to hear this."

Linda jerked her feet away and glowered at Alexa, but the scowl lacked real fury.

"Girlie, this better be good."

Tom yawned and balled his hands into fists, stretching. "I agree. I was dreaming about playing golf and was just ready to tee off."

"Trust me, Tom, this is better than golf. It's better than chocolate and a T-bone steak and cheesecake and coffee and —"

Linda bumped her with her foot. "What is it?"

"Mom rejoined the Arborville fellowship."

Two sets of eyebrows rose.

"And the deacons gave her and Paul Aldrich permission to get published."

They both sat up, making the bed bounce. "What?" They chorused the startled exclamation.

Alexa nodded, smiling so broadly her cheeks hurt.

Linda threw off the afghan and swung her feet to the floor. "When? How?"

Alexa stifled a giggle. Linda at a loss for words was a rarity. "This morning after the worship service in Arborville. The deacons had Mom share her testimony, then my aunt Shelley stood up and said something about not erring, and the congregation voted to let Mom be a member. After that, the deacons took Mr. Aldrich aside and told him they approved him courting Mom."

Alexa flipped her hands outward. "It all happened in one swell foop!"

Linda continued to stare at Alexa with her mouth hanging open. Tom leaned forward and put his hand on Alexa's shoulder. "Honey-girl, I think you mean 'one fell swoop.' "

Alexa laughed, shaking her head. "I'm so excited I can hardly talk."

Apprehension tinged Tom's face. His fingers squeezed gently. "I know you're happy for your mama, but how do you feel about all this?"

Alexa frowned. "What do you mean?"

"Just thinking . . ." Tom scratched his chin, fluffing his snow-white whiskers. "If your mama joins the church, she'll go back to wearing a cap and homemade dresses. If she gets married, you'll be getting a step-daddy and a stepbrother. She'll move in with her husband and his little boy instead of living at the farmhouse with you." He paused, searching her face. "Are you okay with all that?"

She blinked, confused. "Shouldn't I be?"

Linda rounded the bed and sat beside Alexa. She draped her arm across Alexa's shoulders and scowled at Tom. "Now, don't be planting reasons to worry in her head. Let her be! She's happy for our Suzanne, and she ought to be." She tugged Alexa against her side. "I think it's all good news, and I think we should do something special to celebrate." An impish grin dimpled her full cheeks. "Like eating chocolate cake."

"We don't have any chocolate cake."

"So bake one." Linda waggled her eyebrows. "I know how much you like to bake."

Alexa snickered. "And I know how much you like to eat what I bake." She stood. "All right, one rich, gooey, chocolate celebration cake comin' up. And then" — she sucked in a breath — "I think I'm going to look for airline tickets and go home."

For the second time that day, she rendered Linda speechless.

Tom came to life, though. "Home? But what about that DNA test? Don'tcha want to wait and see if that PI is working for your birth mother?"

For reasons she hadn't yet fully understood, the deep need to find her birth mother had eased. Maybe Melissa's unselfishness had erased some of Alexa's resentment. She chewed her lip. "Well . . ."

"And if you leave now, you won't get to go to the concert."

Alexa shrugged. "You could use my ticket. You and Linda could go instead."

Linda found her voice. "Oh, no, you don't. You're not skipping out on me, girlie. Besides, you were looking forward to seeing that reporter friend of yours and the little gal who stayed at the bed-and-breakfast. You gonna skip out on them, too?"

Technically she wasn't skipping out on Briley or Nicci K since they had no idea she'd even be at the concert. But Linda's comment made her reconsider. She had anticipated saying hello to Briley and seeing Nicci K perform. "I guess a few more days won't hurt."

" 'Course it won't." Linda's staunch reply sealed it.

"Okay. I'll stay through the end of the month. But then . . ." She sighed. "Home."

On Monday morning Alexa drove to Indianapolis to visit Melissa. Ms. Reed called Melissa to the parlor, and to Alexa's relief the girl seemed glad to see her. She pulled a photograph from her pocket and held it out. Alexa took it and gazed at the image of a smiling man and woman standing on a small arched bridge. The man held a tow-headed little boy.

"This will be Evvie's family." Melissa tapped the faces. "This is Kristian and Allen. They adopted Rylin when he was a newborn. He's four now. Doesn't he look like a happy little boy?"

Alexa nodded. They all looked happy — the dad, the mom, and the boy.

Melissa cradled her ever-blossoming belly and sighed. "They told me Rylin's been praying for a baby sister, so they were really happy when they found out my baby was a girl." Awe bloomed on her face. "I can hardly believe my little baby is going to be somebody's answer to prayer."

Tears stung behind Alexa's nose. She whispered, "Beauty from ashes."

Melissa tipped her head, her brow crinkling. "What?"

"It's what God does. He takes our ashes — our mistakes — and He makes something beautiful out of them." Just like He had when He'd led Mom to that box behind the garage. "That's because He loves us. He redeems our errors."

Melissa sat in silence for a few seconds, her face reflecting wonderment. Then she blurted, "Guess what else?"

Alexa shrugged and held out her hands in query.

"They had planned to name her Adrianna, but they decided to name her Evelyn instead." Tears winked in Melissa's eyes. "Evelyn Adrianna. Isn't that pretty?"

Alexa nodded. "It's a beautiful name."

"Uh-huh." Melissa took the photo back and gazed at it, joy and pain mingling in her moist eyes. "They took a picture of me, too, for Evvie's baby book so she'll know what I look like. They said I could write her a note to put with it. I've been working on something. It's kind of turned into a poem." She angled a hesitant look at Alexa. "Want to see it?"

"Sure."

Melissa unfolded a slip of paper and pressed it into Alexa's hands. Alexa held the page toward the window and began to read.

My life wasn't ready to call you my own.
I had nothing to offer, not even a home.
Then along came a family who promised to
    be
All the things that I couldn't, and they told
    me,
"We'll love her forever. We'll raise her up
    right.
Her days will be happy. She'll be safe at
    night."
So I collected all the love I could gather,
And I used it for courage to give you over
To the ones who were ready to be Mom
    and Dad.
The parting is painful, but I am so glad

You'll have lots of love from a good family.
My dear little Evvie, please think kindly of
me.

When Alexa finished reading, a veil of
tears made the words shimmy on the page.
"It's . . ." She swallowed. "It's . . ."

Melissa grimaced. "It's corny, isn't it?"
She took the paper back and sighed. "It's so
hard to say what I feel. I wish I was a real
poet."

Alexa impulsively hugged the other girl.
"You are a real poet. A real poet shares her
heart, and you did that."

Melissa pulled back, hope shining on her
face. "Really?"

"Really."

"Then you think she'll understand? She'll
know it wasn't that I didn't want her?"

"You're putting her into the arms of a loving mother and father, Melissa." Unlike her
own mother, who left her in a box to freeze.
"She'll understand."

Melissa blew out a mighty breath, relief
slumping her shoulders. "Good." She
slipped the poem and photograph into her
pocket, and they spent the next hour chatting about other things.

When lunchtime arrived, Ms. Reed asked
Alexa to join them, but she said no. She had

another errand in Indianapolis before she drove back to Tom and Linda's. So she hugged Melissa, cautioning her that she might not see her again since she'd be going back to Kansas soon. She gave Melissa her phone number and Arborville address, and Melissa promised to let Alexa know when Evvie was born.

Lines from Melissa's poem to her baby echoed through Alexa's mind as she drove into downtown Indianapolis. Thanks to Mom and wonderful people like the Dennings, she'd always known love. Her days had been happy. She'd been safe and secure. Everything Melissa wished for her little girl Alexa had received. But her birth mother hadn't bothered to write a note or leave a picture or anything. Did she really want to look into the face of the person who'd abandoned her?

She left the car in a parking garage and walked to Owen Mallory's office. The noon sunshine made her squint but did little to warm her. She was glad to find his door unlocked so she could dart inside out of the cold.

The private investigator sat at his desk, bent over a sheet of paper. He glanced up when she entered. "Well, well, well . . ." He set the paper aside and remained in his chair while Alexa crossed the tile floor. "Funny you'd come in just now."

Alexa draped her hands over the back of one of the plastic chairs. "Why's that?"

He patted the page he'd been examining. "Reading a DNA report. No match to my client."

Alexa borrowed a Tomism. "Told ya."

Mr. Mallory laughed — one short snort of humor. "Guess I'm going to send yours through now and see what happens."

Alexa tightened her grip on the chair. "Would you not, please?"

He frowned, his eyebrows dipping into a sharp V. "What?"

"I'd rather you didn't run my DNA."

"Let me get this straight. You came to me claiming to be the baby I've been hunting, and now you're telling me you're not?"

She shook her head. "I'm not denying I'm the baby your client abandoned. I'm her, all right. What I'm saying is, I don't want to be found." She gave the top of the chair a little smack and took a backward step. "So just tell your client —"

He bolted up and rounded the desk. "Wait a minute." The man's usually emotionless eyes snapped. He stopped within inches of her. "I'm not into game playing, missy. You can't waltz in here wanting things one way and then turn them upside down."

Alexa's heart pounded. Maybe she should have brought Tom with her. But didn't he always say a soft answer turned away wrath? Alexa chose a calm, reasonable tone. "I'm not playing games, Mr. Mallory. This is my life we're talking about. I have a family — a mom who raised me and loves me very much. Sure, I'm curious about the woman who gave birth to me, but I don't need to meet her. She couldn't possibly be better than the mom I already have."

He narrowed his eyes into slits. "You don't know that."

"Actually, I think I do." A smile of fondness formed effortlessly. "I've got the best mom in the world. God handpicked her for me."

He huffed. "Well, you aren't my client, and I have an obligation to follow every lead I'm given. So I'm running your DNA, and I'll give the results to my client. You can't stand in the way."

Alexa nibbled her lip and considered his statement. Finally she shrugged. "Okay. Run it. Like you said, you work for her, and she's expecting answers. But just because we match doesn't mean I'll be willing to meet." She moved to the door. To her relief he didn't follow.

At supper she shared with Tom and Linda about confronting Mr. Mallory. They both scolded her for going to the office alone and made her promise not to do it again. She gave the assurance easily. She had no desire to see that man or his client. She only wanted to go home to Mom and settle into her new routine of having a stepdad and stepbrother.

On Tuesday she slept in and wandered into the kitchen well past the breakfast hour. Linda was bent over rummaging in the refrigerator, her backside sticking out. The clink of jars banging together competed with the radio set to a talk show where two people were arguing. Loudly. Alexa cringed at the ruckus as she passed the radio and eased up beside Linda. She reached over Linda's shoulder for the milk.

Linda rose with a start, nearly clunking Alexa with her elbow. She clutched her chest and glared at Alexa. "Gracious sakes, girlie, don't sneak up on a person like that. You wanna send me to meet my Maker?"

"Sorry, Linda. I didn't mean to scare you." She frowned at the blaring box on the counter. "You'd have heard me if the radio wasn't going full blast. What are you listening to?"

"Humph." Linda marched over and

slapped the Off button. "Tom put it on and then he left. He likes listening to all that jabber. I don't." She balled her fists on her hips. "You missed our morning eggs and toast. I already cleaned up dishes. Are you gonna make a mess now?"

Alexa's stomach growled. She grimaced. "Sorry, Linda, but I think I am. I won't make much of one. Just some cereal or something will tide me over until lunch."

Linda waved her hand and laughed. "Oh now, I was teasing you. I know you always clean up after yourself. Fix whatever you want to. I'll sit at the table and drink another cup of coffee while you eat." She plunked into a chair and sighed. "Can't hardly believe you'll be gone to Kansas soon. Tom and I got used to having our girl around again." She sniffed. "We'll miss you."

Alexa wrapped her arms around Linda from behind and planted a kiss on her plump cheek. "I'll miss you, too. Maybe you and Tom should think about moving to Arborville."

Linda patted Alexa's arms and then pulled loose. "Gracious, girlie, as if we'd want to be the only two pepper flakes in a saltshaker."

Alexa laughed.

Linda laughed, too. "We'll visit, that's for sure, but we're not suited to small-town living. Kinda surprised your mama's taken to it so easily after all her years away."

Sometimes it surprised Alexa how easily she and Mom had settled in. She shrugged, taking a box of cereal and a bowl from the cupboard. "I guess when it's where you're supposed to be, it just . . . works."

Linda watched her pour the cereal and milk, her face puckered into a thoughtful frown. "Do you think it'll ever work for you to join that church in Arborville? Now, I'm not saying there's anything wrong with it. Tom and I enjoyed the singing — oh, the hymns! Those people sing better than some professional choirs I've heard. And the preaching went a little long, but I couldn't find any fault with it even if it wasn't a real minister giving the sermon. It's solid. But the rules . . ." She shook her head. "Could you do all that — the dresses and caps and men and women sitting apart?"

Alexa carried her bowl to the table and sat across from Linda. Her cereal was getting soggy, but she only stirred it around rather than eating it. "I'm not sure. Maybe. Eventually. Especially now that Mom's joining." She released a humorless huff of laughter. "I mean, look at my clothes. I've never dressed like my friends anyway. Putting on the Mennonite-approved dress and cap wouldn't be a lot different than my skirts and blouses, right?"

Linda's gaze roved from Alexa's button-up turquoise sweater to her denim skirt, knee socks, and brown ballet flats. "I dunno. Don't think they'll let you wear orange socks with blue and yellow butterflies with those dresses."

Alexa grinned. "No?" She gave a flippant shrug. "I can live without orange socks."

Linda reached over and cupped Alexa's cheek. "Well, I tell you what, girlie. Tom and I will pray extra hard for you — that you'll know what to do about joining, all right? We want you to be happy."

Alexa raised her shoulder, pressing Linda's hand more firmly against her face. "I am happy, Linda. I really am. I think maybe it's taken me being away from Mom for a little while to fully understand how special she is and how lucky I am to have her."

Linda gave her a little pat and dropped her hand. She pointed at the bowl. "Pray and get to eating before that turns into mush."

Alexa laughed and bowed her head. As she finished her prayer, the back door slapped into its frame and Tom came in.

"Brr," he shuddered, hugging himself. "It's so cold I think I about turned into a giant Fudgesicle. But I got your vitamins" — he handed Linda a small sack — "and I stopped by the post office to check Alexa's box. Would you believe that thing's already collecting junk mail? But I found a letter in it, too. A fat one." He plopped it on the table next to Alexa's cereal bowl. "There ya go, honey-girl."

Alexa glanced at the envelope. Her name filled the center front, written in a precise, flowing script. The return address read *Cynthia Baker Allgood, Indianapolis.*

Linda pointed at it. "You gonna read that?"

Alexa grinned and dipped her spoon. "When I've finished my mush."

CHAPTER 37

Arborville
Suzanne

Suzanne checked the timer on the stove. Five more minutes and the pies would be done. She bounced hot pads against her thighs, eager to take out the last two and then make her delivery to the café. By next Tuesday, Alexa would be here, taking over the pie baking. She couldn't wait to see her girl. And not just because it meant a reprieve from baking. So much had transpired in the past three weeks. She needed to look into her daughter's eyes and make sure Alexa was all right with the changes. Alexa had spent her entire childhood without a father. Would she resent Suzanne for marrying now that Alexa was grown?

Anna-Grace finished scrubbing the worktable clean of the remnants of flour and fruit juices and carried the rag to the sink. As she passed Suzanne, she paused and whisked an uncertain glance at her.

Suzanne forced a smile. "Did you need something, Anna-Grace?"

She kept her lips pressed together, shook her head, and moved on.

Suzanne stifled a sigh. Anna-Grace had hardly said three words since Sunday. Of course, they hadn't been together much. Anna-Grace joined another family for lunch and visiting after church. Then she spent all day Monday at the grade school, helping Steven in the classroom. Monday evening she and Mother sat at the dining room table and worked on wedding favors while Suzanne, Paul, and Danny played a board game in the living room. She'd sensed Anna-Grace watching them, but each time she peeked, the girl quickly averted her gaze.

Maybe she should bring up the subject that had to be tormenting her daughter. But Mother had advised her to let Anna-Grace come to her when she was ready, so Suzanne remained in tense silence, waiting for the storm to erupt.

The stove's timer buzzed. Suzanne turned it off, then removed the two perfectly browned apple pies. She smiled. She might not enjoy baking as much as Alexa did, but her pies smelled just as good. She set them on cooling racks and moved to the butler's pantry to retrieve the carry containers. When she returned to the kitchen, she found Anna-Grace standing in the middle of the floor, her hands twisting her apron and her face wearing a mask of apprehension.

"Cousin Suzy, may I . . . ask you something?"

Suzanne's heart flipped. *It's time, Lord. It's finally time. If only Paul was here, too, to help. Let me answer her questions in a way that brings healing rather than fractures.* She managed a jerky nod. "Of course. You can ask me . . . anything."

"I was surprised by what you said on Sunday. I mean, I already knew Alexa wasn't your biological daughter. My mom and dad mentioned it around Christmastime. But they didn't tell me you'd given up a baby for adoption."

Suzanne swallowed. She inched to the chairs beside the worktable and sank into one. She gestured to the other one, and Anna-Grace sat. Suzanne pressed her palms together between her knees to control her trembling. "It isn't something I mentioned to anyone. They didn't know, either, until recently."

"I see." Anna-Grace looked to the side, worrying her lip with her teeth. "From what you said in service, you were young. And not married." The girl's cheeks flared with red.

"That's true." Surprisingly, her voice emerged calm, devoid of embarrassment. "I made a terrible mistake, and even though God forgave me, I live with the consequences of that choice every day. I've encouraged Alexa to follow the Bible's teaching and remain pure until marriage, just as I know your parents encouraged you, because it's the best way to avoid regrets."

Anna-Grace nodded. She fiddled with her apron, her head low. "Didn't you want to . . . to keep your baby?"

Suzanne wished she could look into Anna-Grace's face, but her daughter kept her head low, so far down that the tips of her cap's ribbons touched her lap. "I wanted to, yes, but I —" She gulped. "It's just that —"

Mother wheeled around the corner, steely determination glinting in her eyes. She rolled her chair so close her knees bumped Anna-Grace's, and she lifted the girl's head with one cupped hand. "What Suzy's trying not to tell you is that I sent her away. I made her give up her baby. I told her it would shame the whole family if people knew she had an out-of-wedlock child." Mother sounded so blunt, so without feeling, but the quiver in her hand and the tears in her eyes communicated her remorse. "There were a whole lot of wrongs done, and most of them for the wrong reasons." She released Anna-Grace's chin and reached for Suzanne. "But God can take wrongs and turn them into rights. He let Suzy's baby grow up in a loving home, and He gave Suzy her own child to love and nurture. We erred, but He was sovereign." She met Suzanne's gaze, her expression tender. "Yes?"

Suzanne nodded. "Yes." She turned to Anna-Grace. Her mouth felt dry, and she licked her lips. "Was there . . . anything else you wanted to know?"

Anna-Grace sat stone still and stared into Suzanne's face for long seconds, appearing not to even breathe. Then she sagged, her air easing out. She shook her head. "No. Nothing else."

Torn between relief and disappointment, Suzanne rose. "Well, then, I better get these pies loaded up and into town before they think I'm not coming." She'd try to find Paul when she was in town, too. She needed a hug.

Franklin
Alexa
Alexa tipped the potato chunks from the

512

cutting board into the soup pot. The potatoes covered the chunks of ham, carrots, and onions already in the pot. She still needed to cut up the cabbage and add a jar of stewed tomatoes, but they didn't take as long to cook as the other vegetables, so she'd add the last two ingredients later. Her mouth watered, thinking about dipping her spoon into a bowl of the flavorful borscht, a recipe she borrowed from the women at the Franklin Mennonite Brethren church. She moved to the sink to rinse the cutting board and knife.

As she turned on the spigots, Tom came in from the garage and crossed to the sink. With a grin he nudged Alexa aside with his hip. "Lemme go first." He held up his hands. "I'm all greasy."

She backed away. "What were you doing out there?"

"Puttering." He lathered his hands with dish soap. "It keeps me out of Linda's hair so I don't get myself in trouble."

Alexa shook her head, laughing. "You might find yourself in trouble if you don't rinse those greasy smears out of the sink."

With a mock look of fear, he grabbed the cleaning sponge and attacked the sink. He finished and yanked a few paper towels from the roll. As he dried his hands, he moved out of her way. He bobbed his chin at the envelope sitting at the end of the counter. "Haven't you opened that thing yet?"

Alexa, scrubbing potato residue from the knife, glanced at the letter and shrugged. "What's the hurry? It's probably like all the others that have come — useless."

He picked it up and pinched it, his brow puckering. "Dunno. This one's a lot thicker than anything that's come. And there's something stiff inside."

Alexa grinned. "If you're so curious, open it yourself."

He stuck his chin in the air. "Well, since you put it that way, I think I will." He slid his thumb under the flap and pulled out several folded sheets of lined writing paper. A white rectangle fell from the folds and slid across the floor. He pinched it up and turned it over.

Alexa shut off the spigots and set the knife aside. "What is it?"

"A picture." He handed it to her.

She examined it while he unfolded the pages. The smiling faces peering up at her from the flat image reminded her of the photograph Melissa had shown her, except this couple had two children instead of one, and they were older. Still, the smiles, the element of happiness, was the same.

She started to give it back to Tom, but something in his expression as he scanned the pages made her freeze in place. "What's the matter?"

Not a hint of teasing showed in his face. "Alexa, I think you better sit down and read this one."

Unease rippled through her. "Why?"

"Because you should." He held the letter toward her.

She backed away. "No. You read it."

"I've been reading it. Now it's your turn."

"You read it to me." She was being childish. She knew it but she didn't care. An unnamed fear gripped her, and she didn't want to touch that letter.

Tom's serious demeanor softened. "Okay. Let's get Linda in here, and I'll read it to both of you. Is that all right?"

Alexa sank into one of the kitchen chairs. "Okay."

Tom retrieved Linda from her little sewing room. She grumbled a bit as they came up the hall, but Tom's shush ended her fussing. She sat next to Alexa, and Alexa automatically reached for her hand.

Tom sat across from Alexa and laid the pages flat on the table. With them upside down, she couldn't read the cursive writing, but someone had gone to a great deal of trouble penning the letter. Alexa pulled in a breath. "Okay. Let's hear it."

" 'Dear Alexa, I saw your photograph on Facebook, and I knew I had to write to you. I believe I'm your mother.' "

Linda gasped. Tom sent her a short frown and went on, his deep voice almost comical as it recited the feminine prose. But Alexa focused less on his voice and more on the content.

" 'When I was a young teenager, I was pretty wild. I didn't have a very good home life, and I suppose you could say I was looking for affection in all the wrong places. I let boys do whatever they wanted, telling myself they loved me. When I found out I was pregnant, I didn't even know who'd done it. It's embarrassing to admit that, but it's true.

" 'I couldn't believe I really was going to have a baby. I was only fifteen — still pretty much a child. So I tried to pretend it wasn't real. Especially when my mom and my latest stepfather didn't even notice. They just berated me for getting so fat. One of my friends guessed the truth, though, and she promised to help me. She's the one I went to when the pains started and I knew you were on your way. You came into the world three weeks before Christmas in my friend's basement while her parents watched movies on television upstairs.' "

Alexa tried to imagine being young, alone, and giving birth without the help of doctors or nurses. She whispered, "She must have been so scared."

Linda squeezed her hand.

Tom angled a worried look at her. "Want me to go on?"

Alexa steeled herself for what would come next and nodded.

Tom lifted the pages again. " 'We didn't have blankets or diapers or little sleepers, but my friend got out an old beach towel. We used it to clean you up as best we could. Then I wrapped you in the towel and held you. And cried. I'd never seen anybody so small and helpless. I had no idea what to do for you. You cried, and I cried, and finally we both fell asleep.

" 'When I woke up, it was morning. My friend said as soon as her parents left for work, I'd have to go home, but I hated my home. I didn't even want to live there. Why would I take an innocent baby into it? But there wasn't anywhere else for me to go. I started crying again. That's when my friend told me about a place in Indianapolis where pregnant, unmarried girls went and had their babies.' "

Alexa jolted. "The home for unwed mothers . . ."

Tom nodded soberly before continuing. " 'My friend called her boyfriend, and he picked us up. He drove us to the street where the home was located and let us out in the alley so nobody at the home would see his car. I wanted to leave you on the back stoop, where you'd be found right away, but my friend said it was more likely someone would catch me. She said I'd get in terrible trouble if anyone saw me. So, instead, she laid you in a box her boyfriend had in the backseat, and she told me to put you behind the garage. She reasoned someone would come out there eventually.

" 'It was so cold that morning. I made sure the towel was tucked in really well, and I pushed the box close to the garage door where the wind would be blocked. My friend wanted to leave right away, but I wouldn't go. I hid behind some bushes and watched. And waited.' "

"Just like Moses's sister in the Bible. Remember?"

Tom went on as if Linda hadn't interrupted, seemingly absorbed by the tale. " 'If somebody didn't come, I was going to take you to the back door, no matter what my friend said. But someone came. A young woman wearing an Amish cap took you out of the box and carried you into the garage. That's when it really hit me what I was doing. I was giving up my baby. It didn't matter that I couldn't take you home. It didn't matter that I had no way to take care of you — I wanted you. And I tried to go to you and get you back, but I was so weak. My friend held on to me. She kept saying we were going to get in trouble. She dragged me back to her boyfriend's car, and he drove us away.

" 'My friend told me I shouldn't worry. She said the people at the home would find a good family for you. After a few days I accepted she was right. I told myself you were better off with someone else. I stopped thinking about trying to get you back again. But I never stopping thinking about you, wondering about you, wishing I could know you.' "

Something tickled Alexa's cheek. She touched her fingers to the spot and realized she was crying. Crying . . . for Mom, who'd never stopped thinking about, wondering about, wishing she could know the baby girl she'd given away. And for her birth mother.

Linda slipped her arm around Alexa's shoulders. "Honey-girl, you wanna stop?"

Tom held up the letter. "There's just a

little bit more. We can wait if you want."

Alexa shook her head. "No. Finish it." She closed her eyes, images of Mom and the woman from the photograph flashing in her mind as Tom read.

" 'Before I became a Christian, I hoped to find you someday. Then after I came to know Jesus as my Savior, my hopes became prayers. Especially when my other children were born, I longed for you, my firstborn. Every December third for the past fifteen years I've closed myself away and spent time praying for you, asking God to guide and protect you and someday let me see you again.

" 'For Christmas this year, my husband hired a private investigator to find you so I could finally tell you how you came to be in that alley and ask you to forgive me for leaving you that way.' "

Alexa choked back a sob. She pressed her fist to her mouth and waited for Tom to finish.

" 'If you are the baby girl I left behind the garage, please know you have a thirteen-year-old half sister named Darcy and an eleven-year-old half brother named Barrett, who are eager to meet you, too. I'm married to Glenn, a fine Christian man, a loving husband, and an amazing father. Even though he isn't your father, he wants to know you and be your friend. Just so you understand, I'm not asking to be your mother, Alexa. I gave up that right a long time ago, but I pray we can be friends someday.' "

Tom stopped, and Alexa opened her eyes. "Is that all?"

He shook his head. "She gives her phone number and an address where you can reach her, then there's a postscript. 'I enclosed a photograph. Please look at Darcy and me. We have a little something in common with you.' "

Puzzled, Alexa reached for the photograph. Linda squeezed in, squinting at the image while Alexa held it up. Linda released a little squawk. "Honey-girl, look at that! All three of you have a beauty mark above your lip."

Alexa touched the spot on her lip. "Then this woman . . . this Cynthia . . . must be my mother."

"It sure seems likely, doesn't it?" Tom slipped the letter back into its envelope and slid it across the table to Alexa.

Linda kept her arm around Alexa, her brown eyes wide. "What're you gonna do?"

Alexa placed her hands lightly over the envelope, her mother's story playing through her mind. "I don't know, Linda. I really don't know."

522

CHAPTER 38

Arborville
Paul

Even though the morning sky was cloudless and only a gentle breeze blew — a mild day for late January — Paul drove Danny to school. The few minutes hardly added up to much when he considered the whole of the day, but they were minutes of solitude with no distractions, minutes that belonged only to them. When he married Suzy, these morning minutes might be the only ones he had one-on-one with his son, so he intended to keep driving Danny the short distance for as long as the boy didn't resist him.

Danny shoved his lunchbox into the belly of his backpack. "Dad, what did you put in my lunchbox today?"

Paul chuckled. "Don't worry. There's plenty enough in there to fill your stomach and even your left leg. You won't go hungry."

Danny crinkled his nose. "That's not what

I meant. I mean, is there anything really good?"

"Well, I wrapped up a piece of peach pie." He'd bought some slices at the café yesterday afternoon — half price since they were the morning's leftovers.

"Did Miss Zimmerman bake it?"

Paul smiled, envisioning Suzy in his kitchen, rolling piecrusts, a smudge of flour on her cheek. "Either her or Anna-Grace Braun. They're the ones baking pies these days."

"Yeah, I know." Danny wriggled as if some inner excitement was trying to break free. "When you and Miss Zimmerman get married, will she bake stuff just for us?"

"I'm sure she will." Paul silently marveled at the miracle that had taken place last Sunday. Suzy overwhelmingly welcomed back into the fellowship, and the deacons giving their blessing on a courtship. He felt like a teenager again — a giddy, head-over-heels teenager. But he'd do things right this time. He slanted a look at his son. "Are you settling in with the idea of adding a mom to our family? I know it's coming a little faster than I'd expected."

"It's okay with me. But I guess it means some things will be different, huh?"

Paul pulled up to the schoolyard and put

the truck in Park. "Yeah. They will." He'd have someone to talk to late at night, someone to share in Danny's upbringing, someone to pray with and laugh with and, God willing, grow old with.

"Yep." The boy sighed. "No more running from my bedroom to the bathroom in my underwear. I'll have to put my pants on first."

Paul burst out laughing.

Danny gawked at him. "It's not funny, Dad. I don't want her seeing me in my underwear."

Paul snagged his son in a hug and planted a quick kiss on his head. "We'll worry about things like that after the wedding, okay? Have a good day at school."

Danny hopped out, and Paul sat in his idling vehicle, watching him gallop across the yard while swinging his backpack in a circle. He rolled down his window and called, "Danny, quit that! You're going to scramble your pie!"

Danny stopped the backpack's flight and aimed a sheepish grin at Paul.

Paul waved and rolled up the window again. He couldn't hold back a chuckle. Danny's idea of change was sure different from his. Suzy would get a kick out of the comment, too. He glanced at his wristwatch.

He was due to arrive at the Goertzens' by ten to finish the addition Daniel Goertzen had started but decided was too much for him to complete. Plenty of time remained for him to drive out to the Zimmerman farm, spend a half hour or so sipping coffee with Suzy. And with Abigail, as the woman now insisted he call her.

Decision made, he angled the truck into a U and headed out of town.

Suzanne

Suzanne stood on the piano bench in the middle of the living room, shivering. "Are you about done? My toes are freezing." She bent over slightly and watched her mother place another pin along the hemline of her dress.

Mother whisked an impatient look upward, two stickpins poking out of the corner of her mouth. She spoke around the pins. "I'm going as fast as I can, Suzy, but you have to stand up straight and stop wiggling. Do you want this hem to be longer on one side than the other?"

Suzanne sighed and straightened her spine. One of the pins holding the dress's placket together pricked her. "Of course not. I just wish I'd —" The doorbell interrupted. Mother looked at Suzanne, and Suzanne gawked back. "Are you expecting someone?"

Mother pulled the pins from her mouth and offered a mild frown. "Now, who would I be expecting at eight thirty on a Wednesday morning?"

Anna-Grace bustled into the room with a dish towel flapping over her shoulder. "Just stay up there, Cousin Suzy. I'll get it."

Suzanne's stomach leaped. Have some visitor witness her on display with a half-pinned hem sagging above her bare calves and feet? "Oh, but —"

Too late. Anna-Grace had opened the door. A familiar male voice drifted from the little foyer and sent her heart into a series of cartwheels. "Good morning, Anna-Grace. Mmm, it smells good in here. More pies?" A slight pause, Anna-Grace's subdued mumble, and then Paul again. "I forgot all about your morning baking spree. Is Suzy too busy to talk?"

Mother called, "Suzy's right here, Paul. Come on in."

Suzanne hissed, "Mother!"

Mother just grinned.

If her dress was buttoned instead of pinned, and if she were half her age and twice as limber, she'd leap from the bench and run out the back door to the cottage,

527

even if the ground was frozen and her feet were bare. But all she could do was cover her left foot with her right, fold her arms across her stomach, and pray Paul wouldn't burst into laughter when he spotted her.

Anna-Grace hurried around the corner and Paul sauntered in behind her. Anna-Grace went on to the kitchen, but Paul came to a halt and his gaze locked on Suzanne's as if some inner radar had directed him. His jaw dropped.

Suzanne's face filled with heat. "H-hi, Paul."

Very slowly his brown-eyed gaze traveled down the length of her frame to her toes and up again, his mouth still slightly ajar. He reached her eyes, and he gulped, finally closing his mouth. Then he shook his head, an expression of wonder on his face. "Suzy, you're . . ."

She cringed.

". . . beautiful."

Mother snickered. Suzanne almost nudged her with her foot, but fear of toppling from the bench kept her still. She flapped both hands at him. "Paul, honestly, I must look a sight. No socks or shoes, my dress half-done, and —"

"You are a sight. A sight to behold."

She swallowed. Warmth flooded her, even

taking the chill from her toes.

He took a step toward her, a smile blooming across his cold-reddened face. "Where did you get the cap? And the dress? I didn't expect . . ." He shook his head again and his breath wheezed out. "Wow."

Mother said, "We've ordered her some caps, but Anna-Grace loaned her one until the order arrives. As for the dress, Shelley's been at her machine night and day since Monday morning." She released a light snort. "That girl claims she's sewn so many dresses she can put them together in her sleep, so she insisted on making Suzy a new wardrobe. She brought over three unfinished dresses last night with instructions to get them fitted so she could finish them today. Suzy's supposed to drop them by Shelley's this morning when she goes in to deliver the pies. So if you don't mind, I'm going to get back to pinning. Suzy, shift." Suzanne made a quarter turn on the creaky bench. Mother grabbed her hem and folded the fabric into place.

Paul moved in front of Suzanne and smiled up at her. "I guess maybe I shouldn't have come without calling, but I wanted to tell you what Danny said this morning. He said things would be different at our house when you move in, and then he said" — he lowered his voice — "he wouldn't be able to run from his room to the bathroom in his underwear anymore."

Both Mother and Suzanne burst out laughing. Mother dropped two pins in her lap and fished for them, still chuckling. "Oh, my, the ideas young ones get. I'll enjoy adding him to my quiver of grandchildren." Her eyes sparkled with mischief. "And maybe even another one or two . . . someday."

Paul's cheeks blazed, and Suzanne experienced a rush of heat. Paul cleared his throat. "Danny seems to be okay with the idea of adding someone to our family. How's Alexa with it? Have you talked to her?"

Mother bumped Suzanne's leg, and Suzanne automatically turned some more. Paul moved with her, keeping himself directly in her line of vision. Suzanne nodded. "She's happy for me, and she asked me to tell you congratulations. But she'll be able to tell you herself soon. She's flying home Sunday afternoon."

"We'll go pick her up together. Danny, too."

Suzanne wished she could leap off the bench into his arms and give him a thank-you kiss. But she had to be satisfied with giving him a big smile. "Thank you. I'd like that."

"Okay. Done." Mother pushed her chair away from the bench and blew out a breath of relief. "Go get changed."

Paul helped her down, his hands lingering at her waist for a moment. Only a moment but long enough to make her pulse pound. He gave her a little nudge and impishly stuck his finger in his mouth. "I just got poked. Go put something less dangerous on. I'll wait for you."

With a giggle she hurried off. With Mother's help she wriggled out of the dress, then quickly scrambled into her customary skirt, blouse, and cardigan over thick cable tights. She'd left her shoes beside Mother's bathroom door, and as she moved to pick them up, she caught a glimpse of herself in the dressing table mirror. She froze, staring at her face framed by a white mesh cap with trailing white ribbons. White, the color of purity. Incongruous. Incongruous with her secular outfit. Incongruous with her past.

"Oh, Mother . . ." The words emerged on a strangled sob.

Mother rolled her chair close, worry pinching her face. "What is it?"

Suzanne touched one of the ribbons. A tear slid down her cheek. "I wish I could meet my groom with a pure soul."

Mother grabbed her hands and forced her around. "Suzanne Abigail Zimmerman, you listen to me. Do you believe that when God forgives, He also forgets?"

Suzanne gulped, shocked by the vehemence in her mother's tone. She considered Mother's question. People sometimes didn't forget, but God wasn't people. She nodded.

"Then what you did with Paul, in God's eyes, no longer exists. That sin is washed clean. Washed clean, Suzy! When Paul sees you coming down that aisle toward him, he will see a pure soul." She gave Suzanne's hands a firm yank. "And I won't let you see yourself any other way."

Suzanne's lips trembled into a grateful smile. She bent over and embraced her mother. "Thank you."

"You're welcome. Now get your shoes on and get out there. Poor Anna-Grace has been baking by herself all morning."

While she and Mother were in the bedroom, Paul had gone to the kitchen. She found him sitting at the worktable with a cup of coffee, watching Anna-Grace flute the edge of the last piecrust. He bobbed his head in her direction and smiled at Suzanne.

"She's finishing up. I told her she should consider joining Alexa in her baking business."

An embarrassed flush stole across Anna-Grace's cheeks. She tucked the pie in the oven, set the timer, then turned a shy look on Paul. "I don't think I'd want to bake so many pies every day the way Alexa does. I'd rather just bake for Steven."

Paul took a sip of his coffee. "It won't be long now, will it? You're getting married next month?"

Anna-Grace nodded and toyed with her apron. "Yes. The eighteenth. Three weeks from today." A dreamy look flitted across her face, and then she gave a little jolt. Her lips twitched into the nervous semblance of a smile. She glanced back and forth between Suzanne and Paul. "H-have you thought about a date yet?"

Paul turned to Suzanne. The tenderness in his gaze melted her, as always. She slid into the chair across the table from him. "We haven't discussed it, but I suppose we should. Arborville weddings are always scheduled when the farmers aren't working their fields, and spring will be here soon." She tipped her head, one ribbon slipping along her neck with a peculiar yet strangely familiar tickle. "Maybe late fall, next year?"

Mother yanked up the cleaning rag and scraped crumbs into her palm. "Seems to me you two have waited long enough. Do you really want a lengthy courtship? After all, you're not seventeen and eighteen anymore."

They should not be having this conversation in front of Anna-Grace. Suzanne released a self-conscious laugh. "I'm sure Paul and I will find a date that suits us." She rose, reaching for the coffeepot. "Would you like a refill?"

"Cousin Suzy?" Anna-Grace took a hesitant step toward the table. Bright red splotches stained her cheeks and throat. She wadded the skirt of her apron into a tangle. "I have an idea. Well, actually, Steven first suggested it, but . . ."

Mother's face pinched into a worried frown. "What is it, Anna-Grace?"

She flicked a glance at Mother and then faced Suzanne again. "Steven wondered if, maybe, you and Mr. Aldrich — Paul — would like to get married the same day we do."

Paul and Suzanne spoke at once.

"That's kind of you, Anna-Grace, but —"

"But that's your day with Steven!"

They both stopped and looked at each other.

"Cousin Shelley could probably get you a dress done in time," Anna-Grace said as if they hadn't interrupted.

In unison they shifted to face Anna-Grace.

"And, Cousin Suzy, you told me you liked the colors I chose. So I know you'd be happy with the decorations. The people coming to my wedding are the same ones you'd probably invite to yours. If you get married the same day as us, you won't have to wait until next year. Like Aunt Abigail said, you've already waited long enough."

Suzanne smiled at the girl, battling tears. "Anna-Grace, that's so sweet and unselfish of you to offer to share your special day with us. But this is meant to be your day with Steven."

"I know, but . . ." The girl inched closer, her Zimmerman blue eyes beseeching. "Steven said, if . . . if I hadn't been given up for adoption, he never would have met me. We wouldn't have fallen in love with each other. We wouldn't be getting married. Steven said . . . and I think he's right . . . that we should be grateful. To you."

Awareness rolled through Suzanne with such force, dizziness struck. She stretched out her hand toward Paul and he caught it. His strong grasp told her he'd understood the unspoken meaning behind Anna-

Grace's words.

One more step brought their daughter to the table. She curled her fingers over their joined hands. She smiled shyly at Paul, then locked her teary gaze on Suzanne. "It would be an honor for me to share my wedding day with you. It's kind of like coming full circle, isn't it?"

CHAPTER 39

Indianapolis
Cynthia

Saturday evening Cynthia waited by the front door. She checked the time on her cell phone. Six fifteen already. If Darcy didn't hurry, they'd be late for the preconcert backstage gathering. Besides, she was starting to sweat, all bundled up in her coat, scarf, and gloves.

She untied her scarf and unbuttoned the top button. Glenn glanced at her. He smiled, shaking his head. "Wonder if anybody plans to sing 'Waitin' on a Woman'?"

Cynthia blasted a short laugh. "Apropos, for sure." Looking toward the hallway, she called, "Darcy, come on! We're going to be late!"

Darcy dashed into the living room, her meticulously curled ponytail cascading from the top of her head and her eyes wide and frantic. "I can't find the backstage passes!" She began rifling through desk drawers, muttering under her breath.

Cynthia walked over and tapped her daughter's shoulder with two slips of tan cardstock. "You gave them to me for safekeeping, remember?"

Darcy sagged and grabbed the tickets. She pressed them to her chest. "Why didn't you tell me? I've been tearing my room apart trying to find them."

Barrett rested his chin on the back of the sofa and grinned at them. "Uh-oh. Mom, better tell her to clean her room before she can go do fun stuff."

Darcy growled. "Batwit, I —"

Cynthia caught her daughter's shoulders and steered her to the closet. "Get your coat and whatever else you need. We'll worry about your room later." They waved good-bye to Glenn and Barrett and dashed across the evening shadows to the car. Darcy bounced in the seat. If the seat belt wasn't holding her in place, she might go through the roof. "Settle down. All your wiggling won't make the car go any faster."

Darcy pressed her folded hands beneath her chin and stared out the window as if wishing could make them magically land in the coliseum parking lot. "I know, but that new singer, the one who's my age — Nicci K — is only going to be at the backstage party for fifteen minutes 'cause she has to get ready to open the show. I really want her autograph. Everybody says she's gonna be a big star someday."

"Only twenty people got backstage passes, honey. She can sign that many autographs in fifteen minutes, so don't worry, okay?"

"Okay." But she didn't cease her restless bouncing.

Cynthia swallowed a chuckle. Darcy's enthusiasm tickled her. She also couldn't squelch her joy at spending the evening with her daughter. She'd been afraid Darcy would ask Glenn to go with her instead, but yesterday at supper she'd asked what Cynthia planned to wear to the concert. When Cynthia said, "Whatever," Darcy rolled her eyes and then rummaged through Cynthia's closet for an outfit. They'd had fun doing a style show for Glenn, and she had to admit she felt young and trendy in her boots, straight-legged jeans, tunic sweater, and scarf. Darcy had good taste.

The parking lot was already crowded with cars. They wasted several minutes finding a place to park and then a few more minutes battling their way through the crowd of people who hadn't scored one of the elusive backstage passes. By the time they reached the doors guarded by two men in black suits and dark sunglasses, Darcy was gnawing her freshly painted thumbnails to the quick in nervousness.

Cynthia handed one of the men their passes. He examined them while Darcy fidgeted and chewed her nails. Finally he nodded at the second man, who opened the door without a word and ushered them inside.

Loud piped music assaulted her ears, and Cynthia cringed, subconsciously rearing back. But Darcy grabbed her hand and pulled her along. "C'mon, Mom! There she is! Let's go!"

Alexa

Linda puffed with exertion and clip-clopped beside Alexa down the curved hallway. Her arms pumped, and sweat beaded on her forehead. "Oh, girlie, these heels are killin' me. Why'd I wear these things anyway?"

Alexa held back an I-told-you-so. Short lace-up boots with rubber soles covered her feet — the perfect walking shoes. Muffled music from the backstage party already in progress carried from the other side of the wall. Alexa didn't slow her pace. "I'm sorry, but if we don't hurry, we might miss Briley.

The ticket girl said he's taking backstage passes and they'll close the doors for good at six forty-five. We don't have time to spare."

Linda huffed out, "How much farther?"

Alexa checked the map she'd been handed at the door. "One more corner." She pointed to the intersection ahead. Excitement stirred in her chest. "That should be it right there. Come on!"

She linked elbows with Linda and propelled her the remaining distance. They turned the corner and encountered two wide-shouldered men dressed in black from head to toe. Before Alexa could ask for Briley, the taller man on the left whipped off his sunglasses and broke into a smile.

"Alexa!"

She released Linda and darted to meet him. He folded her in a hug, rocking her back and forth. She giggled, happier than she'd expected to see Briley again. "Hi!" She pulled back and gave him an up-and-down inspection. "Wow, look at you. You could star in the remake of *Men in Black.*"

Briley laughed, showing his even white teeth. "No, thanks. Observing the whole star-making process is good enough for me. I like what I do."

Alexa gestured Linda forward. "Briley, this

is my friend Linda Denning."

Briley shook Linda's hand, beaming at her. "Hey. Good to meet you." He shifted his attention to Alexa again. "Nicci K's inside. Do you want to say hello to her?"

Alexa cringed. "I'd love to, but I waited too long to get tickets and missed out on the backstage passes."

He threw his arm around her shoulder. "No worries, little sister. Being one of Nicci K's entourage has its privileges. I'll take you in."

She hesitated. "I don't want to get in trouble."

Briley waggled his eyebrows in a familiar gesture of teasing. "Ol' Briley lead you into trouble? Ha! C'mon." He held his elbow to Linda, and she tittered as she took hold.

Alexa glanced at the second guard. He hadn't cracked even the hint of a smile. She whispered, "Maybe we should —"

Briley rolled his eyes and started them in motion. "Stop being a worrywart. Nicole has to leave the backstage party early since she's the first act. If you don't go now, you'll miss her." He nodded at the second guard. "Open up, Patrick, huh?"

Music blasted when Patrick opened the door. Briley gave Alexa a little push through the opening, then followed her in, with

Linda still clinging to his arm. He raised his voice to be heard. "Nicci K's over there, where the crowd has gathered."

The lights were dimmed, giving the backstage space a cloying feeling. But laughter and chatter rose from the group of mostly young people surrounding the teenager. Nicci K sat on a tall stool, with her parents standing sentry behind her, and scribbled her name on the pads of paper people thrust at her. Alexa found herself smiling as she watched the girl. For one so young and so new to the music business, she seemed perfectly at ease.

She shouted at Briley, "Can you take me behind her? I'll talk to her folks."

Briley nodded and steered them around the small crowd. Recognition dawned on Curtis and Kathy Kirkley's faces. Both of them gave Alexa a hug, and then Kathy tapped Nicole's shoulder. The girl glanced back, and her face lit. She leaped off the stool and dove at Alexa with her arms outstretched. "Alexa! Hi!"

Nicole's enthusiastic welcome surprised and pleased her. But as Alexa hugged the girl, she aimed an apologetic look at the others for pulling the singer's attention away from them. Her gaze landed on a junior high–age girl who was staring at her with her mouth hanging open. Alexa experienced a pang of remorse. She'd apparently made the girl jealous. Nicci K needed to focus on her fans. She released the girl and hollered, "You have more autographs to sign." Nicole grinned and hopped back on her stool.

Alexa started to step away, but a frantic motion at the edge of the group caught her attention. The girl who'd stared at her now yanked on a woman's arm and pointed at Alexa while yammering in the woman's ear. The woman, frowning, turned and looked. Alexa gasped. She knew that face.

Cynthia

Cynthia clapped her hand over her mouth to hold back a cry of both exultation and agony. Standing not fifteen feet away was the girl from the Facebook picture.

Darcy clung to her arm, rasping, "Mom, Mom, is it her? Is it, Mom? It looks just like her. You gotta talk to her, Mom. You gotta find out."

Cynthia blocked out Darcy's constant chatter and stared at the girl, who stared back. *Dear Lord . . . Dear Lord . . .* No prayer would form. She tried to calm her raging emotions so she could think rationally. It was dark in the room. Maybe only wishful thinking made her see the girl as the one in the picture hanging on the refrigerator at home. But then why did Darcy see it, too?

While she stood frozen, uncertain, a black woman approached the girl and spoke directly in her ear. Cynthia sucked in a breath. Mr. Mallory had said a girl claiming to be her daughter came to his office accompanied by a black couple. The coincidence was too great. She pressed her trembling fingers to her mouth and whispered, "It's her . . ."

The two men in black suits whisked Nicci K away, and the crowd moaned in disappointment, but then cheers erupted as another singing group entered the room. The throng rushed to greet them. All except Cynthia, Darcy, the girl named Alexa, and Alexa's friend. The four of them remained as still as if someone had driven nails through their shoes. Darcy even stopped bouncing and yanking on her mother and just held tight to her arm.

A look of determination crept over the black woman's face. She curled her arm around Alexa's waist and guided her forward one step. Then two. Cynthia, with Darcy cutting off the circulation in her arm, forced her feet to carry her ahead two stiff steps. Alexa and her friend moved, then Cynthia with Darcy, like chess pieces manipulated by a giant's hand. Finally they stood with a mere foot and a half of space separating them while music blared and people talked and cheered. Not the reunion Cynthia had imagined. But despite the noisy, unconventional setting, a joy unlike any she'd known since the day she asked Jesus to forgive her sins flowed through her and brought tears to her eyes.

"Alexa?" How could one word hold such incredible hope and promise? She gently extracted her arm from Darcy's grasp and reached toward her firstborn. "Alexa . . . it's me."

Alexa

Alexa stared at the face of the woman who'd sent the letter and photograph and then dropped her gaze to her outstretched hand. Long, slender fingers. Like her own hand. Emotions — too many to count — roared inside her. Linda nudged her, the gesture screaming at her to do something. But she didn't know what to do.

With a huff of impatience, Linda caught hold of the woman's hand and gave it several pumps. "You're Cynthia, yes?"

Relief broke over the woman's face. She nodded.

"I'm Linda." She made a face. "We can't

talk in here. Too loud." She pointed to the double doors. "Wanna go out there?"

The woman — Cynthia — looked at the dark-haired girl, who chewed on her pinkie nail. The girl nodded, making her ponytail bounce. Linda bustled Alexa out, and the other two followed. The door closed behind them, sealing most of the noise inside. Comparatively speaking, the hallway was a tomb. They'd be able to hear each other easily now. But no one spoke.

Cynthia stared at Alexa with tears swimming in her eyes and her lips quivering with a timid smile. The girl from the photograph, Darcy, also stared, her blue eyes wide and incredulous. Alexa found herself examining the little beauty mark, a popcorn kernel-sized brown spot, on Cynthia's upper lip.

Alexa said without thinking, "When I was little, Mom tried to wash the spot off my mouth, thinking it was dirt or food."

Darcy giggled, hunching her shoulders. "Mom said she did that to me, too. Kinda funny, really, considering she has the same mark." She stiffened for a moment, then lunged forward and grabbed Alexa's hand. "I'm Darcy. I'm thirteen. I found your picture on Facebook and showed it to Mom and Dad. That's why she wrote to you. I really hope you're my sister because I think you're really pretty. And you even know Nicci K."

Alexa forced a slow breath into her lungs and then let it out, willing her nerves to settle enough to answer Darcy. She couldn't be rude. Not to this child who'd done nothing wrong. "Thank you, Darcy. I think you're pretty, too. I like your hair."

Unexpectedly Darcy caught hold of Alexa's ponytail and gave it a swish with her fingers. "Mine's real straight, like yours, when I don't use a curling iron. Barrett — he's our brother — has wavy hair. And it's sandy blond. Like Dad's. But Mom said I got her hair, as thick and straight as a horse's tail." She flicked an impish grin at her mother, who continued to stare at Alexa with watery eyes. "Don't let her blond hair fool you. Mom's really a brunette. Just like us."

Just like us. Alexa swallowed.

Linda touched Darcy's shoulder. "Were you wanting to collect more autographs? I can take you in, if it's okay with your mama." She bounced a knowing look at Alexa. "Let these two talk."

Cynthia nodded. "That's fine with me." She touched Darcy's arm. "I'll wait for you here."

The girl and Linda trotted off together,

and Alexa was alone with her mother. Her mouth felt like it was stuffed with cotton, but she couldn't waste the opportunity Linda had given her to speak freely. Blinking rapidly in nervousness, she forced herself to look her mother full in the face. "About your letter . . ." Her throat ached. Her voice sounded hoarse. She swallowed again. "Was it all . . . true?"

One tear rolled over Cynthia's bottom eyelashes and raced toward her chin. "Every word."

"Even the part about only wanting to be friends? Because I have a mom." Alexa hoped she didn't crush Cynthia, but she needed to be honest. "I . . . I don't need another mom."

A second tear made its way down Cynthia's face, past the curve of her understanding smile. "It's good you love her so much. She must be a wonderful person."

"She is."

"And your dad?"

Alexa considered Cynthia's simple question. Paul wasn't her dad yet, but she knew him well enough to give an accurate answer. "He's great. I couldn't ask for anyone better."

"I'm so glad."

Her response — spoken with such relief

— reminded Alexa of the poem Melissa had written. Alexa blinked again, this time holding tears at bay. "I'm sorry you had such a rough life. That you couldn't keep me. I'm sorry for you, but I'm not sorry for me. I'm happy. I've always been loved." She risked touching the sleeve of Cynthia's deep-purple tunic. Mom's favorite color — the color of royalty. "Don't feel bad about giving me away. God made sure I landed in the right family."

Cynthia nodded, more tears flowing down her cheeks, and her lips quavered with her smile. She placed her hand over Alexa's. "So you forgive me, Alexa?"

She gave Cynthia's arm a squeeze. "Yes." A weight seemed to tumble from Alexa's shoulders. If she gave a little hop, she might float. She smiled. "Yes, Cynthia, I do."

CHAPTER 40

Wichita, Kansas
Suzanne

"There she is!" Suzanne stepped away from Paul and Danny and wove between other travelers moving down the airport debarkation aisle. She grabbed Alexa in a hug, laughing. "Oh, honey, it's so good to see you."

Alexa returned the embrace, then pulled back and grinned. "Look at you, all Mennonite-ish."

Suzanne touched one of her cap's ribbons. "Do I look strange to you?"

Alexa raised her eyebrows and turned her eyes upward, as if deeply thinking. Then she giggled and grabbed Suzanne in another hug. "You look like Mom to me." Her arms tightened. "I love you, Mom."

Suzanne relished the sweet whisper. She kissed Alexa's cheek and set her aside. "Come. Paul and Danny are here to greet you, too." She led Alexa to the dark-haired man and boy who were already her family in her heart. Alexa hugged them by turn, Paul first with a bit of hesitation, then Danny. She lifted the boy off his feet, making him squawk in mock protest.

She put Danny down but kept her arm draped over his shoulders. She smiled at Paul. "I'm really glad to see you. You can retrieve my luggage from the carousel. Linda sent presents for everybody, and I almost exceeded the weight limit."

Paul laughed. "I can do that for you." He took Suzanne's hand, and the four of them fell into step, with Alexa and Suzanne sandwiched between Danny and Paul. Suzanne couldn't stop smiling. How natural, how right, it felt to walk four abreast.

Paul grabbed Alexa's suitcase, making them all laugh by pretending it was too heavy for him to lift. Then they made their way to Suzanne's waiting car, which would have to be traded soon for something the fellowship approved.

Paul unlocked the doors, then turned to Alexa and Suzanne. "How about if Danny rides up front with me and you ladies ride together in the back? It'll be easier for you to talk."

Alexa joked, "Oh, you mean Mennonite-style?"

Paul grinned.

"Good idea." Alexa snickered. "But let me sit behind Danny so I can kick the back of his seat. I've always wanted to pester a brother that way."

While they drove back to Arborville, Suzanne filled Alexa in on the wedding plans. "I know it's happening awfully fast," she said with a hint of apology, "but after we prayed about it, we really believed it was the best thing to do."

"It is happening fast, but it feels right somehow, too. Kind of like puzzle pieces fitting into place." Alexa gave the back of the front seat a bump with her knee, waited for Danny's yelp, snickered, then turned to Suzanne again. "Have you gone dress shopping already?"

Paul chuckled. "Things are a little different in the Old Order church from what you're probably used to, Alexa. Your mother won't buy a dress."

Alexa frowned. "Then what do you wear?"

"I wear a homemade dress like the one I'm wearing now, only in pale blue."

Alexa touched the attached cape on Suzanne's floral dress. "Don't tell me you're sewing?"

Suzanne couldn't wait to see her daughter's reaction to the answer. "Shelley is sewing it for me. Just like she sewed this dress for me."

Alexa's jaw went slack. "Shelley? Your sister Shelley?"

Suzanne couldn't hold back a laugh. "That's right."

"Wow, Mom." Alexa shook her head, smiling. "Life can turn on a dime, can't it?" Her smile wavered. "And speaking of life turning . . . I met my birth mom."

The casual statement struck like a blow. Suzanne gasped.

Paul glanced in the rearview mirror. "Everything okay back there?"

Alexa grimaced. "I think I just shocked Mom."

"Do you need me to pull over, Suzy?"

Suzanne clutched her chest. "Yes. If you can find a place."

"Will do." Paul slowed and turned off on a dirt road. He drove a short distance, perhaps half a mile, and pulled into a drive meant for farm equipment. He put the car in Park and then angled a worried look into the backseat. "Nobody will bother us here."

Danny released his seat belt and sat on his knees, peering at Suzanne over the top of seat. "Are you okay now?"

Touched by his concern, Suzanne forced a smile. "I'm fine, Danny." Then she turned to Alexa. "Honey, why didn't you tell me before now?"

"It just happened last night." Alexa launched into an animated explanation of receiving a letter and photograph from her birth mother in response to the Facebook picture Linda posted, deciding to send the woman a letter when she returned to Kansas, but then coming face to face with her at the concert. "So Linda took Darcy — Darcy's my half sister — to listen to the bands, and I sat in the lobby and talked to Cynthia the whole time."

Paul said, "Cynthia . . . she's your mother?"

Alexa nodded. "Cynthia Allgood. When the concert was over, Linda and I followed Cynthia and Darcy to their house, because Cynthia wanted me to meet her husband, Glenn, and my half brother, Barrett." She paused and ruffled Danny's hair. "He's a little older than you, kiddo, but only half as ornery."

Danny grinned.

Suzanne touched Alexa's knee. "Did you . . . like them?"

Alexa frowned, as if uncertain whether she should answer. A hint of apology glinted in her eyes. "I did, Mom. They're really nice people. Cynthia and Glenn both had pretty rough childhoods. They met in a counseling group for children of alcoholics when they were college age, and they became Christians the same night. They really worked to turn their lives around and be better parents to their children than what they'd had. I think they succeeded, too. Darcy and Barrett are good kids — really happy and secure."

Paul frowned. "Then is Glenn your father?"

Alexa glanced at Danny before answering bluntly. "No." She gave Suzanne a meaningful look. "Cynthia was only fifteen when I was born, and like I said, she had a rough life."

Suzanne understood. Paul must have, too, because he nodded.

"Mom, your childhood and Cynthia's are like polar opposites. It's amazing to me that she's such a good mom to Darcy and Barrett. You can tell Jesus made a huge difference in her life."

Jealousy tried to worm its way into Suzanne's chest. In one short evening Alexa had gained a great deal of admiration for the woman who'd given birth to her. But Suzanne refused to let the ugly emotion take root. Alexa looked relaxed, happy. She still called her Mom. Suzanne hadn't lost her child, but apparently Alexa had gained something. Paul would call the situation a home run. "So how will you keep in touch?"

Alexa's eyebrows shot up. "You mean, you don't mind if I stay in contact with her?"

Suzanne glanced at Paul. His smile encouraged her. She took Alexa's hand. "It would be pretty selfish of me to keep you from her, considering my contact with Anna-Grace." Contentment eased through Suzanne's frame. "She and I have decided to be good friends."

"Is that enough?" Alexa lowered her voice to a mere whisper, worry crinkling her brow.

A smile tugged at Suzanne's lips. "Oh, honey . . . Good friends is so much more than I ever expected. God gifted me with you, and then He let me be a part of Anna-Grace's life. I'm doubly blessed." Concern nibbled at the corner of her heart. "Do you mind that I'm friends with Anna-Grace?"

"Mind? Mom!" Alexa teasingly huffed and rolled her eyes. "It was my idea in the first place for her to know who you are."

Suzanne choked back a happy sob. Paul reached over the seat and rubbed Suzanne's shoulder.

Alexa's smile bounced from Suzanne to

Paul, approval glittering in her brown eyes. Then she released a light laugh. "It'll be a little tougher for me to be friends with Cynthia since she lives in Indiana and my home's in Kansas, but Darcy and Barrett said they wanted to be pen pals with me. I thought that was cute, and it's a great way for us to get to know each other."

Danny popped up and peered over the backseat like a puppet making its entrance. "Hey! Maybe I can be pen pals with them, too. It sounds fun."

Alexa grinned at him. "I'll ask 'em, Danny, okay?" She faced Suzanne. "Cynthia and I agreed to call each other now and then, and . . . when the kids are on spring break" — an uneasy look crossed her face — "they want to stay at the B and B so we can have some time together." Alexa's expression turned pleading. "Cynthia wants to meet you, Mom, and thank you for being such a great mother to me. And I want you to meet her. You have something really important in common. You both surrendered a baby to another mother's arms, and you both made something good from your mistakes."

Something good . . . Suzanne swallowed happy tears. She couldn't speak.

Alexa gave Suzanne's hands a squeeze. "I've been so mad at Cynthia for leaving me in that alley. It seemed like such a heartless thing to do. But when she asked, I forgave her for abandoning me. After I said it, I just felt . . . free."

Paul placed his hand over their linked hands. "There's healing in forgiveness, Alexa. For the one receiving it and for the one giving it."

"I'll say so." Alexa blew out a breath. "It's so nice to get rid of the bag of boulders I was hauling around. I don't ever want to stockpile that kind of anger at anyone again. It's awful getting stuck in bitterness. Forgiveness is a lot better. It lets you restore relationships, but it also lets you restore yourself."

Suzanne shook her head. "You're really growing up, Alexa. I'm so proud of you."

Alexa held her hands outward, impishness lighting her face. "What do you expect? We Zimmermans are overcomers."

Paul grinned. "Well, Zimmermans soon to be Aldriches, how about we go home?"

Alexa tipped her forehead against Suzanne's, and they smiled into each other's teary eyes. Alexa whispered, " 'Home' sounds perfect."

Arborville
Suzanne peeked around the corner from the

basement doorway. She turned to Anna-Grace, who stood close, and whispered, "It's filling up. Kids will have to sit on laps, I think."

Anna-Grace clasped her hands beneath her chin, nervousness widening her blue eyes. "Are the decorations staying in place?"

Suzanne risked another peek. Plate-sized bows they'd fashioned from strips of burlap hung from each windowsill, the clusters of silk violets and miniature daisies secure in the bows' centers. She nodded. "The masking tape is holding fine. And the candles are all flickering." She grinned at Anna-Grace. "Danny hasn't blown them out yet."

They giggled together like a pair of schoolgirls. From the bottom of the stairs, Shelley hissed, "What are you two doing? Get down here before Paul and Steven see you."

With another burst of girlish giggles, Suzanne looped arms with Anna-Grace, and they descended the stairs in their matching dresses, the white ribbons from the caps bouncing on their shoulders.

Shelley balled her fists on her hips and glowered at them. "Honestly, you two act no older than Ruby and Pearl."

Suzanne and Anna-Grace exchanged smirking grins before clearing their throats simultaneously and facing the self-appointed organizer of the wedding party. They chorused, "I'm sorry." Suzanne's heart danced at the easy camaraderie she shared with Anna-Grace. God had restored their relationship so beautifully.

"Well, no harm done, I suppose. The grooms are holed up in the men's cloakroom, and I doubt they're peeking." The corner of Shelley's lips twitched as if she fought a grin. "Has the whole town turned out?"

Anna-Grace nodded, her eyes reflecting amazement. "Suzy says kids have to sit on laps. I didn't know how many people would be willing to drive over from Sommerfeld, and I didn't know how many people from Arborville would come. After all, Steven and I didn't grow up here, and Suzy's been gone a really long time."

Shelley shook her head and released a heavy sigh. "Oh, Anna-Grace, what a goose you are. Of course people will come celebrate this day with you. Because they love you." Her gaze shifted to Suzanne. "Both of you."

Suzanne touched Shelley's wrist and offered her sister a smile. Shelley placed her hand over Suzanne's, gave a stiff nod of acknowledgment, then turned away. "I better round up the girls. It's almost time to go up." She angled a frown at the cluster of little girls playing a makeshift game of hopscotch in the corner. She huffed. "What were you thinking to have so many junior attendants?"

Of course Anna-Grace had wanted her little sister, Sunny, but Suzanne couldn't choose between her nieces so she'd included Julie, Jana, Ruby, and Pearl.

Shelley continued in her typically straightforward manner. "If Olivia hadn't been willing to help, we would never have gotten the dresses done in time." She whisked a look at Anna-Grace. "If I forget, please tell your mother thank-you for me."

Anna-Grace nodded, and tears stung Suzanne's eyes. How wonderful to hear someone refer to Olivia as Anna-Grace's mother without experiencing the sharp stab of pain and regret. Thanks to God's healing touch, this day was all celebration. The way it should be.

"I'll get the girls settled down, and then I need to go upstairs." Shelley delivered a peck on Anna-Grace's cheek and then treated Suzanne to the same affectionate gesture before dashing off.

Alexa left the cake table, where she'd been adding the final touches to the row of wedding cakes, and moved across the floor to Suzanne and Anna-Grace. Her deep purple dress heightened the gold flecks in her brown eyes.

Love swelled in Suzanne's heart as she watched her precious daughter approach. She automatically reached up and adjusted the white ribbons falling from Alexa's cap, smoothing them down the caped bodice of the dress. She leaned in and pressed her cheek against Alexa's. "You look so beautiful, sweetheart. Thank you for standing up with me today."

Alexa caught Suzanne's hand and swung it gently. "Where else would I be? We've been together my whole life. It only seems right to be at your side when you move into the next phase of living." She released Suzanne and turned a hesitant smile on Anna-Grace. "I'm too new to this Old Order stuff to know if you do the 'something old, something new' tradition, but I wondered . . ." She reached into the pocket sewn into her dress's skirt seam and pulled out a long gold chain.

Suzanne's heart gave a leap when Alexa opened her hand and revealed the locket Suzanne's father had given her mother more than forty years ago.

Alexa held it out to Anna-Grace. "This is

a family heirloom. Grandmother gave it to me, but would you like to wear it today?"

Anna-Grace took the locket and gazed at it for several seconds. "Her betrothal locket, yes?"

Alexa nodded.

"So there's a picture of our grandfather inside?"

Our . . . Suzanne swallowed hard and blinked back tears. She would not greet Paul with a red nose and watery eyes!

Alexa nodded again. "You don't have to if you don't want to. I just thought, maybe . . ."

Anna-Grace slipped the chain over her head and settled the locket in place, directly over her heart. "How does it look?"

Alexa sighed. "Perfect."

Yes, perfect. Suzanne couldn't have chosen a better word. Tears came again. Paul just might have to deal with a red-nosed, watery-eyed bride.

Then Alexa wagged her finger at Anna-Grace. "But it's only a loan. It's covering both the 'something old' and 'something borrowed,' okay?"

The three of them shared a laugh that chased away the remnants of Suzanne's tears. They formed a group hug, which

Shelley quickly disbanded with a tart command.

"Andrew and Clete are at the top of the stairs. Time to go!"

Rachel Ortmann, the cousin serving as Anna-Grace's attendant, hurried over, and she and Alexa organized the little girls in a line from oldest to youngest. Clutching their miniature bouquets of violets and daisies, the girls in their matching yellow dresses marched in a solemn procession up the stairs, past Andrew and Clete, and around the corner.

Rachel and Alexa went up next. At the top of the staircase, Alexa paused and sent a sweet smile over her shoulder to the brides before rounding the corner. Pulling in a steadying breath, Suzanne ascended the final steps and slipped her hand into the crook of her brother's arm.

Anna-Grace, escorted by her dad, entered the sanctuary.

Clete pressed his hand over Suzanne's and whispered, "This is it." He sounded nervous, but he hadn't even hesitated when Suzanne asked him to serve in place of their father. With his square chin and broad forehead, he strongly resembled the dad she remembered. Tears pricked. Would God let Dad know she was marrying the love of her life this evening? She hoped so.

She squeezed Clete's arm, eagerness trembling through her limbs. "Let's go!"

He pressed a quick kiss on her temple, straightened his shoulders, and led her through the doorway.

An entire entourage filled the expanse of floor in front of the dais — the five little girl attendants on the women's side, Danny and her nephew Jay on the men's side, with Alexa, Rachel, Steven's best friend from Sommerfeld, and Paul's chosen groomsman forming a half circle behind the two grooms. Andrew and Anna-Grace moved slowly across the floor, their strides perfectly matched, the way a father's and daughter's should be.

Suzanne and Clete followed the pair along the front women's bench, which they'd pushed aside to accommodate Mother's wheelchair. Mother, Olivia, Sandra, Tanya, and Shelley sat in a row, their smiling faces lifted to the entering brides.

Suzanne returned their smiles with one of her own — a smile moistened by the tears she couldn't prevent from falling. The joy flooding her had to come out somehow, and laughter — even joyous laughter — wouldn't be appropriate. So she let happiness rain down her cheeks.

Andrew and Anna-Grace moved up beside Steven, and finally Suzanne was rewarded with a clear view of her groom. He stood at an angle, his gaze locked on her, his dear brown-sugar eyes glowing with such love and eagerness. A sob rose from her throat and emerged on a little gasp of delight.

She hurried Clete the final few feet and reached for Paul as he reached for her. Their hands joined — a clasp of unity that brought another flow of warm tears, but she no longer cared if her nose was red and her eyes swam. Paul loved her. He loved her unconditionally, the same way her Father-God loved her. Who cared whether her nose was red, blue, or even purple polka-dotted?

Clete and Andrew, in unison, released the brides and moved aside. Deacon Epp, from his spot on the dais, opened his Bible and began to read. The service flowed exactly the way Anna-Grace had planned it, with the exception of four-year-old Jana yawning and scuffing across the floor, her bouquet abandoned on the edge of the dais, to climb into her mother's lap midway through the lengthy sermon. But no one minded. The service was as perfect as the locket of gold glimmering on the bodice of Anna-Grace's pale-blue dress.

Somehow Suzanne's emotion-tightened

tonsils allowed her to pledge her life and love to Paul, and her chest swelled when he made the same vows to her. Finally Deacon Epp offered the words of commitment: "What God has joined together, let no man put asunder." And at last Suzanne lifted her face to receive her husband's kiss. A short kiss, respectful of the watching congregation, but no less heartfelt.

The congregation broke into applause. She and Paul linked fingers and faced the gathered witnesses, and Anna-Grace and Steven also turned. Anna-Grace's fingers brushed Suzanne's hand, and automatically she took hold. She smiled into Anna-Grace's Zimmerman-blue eyes, then leaned forward slightly to catch sight of Alexa and Danny. The two of them had joined hands, and Alexa slipped her hand into Paul's.

Suzanne's vision blurred, and a prayer of pure hosanna winged from her heart. *My heavenly Father, thank You for Your wondrous power to restore and renew.* Then, hand in hand with the ones she loved, Suzanne stepped forward into her God-designed future.

ALEXA'S CHICKEN-AND-SPINACH PINWHEELS

2 large boneless, skinless chicken breasts, rolled flat to 1/4 inch
Handful raw spinach leaves, stems snipped and discarded
1/4 cup crumbled cheese (goat cheese, feta, or another sharp white cheese)
Salt and pepper
1/4 cup butter
1/2–3/4 cup heavy cream

Layer the chicken breasts with spinach, and then sprinkle cheese over the spinach. Salt and pepper to taste. Roll up the chicken over the spinach and cheese and use toothpicks to hold the rolls together. Melt butter in a skillet and brown the rolls on all sides, then transfer the rolls to a baking sheet. (Reserve butter.) Bake rolls for 20–30 minutes at 350 degrees until chicken is done and cheese is melted.

While chicken is baking, add cream to the

butter in the skillet and cook over low heat, stirring frequently. Add pepper to taste.

Remove the toothpicks from the chicken rolls and cut each into 1/2-inch to 3/4-inch slices. Arrange the pinwheels on a serving dish and drizzle with the cream sauce. Serve with rice and crusty rolls, if desired. Serves four.

CYNTHIA'S SWEET AND SOUR PORK CHOPS

4 pork chops, 1/2-inch-thick
2 large green peppers, seeded and sliced
  into 1/4-inch rings
1 large onion, peeled and sliced into 1/4-
  inch rings
16-ounce can whole cranberry sauce
Salt and pepper

Spoon cranberry sauce into a Crockpot.
Layer peppers and onions on the sauce.
Season the pork chops with salt and pepper
and place over the vegetables. Cook on low
6–8 hours (or high 3–4 hours). Serve over
rice, if desired. Serves four.

READERS GUIDE

1. As the story opens, we see Linda and Tom reuniting with Suzanne. But a damper is thrown on the holiday celebration when they learn Suzanne hid the truth from them for twenty years. Why couldn't Suzanne trust their friendship enough to tell them Alexa was not her biological child? Why do we sometimes hold things back, even from our best friends?

2. The chasm between Suzanne and her sister Shelley is deep and wide. While Suzanne appears to want reconciliation, as she's experienced with her other siblings and her mother, Shelley remains aloof and judgmental. The twenty years that have transpired since Suzy went away will never be recovered, but Shelley seems bent on prolonging the rift. Why do family members sometimes hold grudges against one another, clinging to the belief they

have a right to withhold their participation in a restoration of the family unit? How can we work to rebuild strained relationships?

3. Tom and Linda play a very special role in this story — surrogate parents and grandparents for Suzanne and Alexa. Their patience, love, and compassion are unending, and these characters are portrayed as selfless and giving. How might we emulate Tom and Linda?

4. Suzanne and Paul made a mistake in their teen years. But Anna-Grace wasn't a mistake. How do we reconcile an act the Bible calls sin with the result of that act being a much-loved child? Although Anna-Grace's adoptive parents were blessed by receiving the gift of this precious child, the sin Paul and Suzanne committed still carried consequences. How can God take a circumstance that starts out so wrong and make it good and beautiful?

5. Alexa harbored anger and resentment against the woman who gave birth to her. Without knowing all the circumstances, she set her heart against this woman she had never met and nailed her bitterness in

place with much determination, even going so far as to decide exactly what she was going to say to her biological mother when they met. How can we avoid making up our minds to be angry with a person or a situation without knowing all the facts?

6. Cynthia wanted something so badly she lost focus on her family, then felt betrayed by Glenn when he didn't offer the support she expected. Her response was to leave her husband and children — a drastic reaction. Cynthia and Glenn could have avoided the turn of events that resulted in their separation had they prayed together first about hiring the investigator and then communicated throughout the process. How does prayer guide you through difficult situations? Do you make different choices after consulting God than when you make choices on your own?

7. Danny had always been a cheerful and obedient child, but in this story he begins acting out. Paul is faced with the dilemma of trying to determine the cause. When does a parent draw the line at inappropriate behavior if he suspects a child might

be struggling with private pain or confused emotions? Suzy's advice helped Paul decide how to deal with Danny. To whom would you go for advice in addressing a problem with your child?

8. Both Glenn and Cynthia had unpleasant childhoods. Although they'd made commitments to live differently than their parents had, sometimes Cynthia found herself emulating her mother. How do childhood events mold us? How can we break free of harmful patterns and create a better life for ourselves if we've been impacted by negative examples?

ACKNOWLEDGMENTS

Mom and Daddy — Every day I thank God for the parents He gave me. I love you both muchly!

Don — More than thirty years of togetherness . . . What God (and Aunt Linda!) brought together, man has not torn asunder.

Kristian, Kaitlyn, and Kamryn — Being your mom, and now counting each of you as a friend, is one of my greatest joys.

My Sweeties, Bugaboos, and Wugmumps — Each of you, whether born to our family or not, are precious to me. I am so blessed to be your gramma!

The Posse — Love each of you ladies like the sisters I never had.

Connie — You went over and beyond on this one. Bless you, my friend!

The choir at FSBC — Your prayers and support are so very appreciated.

My agent, Tamela — You are irreplaceable!

577

Shannon and the wonderful team at WaterBrook — What a joy and privilege to partner with you. Thank you for your efforts to make the stories their very best.

Finally, and most importantly, God — You make beauty from the ashes of my life, restore me to right fellowship with You when I falter, infuse me with Your strength, and bless the works of my hands. May any praise or glory be reflected directly back to You.

ABOUT THE AUTHOR

Kim Vogel Sawyer is a best-selling, award-winning author highly acclaimed for her gentle stories of hope. More than one million copies of her books are currently in print. She lives in central Kansas where she and her retired military husband, Don, enjoy spoiling their ten granddarlings.

The employees of Thorndike Press hope you have enjoyed this Large Print book. All our Thorndike, Wheeler, and Kennebec Large Print titles are designed for easy reading, and all our books are made to last. Other Thorndike Press Large Print books are available at your library, through selected bookstores, or directly from us.

For information about titles, please call:
  (800) 223-1244

or visit our Web site at:
  http://gale.cengage.com/thorndike

To share your comments, please write:
Publisher
Thorndike Press
10 Water St., Suite 310
Waterville, ME 04901